PEN

Dead Run

Acclaim for P. J. Tracy:

'Outrageously suspenseful . . . the thriller debut of the year
Harlen Coben

'A powerful thriller and an ingenious plot . . . the gripping narrative and vivid characterization make an auspicious debut'
Observer

'A thrilling page-turner with a nail-biting finish . . . the story races along, helped by some sparkling dialogue and colourful characters' *Sunday Telegraph*

'A gripping read with quirky characters and just the right level of thrills and devilish twists' *Guardian*

'Edge-of-your-seat drama' *Star*

'Scary, with dialogue straight out of *The Sopranos* and a plot to rival *Se7en*' *Radio Times*

'A gripping and inventive novel with plenty of nail-biting moments right to the last page. A terrifying read'
Daily Express

'Some of the best new blood in the genre . . . Scary, funny, witty, and genuinely perplexing right to the end'
Glasgow Herald

'An absolute cracker, heavy on atmosphere, lively characterization and snappy dialogue' *Glasgow Evening Times*

'Think *Birdman*, think *The Straw Men* . . . with crackling dialogue and an up-to-the-minute, leave-the-light-on plot, this electrifying debut will match them both'
Mystery and Thriller Club

'Written with such skill and polish you would think it could be Tracy's tenth . . . a strong new voice in the thriller genre'
USA Today

'A soundly plotted thriller that fires on all cylinders'
Publishers Weekly

'Tracy gets her writing career off to a fiendish start . . . a thoroughly enjoyable, unputdownable book' *This Day*

'It's been a long time since I picked up a mystery as riveting and engaging as this one . . . Harlen Coben called it "the thriller debut of the year". He could have dropped the word 'debut' – it's going to be tough for anyone to top it'
Grand Rapids Press

'Look out, thriller world, here's P. J. Tracy . . . one of the most amazing, imaginative, compelling off-the-wall debut novels in many moons' *Denton Record-Chronicle*

'An impressive debut thriller which kept me awake long enough to appreciate the dawn chorus . . . a compulsively readable tale that kept me guessing all the way to the end'
South Africa Sunday Independent,

'A slick enjoyable thriller . . . P. J. Tracy is about to become a household name' *Daily Mirror*

'Tracy's second offering doesn't disappoint . . . Put it with your passport and your money so you don't forget to take it on holiday' *Time Out*

'A tense edge-of-your-seat thriller' *OK!*

'P. J. Tracy's *Live Bait* proves one thing conclusively: that the phenomenal *Want to Play?* was no fluke, and that in Tracy we have an American suspense writer with all the credentials to sit firmly in the upper echelons of top crime novelists'
Barry Foreshaw

'Rich with humour and occasionally moving, this one's a winner . . . her second novel will be as acclaimed as her first'
Irish Examiner

'With generous doses of humour and suspense, this sharp, satisfying thriller will rivet readers from the start'
Publishers Weekly

'A truly brilliant crime thriller, fast-paced and edgy, full of deception and retribution with the essential incredible twist!'
Newmarket Journal

'For those who mourn that Patricia Cornwell ain't what she used to be, Tracy's a wondrous discovery'
Entertainment Weekly

'Eclectic characters and zingy dialogue . . . exhilarating' *People*

'A fun rush of a read . . . the combination of humour and an excellent mystery is addictive' *Rendezvous*

'This is a series well worth shelving with the rest of the aristocrats of mystery writing. Move over, Sue Grafton'
Washington Times

ABOUT THE AUTHOR

P. J. Tracy is the pseudonym for the mother-and-daughter writing team of P. J. and Traci Lambrecht. They are the authors of the award-winning and bestselling thrillers *Live Bait*, *Dead Run*, *Snow Blind*, *Play to Kill*, *Two Evils* and the Richard and Judy Book Club pick *Want to Play?* All six books feature detectives Gino and Magozzi and maverick computer-hacker Grace MacBride. P. J. and Traci both live near Minneapolis, Minnesota.

Dead Run

P. J. TRACY

PENGUIN BOOKS

PENGUIN BOOKS

Published by the Penguin Group
Penguin Books Ltd, 80 Strand, London WC2R ORL, England
Penguin Group (USA) Inc., 375 Hudson Street, New York, New York 10014, USA
Penguin Group (Canada), 90 Eglinton Avenue East, Suite 700, Toronto, Ontario, Canada M4P 2Y3
(a division of Pearson Penguin Canada Inc.)
Penguin Ireland, 25 St Stephen's Green, Dublin 2, Ireland (a division of Penguin Books Ltd)
Penguin Group (Australia), 707 Collins Street, Melbourne, Victoria 3008, Australia
(a division of Pearson Australia Group Pty Ltd)
Penguin Books India Pvt Ltd, 11 Community Centre, Panchsheel Park, New Delhi – 110 017, India
Penguin Group (NZ), 67 Apollo Drive, Rosedale, Auckland 0632, New Zealand
(a division of Pearson New Zealand Ltd)
Penguin Books (South Africa) (Pty) Ltd, Block D, Rosebank Office Park,
181 Jan Smuts Avenue, Parktown North, Gauteng 2193, South Africa

Penguin Books Ltd, Registered Offices: 80 Strand, London WC2R ORL, England

www.penguin.com

First published in the United States of America by G. P. Putnam's Sons,
a member of Penguin Group (USA) Inc. 2005
First published in Great Britain by Michael Joseph 2005
Published in Penguin Books 2006
This edition published 2013
001

Typeset by Rowland Phototypesetting Ltd, Bury St Edmunds, Suffolk
Printed in Great Britain by Clays Ltd, St Ives plc

ISBN: 978–1–405–92663–8

www.greenpenguin.co.uk

MIX
Paper from responsible sources
FSC www.fsc.org
FSC™ C018179

Penguin Books is committed to a sustainable future for our business, our readers and our planet. This book is made from Forest Stewardship Council™ certified paper.

I

Four Corners hadn't been much of a town since October 17, 1946. That was the day Hazel Krueger's father set the Whitestone Lodge on fire and danced naked through the flames in some sort of sorry recompense for all he'd seen and all he'd done in a place called Normandy.

Not that the town had been such a thriving metropolis before that – more like a tiny open spot in Wisconsin's north woods where someone had dropped a lake by mistake – but without the lodge and the trickle of fishermen who made the long drive up from Milwaukee and Madison every summer, the town sort of sat down on itself and started to dry up, corner by corner.

By the time Tommy Wittig was born, the lodge road that crossed the county tar had faded back into the forest, and it was only last week that Tommy, approaching his eighth birthday and given to the solitary contemplation of a lonely child, had ever wondered aloud why the town had been named Four Corners when it had only two.

Grandpa Dale had told him, while walking him out to Whitestone Lake and showing him the crumbled remains of a brick wall that had once framed the base of the old lodge.

'You peel your eyes when you walk through these woods,' he'd said, waving the gnawed end of a briar pipe he hadn't lit in thirty years because he always had his nose stuck inside some engine or other and feared blowing his own head off. 'You can still mark the hole that fire burned in the forest when it jumped from the lodge to the trees. Probably would have burned down the whole damn state if it hadn't started to rain.'

Tommy had marveled at that, wondering where he would have been born if Wisconsin had burned right to the ground that day, and if the flag would have looked funny with forty-nine stars on it instead of fifty.

'Now, if you was a hawk flying overhead, you'd see a fifty-acre circle of second growth, all strangly with those prickery briars that get stuck in your sneaker laces. That was the fire, and I remember it like it was yesterday. Killed this old town, is what it did. Prime white pines was going up like sixty-foot candles on a birthday cake.'

'Was he really naked?' Tommy had asked, focusing on the single part of the story that he found most remarkable. Grandpa Dale had laughed and said that yes, indeed, Mr Everett Krueger had been naked as the day he was born.

'Did old Hazel see him?' Hazel ran the café that sat on the corner next to Grandpa Dale's gas station

– the only other business left in Four Corners – and she was about a hundred years old, as far as Tommy could tell.

That's when Grandpa Dale had squatted down and looked Tommy right in the eye the way he did when something was really serious and he wanted him to pay attention.

'We don't make no mention of that fire in front of Hazel, you understand, Tommy? She was barely older than you when her daddy up and did this thing, and she was right there, watching, just a little girl peekin' through a porthole into hell, watching her own daddy sizzle away into a blackened stick. Can you imagine such a thing?'

Tommy had been trying to imagine it for almost a whole week, and still he couldn't put a picture in his mind of Hazel Krueger as a little girl, let alone one touched by tragedy.

He was straddling his old bike across the street from the café, staring through the plate-glass window, watching Hazel's broad back hunch and move over the grill plate behind the counter. Even through the dust-streaked window, he could see that great pile of too-black hair wobbling on top of her head, and when she turned around to plop a plate down on the counter in front of a customer, he saw the loose skin of remembered chins cascading down over the place where her neck was supposed to be.

Tommy squinted until Hazel's bright red lips were a blur and her wrinkles disappeared, and he still couldn't see the little girl under all those years.

On the other side of the plate glass, Hazel looked up and caught sight of him and wiggled her fingers and Tommy waved back, suddenly shy. For all the years of his life she'd just been old Hazel with the arms so big they could squeeze the squeaks out of you, and the crazy hair, and the free french fries anytime he set foot inside the café.

But ever since Grandpa Dale had told him the story of how Four Corners became two, Hazel had seemed like a different person – an exotic and interesting stranger who'd watched her own daddy burn to a cinder.

He heard the old Ford pickup when it was still a good quarter mile behind him, and he trotted his bike onto the shoulder close to the trees and looked around frantically. 'C'mon, boy! C'mon, where are you?'

The pup was an early birthday present, little more than a black-and-tan fluffball with too-long ears and too-big feet and a penchant for wandering. The dog had absolutely no sense when it came to cars.

'Hey, pup!' Tommy laid down his bike and squatted, peering into the trees that marched nearly up to the tar across the road from the café and the gas station. There were ghostly tendrils of morning ground fog still hugging the trunks, and he dearly hoped the pup would come out on his own, because Tommy didn't want to go in there after him. It looked like a scene from one of Saturday night's

Creature Features, when mist started floating around crooked graveyard tombstones and you just knew something bad was coming any minute.

It startled him when the pup came bounding out of a dew-speckled fern bank and jumped into his arms, grinning. A wet, busy tongue found his ear and made him giggle just as the battered white pickup topped the rise that dipped down into the down. 'Hold still, you squirmy worm,' he said as he hugged the pup close to his chest as the truck passed slowly, then turned left into Grandpa Dale's station. Tommy's mom leaned out the passenger window and crooked her finger at him.

The pup galumphed after him as Tommy pedaled across the road to the station. Halfway there, the oversized feet tangled and set the pup tumbling like a fuzzy roll of black-and-tan yarn. He scrambled upright, shook his head, then sat down abruptly on short, crooked haunches and let out a plaintive yip.

Jean Wittig watched out the truck window, shaking her head. She was a pretty blonde woman with fair skin just beginning to show the cruelties that the sun inflicts on a farmer's wife. 'You need to watch that pup on the road, remember.'

Tommy screeched the old bike to a halt next to the truck and looked up at his mother. 'I will,' he said, solemn with the weight of this responsibility.

'We might be late, so remember to help with the milking, and anything else Grandpa Dale asks you to do. What are you grinning at?'

'Nothin'.' Tommy kept grinning.

'Think we're going birthday shopping, don't you?'

'Uh-huh.'

Harold Wittig leaned forward and peered past his wife out the window at his son, affecting surprise. 'Somebody's havin' a birthday?'

Tommy's grin widened.

'Hell, we're just goin' to Fleet Farm to pick up some new parts for that old milker.'

'Don't say "hell" in front of the boy, Harold.'

Harold rolled his eyes and got out of the truck to pump gas.

'Here, Tommy.' His mother handed him a dollar bill. 'Run over to Hazel's and get us two donuts for the road. Those ones with the jelly filling.'

'Hey, Mom, did you know that Hazel watched her daddy burn in a big fire a long time ago?'

'Oh, Lord. Harold . . . ?'

'Wasn't me. Talk to your dad.'

Grandpa Dale chose that moment to walk out of the station, and Jean fixed him with a look that made Tommy decide it was a good time to go get those donuts.

The café was bustling this morning, with all three of the booths and half of the counter stools filled. Hazel was manic, propelling her bulk from grill to booth to refrigerator to counter with a speed that was absolutely amazing for a woman of her size.

Tommy suffered a pat on the head and a cheek tweak from Pastor Swenson and his wife, respectively, nodded like he'd seen his dad do at the two hired hands who were helping put up hay at the farm, and eyed with some interest the two families in the other booths and a lone woman at the counter. Not many strangers found themselves on the mile-long strip of tar that passed through Four Corners as it connected County Road Double-P to County Road Double-O, and this many at one time was downright unheard of.

'Here you go.' Hazel distributed five plates at one booth, all expertly balanced on her slablike arms, then pulled a map out of her pocket and slapped it down on the table. 'But like I said, all you gotta do is head up to Double-O, hang a left, then keep going. You'll hit Beaver Lake in under an hour if you don't get the itch to wander off the county roads again.'

A frazzled-looking woman in sunglasses with tiger stripes on them took the map and tucked it into her purse. 'We'll take the map, just in case.'

'Suit yourself.' Hazel poked her fists into hips like bread dough and looked down at Tommy. 'Well, Tommy Wittig, as I live and breathe I swear you've grown a foot since I saw you last!'

Tommy blushed because Hazel saw him almost every day of his life, and he was sure everyone in the café, stranger or not, knew that.

'Must be because your birthday is tomorrow and you're growin' so fast.' She tipped her head sideways, and for one terrible minute, Tommy thought that pile of black hair was going to fall right off and land at his feet like some dead animal.

'I need two donuts really quick!'

Hazel laughed a big laugh, like a man, then went behind the counter and opened the glass case where her home-made donuts were laid out like jewelry. 'What kind today, honey?'

Tommy looked up at that broad, sagging face with its familiar smear of red lipstick, and the dark eyes that always twinkled, and thought how silly he was to have been so leery of old Hazel this past week, to have thought of her as a stranger.

'Hazel?'

'What, hon?'

'Um . . . I'm sorry . . . well . . . I'm sorry your dad died.'

Hazel's face went quiet then, and she looked at him for a long time. It was sort of a grown-up look, and in a funny-nice kind of way, it made Tommy feel old. 'Why, thank you, Tommy. I appreciate that,' she finally said, and then she took one of the little white bakery bags that she put donuts in off a stack on the case and shook it open.

By the time he got back outside, the mist was gone from the woods across the road, and Grandpa Dale was standing next to Dad at the pickup truck, hands shoved deep in his coverall pockets. If Mom had scolded him for telling the story about the lodge fire and Hazel's dad, it was over now, because all three of them were smiling around a secret. They stopped talking abruptly when they saw him coming, and Tommy knew they'd been whispering about his birthday present.

He walked toward the truck slowly, his eyes on his dad in absolute adoration, pushing back the nagging thought that if Hazel's daddy could die, then maybe other daddies could die. But not his. His was the tallest, broadest, strongest dad in the world, and even fire couldn't hurt him. Sometimes he'd catch a head-butt from one of the cows clattering out of the barn after milking, and he'd holler after her that she was a goddamn milkin' whore, and Mom's face would get all stiff and she'd tell him he'd burn for taking the Lord's name in vain, and that's when he always said he was too full of vinegar to ever catch fire.

His father laid a big, work-roughened hand on his shoulder as he passed and squeezed a little. 'Be good, son.'

'Yes, sir.' His shoulder felt cold and light when his father took his hand away and climbed into the truck.

'Thanks, honey.' His mom took the donut bag and leaned out the window and planted a kiss on his head. 'You be good, now. See you at suppertime.'

Grandpa Dale walked him out to the center of the road and they stood there, waving after the pickup as it roared away around the curve toward County Road Double-P. The pup sat crookedly at Tommy's side, leaning against his leg, pink tongue lolling.

Grandpa Dale put his hand on Tommy's shoulder. It wasn't nearly as big as Dad's hand, or as warm.

'Unusual number of strangers in town this morning.' He nodded toward the two unfamiliar cars parked on the side street between the station and the café.

'They got lost,' Tommy said.

'I figured. Pumped nearly thirty gallons of gas already just on those two.'

'That's a lot.'

Grandpa Dale nodded. 'Your grandma's in there working on the books today. Guess she could pump gas with the best of them if the need arises, which means maybe you and me could go fishing in a bit, if we had a mind to.'

Tommy grinned up at him, and Grandpa Dale ruffled his hair.

A quarter mile north of town, Pastor Swenson's twin sixteen-year-old sons, Mark and Matthew, were working in the Wittigs' roadside pasture. The house and hundred-year-old barn were behind them, etched against a cornflower sky at the end of a drive as straight and true as the rows in Harold Wittig's cornfield. Behind the barn, Whitestone Lake lay like a giant blue plate in a necklace of cattails.

A prime herd of Holsteins grazed close to where the boys were repairing the white board fence, near a sign that read 'Pleasant Hills Dairy Farm.' Jean Wittig had painted the sign herself with green enamel left over after Harold touched up the old John Deere, and everyone agreed that on the whole, the sign looked mighty professional. The P in 'Pleasant' was canted slightly to the right, as if it were in a hurry to catch up to the other letters, but Harold thought that gave the sign zip, and he wouldn't let Jean repaint it.

Mark and Matthew had their headphones on full blast, listening to their favorite heavy-metal bands, so they didn't hear the truck making the turn off Double-O, and wouldn't have thought much of it, even if they'd looked up and seen it coming. It was a sight they were used to – just a truck that looked like all the other dairy tankers traveling from farm to farm on Wisconsin's secondary roads, taking on raw milk from the state's productive herds. It had a dusty white cab and a shiny stainless-steel tank that looked like a giant's Thermos bottle. 'Good Health Dairies' was spelled out in royal blue lettering along its length.

The truck was going forty miles per hour when it hit the place the tar had buckled in yesterday's afternoon heat, right at the end of the long driveway leading back to the Wittig farm. The cab's right front tire bounced violently over the worst of the break, then veered into the soft pea gravel of the shoulder. There was a long, high-pitched squeal as the driver slammed on the brakes, and then, its forward momentum diverted, the truck began a sickening lurch to one side. It balanced on its left wheels for an endless moment, as if giving the driver time to think about what was to come, then jackknifed and crashed to its side and slid across the asphalt with a deafening metallic screech.

Wide-eyed and terrified, the driver lay pressed against his door, the metal handle poking into his ribs, his hands still frozen in a white-knuckled grip around the steering wheel. The cab was pointed toward a distant cluster of farm buildings, and through the stone-pocked windshield, he saw two boys running toward him down the dusty drive. In an adjacent pasture, a tight cluster of panicked Holsteins was running the other way.

'Shit,' he finally managed in a shuddered exhale that broke the word into half a dozen syllables. He flexed his fingers on the wheel, wiggled his toes, then released a shaky, breathy laugh, giddy to find all his body parts intact. His smile froze when he heard the compressor behind the cab kick in, and vanished altogether when he glanced at the dashboard and saw the needle on the bulk tank gauge dropping slowly.

'Sweet Jesus,' he whispered, groping frantically for the small computer unit built into the console. He depressed the large red button in the middle, then hit the send key. A message appeared on the tiny screen, blinking innocently in large, baby blue letters.

SPILLED MILK
SPILLED MILK
SPILLED MILK

Mark and Matthew were almost to the truck, running flat out, legs and arms and hearts pumping hard. They dropped like stones a few yards shy of the truck and, for one terrifying instant, saw horror in each other's eyes.

On the other side of the pasture, the cows in Harold Wittig's prime herd of Holsteins began to sink to their knees.

Half a mile downwind in Four Corners, the screeching noise had split the quiet morning like a thousand fingernails scraping down a blackboard. The puppy wailed and batted at his ears; Grandpa Dale and Tommy both covered theirs with their hands. For a second, Dale wondered if those Swenson boys had taken out Harold's old John Deere and tipped it over in the road again, but he dismissed the possibility almost as soon as he thought of it. The horrible noise was going on much too long for that, spearing into his brain, making his eyes hurt.

The curious and the worried had already started to come out of Hazel's by the time the awful noise had stopped, all of them looking up the road toward the Wittig farm, shading their eyes in the bright light of morning. The pastor and his wife were the worried ones, thinking of their sons working up there. The sudden silence was almost more upsetting than the sounds of the crash had been, and they both moved quickly toward where they had parked the big Chevy in front of the café. The others were wandering right into the middle of the road, as if that would help them figure out what had happened over a hill and out of sight.

Inside the café, Hazel was waiting impatiently for the donuts she'd just put in the fryer to finish so she could follow her customers outside and investigate for herself. Excitement of any kind was a rare thing in Four Corners, and not to be missed. When she finally lifted the basket and hooked it on the edge of the fryer – another perfect batch – she had only enough time to glance out the window and marvel at the sight of her customers prayerfully sinking to their knees, some of them right in the middle of the road, before her candy-red mouth sagged open and her throat started to close.

When Dale saw the first person go down just a few yards away, he scooped up Tommy in one arm and the pup in the other and tried to race away, but already his heart was pounding too slow for that. He never felt the pup slip from his grasp and tumble to the asphalt, but he never let go of Tommy, not even when he finally fell.

2

Ricky Schwann was freezing his ass off. Damned water in this quarry never warmed up, no matter how hot the summer. It was great when you needed to quick-chill a case of brews, but it really sucked when you were two hundred pounds of muscle in a pair of swimming trunks and had to dive in after it. Ricky had worked hard his senior year at Paper Valley High to get down to five percent body fat, but now he was wishing he'd porked down a few more Big Macs, just for the insulation.

Ten feet down into the black water, his lungs were already starting to burn and his eyes hurt from the cold. He squeezed them shut. The water was so black that you couldn't see more than a few inches anyway. He yanked hard again on the rope that tethered the case of beer he was after, but it wouldn't budge. He was going to have to go all the way down. Five, ten more feet, he figured.

He went hand over hand down the rope until he felt it veer sideways, snagged on whatever it was that was holding it down. He jerked on the rope and felt it loosen, then opened his eyes in time to see another pair of eyes floating toward him. They were blue, just like his, but wide and empty.

*

'What'd I tell you?' Deputy Bonar Carlson was leaning forward in the passenger seat of the patrol car, jabbing a chubby finger at the windshield. 'Look at the top of those Norways. Yellowing already, and August is still a youngster.'

Sheriff Michael Halloran kept his eyes on the twisting strip of tar so he wouldn't run into one of the Norway pines that Bonar wanted him to look at. The forest moved in on everything man-made when you got this far north in Wisconsin, and roads were no exception. He felt like he was driving through a tunnel. 'We are not having a drought,' he said. 'You're doing that Chicken Little thing again.'

'It's going to be a bad one. Maybe as bad as 'eighty-seven.'

'That's such a load of crap. We nearly drowned in June. Broke every record in the book for rainfall.'

Bonar snorted and flopped back, sticking a thumb under the seat belt to ease the pressure on his considerable, cherished stomach. 'That was then, this is now. Just wait until we get to the lime quarry. I'll bet the water is at least a foot low, maybe two.'

'No way.' Halloran eased the car around an unbanked turn, watching sunlight dapple the road ahead like a strobe. He'd known since the fifth grade that only a fool questioned anything Bonar stated as fact, but he just couldn't help himself. One of these days, he was going to prove him wrong about something. The law of averages was on his side. 'Did I miss the turn? Feels like we've been driving for hours.'

'Fifty-seven minutes from the office to the lime quarry, and that's if you don't run into a deer or a bear. How long since you've been up there?'

Halloran thought about it for a minute, and then got sad. 'Senior-class party.'

Bonar sighed. 'Yeah. Gives me the creeps every time I pass the place. Haven't dipped a toe in that water since.'

The old lime quarry they were heading for hugged the northern county line, about as far from human habitation as you could get in this part of the state, making it an ideal party site for every teenage bash since the quarry and kiln had closed in the '40s. Fifty feet down from ground level, the lime had petered out and buried springs had bubbled up, filling the ugly machine-made hole with icy water. Halloran had always liked thinking about that – man working decades to make a piece of earth ugly, nature covering the scars in a blink, if you just left her alone to do her job.

But the water and the isolation made the place a magnet for kids and kegs, and every now and then something bad would happen. Like at the senior-class party nearly twenty years ago, when Howie Dexheimer dove into that cold black water and disappeared, as if the quarry had swallowed him whole. Every diver in the county had worked the deep water for weeks but never found the body. As far as anyone knew, Howie Dexheimer was still down there.

'You think it's him?' Bonar interrupted Halloran's thoughts as if he'd been following them.

'Lord, I hope not. I sure don't want to see Howie after twenty years in the water.'

When Bonar was thinking hard, his whole face screwed up. 'Might not be so bad. Water's too damn cold for anything to live in, including most bacteria. The body could be almost perfectly preserved if the alkaline content isn't too high.'

Halloran winced. The idea of a perfectly preserved Howie was almost worse.

Fifteen minutes later, he found the two-lane dirt track that made a hole in the woods. Deputy Walter Simons was blocking the access with his legs spread and his arms crossed over his chest, a banty rooster with an Elvis haircut trying to look like Colossus.

Halloran pulled up alongside him and opened his window. 'Tell me something I don't know, Simons.'

Simons swatted ineffectually at a congregation of deerflies buzzing around his head. 'Goddamn deer-flies bite like a son of a bitch, did you know that?'

'I did.'

'Well, it isn't poor old Howie Dexheimer, anyway. I caught a glimpse just when they were pulling him out, and Howie never had hair that long.'

'Hair grows after death,' Bonar told him.

'Go on.'

'So some people say.'

'Does it tie itself up in a ponytail with a rubber band?'

'Hardly ever.'

'Well, there you go. Besides, Doc Hanson says this was an older guy, mid-twenties at least, and not in the water that long. No ID, no nothin'. Naked as a jaybird. You want to send Cleaton back out here with the squad? Another ten minutes out in these bugs and I'm going to be a pint low.'

About a tenth of a mile in, the two-lane track broadened onto an open grassy area clogged by cars – Doc Hanson's old blue station wagon, three patrol cars that had responded to the call, and a brand-new Ford pickup that would have eaten up a year of Halloran's salary. Had to belong to the kid who had called it in, he decided. These days half the kids in the district got new trucks just for graduating.

Just beyond the makeshift parking lot, an earthen ramp that had once been access for heavy machinery led down to the water. They'd called it 'the girlie road' in the old days, and no self-respecting, testosterone-crazed teenage boy would ever set foot on it. There was only one acceptable entrance into the water for them.

Halloran's eyes shifted to either side of the ramp, where the quarry walls rose a good fifteen feet from the black water. Mature trees leaned over the rim as if peering downward, and frayed ropes hung from many of the bigger branches. He and Bonar had hung ropes just like them when they were young and immortal, swung on them like foolish apes until they arced over the water and let go. Timing had been everything. You let go too soon, and you landed on the jagged rocks that climbed the ridge wall. That had been the thrill of it, and with the sharp and fearful eye of maturity, Halloran thought it was pretty much a miracle that they had survived their own stupidity.

He glanced over at five teenagers tangled together in a distressed knot near one of the county cars. Their expressions cycled through the spectrum of human emotion – shock, horror, fear, fascination, and back again – as they tried to make sense of their gruesome discovery. He recognized Ricky Schwann, a full head taller and a few shades grayer than the rest of them.

Halloran and Bonar ignored the kids for the moment, got out of the car, and headed down the rock-strewn slope to the little beach below, where Doc Hanson's crouched form was partially blocking the view of what Halloran dearly hoped was an intact body. Initially, all he could see of it was a head and a pair of legs so white they looked like they belonged on a plaster statue. As they drew closer, the doc got up and took a step back, giving them their first look at the torso.

'Oh, man.' Halloran's cheeks went up and his mouth turned down when he saw the band of neat, pencil-sized black holes that stitched a perforated line across the white flesh of the dead man's chest. 'We just figured it for a drowning.'

Doc Hanson was holding his gloved hands away from his sides so he wouldn't forget and shove them in his pockets. 'So did I, until they pulled him out.'

He stooped and moved a tangled clump of wet hair away from the open filmy eyes. 'You know him?'

Halloran and Bonar both took a long look at the frozen face, then shook their heads.

'Me either. And I figure I know just about everybody in this county. Hell, I delivered half of them. But I've never laid eyes on this boy.'

'Identifying marks?' Halloran asked.

Doc Hanson shook his head. 'No freckles, no moles, no scars, no tattoos. He might have had something on his back, but there isn't much left of it anymore. You want me to roll him?'

'Lord, no,' Bonar said, already picturing what that many exit wounds might have done to the body. 'It looks like somebody tried to cut the poor guy in half.'

Doc nodded. 'Eight full penetrations, head-on, another one that scraped his left side, see?' He pointed to a raw strip where tissue had been burned instead of blown away. 'Mowed him down, is what they did. Looks like NATO rounds some fool fired on full automatic, which is flat-out overkill. That stuff fragments like crazy. One good chest hit like any one of these' – he gestured at the body – 'and the job's done.'

Halloran looked curiously at the kindly, time-worn face of the doctor who'd delivered him, who'd given him lollipops with every childhood vaccination and mixed india ink with the plaster so he could have a 'manly-colored' cast when he'd broken his wrist in second grade – not the kind of man you'd think would know a whole lot about the end results of automatic rifle fire. 'NATO rounds, Doc?' he asked softly. 'You learn about those in med school?'

The softening jowls under the old doctor's jaw tightened a little. ''Nam,' he said in a way that made the single syllable sound heavy and dark and final.

Halloran and Bonar shot each other a look. You could know a man for all of your life, it seemed, and still know so little.

The sound of spilling water made them all look toward the ramp, where a diver was emerging, looking strange and shiny and alien in his scuba gear. Halloran thought of old monster matinees and wished he was at home watching one now.

The diver pulled off his mask as he waded toward them. 'You're going to need a couple more body bags down here.'

Within the hour, there were two more bodies lying on the tiny beach – one younger, one older, but both as nude as the first, with similar chest wounds. Doc Hanson had two unhappy deputies move the corpses until they were in the order he wanted.

'There,' he said, finally satisfied, gesturing Halloran and Bonar over to where he stood at the feet of the body in the center of the ghastly trio. 'Now look at the wounds, left to right. Looks like the bullet holes almost sew them together, doesn't it?'

Halloran squinted, narrowing his eyes to tighten his line of vision so he saw only the wounds, not the human bodies the bullets had punctured. 'This is the way they were standing when they were shot,' he said quietly, and Doc nodded.

'Just so. Right-handed shooter, sweeping left to right.'

Bonar's lips were pushed out, as if he'd just tasted something very bad. 'Why not a left-handed shooter, sweeping right to left?'

Doc Hanson hesitated before he responded, as if he were reluctant to confess that he knew the answer. 'There's a burst when you fire an automatic rifle, Bonar – the bullets come so fast when you pull the trigger that if you're not used to it, you get a heavy cluster before you start your sweep. See the man on the left, the one we pulled out first? Nine shots. He was the first in line. The one in the middle was hit five times, the one on the right only three. So this is what happened. Someone lined these men up and executed them all at once.'

There was a hollow sound to Doc's voice that kept Halloran from looking at him. He looked at the bodies instead. 'You've seen this kind of thing before?'

Doc Hanson shoved his hands in his pockets, then pulled them out and looked irritably at the latex gloves he'd just ruined. 'Not in this country.'

3

Grace MacBride was standing at one of the open mullioned windows on the third floor, resting her eyes on the greenery outside while several computers hummed behind her. She was finally growing used to the new office, to lush treetops outside the window instead of the Minneapolis skyline, to the relative quiet of the exclusive Summit Avenue neighborhood instead of the brash bustle of the warehouse district.

Moving the Monkeewrench office into Harley Davidson's mansion was supposed to have been temporary, but it was almost a year since they'd abandoned the bloodied loft that had been home to their company for ten years, and not one of them had even suggested looking for another space. It was comfortable here – Harley saw to that – and for a quartet of societal rejects that comprised all the family any of them had, a home seemed a proper environment.

Besides, Charlie liked it here. He was sitting perfectly upright in the ladder-backed wooden chair next to her desk, haunches and four big feet crowded onto the small seat, what was left of his tail sticking through the back. His brown eyes followed every move she made. She laid a hand on the top of his wiry head and he closed his eyes. 'Two days,' she said, and the dog sighed.

Grace was dressed for travel, which meant she was wearing two guns instead of one – the Sig in the shoulder holster low under her left arm; the derringer tucked into one of the tall English riding boots she wore every time she left her house. Her jeans and T-shirt were lightweight in deference to the August heat, but they were still black. Something about the color made her feel safe and hidden and powerful, and she couldn't discard it any more than she could discard the boots and the guns. The one day in eleven years she had tried, a man with a gun of his own had come calling, reminding her that such a venture was pure folly. Life was dangerous, and facing it unarmed was simply too risky.

She turned away from the window when she heard the first muffled footfalls on the carpeted stairs two floors down, and then the strident hum of the small elevator that served this wing of the house. She knew it was Harley and Roadrunner on the stairs, and Annie on the elevator, but still, her stomach clenched and she automatically laid her hand on the Sig. She didn't lower it until she heard Harley bellow from the first landing, 'Coming up, Gracie!' Harley knew she had her hand on the gun. She really loved him for that.

Roadrunner was first through the door, his six-foot-seven-inch, sapling-sized frame clad in his customary one-piece Lycra biking suit. Today's selection was navy blue with a red swoosh across the back. 'I don't care how rare it is or how much it cost,' he threw over his shoulder at Harley. 'It's still ugly.'

Harley stomped in behind him, a massive, bearded man with beefy, tattooed arms wrapped lovingly around a monstrous clay pot that presumably held the item in question – some sort of cactus bristling with three-inch quills. 'And that coming from a man who painted his friggin' kitchen pink.'

'It's not pink, it's cerise, and the guy at the paint store said it was one of their most popular interior colors.'

'It's baboon-butt pink, Roadrunner, and the guy at the paint store should be imprisoned for telling you any different.' Harley tenderly placed the cactus down in the corner and backed up to admire it. 'What do *you* think, Gracie? It looks great there, doesn't it?'

Harley was a man of great passion, and when he found something new that struck his fancy, he went after it zealously. He had amassed a world-class collection of vintage motorcycles and a wine cellar that could reduce a sommelier to tears, and Grace understood those things, because they were utilitarian and therefore worth the time and expense. But after the Monkeewrench crew's recent trip to Arizona, he'd developed an unlikely obsession with cacti and now had an entire room downstairs filled with the things, which baffled her – they simply weren't useful. 'I guess we won't have to worry about watering it,' was all she could muster.

Harley gave her a look of crushing disappointment. 'I was expecting a little more from you, Grace. And by the way, if you hear a strange, clattering sound, ignore it – it's just my heart breaking and shattering on the floor.'

Grace couldn't help but smile. 'Sorry, Harley. I just don't get it.'

'Neither do I.' Annie Belinsky fluttered into the room in a dress made to look as if a thousand silk butterflies were feasting on her body every time she moved. She had tiny feet and a rosebud mouth, but everything else about Annie was pure, queen-sized Renaissance, and her parading around in that dress in front of Harley all morning had been like dragging a side of bacon in front of a starving dog. She stood in front of the cactus with her hands on her hips and a stern look of disapproval on her face. 'I thought we agreed you'd keep your acupuncture experiments downstairs.'

'I told you, this is a special cactus and it's brand-new. I want to keep an eye on it until it gets acclimated.'

Annie rolled her eyes. 'You're losing your mind, Harley. Why couldn't you fixate on something pretty, like orchids?'

'Orchids are *chick* plants,' he said in disgust. 'But the cactus is tough, a take-no-prisoners kind of plant.

I like to think of them as the botanical equivalent of me – all man.'

'Yeah – annoying as hell.'

'The kind of man who could take that dress off your big, beautiful body with his teeth, one piece of silk at a time.'

'Pig.'

'Hey, I knew those little fluttery things were silk, didn't I? I just can't figure out what's holding them on . . .' He reached for her dress, but Annie slapped his hand and turned toward Grace in exasperation.

'I'm being mauled. Can we get out of here yet?'

'Almost ready. I'm just burning the last disk.'

It was their fourth month taking the Monkeewrench computerized detective software on the road, donating their time and equipment to local police departments that were coming up empty on homicides that were, or might be, serials. Over the past ten years, the software that Monkeewrench had produced – particularly the games – had made all the partners extremely wealthy. But the last game they created spawned a string of grisly murders, and the names and faces of the victims haunted them still. So they were doing penance the only way they knew how: by turning the computer genius that had sparked those killings against other killers, wherever they could find them. They'd brought down two already – one in Arizona and one in Texas.

We're batting a thousand, Grace thought, but philanthropy in this arena was an exhausting and depressing endeavor. There were too many killers out there, too many police departments ill equipped to sort through and collate the volume of information that always accompanied such investigations. Their new software was amazingly effective, making connections in seconds that would normally take months of legwork, but it was the only prototype in the world, and picking a single case to work from the hundreds of urgent requests had become an ongoing moral dilemma.

Today she and Annie were driving to Green Bay to set up for a case that they wouldn't have given a second glance if Sharon Mueller hadn't asked them to take it on. Once Sheriff Halloran's deputy in Wisconsin, now on temporary loan to the Minneapolis FBI office as a profiler, Sharon was convinced a serial killer was just beginning a spree in the Green Bay area, even if her superior at the FBI wasn't. Special Agent in Charge Paul Shafer refused to authorize bureau time and resources on what seemed to be three very dissimilar murders, so technically Sharon was off the clock on this weekend jaunt. The Green Bay police didn't see a connection either, but they had three unsolveds on the books and were more than happy to take any help Monkeewrench was offering free of charge. After reviewing the file, the Monkeewrench crew wasn't so sure they had a serial, either, but Sharon had nearly died saving Grace's life last year, and if she'd asked them to go to the moon, they would have found a way.

Harley sank down into the broad, padded leather chair at his workstation and propped his jackbooted feet up on the desk. 'So what do you think? Is Sharon going to stay in Wisconsin?'

Annie was delicately picking through a drawer in her desk, trying to capture a favorite tube of lip gloss without chipping her manicure. 'Who knows? She's got the cushy FBI job here if she wants it, but then again, Mr Dreamboat is waiting for her in the sticks.'

Harley blew a raspberry. 'Mr Dreamboat is a dumbshit, or he would have dragged her back to Wisconsin a long time ago.'

'I thought you liked Sheriff Halloran.'

'I do like him. He's a hell of a sheriff and a hell of a nice guy, but that doesn't make him any less of a dumbshit. If I had some red-hot pixie like Sharon all googly-eyed over me, I sure as hell wouldn't be cooling my heels in the hinterlands, waiting for her to come knocking. Even the Italian Stallion knows better than that, doesn't he, Gracie?'

Grace gave him one of those long, steady looks that frightened children and strangers, but it didn't work on Harley at all.

'Leo Magozzi's just not the kind of guy who lies in the weeds with his fingers crossed,' he went on. 'I'll bet he's been on your doorstep every night since we got back from the Southwest, hasn't he? Halloran could take a lesson from that guy.'

Annie drummed her rainbow nails on her desk, instantly capturing his attention. 'For a man with no discernible love life, you're pretty free and easy with the sage advice.'

'What do you mean? I have several discernible love lives.'

'I'm talking about relationships where you actually know the other person's name. Come on, Grace. I told Sharon we'd pick her up by ten.'

The computer Grace was working on chimed, and she pulled the finished disk from its drive. 'Okay, that's the last one.'

She patted Harley on the head as she passed his desk on the way to Roadrunner's bank of computers. He turned off the monitor before she got close enough to decipher the scrolling lines of code.

'Something you don't want me to see?' she asked, a little amused.

Roadrunner lifted one angular shoulder. 'It's a surprise Harley and I are working on.'

'Really?'

'Aw, shit.' Harley came storming over. 'You didn't let her see it, did you?'

'No, I didn't let her see it . . .'

'See what?'

Harley folded his arms over his chest and grinned at her. 'Never you mind. Besides, if we told you, you'd be an accessory, and this has got to be the most illegal thing we've ever done.'

'I like the sound of that.'

'I went on the criminal justice board. Fifty, sixty years if we get caught.'

'And I like the sound of that,' Annie drawled from the doorway.

'You're going to call when you get there, right?' Roadrunner asked Grace.

'Of course we will.'

'Because your cell phones probably won't work, you know. I checked it out. There are hardly any towers in northern Wisconsin.'

'Excuse me?' Annie sounded like a kid who'd just learned that Santa Claus wasn't real.

Roadrunner sighed. 'No cell towers, no cell coverage. Northern Wisconsin is pretty much a wasteland when it comes to telecommunication. You might not be able to call out until you get close to Green Bay.'

Annie looked at him as if he'd lost his mind. 'That is absolutely impossible. I called Paris from the top of the ski lift on Aspen Mountain last winter, and Aspen is *wilderness*.'

'Yeah, right,' Harley scoffed. 'That's why every friggin' couture house in the world has a shop there. Let me tell you, you haven't begun to see wilderness until you've been to northern Wisconsin.'

'Like you would know.'

'Well, as it happens, I do know. Drove an Ojibwa friend up to the Bad River Rez once. Saw nothing but black bear for about three hours straight, and not one of them was carrying a cell phone.'

'See?' Roadrunner said to Grace, his forehead wrinkled with worry. 'You're going to be totally out of touch for a really long time.'

Grace smiled at him. Roadrunner somehow managed to be both the child and the fretting mother of the Monkeewrench crew. His outlook had always been dark, his general philosophy one of blanket pessimism. 'It's only a six-hour drive, Roadrunner.'

'Yeah, well, a lot can happen in six hours. The car could blow up. You could hit a moose or have a blowout, and then veer off the road into a tree and lie there unconscious with all your arms and legs broken . . .'

Harley smacked him on the back of the head.

Ten minutes later, Harley, Roadrunner, and Charlie stood at the end of the driveway like three abandoned puppies, watching Grace and Annie pull away in Grace's Range Rover.

'We should have gone with them,' Roadrunner said.

Charlie whined his agreement.

'No room in that puny little SUV for two big, strapping men like ourselves and three women with all their makeup. Annie took a friggin' trunk, can you believe that? For a weekend in Green Bay, where nobody ever wears anything except Packers sweatshirts.'

'We could have taken the RV . . .'

'Damnit, Roadrunner, how many times do I have to tell you not to call it that? It's a luxury motor coach.'

'Whatever. We could have taken it. There's plenty of room for all of us.'

Harley stared at the clump birch in the yard across

the street. He rocked back and forth on his run-down heels. 'I hate goddamned Wisconsin.'

'The Harley-Davidson plant is in Wisconsin.'

Harley's big head moved up and down a little. 'Yeah. There is that.'

A lot of people assumed that Chicago was the windiest city in the country, just because of the 'Windy City' moniker someone had slapped on the place more than a century ago. The truth was that Chicago wasn't anywhere near the top on any known list, and Minneapolis was windier by a whopping tenth of a mile per hour. Perched on the northern edge of the Great Plains, it was an easy target for the prairie winds that swept across the Midwest during the summer, which made the warm months tolerable for a population that wore parkas six or seven months out of the year. But every August, the prairies seemed to run out of breath, the wind stopped, and the heat settled over the city like shrink-wrap.

Grace had never minded the heat – or the cold, for that matter. Even after eleven years in the state, she was still baffled by the local fixation on the weather. But Annie had succumbed to the obsession almost immediately. Like almost every other resident, she watched every weathercast on every channel every chance she got, and spewed statistics like a meteorologist on uppers. They'd been in the car exactly two minutes when she started tapping the digital temperature readout on the dash.

'Lord, would you look at that. Eighty-eight degrees and it's not even ten in the morning. Another hour and we'll be fish poachin' in a kettle.'

'We'll turn up the air-conditioning.'

'Hah. As if air-conditioning could put a dent in the dew point we're expecting today. Did you hear how high it's going to be?'

'I don't even know what the dew point is.'

'Honey, no one really knows what the dew point is, but it's going to be bad. Tropical. And Fat Annie is going to suffer. Is that Sharon?'

Half a block ahead, Sharon was standing at the curb outside her apartment building, wearing her little navy FBI pants suit and her dreadful black lace-ups. She wore her brown hair in a short pixie cut, and would have been button-cute if it hadn't been for the mean-little-dog expression on her face. She had a big leather handbag over one shoulder and a canvas duffel at her feet. 'Look at that bitty thing. Was she that short last week?'

'Shorter. She was sitting down.'

The three of them had arranged to meet at a bar and grill on the fringes of downtown to take a look at the documentation Sharon had gathered on the case. She had already commandeered a large booth in the back by the time Grace and Annie had arrived, and was frightening the regulars with a spread of autopsy photos she'd laid on the table. 'Are those all from the Green Bay case?' Grace had asked, and Sharon had swept the photos aside immediately.

'Lord, no. I just take these along whenever I'm going out alone. No one hits on a woman looking at dead people.'

Grace smiled at the memory, as she had smiled then. Most women would have worn a ring on their left hand to avoid unwanted male attention; Sharon brought pictures of corpses, and Grace liked that about her.

Annie rolled down her window when they pulled up to the curb. 'Sharon Mueller, what on earth are you doing standing out there in this heat, especially in that sorry synthetic getup?'

Sharon stepped up to the window and breathed mint into the car. 'I am a representative of the Federal government, and this is my Federal government outfit. In the back?' She hefted her duffel.

Grace nodded and got out to open the back gate for her. As Sharon tossed her duffel in, she eyed Annie's trunk suspiciously. 'Somebody planning to stay awhile?'

'Only the weekend, honey,' Annie answered as she climbed out of the passenger seat and held the door open for Sharon. 'I bring at least two trunks for anything longer than that. Now, you come on up here and sit in the front. I'll be needing the backseat to accommodate this dress. If it gets wrinkled, the appliqués poke out this way and that, and I end up looking like I've been run through a paper shredder.'

'It's a pretty amazing dress,' Sharon said, giving her the once-over.

'I knew there was hope for you, darlin'.'

After a minute on the road, Sharon said, 'This feels weird.'

'What, the car?'

'Nah. Going on a road trip with a couple of women.'

'You've been on road trips with men?' Annie asked from the backseat, immediately intrigued.

'A couple. I wouldn't recommend it, though. Guys have this thing about getting from point A to point B as fast as possible. No side trips. They never want to stop and look at anything. And they never have to go to the bathroom either.'

'Yeah, yeah, I know all that, but who'd you go on a road trip with? Sheriff Halloran?'

'God, no. Elias McFarressey. He played the accordion, among other things.'

Annie's jaw dropped. 'You dated a man who played the accordion?'

'It was Wisconsin. You kind of had to be there.'

'I'm seeing Lawrence Welk.'

'It wasn't quite that bad. Grace, do you know where you're going?'

'I figured I'd head east until you tell me to make a turn.'

'That'll work. I'm better than any GPS, at least in Wisconsin.'

'Good thing, because I don't have one.'

'I thought all these fancy rides had GPS.'

'Grace wouldn't hear of it,' Anne said. 'Too Big

Brother. They always know where you are with a GPS.'

Sharon cocked her head at Grace. 'And who is "they"?'

Grace shrugged. 'Could be anybody.'

4

Down the long drive that led to the Wittig farm, behind the barn and out of sight of the road, three figures in bulky white suits stood motionless in the tall grass bordering a paddock fence, looking as alien in this landscape as the barn would have looked on the moon.

Through the thick transparent shields in their helmets, three pairs of busy eyes watched the slow progress of a big green tractor with a blade doing work it was never designed for. Flattening the grass with heavy, dirt-caked treads, the machine lumbered inexorably toward a lip of land behind the paddock that sloped down to a small lake. Behind the tractor, at the end of a long chain with links as fat as a man's fist, the dairy tanker followed as obediently as a dog on a leash.

Behind his shield, Chuck Novak's lips compressed and he tasted salt. Rivulets of sweat were coursing down his reddened face – sweat born as much of fear as of the unrelenting heat that turned the heavy suit into a portable sauna. His companions were sweating, too, but their expressions revealed none of the nervousness that was churning in Chuck's stomach like acid in a Mixmaster. Maybe they weren't afraid. Maybe they'd understood the hurried lecture about vacuums and pressure and molecular weights that was so far beyond Chuck's high-school education it might as well have been delivered in Chinese – maybe they were a hell of a lot more certain than he was that all the gas had long since escaped from the milk truck's stainless-steel tank, just like the Colonel had said.

But if that was true – if there was no danger whatsoever that any of the lethal gas lingered – why the hell did they have to wear these suits? Why had all the others been pulled back out of range until they were finished with the truck?

Because somebody wasn't one hundred percent sure, Chuck thought.

He blinked sweat out of his eyes and watched the tractor grind to a halt at the edge of the slope, then ease back to put slack on the chain. For a long moment, none of the three white-suited men moved, then one of them waddled toward the back of the tractor to release the chain. The second man headed toward the front of the truck, and after taking a deep, shaky breath of canned air, Chuck brought up the rear.

The thick, bulky gloves attached to the arms of their suits foiled dexterity, and it seemed to take them a long time to release the chain from the oily undercarriage of the truck. By the time it was accomplished, the tractor had already positioned itself to the rear, its massive blade raised slightly and ready to push. In a stiff-legged hobble, the three men moved as quickly as possible to one side, near the edge of the slope, so they could watch the truck go over.

Someone should at least say some words, Chuck thought, looking first down the hill that slid into the lake, then back up at sunlight glinting off the truck's windshield. After all, there was a man in that truck, and this was his burial. He had a mental flash of Alvin slumped across the seat, the cab around him splattered with things he didn't want to think about, and the bitter taste of nausea crawled up his throat. He stiffened immediately. Even worse than the memory of what had been left of Alvin was the prospect of throwing up in a contained suit.

Bless him, Father, for he has sinned, he thought, paraphrasing the beginning of every confession, but by then the tractor's blade had cupped the truck's rear bumper and the big engine was growling.

There had been some concern about the truck tipping as it rolled down the slope toward the lake, but the distance was short, the angle of descent was steady and relatively shallow, and the truck went in almost gracefully, like some gallant old ship consigned to a watery grave. Momentum pushed it through a bank of cattails to a sharp dropoff, and then its great weight pulled it promptly down to a muddy bottom.

Thirty feet deep, their diver had said – cold, springfed, and apparently stocked with walleye. Chuck smiled a little at that, remembering that Alvin had been a fisherman. He thought of the water filling the cab, buoying the dead man up to gaze sightlessly out the windshield at all those fish.

He stood at the edge of the hill for what seemed like a long time, staring down at where the dark water had closed over the shiny steel tank, and then he heard the impatient revving of the tractor behind him.

Turning, he saw the massive blade almost hidden behind a messy pile of black and white and red. As the tractor inched forward, its treads biting into the soft manure-rich soil in the paddock, the pile shifted and started to tumble sickeningly.

Shit, Chuck thought. Now came the hard part. Dead cows wouldn't roll down that hill to the lake with the same ease and dignity as the truck.

He shuddered and turned away, imagining a log-jam of Holsteins at the bottom of the hill, bobbing around in the shallow water at the lake's edge. There was going to be some handwork involved here, and he wasn't looking forward to it.

5

Three and a half hours into the trip to Green Bay, Grace heard a telltale click and glanced right, where Sharon was slouched in the passenger seat, her hands at war with her shoulder harness. This was the universal background music of women traveling by car, Grace mused – the click and rattle of seat belts being constantly adjusted to pass between the breasts instead of smashing one of them flat.

'Damn seat belts,' Sharon muttered. 'If one of these things ever dared press against a man's balls, you can bet your life the designer would end up hanging by his.'

Annie chuckled from the backseat, unbuckling her own seat belt quietly – very quietly, so Grace wouldn't hear.

'Honey, you think you've got it bad? You should be toting my cargo. I swear I added a bra size at that diner, and I still haven't figured out what the hell I ate. Everything was white. Hey, Gracie, just how lost are we? I haven't seen a house or a car in about a million miles.'

Grace had never understood the concept of being lost. It was one of those things you had to learn in childhood, a sense of time and place that only had meaning if you belonged somewhere, if you were expected. No one had ever expected Grace to be anywhere, and therefore she had never been late, never been missing, never been lost.

Once when she was very young, she'd ended up in a night-darkened alley in some city or other – cities were basically the same, and differentiating them by name was not a priority in her memory – and there she had watched with unabashed amazement as an ageless, ragged-looking creature poked a needle into her arm. Oblivious to her audience of one, the woman performed her self-destructive magic act on the stage of Grace's curious child-stare, eventually raising foggy eyes and saying, 'Hey, kid. What the fuck are you doing here? You lost, or what?'

At the time, she'd thought it was an odd question. How could she have been lost? She was standing right there. Even then, in a city with no name and an alley with no hope, Grace hadn't felt an inkling of that impending panic others felt in unfamiliar surroundings, or when they didn't know precisely where they were. You were always *somewhere,* right?

So she didn't understand the apprehension that had crept into Annie's voice as they drove deeper into a maze of twisting, empty country roads that coiled through the northern Wisconsin wilderness. 'We're not lost, Annie, it's just a detour.'

'So said Hansel to Gretel,' Annie grumped. 'And we turned off the detour an hour ago to go see that silly ol' barn, which, incidentally, was almost the very last sign of human habitation I've seen. Lord knows where we are now.'

'My fault.' Sharon gave her a sheepish shrug. 'Mea culpa.'

'Oh, honey, don't apologize. That barn was the most amazing thing I've seen since the day Roadrunner took his shirt off. I just didn't realize it was the gateway to hell.'

Annie looked out at the tunnel of towering white pines that crowded the strip of tar like silent spectators at a parade. The thick trunks seemed to swallow the light, offering occasional strobe-light glimpses of what lay within. She had no idea what might be lurking out there in the shifting shadows, but she was quite certain it was unpleasant. 'This is absolutely the spookiest place I have ever been in my life. I never heard of anyone famous from Wisconsin, and now I know why. Nobody lives here.'

Sharon turned around in the front passenger seat and lowered her sunglasses so Annie didn't look orange. 'Ed Gein was famous. He lived here.'

'Never heard of him.'

'He used to kill people, grind them up, and eat them.'

'Hmph. Well, apparently he ate them all.'

Sharon smiled at her, and the pull of muscles puckered the small, circular scar on her neck. Every time Annie noticed it, she remembered a pool of blood on the floor of the Monkeewrench warehouse, a smeared trail leading away where Sharon had crawled on her belly to get upstairs and save Grace.

'There aren't many people up here,' Sharon said. 'Mostly state forests. This far north, they just seem to go on forever.'

'Speaking of which, I've been keeping an eye on that little ol' compass up there on the dashboard. It's been pointing north an awful long time, and I just don't think Wisconsin is all that tall. Maybe we should see if we can't find a right turn before we hit the North Pole.'

'Looks like we're about to get a chance to do just that,' Grace said, tipping her head toward a small sign coming up on the right that read, 'Four Corners → 2 mi.'

'Praise Jesus.' Annie sighed. 'Civilization.' She patted the dark bob that had become her signature hairstyle over the past year, then fished a compact and a tube of lip gloss from her purse. From what she'd seen at the Holy Cow Diner, more than a few of the Wisconsin country women rivaled her in girth, but they didn't know beans about presentation. It was Annie's job as a fashion missionary to show them the way.

She had the lip gloss at a critical point in the application when the Range Rover suddenly backfired, then lurched, sending a streak of magenta across her upper lip. 'Damnit, Grace. What'd you do? Run over a reindeer?'

But Grace didn't answer her. Sharon was looking

curiously at the gauges on the dash, and Annie suddenly noticed the kind of silence that didn't belong in a moving car. She looked out at the trees passing ever more slowly. 'Oh, for God's sake. Did this thing just up and quit?' This was flabbergasting. Grace's car would never break down. It wouldn't dare.

'Looks that way,' Grace said calmly, adjusting her left hand on the wheel to compensate for the sudden loss of power steering, trying to restart the car with her right. There was no response when she turned the key, and the only sound in the car was the muted hiss of the tires on the road.

Grace never actually frowned, at least not like other people. But something showed in her eyes, even as her face remained expressionless, almost as if they were turning inward to examine the emotions that others rarely saw. It wasn't a conscious thing – just a lesson learned long, long ago, that if you kept your feelings to yourself, people couldn't use them against you. At the moment, her dominant feeling was rage, directed toward her mechanic in particular and internal combustion engines in general.

You can't control everything. A smug, condescending psychiatrist had said that to her ten years ago, demonstrating his mastery of stating the obvious. Of course you couldn't control everything. Grace had learned that when she was five. But you could anticipate and prepare for any eventuality your imagination could come up with, and she was very good at that. The worst-case scenario was her specialty.

Not once did she consider that the Range Rover would start again, or that some Good Samaritan would come along to lend a hand and give them a ride. These were things that happened in some perfect, predictable world, but Grace had never been there. In her world, they were going to end up walking, and that's what she prepared for.

Her eyes scanned the side of the road for anything resembling a turnoff as the Range Rover slowed. They'd almost exhausted the last of their momentum when she spotted a dirt track making a doorway into the woods on the right. 'Is that a driveway?'

'Maybe . . .' was all Sharon had time to say before Grace turned the wheel and the Range Rover shot forward on the track's initial downward slope. Pine boughs slapped against the windows as the car lumbered around one sharp turn, then another. They were well into the woods by the time the car coasted to a stop. The shiny Range Rover sat in the middle of the shaded greenery like a black mistake, and for a moment, the only sound was the engine ticking as it cooled.

'That was exciting,' Sharon finally said. 'I liked the part where we zoomed down that little hill and almost ran into that tree. You know, I'm not sure how it works in the city, but over here if you're having car trouble, you just pull onto the shoulder.'

Grace unbuckled her seat belt and popped the hood. 'If we have to leave the car, I want it out of sight. We've got a fortune in hardware back there, most of it one of a kind.'

Annie was peering out her window, her breath fogging the glass. 'This is not a driveway.'

'It could be an old logging road,' Sharon suggested. 'And it looks like it might cut through the woods over to Four Corners. I bet we could walk it easy.'

Annie was horrified. 'You mean *outside*? It's a million degrees out there, and you want me to go hiking through the woods? Have you seen my shoes?'

But by then Grace and Sharon had both opened their doors, and a wave of heat had rolled into the car, obliterating what was left of the air-conditioning. 'Oh, for God's sake,' Annie grumbled, following them out, catching her breath when the full force of the afternoon heat hit her. She fluffed out her dress and minced her way to the front of the Rover, careful not to let the spiky heels of her pumps touch the forest floor. 'Well, open this thing's mouth so we can fix it and get out of here.'

'Annie, you don't know a thing about cars,' Grace reminded her.

'I know you look under the hood when they break. Besides, I'm an intelligent woman, and it's just an engine – how hard could it be to figure out? Maybe one of the gerbils died.'

Grace raised the hood and stood back a little, amused by Annie's look of concentration as she peered inside.

'This is so disorganized. Is it supposed to look like this?'

'Sort of.' Sharon leaned forward, then tipped her head to look at Grace. 'What are you thinking?'

'That we need a tow truck.'

Annie looked at the obviously useless engine as if it were a puppy that had just wet on the rug, then flounced back to the car and snatched her cell phone from the backseat.

'Not a lot of towers around here,' Sharon said, but that didn't stop Annie from waving the phone around like a magic wand as she spun in a slow circle, trying to snatch a signal out of the hot, heavy air. She tried Grace's phone, too, just in case hers was in some way inferior, then let her hands drop to her sides, thoroughly indignant. 'This is outrageous. It's the twenty-first century, we're in the most technologically advanced country in the world, and I cannot make a phone call. How do people live like this?'

For a moment, the three of them stood quietly, looking around. There was a deep, unnatural silence to the shadowy forest, as if it weren't a real forest at all, just a movie set. It was Grace who finally uttered the words Annie dreaded most.

'I guess we walk.'

Annie looked down helplessly at her beautiful, fluttery silk dress and her beautiful four-inch heels.

'I've got some extra tennies in my bag,' Sharon offered.

'Thank you,' Annie said, then thought about it for

a minute, considering what was really important. 'What color are they?'

As it turned out, they were lavender high-tops, and as Annie looked down at the rounded toes, damned if she didn't like what she saw.

'You look ridiculous,' Grace said.

'I refuse to entertain fashion criticism from a woman with a hundred black T-shirts. Besides, you put some heels on these things and they just might work.'

The logging road, if that's what it was, quickly deteriorated to a narrow dirt path pocked with the sliced prints of deer. Eventually, even the tracks of animals disappeared under a thick carpet of crackling, rust-colored needles. On either side, the forest thickened and darkened, with the lacy fronds of giant ferns quivering at their passage.

Annie eyed the foliage suspiciously, thinking it looked entirely too prehistoric for her taste. And it wasn't just the tropical heat or the mutant ferns that reminded her of *Land of the Lost* – everything about this little excursion had set them back ten thousand years. 'This is absurd,' she mumbled, shifting the strap of her voluminous shoulder bag. Grace had tried to talk her out of taking it, but the day Annie went anywhere without her makeup would be the day they put her in the ground. 'An hour ago, we were three intelligent, successful women in a seventy-thousand-dollar car with cell phones and some of the most advanced computer equipment on the face of the earth, and now we're slogging through a primordial forest like the Barbarella triplets.'

Sharon laughed. 'Nature's the great equalizer.'

'Nature sucks. It's hot and sticky, and it smells like dirt out here. And by the way, would you two waifs slow down? You're with a size-large woman who's wearing flat shoes for the first time in her life, and this path is a death trap. There are tree roots poking out everywhere. Somebody should pave this thing.'

The ninety-degree heat made short work of Annie's laundry list of grievances about the great outdoors, and silence closed around their little parade. The farther into the woods they went, the more the forest seemed to press down on them as giant pines linked boughs overhead, creating a dark, aromatic canopy. The silence was as dense as the tightly packed carpet of dried needles underfoot, and as oppressive as the weight of air so still it almost seemed to have substance.

Eventually, the trees seemed to thin a bit, and then abruptly, the woods opened before them, like a door onto a lighted room. They took a step out of the trees onto a circle of old, broken asphalt that formed a crude cul-de-sac. It narrowed into a strip of potholed tar that intersected a road a hundred feet ahead.

'Thank God,' Annie muttered, fanning her perspiring face with a plump hand. 'Damn woods is like a sauna.' Then she raised her hand to shield her eyes from the bright afternoon sun and looked around.

'Good heavens. Is this supposed to be a town?'

There was an old frame house nearly backed into the woods on their right, a pair of concrete-block buildings up on each corner, and not much else.

'At least there's a gas station,' Sharon said, nodding at the rusting hulks of old cars jammed together behind the building on the left.

'Well,' Annie said, plucking at her bodice. 'Good luck to us all if that's the Range Rover service center.'

Sharon smiled. 'You might be surprised. Some of these small-town mechanics can fix just about anything.'

Grace stood very still for a moment, watching, listening, trying to shake the feeling that she'd just crept uninvited through someone's back door. 'All we need is a phone,' she finally said, and started toward the gas station.

Up at the intersection, they all hesitated and squinted up and down the empty two-lane road. The woods on the other side looked almost solid, like a living green glacier moving inexorably to swallow whatever puny structures man had erected here. To the left, just past the gas station, the road curved quickly out of sight into the thick woods. It disappeared just as quickly to the right over the crest of a small hill. There was no movement and no sound. Grace could almost hear herself breathe.

Annie looked around, irritated. 'Four Corners, my foot. There are only two corners in this town. Talk about delusions of grandeur.' The silence seemed to swallow the echo of her voice, and she frowned abruptly. 'Damn, it's quiet here.'

Sharon chuckled. 'You've never spent much time in the country, have you?'

Annie snorted. 'Of course I have. The country's what you drive through on the way from city to city.'

'Well, this is what it's like when you get out of the car. It's a hot, lazy, summer Saturday in a little nowhere burg, and quiet is one thing you get in abundance in a place like this.'

Grace thought about that. Sharon was the native, the country deputy from Wisconsin, and as alien as this kind of quiet was to Annie and Grace, Sharon accepted it as perfectly normal, and Sharon would know. Still, she felt uneasy.

It wasn't just that there were no people in sight – that wouldn't have been so odd in a little town where the census takers probably counted on their fingers – but there was no evidence that there were people anywhere. No radios, no dogs barking, no muted laughter of children in the distance – no sound at all.

She looked at the building to their right, at the sign hanging from a wrought-iron bracket with letters spelling out 'Hazel's Café.' To the left was the gas station, obviously showing its best side to the highway. The two old-fashioned pumps squatted on a concrete island between the building and the road, their metal cases polished and oddly clean. A faded blue sign hung on a tall metal post, advertising 'Dale's Gas' in white block letters. At least the door was wide open, suggesting that someone might be inside, out of the heat.

Her boots clicked on the concrete as she crossed the apron toward the door. It seemed strange not to hear the syncopated accompaniment of Annie's omnipresent high heels next to her, just the soft slap of the borrowed high-tops and the leather squeak of Sharon's lace-ups. It bothered her that she could hear these sounds so clearly.

The gas station was as empty and still as the town itself. Grace stepped inside, listened for a moment, then moved toward an interior doorway that opened onto a darkened, deserted garage. Her nose wrinkled at the ripe smells of old oil, gasoline, and solvents, advertising that this was a working garage, even though the picture didn't match the smells. From what she could see in the shadowy garage, the entire place was coated with layers of grime that could probably count the years like rings on a tree. But the inside of the station proper seemed almost spit-shined. Hands that touched an oil can apparently never made it to the register. There wasn't a single greasy fingerprint smeared across its keys or the white Formica countertop it sat on. Even the inside of the window bore the streaked circles of a recent washing, which seemed strange since the outside of the glass was still spotted from the last rain.

Sharon was preoccupied with a map of Wisconsin tacked to one wall, but Annie was looking around the station, hands on her hips. 'Good Lord, who owns this place? The Amish?' She ran a fingernail over the top of the counter, then inspected it. 'Harley's kitchen should be so clean.'

'Oh, boy.' Sharon was tapping a point in the map. 'You are here,' she pronounced. 'We're a little more off the track than I thought.'

Grace looked over her shoulder and winced. 'Looks like we're still about a hundred miles from Green Bay.'

'I'd better call them, give them a heads-up on the delay. I told the detectives we'd be there by four, and there's no way we're going to make that.' Sharon went to the phone on the counter, picked up the receiver and put it to her ear, then frowned and pushed the disconnect button a few times before she hung up. 'Damn thing's broken.'

Annie rolled her eyes and turned in a flutter of limp silk, grumbling about small towns stuck in the dark ages, cars, heat, humidity, and the telecommunicating world in general. She kept up her monologue as Grace and Sharon followed her all the way across the crumbling side street and up the three concrete steps that led to the café's screen door. 'I'm going to order myself a quart of iced tea and then –' She stopped in mid-sentence as she opened the door, then released a great breath. 'All right, ladies. This is starting to get a little weird.'

Grace eased the screen door closed behind them, and the three women stood there for a moment in the silence, staring at the empty booths, the empty stools by the counter, the empty galley cooking area behind it. Everything was spotless. If it hadn't been for the odors of fried food and baked goods still lingering under an acrid, antiseptic smell, Grace would have thought the place hadn't been a working café for years.

Sharon went to the counter and picked up the phone that sat by the register. She looked sheepishly at the other two when she put it down again. 'So the phones are out all over town.' She shrugged. 'Probably takes the phone company days to get out to a little spot like this and make repairs.'

Annie raised one perfectly arched brow. 'And the people?'

'Who knows? Fishing, town picnic, siesta . . .' Sharon looked from Annie to Grace, saw the uncertainty in one face and the hard tension in the other, and realized for the first time how very different they all were. She knew the origins of Grace's paranoia – hell, if she had lived with a serial killer's bull's-eye on her for ten years, she'd be paranoid, too. And from the first time she'd met her in the hospital, she'd pegged Annie as a woman who'd learned the hard way not to trust in much. But Sharon had her own history now – had been living on the edge of panic for months, ever since she'd taken a bullet in the Monkeewrench warehouse. But for the first time since she'd felt that slug plow into her neck, she felt oddly comfortable and safe in this place where the emptiness and quiet were so disturbing to the other two.

She laid her shoulder bag on the counter and sank onto a stool. 'Okay. I get that you're weirded out by this place, but what you have to understand is that this is normal. I spent most of my life in a little town not much bigger than this, and you know the first time I locked a door? When the FBI put me in that Minneapolis apartment nine months ago, right after I got out of the hospital.'

Annie scowled at her. 'These are businesses. You don't walk away from a business on a Saturday afternoon and leave the door unlocked, no matter where you live. That's just plain crazy.'

Sharon sighed. 'I'm telling you, that's the way it is in a place like this. What customers are they going to miss? Their neighbors? They'd probably help themselves and leave the money on the counter. And neighbors don't steal from neighbors out here. Grace, what are you looking for?'

She'd been wandering around the café, eyes sweeping the floor, the empty booths, and finally the front window. 'Hmm?'

'You see something out there?'

'Outside? No. But I'm going to take a walk, check out the house we passed on the way in. Be right back.'

Grace started to walk around the side of the café toward the frame house behind it, then stopped, blue eyes riveted to the small metal box bolted into the concrete block. A fat sheath of PVC snaked down from the bottom into the ground. She walked a little closer to read the name of the local telephone company imprinted on the box, just to make sure, then felt a shot of adrenaline fire at her heart. The PVC sheath, and the cluster of wires within, had been sliced through.

Grace froze in position, moving only her eyes, and felt her hearing sharpen, trying to pull sounds out of this eerily silent place.

Kids, she told herself. *Kids with a pocketknife and a serious streak of ill-guided mischief.*

After a few moments she moved slowly, cautiously, circling the gas station until she found its phone box and severed cord sprouting ragged wire ends. Her mind was moving at light speed, compensating for the restraint she forced on her body.

She found the outside phone box on the house, another clean cut, and then moved warily to the front door, opened it, looked into the shadows, and listened. It wasn't necessary to search the place. She knew instantly that there was no one inside.

She closed the door to the house quietly, then stood there on the stoop for a moment, looking, listening, longing for a breeze to ruffle the silence that threatened to smother her.

She didn't care what Sharon said about normalcy and small towns and unlocked doors on a Saturday afternoon. She couldn't think of any of that now. She was too busy listening to the voice in her head that said they weren't supposed to be there.

6

Sheriff Michael Halloran was sitting in his office on the second floor of the Kingsford County Government Center, his chair turned toward the big window that looked out over Helmut Krueger's dairy farm.

He'd never heard anyone describe Bonar Carlson as brilliant, but the man saw more than most and paid attention to details that the rest of the world glossed over. That was part of what made him such a good cop. Halloran was now seeing what Bonar had noticed a long time ago, and it made him feel a little inferior, like he'd been walking around with his eyes shut for most of the summer.

Helmut Krueger's pasture wasn't nearly as lush and green as it should have been; it had that autumn cast that happens when grass starts to dry from the roots up and the yellow shows through. And if that wasn't enough to confirm Bonar's predictions of drought, all you had to do was look at the herd of Holsteins. They were crowded into a black-and-white jumble today, butts out like football players in a huddle, tails beating ineffectually at the plague of biting flies that could take a hundred pounds off a heifer in a matter of days.

Bugs of one sort or another were a constant bother

during any Wisconsin summer, but when drought threatened, the mosquito population went way down while the deerflies, horseflies, and stable flies reproduced in epidemic numbers to torment the daylights out of farm animals.

The signs had all been there in front of him, and Halloran hadn't seen them. It made him question his own powers of observation, made him wonder what he was doing in a job where success often rested on seeing what other people didn't.

Like this case. This was his second homicide case in as many years, after a decade of thinking that breaking up a bar fight was going to be the pinnacle of his law enforcement career. No way did that kind of background prepare you for making sense of three bodies that looked like war casualties dumped in a rural swimming hole.

He looked down at the case file cover sheet on his desk, the blank lines taunting him with all he didn't know.

Bonar gave the doorjamb a cursory rap on his way in, heading straight for the chair opposite Halloran's desk. When he sat down, the cheap vinyl wheezed like a defective whoopee cushion. 'I've got a thumbprint on my birth certificate,' he said without preamble. 'You do, too.'

'I do?'

'You were born at Kingsford General, right?'

'Right.'

'Then you were printed.'

Halloran lifted a pen. 'Should I be taking notes?'

'Most hospitals print newborns right in the delivery room. Feet, hands, thumb, something, so they don't send the wrong baby home with the mother. So what I want to know is, how hard would it be to print a full set off every kid when they were born and put them in some kind of a database?'

'Gee, Bonar, you've got the makings of a despot.'

'Do you know how many bodies go unidentified every year? How many families sit around waiting for someone to come home, and all the time they're in the ground somewhere under a John Doe marker?'

Halloran sighed. 'I'll take a wild guess here. Nothing came up on the prints, right?'

'Not in AFIS, or anywhere else they let us look. And I don't mind telling you I was pretty surprised that not one of the three had an arrest record. It seems obvious that they were running in a pretty rough crowd, and not one of them did time? That almost defies logic.'

Halloran started making folds in the case cover sheet. 'Maybe they were just nice young men who got caught in the wrong place at the wrong time.'

'You're going to have to do some fast talking to convince me that an execution with an automatic rifle was just some kind of unfortunate turn of events.' Bonar pulled a flattened Snickers bar out of his pants pocket, ripped it open, and took a huge bite. 'Any luck with Missing Persons?'

'Nothing on our sheets. I've got Haggerty posting the photos on the nationwides, for all the good it will do.'

Bonar dabbed a fleck of chocolate from his lip with his little finger. 'These boys are pretty fresh. Maybe no one's missing them yet.'

'Could be. The autopsies might give us a place to start, but that's going to take a while. Doc says the state boys at Wausau are backed up with that multiple on Highway 29.'

Bonar sighed and got up to throw his Snickers wrapper in the garbage can. 'You want to tell me how we're supposed to solve a triple homicide without knowing who the victims are?'

Halloran went back to folding the paper on his desk. 'How many automatic rifles you figure we've got in this neck of the woods, Bonar?'

'Probably one or two more than Fort Bragg.'

'And who uses them?'

Bonar thought about that for a minute. 'Well, we busted Karl Wildenauer for blasting ducks with one last November.'

'Besides Karl.'

'Green Bay took a couple of AK-47s in that cocaine bust last week.'

Halloran scribbled on a notepad. 'Okay. Drug dealers.'

Bonar made a face. 'Kingsford County may have a few teenagers trying to grow pot in their folks' corn patch every now and again, but I doubt they've got firing squads on retainer. The real serious bad boys usually do their dealing in the cities.'

'So maybe it's city business. Maybe this was a body dump, pure and simple. Wouldn't be the first time. How about if we send the morgue shots to some of the narc divisions around the state, maybe even Chicago, see if anybody recognizes them.'

'That's an excellent thought.'

'Thank you. Now tell me who else uses automatic rifles, just in general.'

Bonar rolled his eyes to the ceiling and started rattling them off: 'Military, organized crime, militia crackpots, collectors – and we have a fair number of all of those in the Dairy State.'

'That's about the same list I came up with, and I'm thinking that if our three victims were involved in any one of those, Milwaukee might be able to help us out with an ID.'

'The FBI?'

'And maybe the ATF – I'd be willing to bet they both have lists nobody else gets to see.'

'I take it you feel like spending the rest of the weekend jumping through flaming hoops.'

'Not particularly. I was hoping we could grease the wheel a little. What about that buddy of yours you used to play poker with? Doesn't his son work for the Feds?'

Bonar clucked his tongue. 'Not anymore. Poor kid had some nervous troubles a while back and had to resign. I think he's managing a Dairy Queen in Fond du Lac now.'

'Sorry to hear that.'

'It's not all bad. We can probably get free ice cream whenever we're in the neighborhood.'

'Terrific. In the meantime, let's fax off the morgue shots and prints to the Milwaukee SAC anyhow, cover all our bases.'

'Sure, we can go the horse-and-buggy route if you want. Or you could just call Sharon in Minneapolis and tell her to run it through.'

Halloran pretended he hadn't heard that and started shuffling through papers on his desk. 'What's the SAC's name again? Burt somebody?'

'Eckman.'

'That's right. You want to put together a package while I jot him a note?'

Bonar cocked his head curiously. 'You've got a direct line to the FBI, and you're not going to use it because . . . ?'

Halloran continued sifting through papers urgently until he found a blank fax cover, then began filling it in with a surgeon's concentration. He ignored Bonar for as long as he could, until he was hovering over Halloran's desk like a sadistic Goodyear Blimp.

'Call her, Mike. Purely business.'

Halloran laid down his pen very carefully. 'Do not try to come up on that kind of crap sideways, Bonar. Sharon and I don't talk anymore, and you know it.'

'Yeah, I know it, and it's a damn shame, if you ask me.'

'I didn't.'

'You're going to have to talk to her sometime. Technically, she's still a Kingsford County Deputy.'

'Only until Monday.'

'Huh?'

'That's when her leave expires. If she's not at roll call Monday morning, she's out.'

That put Bonar right back down in his chair, staring at his old friend across the desk. 'Jesus, does she know that?'

Halloran nodded shortly. 'Official notification went out a month ago. Certified. She got it.'

'You sent her a letter telling her she was out? A *letter*?'

'Thirty days' notice in writing. That's the law.'

'A phone call might have been nice.'

Halloran laid down his pen and looked Bonar in the eyes. 'This is the way it is. I've got a department to run; I've got a hole in the roster I've been working around for months, ever since Sharon took her so-called "temporary leave," and I've got a phone that rings anytime a deputy of mine takes the trouble to dial the number. Sharon stopped returning my calls months ago, and I got tired of talking to her machine. Now. Do you want to keep riding me about Sharon, or do you want to hear my other idea on how to ID our three sinkers?'

Bonar leaned back and folded his arms across

what he could still find of his chest. 'I'd really like to keep riding you about Sharon, but if it'll make you happy, I'll listen to your idea first.'

7

It was the third year the Minneapolis Police Department had sponsored a Fun Fair for the Youth in Crisis Program, and this one promised to be the most successful yet. It was nearly four o'clock already, but the park was still jammed with parents and kids, and most of the cops who weren't on duty were either volunteering at one of the booths or enjoying the festivities with their own children in tow.

Detective Leo Magozzi had just finished his volunteer stint selling hot dogs in the food tent, and now it was time for some real fun. He bought three tickets for the dunk tank from a new hire out of Fraud, politely laughed at his lame '*drunk* tank' crack, then got in line under the bright August sun with about twenty other people, including Chief Malcherson. Tall, light-haired, and icy-eyed, the man looked far too Nordic to carry off summer wear. It was the first time Magozzi had ever seen the painfully genteel man in anything other than a very expensive suit, and it was a little unsettling. Even the Chief himself seemed slightly at odds in his alien skin of lightweight shirt and slacks, his hand straying every now and then to his tieless collar, as if searching for a missing body part.

'Afternoon, sir. I'm glad you could make it today,' Magozzi greeted him.

Malcherson gave him just a hint of a droll smile. 'I'm happy to be here, Detective. Although I must admit I'm feeling slightly guilty about standing in this line, planning to willfully contribute to the discomfort of one of our own.'

'You're in good company, sir.'

'I see that. And it *is* for a good cause.'

'That's exactly right, sir, and if it makes you feel any better, I know for a fact that Detective Rolseth is delighted for the opportunity to make such a substantial contribution.'

That, of course, was bullshit, and everybody, including Chief Malcherson, knew it. Gino Rolseth, Magozzi's partner and best friend, was mad as hell to be the main attraction today, but he really hadn't had much say in the matter. Earlier in the week, an anonymous donor had offered to match this year's Fun Fair proceeds, but only under the condition that Gino take the perch above the dunk tank.

Gino had immediately thrown a world-class fit, refusing flat-out, but once word got out in Homicide, everybody was quick to remind him that his refusal would be tantamount to ripping food from the mouths of needy children in danger of turning to the streets, et cetera, et cetera.

Nobody knew who was behind it – they all had their theories – but one thing was certain: it would be the only case Gino would be working until he figured it out.

Magozzi and Malcherson both cringed a little when they heard a loud salvo of hoots and hollers coming from the front of the line. A few minutes later, skinny little carrot-haired Detective Johnny McLaren was practically jigging toward them, a bright blue snow-cone smile plastered on his sun-pinkened face.

'Man, was that great! You should have seen the expression on his face when the ball connected and he went down. Glad I'm on vacation next week, is all I have to say.' He turned toward Malcherson. 'Come on, Chief, you've gotta know who's behind this. You took the call, right?'

Chief Malcherson's expression was stone. 'I truly have no idea, Detective. I was hardly in a position to press the matter of identity, given this very generous individual's adamant wish to remain unnamed.'

McLaren smirked a little and rocked back and forth on his feet, trying to decide whether or not to believe him. 'Okay, sure, Chief. The whole gift horse thing. Well, good luck, guys. I'm going to go buy myself another ticket.'

'I can *not* frigging believe that you, of all people, my own partner for Christ's sake, actually participated in this travesty.' Gino was sitting morosely at a sunny picnic table with Magozzi, slurping the sticky remains of a snow cone out of its limp paper holder. He'd exchanged his soaked swimming trunks and

T-shirt for jeans and a vintage bowling shirt that had seen better days, probably sometime during the Korean War.

Magozzi did his best to look contrite. 'The Chief and I were actually having second thoughts there for a while, but when we saw your own daughter dunk you, that pretty much nailed it for us.'

'Yeah, but I've got an avenue of remuneration for that little traitor – Helen's going to be fifty before I let her get her learner's permit. Damnit, I knew I should never have let her go out for softball.'

'Well, if it's any consolation, I'm feeling pretty bad about the whole thing. Hell, I had no idea I could still throw like that.'

Gino glared at him. 'Yeah, right, and neither did the Chief, who I just found out was an all-star frigging pitcher at the U of M. I'll tell you what – you find out who the comedian is who set me up and maybe I'll think about forgiving you.'

'The Chief doesn't even know who it is.'

Gino scowled and scrubbed at his blond brush of wet hair. 'Yeah, right. You know what I think? I think this whole thing was a departmental conspiracy, and ten bucks says McLaren was the mastermind, the little Irish rat. I bet there isn't any anonymous donor, and you guys are all busting a gut right now.'

'Nope. I saw the wire-transfer number on Malcherson's desk the other day. Looked legit to me.'

'No kidding? Did you check it out?'

'Hey, I'd step in the line of fire any day for you,

buddy, but I'm not willing to lose my job over this.' Magozzi paused for a meaningful moment and then grinned. 'I did give it to Grace, though.'

Gino's scowl melted faster than his snow cone had. 'You are officially off my shit list, buddy.'

'Glad to hear it.'

'Okay, so spill it – justice awaits.'

'I don't know anything yet. Grace didn't have time to check it out before she left for Green Bay.'

'Damn, I forgot about that. When's she coming back?'

'In a couple days.'

'Oh, man, I can't wait that long.' Gino brooded over his predicament for a few moments, then looked at Magozzi triumphantly. 'Hey, what about Harley and Roadrunner? They can run the number just as easily as Grace can, and I bet they're bored out of their skulls without two high-maintenance women in their hair. We can take them out for beer and burgers later for their trouble.'

'It's Saturday night. Don't you have a hot date with the wife and kids?'

'The wife and kids are deserting me for a pizza party for Helen's softball team.'

'You're passing up pizza?'

'It's at one of those hideous theme restaurants where they let toddlers run amok and wallpaper with pepperoni. I have standards, you know. Besides, it's an all-girl thing.'

'What about the Accident? Isn't his manhood

going to be adversely affected by going to an all-girls thing?'

'Gender discrimination doesn't start until age five.'

Magozzi shrugged. 'I'll give Harley a call.'

Gino beamed at him. 'You're the man. Hey, buy me a hot dog, I'm starving.'

As Magozzi reached for his wallet, his cell phone chirped. 'Go on,' he said, passing over a twenty. 'Gotta get this.' He was foolishly hoping that perhaps Grace MacBride had been overwhelmed with the sudden need to hear his voice. This had never happened before, but sometimes you just had to hold on to the dream.

He was hanging up as Gino wandered back to the picnic table, loaded with three footlongs, two bags of mini-donuts, and an unidentifiable deep-fried thing on a stick.

Gino handed over two dollars in change.

'That's *it*?'

'Hey, it's for a good cause, that's what you kept telling me. Was that Grace?'

'Nope. Our old buddy Mike Halloran.'

It took Gino a couple of seconds to place the name. 'No kidding? How the hell's life in the Cheese Belt?'

'Pretty interesting, as of this morning.'

'Yeah? What's up?'

'They pulled three bodies out of a swimming hole this morning, figured them for drownings. But when they laid them out, they saw a whole lot of holes that shouldn't have been there. Somebody took a swipe at them with an automatic, the coroner thought maybe an M16.'

'Now that's something you don't see every day.'

'Not outside a third-world country, anyhow. All the shots lined up, too, execution-style.'

Gino took a monstrous bite out of a mustard-and-onion-slathered dog. 'Jesus. What a way to spend a Saturday. But why did he call you? Does he think there's a Minneapolis connection or what?'

Magozzi shrugged. 'They don't know where to start, because they can't ID the bodies – totally nude, no identifying marks, and no hits on the fingerprints. Halloran was hoping Grace would run the morgue shots through her facial-recognition software, see if anything popped that way.'

'So why didn't he just call Sharon? They're practically driving past his front door.' Gino polished off his first dog and started in on the second one.

'Because Halloran had no clue Sharon was on her way to Green Bay with Grace and Annie.'

Gino's brows lifted. 'I thought those two were a hot item.'

'It's hard to date when you live two hundred miles apart.'

'What's wrong with phone sex?'

'I didn't ask.'

'Christ, I hope she didn't dump him for a suit.'

'We didn't get into particulars.'

'Did you call Grace?'

'No answer on her cell. I left a message.' Magozzi eyed Gino's deep-fried-thing-on-a-stick. 'What the hell is that?'

'Dill pickle.'

'That's disgusting.'

'Like you would know.'

8

When Grace finished checking all the phone lines, she walked back to the street in front of the café and stood there for a moment, listening. The only sounds she heard were Annie's and Sharon's muffled voices coming from inside, but when she turned to look, the glare of the sun bouncing off the big plate-glass windows nearly blinded her.

They looked up when Grace pushed open the screen door. Annie and Sharon were sitting at the counter, sipping from soda cans taken from the glass-fronted cooler, Annie waving her cell phone, trying to find a signal. 'This piece of crap is hopeless. Doesn't work outside, doesn't work inside . . . You find anybody, darlin'?' She handed Grace a bottled water and tucked the useless phone back in her purse.

Grace shook her head, opened the bottle, and took a quick drink before she spoke. 'Someone cut all the phone lines.'

'*What?*'

'Right below the feeder boxes. On the café, the gas station, and the house.'

All three were silent for a moment.

Sharon finally said, 'Kids, maybe.'

'Maybe.'

Annie was watching Grace's face. 'What are you thinking, Grace?'

'That we should get out of here.'

Annie sighed, took a last drink from her soda can, and pushed herself up off the stool. She went over to the cooler, grabbed three bottles of water, and set one on the counter in front of Sharon.

'What's this for?'

'Tuck it in your bag, darlin'. It's mighty hot out there, and it appears we're going to be doing a little more walking.'

'You're kidding, right? According to the map in the gas station, it's at least another ten miles to the next town, and that's after we hoof it all the way back to the truck. Can't a couple of techno-whizzes like you fix the phone lines?'

'It's a twenty-five-pair cable,' Grace replied. 'That's a lot of splicing. It might take a couple hours.'

'By which time the people who live here will probably be back from wherever they went and will be happy to give us a ride. In the meantime, we've got food and drink and a place to get out of the sun . . .'

Annie looked at Sharon as if she'd lost her mind, forgetting for a moment that not everyone in the free world knew that when Grace said 'we should get out of here,' it was like a Seeing Eye dog jerking a blind person out of the way of a runaway bus. 'We should leave now.'

'Okay,' Sharon continued, trying to be reasonable. 'How about this. You and Grace stay here, start working on the phones, and in the meantime, just to cover all our bets, I'll start walking, maybe get lucky and catch a ride. No offense, Annie, but it's over ninety out there, and I'm guessing aerobics isn't your . . .'

'Quiet.' Grace had moved quickly, almost soundlessly, over to the screen door, where she stood with her eyes closed and her concentration focused in a cone of awareness that headed left past the gas station, around the curve that disappeared into the woods. What she'd heard had been nothing specific, nothing immediately identifiable – just a faint, muted roaring sound that didn't belong.

'Something's coming' was all she had time to say.

Harold Wittig slammed the gearshift into park and draped his wrists over the pickup's steering wheel, his lips tightened in annoyance. He lifted one arm and wiped his sweaty forehead on his sleeve, promising himself for the hundredth time that he was going to junk this damn truck and get one of the big new Fords with an air conditioner that would turn a two-dollar whore frigid. Damn, it was hot, and the day had been one disaster after another.

First a flat tire on the way into Rockville this morning, then Fleet Farm hadn't had Tommy's birthday bike assembled and they'd had to wait two hours while a couple doofuses fumbled around with Allen wrenches and a forty-page instruction manual, then Jean got her period and made him run into the store to buy a box of Tampax and he thought he'd die right there at the checkout when the pretty young cashier had smiled sweetly and said, 'Just the Tampax? Is that it?' and now this. Christ, what a day.

He glared out the dusty windshield at the empty jeep on the side of the road and the two orange-and-white sawhorses topped with blinking yellow lights, blocking both lanes. Two men stood in front of the roadblock, wearing camouflage and combat boots and the earnest expressions of little boys playing soldier. M16s that Harold dearly hoped weren't loaded with live rounds were slung over their shoulders. The way his luck was running today, one of them would probably walk up to the truck and shoot him in the head.

Jean was leaning forward in her seat, as if another inch closer to the windshield would make the reason for the peculiar roadblock perfectly clear. Her face was dewy with the heat, and her lips were folded in on each other in that slightly alarmed expression she always wore when something didn't make sense. 'What are they? Soldiers?'

'Looks like. Probably Guard.'

'What are they doing? Why do they have the road blocked off?' Her voice was rising up the scale as a seed of panic germinated, and Harold knew her imagination was already running wild, manufacturing improbable scenarios of tornadoes, floods, riots, and any of the other disasters that brought the National Guard out into the civilian world.

'Relax, honey.' He laid a comforting hand on her knee. 'They're just weekend warriors, and they've got to practice somewhere.' But the truth was that he felt a little tickle of unease on the back of his own neck as one of the young men headed toward the driver's side of the truck. This one was fair and freckled and sporting a brand-new sunburn, but he had the bearing down pat: straight back, clipped movements, and that tucked chin you see only in the posture of a military man at attention. 'Afternoon. What's up, soldier?'

The soldier stepped right up to Harold's open window, his rifle now casually at his side, and gave them a friendly nod. 'Afternoon, sir, ma'am. I'm afraid the road's closed temporarily. We're detouring traffic up to County S –'

'What do you mean, the road's closed? Why?'

'Military maneuvers, sir. Your tax dollars at work.'

Jean breathed a sigh of relief, then felt irritation rise to fill the empty space where panic had lived just a moment before. She'd been prepared to deal with catastrophe, but not inconvenience. She brushed a clump of damp blond curls from her forehead and started fanning her face with the Fleet Farm sale flyer. 'What do you mean, military maneuvers?' she snapped at the young soldier, and Harold had to smile as the man's brows shot up in surprise, almost pitying him for being stupid enough to put a roadblock between Jean and her shower on the first day of her period. 'We live on this road and there were no military maneuvers going on here when we left this morning.'

Harold started to give the soldier an apologetic grin, but something in the man's face made his smile falter. The stoic, soldierly countenance was suddenly gone, replaced by a ripple of confusion and maybe even a little fear, and that made him nervous. Men in uniform weren't supposed to be confused or fearful, and when they were, bad things happened. 'Uh . . . you say you live on this road, ma'am?'

'That's right. About a half a mile the other side of Four Corners. The big farm on the left. And now we'll thank you to move that little barrier out of the way so we can get home to our son.'

The soldier was very still for a moment, then he took a breath and put the tough face back on. 'I'm very sorry, ma'am, but I can't do that. We have orders not to let anyone by.'

'You have *orders* to keep me from going home?' Jean asked incredulously, leaning forward in her seat so she could shoot a withering glance in the soldier's direction. 'I don't think so. Now let us by or we'll drive right over you and your roadblock.'

Oh, this was just terrific, Harold thought. He was planted smack-dab in the middle of a firing zone between a raging woman and a stressed-out kid with a firearm. He gave Jean a warning glance, then turned back to the soldier, forced a thin smile, and tried his best to sound reasonable, even though his patience was fraying. 'Listen, soldier, we just want to get home to our boy. Surely you can understand that.'

'I do, sir, but we have our orders,' he repeated.

'And just what are we supposed to do? Drive around until you're finished playing your war games?'

'That's up to you, sir. I'm just doing my job.'

'This is not your job. I want to speak to your commanding officer right now. And if you don't make that happen, I'm going to turn this truck around, find the closest phone, and you can make your explanations to the Missaqua County Sheriff's Department.'

The soldier was clearly distressed now, his eyes darting back and forth between them, and Harold thought he saw a flicker of guilt and remorse in his eyes. 'Would you wait just a moment, sir, ma'am?' I'm going to have to call this in.' And with that, he spun smartly on his heel and double-timed it back to the sawhorses where the other soldier stood watching.

Startled by his sudden departure, Harold felt the little tickle on the back of his neck intensify, and he nearly jumped out of his skin when Jean touched his hand.

'Something's wrong,' she whispered, and he heard the tremor in her voice and felt its echo deep in the pit of his stomach. 'Something happened, something they won't tell us . . .'

'Honey, take it easy.' Harold covered her hand with his and squeezed, trying to dredge up a reassuring smile. 'These boys can only do what they're told.

If he has orders to block the road, he'll keep his own mother out, but a higher-up will straighten him out.'

He watched the two soldiers through the windshield. Freckle-face was over at the jeep, talking to somebody on the radio; the other one kept his eyes trained on the pickup.

Harold rubbed at the sweat trickling down his neck. Damn truck was a sweatbox when it wasn't moving, and this was taking too damn long. 'Wait here. I'm going to see what the holdup is.'

Freckle-face had just signed off the radio when he heard the long screech of the truck door opening on rusty hinges and saw Harold Wittig step down onto the road. His first thought was how much the man looked like a comic-book Superman, with a curl of black hair over his forehead and the arms and shoulders of a weight lifter. His second thought was barely a thought at all – just an animal's instinctive response to stimuli. He spun in place like a deadly ballerina, swinging his rifle around to point directly at Harold Wittig's midsection, and even before he had completed his turn, his partner was down in a crouch with his rifle aimed. 'Hold it right there!'

Harold stopped dead and gaped at the rifles in utter disbelief. He finally remembered to blink when his eyes started to burn. He closed his mouth to swallow, then asked quietly, 'Are you boys out of your minds? What the hell do you think you're doing?'

The soldier's voice was a little shaky, but the

muzzle pointed at Harold never wavered. 'We're just doing our job, sir.'

Harold stared at him, incredulous. 'Your job? It's your job to point a weapon at an unarmed civilian? It's your job to keep people from going home?' He started to take a step forward.

'*Sir!*' The soldier rattled the strap on the M16 as he jerked it to brace on his hip.

Harold froze.

'Please don't move, sir.'

Goddamn weekend warriors, Harold thought, suddenly furious that a couple of toy soldiers who came out only once a month to play had the nerve to point guns, loaded or not, at one of the taxpayers who paid their salaries. He squared his shoulders and dropped his head and looked from one to the other. 'You boys have just bought yourselves a world of hurt . . .'

'Harold?'

Confused by the unexpected sound of his wife's voice, Harold swung his big head around to see Jean out of the truck, cowering by the right fender, terrified eyes jerking back and forth from her husband to the rifles. Jesus Christ, he would never understand women. She wouldn't eat eggs for fear of clogging an artery forty years down the line, but she'd walk out in front of two M16s as if she were made of Kevlar.

'Get back in the truck, Jean,' he said calmly, because even though he was sure – absolutely sure –

those guns weren't loaded, he didn't need her out here complicating matters.

She looked at him for a moment, then turned and got back into the truck.

'You too, sir,' Freckle-face called out, gesturing with his rifle. 'Back in the truck, please. Now. You're almost cleared for entry. I'm just waiting for a call-back. It should only be another minute or so.'

Harold glared at him for a second, then climbed up into the truck. He glanced at the tears coursing down his wife's face, saw the violent trembling of her hands, and for the first time in his life, wanted to harm another human being. Two of them, in fact. For right now, there wasn't a whole lot he could do with a couple of puffed-up hotshots who might or might not be carrying live ammunition, but by God, the second he got near a phone he was going to burn up the wires all the way to Washington if he had to, and see these assholes up on . . .

Wait a minute, Harold.

He'd been staring at the soldiers by the jeep, vision and mind clouded by the red blur of impotent fury, and goddamnit, he hadn't seen it, hadn't seen what any clear-eyed fool would have noticed right off, and now he felt a ball of fear that clenched at his stomach and almost stopped his heart.

'Jean,' he whispered, eyes straight ahead now, lips barely moving, sweat rolling down from his forehead like someone had just turned on a faucet. 'Get down on the seat and hang on.'

The funny thing was that Jean, as strong-minded a woman as he'd ever known, did as she was told without a second's hesitation, probably because she had known long before he did how wrong things were here. 'Are we going to find Tommy?' was the only thing she asked.

'That's where we're going.'

Harold eased the gearshift out of park, slowly, carefully, sliding his butt forward on the seat until he could barely see over the wheel, and then his lug-soled lace-up punched the accelerator and the old Ford leaped forward and smashed through the sawhorses like a crazed bull going through a barn wall. Shards of wood were flying everywhere, and the engine was roaring so loud that they could hardly hear the gunfire that was shattering the windows around them.

Annie and Sharon had moved up next to Grace at the café's screen door by the time the distant popping sound started to syncopate the roar of whatever was coming.

Annie was pretty excited. She'd already identified the roaring as the approach of a big pickup – she'd spent a fair amount of time in those during her Mississippi youth, both upright and reclined – and at this point she wasn't at all particular about the mode of transportation arriving. Just so she didn't have to walk ten miles in this heat or spend two hours trying to patch twenty-five telephone wires. The popping was troublesome, though. 'What is that? Firecrackers?'

'Automatic rifles,' Sharon replied without a trace of doubt, slipping her weapon from her leather shoulder bag, and Annie's vision of rescue by some husky country good ol' boys took a dark turn.

Grace already had her Sig in her hand. Over the years, her survival instinct had been honed down to the most primal level. She never stopped to analyze, to moralize, to ethically weigh the wisdom of pulling her gun. If she sensed danger, the weapon came out of the holster. It was that simple. And automatic rifle fire didn't belong in the Wisconsin countryside.

She was still looking through the screen door to the left where the road curved into the woods, and then they all heard it and saw it at the same time: a battered white pickup roaring around the curve and into the town, zigzagging crazily, steam pouring out of the grill, the shredded rubber of its tires slapping the tar while sparks flew from the undercarriage.

Grace flung out an arm, saying, 'Back! Back!' and pushing Annie and Sharon away from the door and the big front windows, her first fear being that the truck would veer into the café, shattering the glass. Instead, the roaring sound ended abruptly with the sudden death of its engine, and the truck came to a wheezing stop in the middle of the street directly in front of the café, its windows shattered, its side peppered with what had to be bullet holes.

In the next heartbeat, a jeep came careening

around the curve and screeched to a halt inches behind the crippled truck, and Grace and Sharon both started to raise their guns. But then two soldiers jumped out, automatic rifles leveled at the truck, both of them red-faced and screaming, 'Get out! Get out! Get out!' and for the very first time in more than a decade, Grace was holding a gun in her hand and wasn't certain what to do with it. Pulling her gun at the sound of automatic weapon fire had seemed perfectly sensible, but when the fire was coming from men in uniform, it changed everything. She caught a glimpse of Sharon's gun in her peripheral vision, frozen at half-mast as hers was.

The soldiers were yelling, the damaged passenger door screamed as it was flung open, and then there was silence so deep that Grace could hear the bright tinkling of shattered glass tumbling to the asphalt. A pretty blonde woman in a print dress stepped down from the truck and would have collapsed, had she not been supported by the strong hands of the man who climbed down behind her. Grace had a millisecond to see the flash of a gold wedding band on the man's left hand and a skim of white slip showing below the hem of the young woman's dress before the soldiers opened fire.

The man fell first, a red blossom erupting on the blue of his denim shirt. And then new red flowers bloomed all over the woman's dress and she began to sink to the ground.

For an instant, Grace, Sharon, and Annie were

frozen in place like mannequins on display – three women with their breath caught in their throats, standing ten feet behind a plate-glass window in plain view of anyone who happened to look.

But the guns kept firing, and when the man and the woman fell, that single heartbeat of immobility was over. The three women dove to the floor as one, below the sight line of the windows, and started scrambling on hands and knees toward the café's back door. They slipped outside with the guns still firing behind them, bolted across the narrow strip of grass between the café and the frame house, then into the woods.

That was the great thing about women, Grace thought. Forget the female reputation for endless speculation and discussion – when things went south, women didn't stop to analyze. Even women with guns in their hands deferred to instincts honed by centuries. Warning. Danger. Run. Hide.

9

A few yards into the trees, the relative darkness of the forest closed around the three women, giving the illusion, if not the reality, of safety.

And then the shooting stopped.

It was deathly still again – quiet enough to hear the muffled voices of the soldiers in the street in front of the café, even with the buildings and trees between them – quiet enough for the soldiers to hear them if they made too much noise.

The three women froze, moving again only when new noises broke the silence – another vehicle arriving in front of the café, then more voices that sounded like mad dogs barking.

More soldiers, Grace thought. *But how many more, where are they coming from, and why the hell did they shoot those people down?*

She remembered last October, when the entire city of Minneapolis knew that a killer would be at the Mall of America looking for the next anonymous victim; and she remembered how many people went to the mall anyway, blinded by that ingrained belief that bad things happened to other people, not to them. Grace had never thought that way. If there was a bad thing in the neighborhood, it was surely coming for her next, and the very first thing you did was try to get the hell out of there.

Her eyes searched the trees until she caught a glimpse of the old logging road, and when she started to move toward it, Annie and Sharon followed. Apparently all of them had the same thought in mind: getting back to the Range Rover, to the highway they'd come in on, away from whatever nightmare was happening in this town.

The going was easier on the old overgrown logging road. They moved quickly and silently past lacy banks of ferns so tall and thick that they brushed against their hands as they passed. Grace stayed in the lead, stopping every few yards to listen, long after the sounds from the street in front of the café had faded into the distance.

When they came to the place where the path angled left, Grace stopped again, but this time she went so still and rigid that Annie and Sharon both stopped in mid-step behind her, eyes wide to pierce the gloom, finally focusing on what Grace had seen before them. None of them breathed.

Several yards ahead, nearly obscured by the drooping arms of a big white pine, a soldier leaned casually against the tree, looking directly at them.

Sharon's fingers twitched ever so slightly.

Don't do that. Don't reach for the gun. You should have had it in hand anyway, you idiot, because now you don't dare move a muscle, you don't dare unsnap the holster because a tiny noise like that could get us all killed. And what the hell do you think you're going to do with it anyway? You've never shot anyone in your life, even that one time you should have, and now you're planning to start with a man in uniform? Jesus God, you don't even know what's going on here, you don't know who the bad guys are, and what if those people in the truck were terrorists planning to blow up the country and you shoot the brave soldier risking his life to defend his country just because he has a gun bigger than yours and you're scared? Think, goddamnit. Think like a cop, not like a woman.

She eased a quiet breath into her lungs and expelled it slowly, silently, her eyes on the soldier, trying to figure out if he was really looking right at them or if it only appeared that way.

After an endless, heart-stopping moment, he turned his head to the side and said, 'Pearson, you got a cigarette?' and then all three women looked in the direction he had turned and saw things that hadn't been readily visible before: another soldier standing a few yards to the right of the first, filtered sunlight glancing off the metal barrel of a gun, and farther away still, the distinctive shapes of other heads and shoulders, shifting slightly to relieve stiff muscles.

'They didn't say we could smoke out here.'

'Yeah, well, they didn't say we could take a piss, either, and you didn't let that stop you.'

'All right, all right, just a sec.'

As the two men moved together and dipped their heads to share a light, Grace sidestepped ever so slowly off the path, into the trees, and ducked into the lush cover of a thick stand of the giant ferns. She kept her head above the level of the greenery until Annie and Sharon were settled on their bellies beside her. When she was sure she couldn't see either one of them, even this close, she eased all the way down, closed her eyes, and listened to the pounding of her heart. It seemed terribly loud, and yet the rest of the woods was so quiet that she could hear the soldiers' conversation over it quite clearly.

'We're too tight here, Durham. We should spread out more.'

'Tight on the funnel points, Pearson. Perimeter 101.'

'You ask me, it's a waste of time. If we pulled everyone in off the perimeter, we could be out of here a hell of a lot sooner.'

'If somebody else gets through, it wouldn't matter how fast we pulled out. Containment. That's what it's all about now.'

Silence for a long moment, then the sound of a throat clearing. 'It wasn't supposed to go down like this.'

'It never is. And then the wild card shows up. Anybody with half a brain would have turned around at that roadblock instead of crashing through it.'

'I heard their kid was in here, Durham. What if there are other people out there like that? People who weren't here when everything went to hell, on their way back home right now? Then what?'

'You know damn well what. We follow orders, just

like Zacher and Harris did. Look at it this way, Pearson. Everyone they knew is dead anyway. Not a lot to come home to. Bottom line, anybody gets into this town, they don't get out, fucking period, end of story.'

And there it was, Sharon thought, as clear as new glass. The man and woman in the pickup had not been terrorists, drug runners, foreign agents, or any of the other things her mind had been buzzing through, searching for something that might explain, if not justify, being gunned down by American soldiers. They'd simply been in the wrong place at the wrong time.

Just like we are.

'Goddamnit, Durham, this is a fucking nightmare. Somebody's going to find out.'

'Not if we do our job.'

Right next to her, Sharon heard Annie take a soft breath. And then a plump hand moved a fraction of an inch in the darkness beneath the greenery, and a rainbow fingernail touched her hand. It startled her at first. She'd never seen Annie touch anyone. For the first time in nearly twenty years, she felt a sharp sting behind her eyes. She'd been alone for a very long time.

On Sharon's other side, Grace had rested her forehead on the tops of her hands, eyes closed. *Too close,* she was thinking. *Too damn close.* They'd almost walked into those soldiers, and it was her fault. She had been in the lead and she'd almost gotten them all killed. She put the guilt away, back in the place where she carried all the guilt for so many other things, and began to inch backward on her belly, deeper into the woods, farther away from the path. She moved very slowly, careful not to disturb the fronds overhead, because there could be no more mistakes. After several minutes of this painstaking, backward belly crawl, they were deep enough into the cover of the trees to rise to their hands and knees and begin the agonizingly slow, silent crawl away from the soldiers, away from freedom, back toward the town.

After what seemed like a very long time, they reached the edge of the woods behind Four Corners and lay abreast in the cover of a thicket of young locust trees.

Grace examined the strip of lawn that lay between them and the frame house behind Hazel's Café, then looked carefully in every direction, focusing longer on the shadows behind them. Those men in the woods had been so hard to see until they were almost on top of them. There could be a dozen of them within spitting distance and she wouldn't know it.

She closed her eyes and took a deep breath, forcing herself to clear her mind and concentrate only on the needs of the moment, and what they needed at the moment was a place to hide, a relatively safe place where they could consider all they'd seen and heard and decide what to do next.

Her gaze fixed on the storm-cellar door that slanted up to the foundation of the frame house. In front of the door was a bare patch of grass, indicating frequent use – maybe it was unlocked, too, like everything else in this town.

Grace looked over at Sharon and Annie, held up one finger that told them to stay put, then sprang away, darting across the grass, grasping the handle of the heavy wooden door and heaving it upward. The hinges moved easily in their oiled casings. She laid the door to rest on a concrete block obviously placed for that purpose, then looked down a short, steep flight of concrete steps. There was another wooden door at the bottom. Without a moment's thought to what she would do if there was someone behind that door, she scrambled down the steps, turned the old metal knob, and pushed inward.

A wall of cool, dank air rushed past her like a chilly ghost anxious to warm up. Goose bumps rose on her arms, as much from the temperature change as from anything lurking within. Her hand closed tighter on the sweat-slicked grip of her Sig as she let her eyes adjust to the gloomy space, barely illuminated by the thin, brownish light that filtered in through window wells near the ceiling. Sweating rock walls shored up the foundation, and rough-hewn uprights marched across a packed earth floor. Stacks of cardboard boxes with sides bowed and sagging from the damp climbed around some of the posts like moldy pyramids.

Grace moved silently through the clutter, zeroing in on every shadow that had the potential to conceal, then hurried back up the concrete steps to wave Sharon and Annie in. She watched as the two women crossed the lawn in the kind of fearful, crouching run you saw in war movies, not in real life.

Once they all were safely inside and the doors were closed behind them, Annie made a beeline for an old, four-legged concrete sink – to get a drink, wash her hands, rinse out her dress, who knew with Annie – but Grace grabbed her arm and pointed silently toward the ceiling. Even turning on a faucet wouldn't be safe if there was someone upstairs.

She moved to the flight of open wooden steps leading up a dark passage to the first floor, Sharon and Annie right behind her. At the top, she stopped and pressed her ear to the door, holding her breath, listening for a long time before turning the knob.

The door opened onto a central hallway that bisected the house from front to back. To their right was the front door that Grace had peered through earlier from the other side, when she'd been standing on the stoop, wondering who on earth would cut all the phone lines in this little nowhere town.

They moved soundlessly through the house in a stealthy, tiptoe exploration, stopping briefly at the open, double-hung windows in the living room to look and listen. There were no sounds coming from the street anymore, and that in itself was chilling. There should be noise after a slaughter, Grace thought – the wail of sirens and people to mark the terrible occasion. And yet there was nothing.

In the kitchen, at least, they found evidence that someone actually lived in this town – there was an unopened package of four pork chops floating in a bowl in the sink. The three women raised their heads from the sink and looked around, more wary than ever that this abnormally deserted town had been normal not so long ago, populated by normal people who took pork chops out to thaw for supper.

The bedroom and bath belonged to an older woman, filled with a lifetime of knickknacks, crocheted doilies, and bizarrely, an old stuffed animal propped carefully against the pillows on the bed. Grace imagined a carnival game fifty years past and an aging woman's memories of a lanky boy and better times. The pervasive, sickly-sweet smell of cheap perfume that's been in the bottle too long lingered in the stifling air.

Sharon sat on the bed and reached halfheartedly for the phone on the nightstand. She knew it wouldn't work. It was just something you did. 'You heard them,' she said, putting down the useless phone. 'They're all dead. Everybody who lived in this town. The woman who lived in this house.'

Grace and Annie just looked at her. Well, yes, that was probably true, but that didn't mean there was any reason to just blurt it out like that.

'And they're not soldiers. Our soldiers do not kill civilians. They do not shoot down people in the street.'

Grace didn't think it was necessary to remind her

that such unthinkable things had indeed happened, in this country and others. Sharon knew that as well as any American. But good soldiers and good cops had a bond and common purpose that Grace had never experienced. She'd been on the other side too long, glimpsing it only through Magozzi's eyes. And Annie didn't bother herself with such trifles, never trusted a man inside or outside of a uniform, as far as Grace knew.

'It wouldn't be the first time the military tried to bury a screwup,' Annie said tactlessly. 'Maybe it's not soldiers – maybe it's some fringe group of whackos with a charge card at the local surplus store, but it could be either. And in the long run, what does it matter? These are not nice people.'

Sharon narrowed her eyes. 'You sound like every conspiracy theorist I ever met. Do you really think soldiers just walked into this place and started shooting everybody?'

Annie found a little boudoir chair at a makeup table that interested her. It held a jumble of cosmetics tubes and jars and a surprisingly neat row of nail enamel in every color of the rainbow. She picked a jar of purple with sparkles in it and held it up to the window. 'I'll tell you what I think. I think something unexpected happened here – an accident, maybe – and those assholes in camouflage, whether they're soldiers or not, are trying to keep it quiet, and they're willing to kill people to do it – including us, just because we happened to stumble onto the place.'

Grace was watching Sharon's face, thinking this was harder for her. She was a good cop, like Magozzi. Believing the worst of the people you thought shared your ideals was almost impossible. 'Annie's right about one thing,' she said. 'Who or what they are doesn't make a whole lot of difference at this point. We need to get the hell out of here. Those men are all over the woods, and eventually they're going to find the Rover, then there won't be a place in this town that's safe.'

'Oh, Lord,' Annie whispered, staring into the mirror as if she were seeing something that wasn't her reflection. 'That's not the only thing they're going to find. We left our purses in the café.'

Sharon closed her eyes. 'Oh, Jesus.'

Grace blew out a long sigh and glanced out the window. 'What time does it get dark?'

'Seven-thirty, eight,' Annie said immediately, but Sharon shook her head.

'That's Minneapolis. It's a half hour earlier this far east, earlier still in woods like these.'

Grace was weighing the risks of trying to escape in daylight against waiting another hour until dark. It was one of those decisions that could either save your life or get you killed, and it never occurred to her to let someone else make it. 'We'll wait for dark,' she decided. 'If it seems safe, we can pick up the purses on our way.'

'And just how are we supposed to get out?' Sharon asked. 'Those guys are too hard to see in the woods, and we sure as hell can't just stroll down the road . . .'

'Not on it, but right next to it, down in the ditch, on our bellies again if we have to. And not back the way we came in. We know there are soldiers covering that end of town, so we'll try the other direction. Even if they're patrolling the road itself, they'll do it by jeep, and we can hear them coming.' She looked at Sharon specifically. 'How does that sound?'

Sharon almost smiled. That Grace had asked the question at all was simply a courtesy, because ultimately, Grace MacBride would do what she wanted to do. 'Actually, it sounds wrong. I've got a gun and two badges, and I'm supposed to be chasing bad guys, not running away from them.'

'Honey, not even Rambo would take on these kinds of odds,' Annie said.

'Yeah, I know,' Sharon said, stretching her arm until the fingers of her right hand brushed the long, silky fur of the stuffed animal next to her on the bed. Suddenly she went still, frowning. The fur felt . . . sticky. She focused on the strands twined in her fingers, then raised her gaze slightly and stared straight into the glassy eyes of a very dead Yorkshire terrier. Some awful liquid had oozed from its open mouth to puddle and congeal beneath the fur of its chest – the very fur she had been stroking. 'Oh, shit,' she whispered, launching herself off the bed, holding her hand at arm's length. 'That's a real goddamned dog.' Then she raced into the bathroom.

Grace and Annie moved to the bed and stared

down at the pathetic pile of fur. From this angle, it still looked remarkably like a stuffed animal; they had to bend even closer to see the extent of the horror that had sent Sharon on her first solo flight of the day.

Annie squeezed her eyes shut as Grace handled the dog, slipping her fingers into its long hair, searching. Finally she straightened.

'There isn't a mark on that dog,' she said quietly.

Annie wrinkled her nose. Unlike Grace, she wasn't all that familiar with death. As a matter of fact, she'd seen only one dead person in her entire life, and since she'd inflicted the damage herself, the grossness of it hadn't really bothered her that much at the time. But this was disgusting. 'It looks like it threw up. Poison?'

Grace shrugged. 'I suppose it could have been. Or any number of natural causes, for that matter. Death is seldom a pretty event.' She looked down at her hands and hoped Sharon would finish in the bathroom soon so she could wash them.

10

Roadrunner was pacing back and forth across the considerable length of the office, his shoes screeching on the polished wood with each pirouette and about-face. Harley hunkered down a little lower in front of his computer screen, trying to ignore him as he worked on a trace of the bank account that had financed Gino Rolseth's humiliation by dunk tank – a simple enough task if you didn't have a string bean in Lycra melting down in front of your eyes.

'Goddamnit, Roadrunner,' he finally snapped. 'You're wrecking the floor.'

'I am not. I'm wearing sneakers.'

'Okay, how about this? *You're driving me fucking crazy.* I can't work with you clumping and screeching all over my quarter-sawn oak. And you're upsetting Charlie. Look at him. He's frowning.' Harley nodded toward Grace's morose-looking wirehaired mongrel, who had assembled himself on a stool at a small bistro table in the corner.

'He's frowning because you gave him too much ice cream. You know it gives him headaches.'

Charlie's head lifted and his little stump of a tail wiggled when he heard 'ice cream.'

'Does that look like a dog who gets ice-cream

headaches? I don't think so. Did you feed him his chicken stew yet?'

Roadrunner stopped pacing. 'Chicken stew?'

'Yeah, it was in that square plastic thing . . . Oh, Jesus, don't tell me you ate the dog's food.'

Roadrunner turned a vibrant shade of crimson. 'I thought Grace brought that over for us.'

Harley put his head in his hands. 'One day I'm going to replace that little toy brain of yours with the brain of a human being.'

'How was I supposed to know? It didn't look like dog food. It didn't *taste* like dog food . . .'

'Lucky for you, it's not. That dog eats better than we do.' He looked over at Charlie. 'Well, buddy, looks like you and me are going to have to get some pizza. What do you think of that, boy?'

Charlie lowered his head and whined.

'No pizza? What kind of a slob are you?'

'He's not hungry, he's worried, and you should be, too. It's already five o'clock. They were supposed to be in Green Bay by four.'

'I keep telling you – they're women. God knows how many times they had to stop to eat or put on lipstick or stretch their legs or whatever else it is women do that makes road trips so damn irritating. And on top of that, Annie's with them. Do you know how many vintage clothing stores there are between here and Green Bay?'

Roadrunner folded his arms huffily across his hollow chest. 'This isn't like them, and you know it.

Grace promised to call, and she hasn't. And when Annie has an appointment, you can set a clock by her. Worse yet, none of them are answering their cell phones. Something's wrong.'

Harley raked his black beard, reluctant to admit that Roadrunner had a point, because to do so would be admitting that something *was* wrong. 'Maybe they're already there and they just haven't had time to call. This wasn't a pleasure cruise, you know. They have work to do.'

'Are you saying Grace and Annie just forgot to call?'

Harley sighed. 'Grace left a sheet with contact numbers on it, right?'

Roadrunner nodded.

'Okay, genius, why don't you call Green Bay and find out if they showed yet?'

Roadrunner started pacing again, faster than before. 'Yeah, but what if they're not there?'

'Jesus. You run yourself ragged worrying about them, and now you're afraid to call and find out if you should be worrying at all?' He stretched out his hand and waved it impatiently. 'Give me the damn number and go take a Valium or something.'

'Nice of you to ferry me all over town like this, buddy.'

'No problem.' Magozzi took a turn off Snelling and headed back into the residential checkerboard of one of St Paul's older neighborhoods. 'But as long as I'm over here, I should take a drive past Grace's house while she's gone. Just to keep an eye on things.'

Gino rolled his eyes. 'Uh-huh.'

'Seriously. It's not the best neighborhood, you know.'

'Yeah, right. You can always spot a crime-ridden neighborhood by all the tricycles in the yards. And those kids in that plastic wading pool over there? Talk about your unsavory types. Look at 'em. They're probably planning a heist right this minute.'

'Oh, give me a break. It's just a few blocks out of the way.'

'Twenty-two, to be exact. And the point is, my friend, you got it bad.'

'Meaning what?' Magozzi pulled to the curb in front of Grace's little house and stared at the lifeless windows.

'Meaning you're mooning over an empty house, buddy, just because your girlfriend lives there. Shit, I haven't done that kind of stuff since high school.'

'I am not mooning over an empty house. I am looking for burglars and arsonists.'

Gino snorted. 'Special Forces couldn't break into Grace's house, and you know it. Damn thing's probably rigged to self-destruct if the paperboy steps on the front mat.' He leaned across the front seat and looked out Magozzi's window. 'Man, the only yard in the city sadder than yours is Grace's. Between the two of you, you've got the landscape sense of a fire ant. Nobody's trying to kill her anymore, so why doesn't she put some shrubs or something around that place? Looks like nuclear winter.'

Magozzi sighed and pulled away from the curb. 'She likes it that way.'

'Why doesn't that surprise me?'

Ten minutes later, they pulled into Harley's driveway and Gino wasted no time in pointing out the superior landscaping. 'Now here's a yard. Living grass, mature trees, and nice, big shrubs with those puffy white things all over them.'

'Flowers. Why are you suddenly so obsessed with people's yards?'

'I'm not. All I'm saying is that there's nothing wrong with a little pride in ownership.'

'Uh-huh. Angela finally made you dig out that flower bed she's been talking about for three years, didn't she?'

'That's not the point.'

Magozzi smiled. 'Right. Pride in ownership.'

'Exactly. By the way, I got all my plants at Uptown Nursery, and Lily Gilbert gave me twenty percent off, and if she knew what your yard looked like, she'd probably donate everything.'

'I'll think about it.'

He and Gino got out of the car and headed up the front walk, Gino lagging behind as usual. He'd always taken it slow on the way up to Harley's house, and Magozzi used to think it was because the grandeur of the place intimidated him. But now he was beginning to suspect that Gino had been examining the garden layout all along, making mental notes that he could use later to impress Angela.

'You sure Harley said to just walk in?' Gino had finally caught up and was now standing at the mansion's massive front doors, staring at the huge iron demon face that served as a knocker.

'Yeah. He said come in the front, look for the beer, and we'd know where to take it from there.'

'Great. A treasure hunt in Frankenstein's castle.'

The heavy oak doors swung open with surprising ease – just like they always did in old horror movies, Gino was thinking, as they let themselves into the vast foyer. All the dark wood and Titan-sized antiques inside added to the sense of foreboding that had started with the demon door knocker, but Gino was quick to home in on the one ray of sunshine amid all the gloom and doom: sitting on an elaborately carved, marble-topped table in the middle of the parquet floor was a champagne bucket filled with ice and bottled beer. A hastily scrawled note beside it read: ''Vator to 3rd fl, bring the beer.'

Gino brightened immediately. 'I love this guy,' he said, scooping up the ice bucket. 'He moves his ten-million-year-old vase to make room for some Rolling Rocks. Talk about getting your priorities straight. Now where the hell's the elevator? This place gives me the creeps.'

Since neither of them had ever ventured much farther than the foyer without an escort before, it took them a while to negotiate the dizzying maze of rooms and doors, stairways and dead-ends, before finally ferreting out the understated mahogany panels that opened onto a high-tech elevator. By the time they were finally lifted up to the third-floor office, Harley was waiting for them at the doors, a huge grin plastered across his face. 'Don't tell me the super-cops got lost down there.'

'Hell, no, we were just giving your Minotaur directions,' Gino grumbled, handing over the beer bucket. 'Next time you invite guests over for an unguided tour, you might want to think about laying down glow-in-the-dark footprints.'

Harley let out a belly laugh and gave them each an affectionate slug on the arm. 'Come on in, grab a beverage, and make yourselves comfortable. I'm still working on your little project, Rolseth, but we'll get to the bottom of it.'

Gino was visibly grateful, which was no small feat for him. 'Thanks, man. I really appreciate this.'

'No problem. And I gotta tell you, this whole plan was nothing short of pure, diabolical genius, and I mean that in the nicest possible way. Makes me jealous I didn't think of it myself.'

Roadrunner was waiting to greet them, too, but hanging back a little, as he always did. He gave them a goofy smile and an awkward wave. 'Hey, Magozzi, hey, Gino.'

'Roadrunner! What the hell – you been working out or something?' Gino asked.

Roadrunner examined his shoes while he turned a

thousand shades of red. 'Not really. Just biking a lot.'

'Yeah? Well, the Arizona sun was good to you.'

He looked up hopefully. 'I did get a little color when I was down there, huh?'

Harley rolled his eyes at Magozzi. 'Yeah, right. He still looks like a lefse to me. Come on, buddy, let's you and I pull up some chairs and trade gossip while those two discuss sunscreen.'

They hadn't made it more than two steps into the main room when a furry rocket came barreling toward them and skidded to a halt in front of Magozzi. Charlie submitted to a few moments of chin-scratching, just to be polite, but it was pretty clear that this was not the dog's final destination. Trembling with excitement, he gave Magozzi's hand a quick, apologetic swipe with his tongue, then bounded toward Gino, who dropped down on all fours and started blubbering to the dog as if he were his only child. It was disgusting.

Magozzi shook his head sadly. 'Sometimes that dog makes me feel undervalued.'

'Tell me about it. I've been feeding him Ben & Jerry's all day, and this is how I rate.' Harley waved Magozzi over to a pair of chairs on the far side of the room, opened some beers, and spoke in a low, quiet voice, making sure he wouldn't be overheard. 'Have you heard from Grace?'

'No . . . why? What's wrong?'

'Nothing, I don't think. It's just that Roadrunner was freaking out before you guys showed up, and I don't want to get him started again. If he gets any hotter, his suit is gonna melt into a puddle of Lycra, and I don't think any of us want to see him naked.'

'Uh . . . I'm not sure I understand.'

'Oh, yeah, sorry. Well, maybe you knew, maybe you didn't, but Grace, Annie, and Sharon were all supposed to be in Green Bay at four. So four comes and goes and by five, we still hadn't heard from them and we couldn't raise them on their cells. That's when Chicken Little here starts proclaiming the end of the world, because they should be somewhere near Green Bay by now, in which case their cells would work. I tried to calm him down – give them another hour, I told him, but you know how he gets. So I called the Green Bay detectives they're supposed to be meeting, and it's the same story there. Hadn't called, hadn't shown, hadn't checked in to their hotel, couldn't be reached on their cells. I tried very politely to convey my concern to those no-neck cheeseheads, but the bastard hung up on me, and now it's way past six, and even I'm starting to get a little worried. They always call. They *promised* to call. It's just not something they'd blow off unless something was wrong.'

Magozzi felt a little tickle of apprehension, then reminded himself whom they were talking about. 'Come on, Harley. This is Grace and Annie. Even if anyone were stupid enough to try to give those two trouble, it's the perps you should be worrying about. Plus, they've got Sharon with them. Those three together could probably take down a small country if they had to . . .'

Harley was shaking his shaggy head. 'Okay, this is the problem with homicide cops. Somebody mentions trouble, you automatically think bad guys. Roadrunner's been talking car wrecks.'

Magozzi actually felt his brain screech to a halt, and pictured little nerve impulses putting on their back-up lights and heading in a different direction. Harley was right about the way his mind worked, but it wasn't just because he was a cop. The notion of extraordinary Grace being vulnerable to something as ordinary as a car wreck had never occurred to him. 'Shit,' he mumbled, starting to rise from his chair. 'I'll call Wisconsin Highway Patrol, have them check the accident reports. . . .'

'Don't bother. Already did that, and the prick at WHP didn't have a very cooperative spirit, if you know what I mean, so we plugged into the statewides and looked for ourselves. Nothing. At least, nothing that's been reported yet. We've got a tag alarm on the website if anything comes in, so we're covered there.'

Magozzi eased back down in his chair, took a careful look at Harley, and felt that trickle of apprehension swell and roll in his belly.

Gino ambled across the room and stood over them, his hands in his pockets. 'What are you two whispering about? You sound like a couple old ladies.'

Magozzi glanced at Harley, then slid his eyes over to where Roadrunner was pacing again. 'Roadrunner's a little worked up.'

Gino shrugged. 'Of course he's worked up. The ladies are missing. He told me.'

'Not missing. Just late.'

'You gotta be kidding. Those three? Ten minutes over, they're late. This long? They're missing.'

11

It was after six when Halloran dialed Grace MacBride's cell number again and got the same canned voice telling him to leave a message. He'd already left three and decided a fourth would probably cross the line between urgent and rude – not a prudent thing to do when you were begging a favor.

He'd been telling himself that the urgency he felt was purely professional. He'd convinced himself that they needed Grace's facial-recognition software to help ID the bodies from the lime quarry. And if he was going to drive the morgue shots down to Green Bay tonight, he wanted to get on the road before dark. But there was another little voice inside that kept asking if maybe the urgency didn't have something to do with Sharon Mueller and the possibility of seeing her. Halloran dearly hated those little voices.

Bonar strolled in just as he was hanging up the phone. 'Just take a look at this,' he said, holding his arms out and turning sideways.

'What am I looking at?'

'Please. Surely you can see that I'm becoming emaciated. Wasting away before your eyes.'

'Really? Then congratulations. You're pregnant.'

Bonar dropped his chin to look down at his stomach. 'That's bloat from malnutrition. Plus, they're going to be out of the special at the diner if we don't get over there.'

'What's the special?'

'Chicken-fried steak in milk gravy.'

Halloran sighed and pushed away from his desk. 'God, I love that stuff.'

'Who doesn't?' Bonar picked up the phone and pushed a number he'd memorized about a million years ago. 'Cheryl? This is Bonar. Put a couple of those specials on the back burner and guard them with your life, okay?' He hung up the phone and frowned. 'Don't you think it's kind of funny that a woman that old is named Cheryl? Her name ought to be Emma or Violet or something.'

Halloran considered that while he slipped a clip in his weapon and snugged it down into his belt holster. 'Never thought about it. How old do you suppose she is?'

'She's seventy-three. Criminy, Mike, you've seen her almost every day of your life since you were a kid. How can you not know how old she is?'

'Maybe because I was never rude enough to ask.'

'You hardly ever have to ask a woman anything straight-out. You just have to listen close. That's your problem, you know.'

Halloran grabbed his cigarettes out of the drawer

and closed it just a little harder than necessary. 'Who says I have a problem?'

'You've got lots of problems. Women just happen to top the list. You can't even get Grace MacBride to call you back, and she doesn't even know you well enough to dislike you yet.'

Halloran ignored the dig. 'I'm thinking of just driving those morgue shots over to Green Bay so they'll be waiting for her.'

'Why don't you just fax them?'

'Magozzi says the program works better with the original photo, and I want the best shot we can get. I don't suppose Wausau has any news about the autopsies yet?'

'They do, and you're not going to like it. The ME called about a half hour ago. He took custody of our three bodies this afternoon and was prepping for the autopsies when the Feds charged in like the cavalry and rode off into the sunset with them.'

'They took our *bodies*?'

Bonar nodded. 'Uh-huh.'

'They can't do that.'

'They can, and they did.'

'Just when did you plan on telling me all this?'

Bonar shrugged. 'After supper. Why ruin a good meal with something you can't do anything about anyway?'

Halloran snatched the phone and started pushing buttons. 'Goddamnit, Bonar, you think I'm going to sit on this? I'm going to get some answers right now . . .'

'I already called them.'

'Who?'

'Whoever you're trying to call. And I already asked all the questions you're going to ask. That's what you pay me for, remember?'

Halloran was still miffed, but he replaced the receiver. 'Oh, really. Okay, then give it to me, starting with who the hell gave those Federal body snatchers carte blanche at a Wisconsin ME's office.'

Bonar sighed and took a seat. 'The Federal judge who signed the warrant, that's who. I'm guessing those prints we sent to Milwaukee got some attention after all.'

'So what did they tell the ME?'

'Nothing. They just slapped down the warrant, said it was a Federal case now and they were taking over. He didn't know a thing about it until they came waltzing in, and neither did anybody else down there, including the director of the lab.'

'What the hell would make them move so fast?'

'That's exactly what I wanted to know. So after I hung up with the ME, I gave Milwaukee a call and spent another fifteen minutes talking to every FBI buck-passer in the whole God-blessed office, learning exactly nothing except that anybody who knows anything about this is either out of the office, out of town, or just plain out. They ran me around in so many circles, I'm still dizzy.'

'So much for interagency cooperation.'

Bonar nodded sullenly. 'They said to call Monday.'

'Right. Like the weekend will make a difference. Damn, this really pisses me off. If there's a Federal crime involved, fine, they can have it, but at least they could have given us a courtesy call.'

'So what do you want to do? We're kind of paralyzed here.'

'We're more than that – we're out of the loop. But I'd sure as hell like to find out what's going on and get a leg up on the FBI, just so I could rub it in their faces Monday morning.'

'Me, too.' Bonar let his eyes drift thoughtfully to the window and the cow pasture beyond. 'Of course, Sharon could probably find out for us in five minutes, if you'd just swallow your pride and give her a call . . .'

Halloran kept his expression perfectly flat and unreadable, but Bonar's eyes had zoomed in on him in one of those spooky looks that made Halloran feel like he was getting an X-ray.

After a few moments, Bonar was grinning smugly. 'So you did try to call her.'

'Well, yeah, sure, I tried her a couple times,' he said, going for nonchalance. 'When I couldn't get ahold of Grace, I thought maybe I could reach her through Sharon.'

'You don't have to explain yourself to me.'

Halloran grabbed his phone irritably. 'I wish you'd stop reading my mind. It's creepy.'

'I'm no mind reader – you're just totally transparent. Who are you calling?'

'Green Bay.'

Bonar's heavy brows went up. 'You're going to call Sharon out of a meeting?'

'I am.'

'Uh, excuse me, but first you threaten to fire the woman, and now you're going to ask for a favor?'

'That's the plan.'

'This should be interesting. You do know that if chicken-fried steak sits in the gravy too long, the breading gets all mushy.'

Halloran almost smiled. 'I do know that.'

The lead detective in Green Bay was a fast talker with a broken-glass voice that sounded more blues singer than cop. Halloran picked up the hint of an East Coast accent. Detective Yustin was cordial enough, but a bit bent out of shape, understandably so.

'No sir, Sheriff Halloran, haven't heard a word, can't raise them on their mobiles, and they were supposed to be here two hours ago. Four o'clock, Miss Mueller said, give or take, and it's after six. Don't get me wrong – this is a favor they're doing us, strictly gratis, so I'm not complaining, but I have four other guys here since three and I'm doing the overtime math in my head, you know? And overtime math is like tax-audit math – it never adds up the way you want it to.'

Having never been audited, the whole tax analogy

was lost on Halloran, but he understood the sentiment. 'I'd be grateful if you could tell Agent Mueller to give me a call as soon as she gets there. I won't keep her long, but it's fairly urgent.'

'These ladies are a hot ticket today.'

'What do you mean?'

'I mean you and me aren't the only people looking for them. I got a call from Minneapolis earlier.'

'Huh. You get a name?'

'Yeah, sure, a tough guy, said his name was Harley Davidson, if you can believe that, and when I told him they weren't here yet, he got a little testy and proceeded to tell me how to do my job. Put out a watch for the car, call in the troops, like that. And this was when the ladies were only an hour late. Hell, if I put out calls every time somebody was an hour late, my fourteen-year-old would be on our most-wanted list, you know? The guy sounded a little too tightly wound to me. I'm thinking jealous boyfriend, if you're curious.'

Halloran smiled a little. 'Actually, he's the business partner of the two women Sharon Mueller is bringing along.'

'You mean the two incredibly generous women who are donating their time and software to help me out?'

'The very same.'

'Oops. Guess I have some apologizing to do. You mind if I ask you a question?'

'Fire away.'

'Well, this software has to be worth a billion dollars, and they're giving it away? Maybe it's just me, but I don't understand philanthropy when there are that many zeros attached.'

Halloran said, 'From what I understand, all the partners made some serious money on their software company, but one of their games got a lot of people killed.'

Detective Yustin grunted. 'The Monkeewrench murders last October.'

'Right.'

'So this is, what? Some kind of penance?'

'Maybe. Hell, I don't know. Maybe they'd give this stuff away anyway. They're nice people, every one of them.'

'Well, that's good to know. I'll pass on your message to Agent Mueller when she arrives, Sheriff.'

By the time Halloran hung up with Detective Yustin, Bonar was over at the credenza, finishing a call on another line. He gave Halloran a dark look. 'That was dispatch. Gretchen Vanderwhite's missing.'

'The cake lady?'

'Yeah. She was hand-delivering a cake to a wedding over by Beaver Lake this morning; stopped to pick up Ernie's insulin at the pharmacy on the way, and was supposed to be back in plenty of time for Ernie's next shot. He's an hour overdue already.'

'Is Ernie still driving?'

'Nah. He can't see a fly on the end of his nose anymore. Doc Hanson's on his way over there now to shoot him up. Dispatch called the bride's family. Gretchen never showed, and boy are they pissed. The bride and groom had to cut a grocery-store angel food for the pictures, and the bride cried during every damn one of them.'

Gretchen Vanderwhite had started baking cakes about the same time the first McDonald's opened in Green Bay. She'd taken a fancy to the big sign that kept track of the number of burgers sold, and decided to put one up in her own yard. Everyone had gotten a chuckle out of that in the beginning, but then the numbers had started to climb and Ernie'd had to get a bigger sign. The last time Halloran drove by their farm, the sign had read more than four thousand, and as far as he knew, she'd never missed a single delivery. 'We gotta move on this, Bonar,' he said.

'I know.' He was already punching numbers into the phone. 'I'll sweet-talk Cheryl into running our dinners over here, then we'll get things moving before you have to head to Green Bay.'

'That's on hold for a while. They're not there yet.'

Bonar looked up. 'What do you mean?'

'Just that. They haven't showed up, haven't called. They're two hours late.'

Bonar's fingers froze over the buttons. 'That doesn't sound like Sharon. That woman would be ten minutes early for her own execution.'

'Apparently, it doesn't sound like Grace or Annie,

either. Harley Davidson already called Green Bay a while ago, all hot and bothered.'

Bonar pushed the disconnect button and just stood there a moment, lips pushed out almost as far as his gut, his thick brows coming down like a couple of furry blinds. 'Do you have Davidson's number? Maybe Grace checked in with him since then. They're a pretty tight crew.'

'No. But Magozzi can probably reach him.' Halloran picked up the phone, thinking he hadn't made this many calls to the Minneapolis detective since the Monkeewrench case. Something about that gave him a bad feeling.

When Magozzi saw the Wisconsin area code on his caller ID, he nearly put his thumb through the talk button answering it. He was more than a little disappointed to hear Halloran's voice on the other end instead of Grace's, but it was a call he was about to make himself anyhow – the Sheriff had just beat him to the punch.

When he hung up ten minutes later, he felt like an injured deer in a pack of wolves. Roadrunner and Harley had mobbed him during the conversation, straining to hear what Halloran was saying. He caught beer breath from Harley on one side and lime breath from Roadrunner on the other, which seemed peculiar, although nothing really surprised Magozzi anymore when it came to the odd man-child with the mind of a super-computer. For all he knew, the guy subsisted on an all-citrus diet. Gino was taking it all in from a big leather office chair, with Charlie at his feet, head lifted in rapt attention. It was the perfect portrait of a country gentleman and his loyal dog, sans the smoking jacket and hunt prints.

'Okay, Halloran just got off the phone with Green Bay before he called me, and they're still not there. But you probably already figured that out.'

'Yeah, yeah, yeah,' Harley said impatiently. 'Jump to the good part where you asked if he could help us out and then you were really quiet for a long time.'

'He's going to do what he can.'

'Which is?' Roadrunner asked.

'He'll get out a statewide APB on the Rover ASAP, plus he's going to make some personal calls to the counties they'd drive through and ask for some extra pairs of eyes out on the roads looking. I guess they have a pretty tight Sheriffs' Association over there and, according to him, they all owe him favors.' He stood up slowly, as if he didn't completely trust the ability of his legs to hold him, and looked at Gino. 'You want to come along?'

'Give me a sec.' Gino patted Charlie on the head, then pulled out his cell phone and pushed a single button. 'Hey, Angela . . . Jesus, what's that noise? Oh, yeah? Well, it doesn't surprise me. I had that kid pegged as Satan's spawn years ago. Listen, the thing is, I'm probably not going to make it home tonight. You know that strip bar near Marshfield you never let me stop at? Hell, no, we're not going to bust them, we just want to watch, maybe get a lap dance or two . . . Of course we'll be careful, don't worry, Magozzi told me all the women are behind glass.' Gino clicked off, ruffled Charlie's ears one last time, then pushed himself up out of the chair.

Roadrunner and Harley were staring at him. 'You're going to a strip club in *Marshfield*?' Harley asked.

Gino rolled his eyes. 'Christ, of course not. We're going to Wisconsin to find the ladies.'

'Just like that?'

'Just like that.'

Magozzi was already halfway to the door when Gino caught up to him. 'I'm probably jumping the gun here, Gino.'

'Probably.'

'You talked to Angela earlier, right?'

'Yep. Called her after Roadrunner told me what was going on. Figured you'd want to head over there.'

'What'd she say?'

'She wanted to know why we hadn't left yet.'

Magozzi smiled. 'I love Angela.'

'Me, too.'

'We don't even know which road they took.'

Gino shrugged. 'We're detectives. We'll figure it out.'

Roadrunner and Harley were right behind them before they got to the elevator. 'We can all go together in the rig,' Harley said.

'Actually, we'll need the radio in the unmarked –' Gino started to say.

Harley slapped him good-naturedly on the shoulder and nearly knocked him down. 'My friend, we got more communications in that rig than you've seen in your life, police band and any other band you can think of. You can call the goddamn space station if you want.'

Gino raised his brows. 'No shit?'

'No shit. Besides, the computers might come in handy.'

Having all of them in the elevator at the same time was tight, and Gino looked worried. 'You got a payload limit on this thing?'

'Damned if I know,' Harley replied, and pushed the down button.

12

Twilight had leached the color from the town of Four Corners. It lay silent and still in the deepening shadows, like an old black-and-white photograph. The street was empty, the buildings were starting to disappear into their own darkness, and the silence was total.

Inside the little house behind the café, Annie turned the bathroom faucet a fraction of an inch and washed her hands under a trickle of water. They had to be careful, Grace had said. The pump had already kicked in once when they'd washed their hands after handling the dead dog, and the noise had sounded like an explosion in the unnatural quiet. If they used too much water, it could happen again. Annie frowned, remembering the long list of things Grace had warned them to be wary of – things Annie wouldn't have thought of in a million years.

She bent her head over the sink and pressed some cool water against her eyes. Damnit. After more than ten years of full-blown paranoia, every sense on high alert at all times, Grace had started to get a little better. Closing the books on the Atlanta horror had helped, so had her relationship with Magozzi, but all that progress had been erased in a few hours, as if it hadn't happened. The old Grace had settled in for another long stay.

It was almost fully dark already – time for them to leave the house – and they were each taking a turn in the bathroom while the other two watched the windows, front and back. *But don't flush. And don't use the toilet paper roll. It's wooden and loose and might clatter. Take some sheets off the fresh roll on the back of the can.*

Even Sharon had raised her brows at the thought process that pulled that little detail out of the murky realm of possibility. Grace wasn't leaving anything to chance anymore.

Annie could barely see herself in the tiny medicine-chest mirror, and she decided that was a good thing. She'd caught a glimpse earlier, before the woods had swallowed the sun, and had barely recognized her own reflection. It wasn't the grime on her face or the running mascara or even the disheveled hair, as much as that distressed her. What Annie had inside could shine through all things superficial – but there was something in her eyes that made her look like a stranger, something she hadn't seen there since her seventeenth birthday, on the night she'd discovered what knives could do.

When she was finished in the bathroom, she went to stand next to Sharon at the kitchen window. She wrinkled her nose at the faint odor coming from the pilot lights of the old-fashioned gas stove. 'Your turn,' she murmured.

Sharon nodded absently, still staring at the dark

backyard and the black woods beyond. She looked a little brittle to Annie. 'How long have we been in here?'

'About forty minutes. Too long, according to Grace.'

'She's right. It's starting to feel safe.'

'It isn't. Too easy to get trapped in here.'

'I know.' Sharon stepped away from the counter, then stopped and looked down at the old wavy linoleum beneath her feet. 'When I was little – five or six, maybe – our barn caught fire one night, went up so fast there was no time to get the cows out. But the horses had an outside door of their own, always open, so they could run in and out and get away from the bugs. So the timbers were falling and the cows were bawling and starting to cook and you could look through the big open door into where the horses were all bunched together in the smoke and the flames, screaming, kicking at each other, looking right out the door they ran in and out of a hundred times a day.'

Annie just stood there as Sharon walked away, looking out the window at the darkened backyard, at the clothesline over in the corner, at the zinnias someone had planted around the poles, feeling a little silly for watching for armed soldiers coming to kill her. Suddenly, it just seemed too surreal, and she could feel her mind slipping, telling her that this was simply too preposterous to be believed. Surely there wouldn't be soldiers in a place with zinnias and clotheslines, and even if there were, surely they wouldn't be bent on murder. They were panicking, jumping to conclusions, following Grace's paranoia when they were really perfectly safe here . . .

And then she closed her eyes and saw a burning barn and wanted desperately to get out of the house. *Right now.*

Three minutes later, they were all huddled around the front door, peering through the glass panel at the top. There was nothing out there, just a hint of light at the top of the trees that towered around the town, advertising that somewhere beyond their view, the moon had risen. Apparently, it was high enough to start painting the shadow of the café on the grass between it and the house.

And then part of the shadow moved.

Grace froze, afraid to look away, afraid to blink, but everything was still. Maybe her eyes were tired, playing tricks, or maybe an errant breeze in this breathless air had moved a single leaf on a bush. But Annie and Sharon had seen it, too. They were already moving toward the basement door, down the steps without a sound. Grace followed, turning on the top step and starting to close the door. Had it squeaked when they'd opened it? She couldn't remember.

Outside the house, two shadowy figures crept up to the front door and immediately dodged to either side, flattening their backs against the siding. A shower of loose paint chips crackled softly, then fluttered down to the cement stoop.

Grace froze at the top of the basement stairway, the door an inch from closing. In this too-quiet town where the absolute silence had been ruptured only intermittently – by gunfire and jeeps and soldiers unconcerned with making noise – the faint shussing she'd just heard outside was menacing in its subtlety. Seconds passed, almost a minute, but she heard nothing more. She released her breath slowly, then took another step down and closed the door behind her. The latch engaged with a soft click.

Outside on the front stoop, one head jerked, cocked an ear toward the door. His partner looked over at him and lifted his brows in a question. *Did you hear something?*

They both listened, eyes narrowed on each other, palms wet on their rifle grips. After a sixty-second count, they entered the house quietly, the muzzles of their rifles swinging in a deadly double arc.

Down in the basement, Sharon and Annie waited for Grace on either side of the wooden door that led up the back concrete steps and through the storm door to the backyard. Neither of them made a move to open it. Maybe they were waiting for the last possible second before they risked making noise, or maybe they were just terrified of what might be waiting for them on the other side.

Grace reached past them for the metal knob, then froze when she heard a floorboard creak overhead.

The three women were rigidly still, their eyes rolled

upward to look at the basement ceiling. Not one of them doubted the cause of that long creak above their heads. Even though there hadn't been another sound for almost a full minute, they all knew. Somebody was upstairs.

A few seconds later, Grace felt a breath of air, the soft pulse of a baby's exhale touching her face. *Air exchange! Air exchange!* The thought screamed like a Klaxon in her head.

Someone had opened the door at the top of the stairwell.

The women stood motionless in the black basement while beads of silence gathered on the string of time. Grace was looking over her shoulder in the direction of the stairwell, listening, waiting. The Sig felt heavy hanging in her right hand.

They're up there. Men with guns a lot bigger than this one are standing up there at the top of the stairs, wondering if the treads will creak under their weight, listening for sounds from down here before they risk the first step . . .

When it finally came – the barely audible tap of a rubber sole against the wood of the first riser – it was almost anticlimactic.

First step.

Grace's hand began to turn the knob . . .

Tap. Second step.

. . . farther to the right in perfect, beautiful silence . . .

The third riser creaked faintly just as the latch eased free of its housing and Grace pulled the door open slowly, not too far, just a crack, just big enough for Sharon to slip through silently, silently . . .

Grace never heard the next step, but she knew when it happened, because she felt the weight of that oh-so-silent boot coming down, as if he were treading on her chest instead of the fourth step down . . .

Sharon slipped through the doorway like a floating shadow. She rounded her back and went up the first few concrete steps bent in half, then squeezed to one side. The presence of the slanted overhead door bore down on her like a great, invisible weight. A few of her hairs brushed against its splintery underside and pulled free from her scalp.

In what had to be the most graceful movements of her life, Annie followed like water flowing uphill. She squeezed next to Sharon, every muscle in her body screaming with tension.

Grace felt the mass of their three bodies crowding the small space as she took a silent step after Annie, then turned and pulled the door closed behind her. *How many steps have they come down now? Are they at the bottom, on the dirt floor? Can they see the door yet?* She gritted her teeth and started to ease the knob back to its resting place, a millimeter at a time.

And then she heard them on the other side.

Sharon's hands went up instantly and pressed against the slanted door over her head. Someone on the other side of the door in the basement was talking, heedless of noise now. Apparently, they'd decided that the building was empty. She couldn't make out the words, just syncopated mumblings muted by the heavy wooden door. Stupid men. Stupid, stupid men. They hadn't checked behind door number two. Yet. She tightened her stomach muscles and pushed the overhead door up an inch, then another and another.

Annie's eyes lifted as a slice of muggy air wafted into the tiny space, then she straightened slightly and poked her head up into the night. *Silly,* she thought. *What are you going to do if there's someone out here? Just sink back down and take odds on who'll find you first? The guys outside or the guys inside?* She moved quickly then, up the rest of the steps, turning to hold the heavy door by its handle while Sharon and Grace crept up after her. The three of them shared the weight, easing it carefully back down until it stopped soundlessly in its frame. Still bent over, they froze at the unmistakable sound of the inner door opening, and then a low-pitched voice, muffled only slightly by the outer door and the three feet of space that separated it from their ears.

'Come on. Let's go out this way . . .'

Before the man had finished his sentence, they were halfway across the yard, sprinting silently on the balls of their feet, heading for the side of the house. They'd just ducked around the corner and pressed their backs to the siding when the outer storm door began to lift from its casing.

'So now what, the gas station?' The man's murmur traveled clearly in the silence, snaked around the corner, and pinned the three women in place.

'Then the café . . .' Their voices receded as they turned away and started moving across the house's backyard in the opposite direction.

For a few moments, the women remained flat against the side of the house, watching, listening, waiting for their hearts to slow down.

Grace's eyes were wide open, but she couldn't see a thing. Somewhere the moon was probably washing open fields with pale yellow light, but it hadn't risen high enough to shine down into the hole in the forest that was Four Corners. For all she knew, this kind of utter darkness was common in a place so far from the reflected glow of city lights, but even she knew that this kind of utter silence wasn't common anywhere.

No sleepy bird sounds, no croaking frogs, no mosquitoes, for God's sake.

Gradually, her eyes adjusted to the black night, and shadows began to separate into distinctive shapes. Directly across from where they stood, an elderly, virtually impenetrable hedge of lilacs ran the length of the house, up to the café beyond, all the way to the shallow ditch bordering the road. They crept quietly across the grass into the deeper blackness of the hedge's shadow, then inch by cautious inch, they made their way to within a few yards of the highway. The three dropped simultaneously to their bellies in the dirt.

Straight ahead, a hint of starlight played off the pebbled surface of the two-lane strip of tar. To the left, past the hulking outlines of the café and the gas station beyond, the black mouth of the forest swallowed the road.

To the right, the direction they had chosen, the delineation between the dark highway and the darker sky was almost indiscernible, and the road simply disappeared over a small rise. Nothing moved. Nothing made a sound.

Grace glanced at Annie on her left, saw a glitter of white where the eyes would be in a nearly invisible face, and then began to wriggle forward, past the shelter of the lilac hedge, down into the shallow, grassy ditch. There was no way they could risk getting in and out of the café now – only a faint hope that the purses might not be seen in the dark.

With virtually no sounds to hear other than the ones they made themselves, and no light by which to see, Grace's other senses seemed to sharpen and overlap, as if to compensate. She could smell the oil from her gun, caught a whiff of brackish water from somewhere up ahead and, breathing through her mouth, tasted something she could only describe as green.

After the first few yards, Annie decided that crawling on your belly was one of those activities you very sensibly gave up when you started to develop breasts. She felt as if she were trying to propel two ripe cantaloupes through grass so long and slick that even the insides of her feet had trouble gaining traction.

It was a relief when she sensed the floor of the ditch sloping down, even as the highway sloped up. *Good,* she thought, thinking that if it went deep enough, they could crawl on their hands and knees instead of trying to slither on their bellies. Snakes with legs, she decided, would be every bit as handicapped as people without them. It all depended on what you got used to.

The ground beneath the thick grass was dampening with every push forward that Grace made. When the fingers of her left hand dipped into standing water puddling around the roots, she bent her right elbow to keep her gun clear of the water. A few more yards, and she felt the giddy relief of a floating sensation as she pushed into water deep enough to displace part of her weight.

By now the ditch had widened slightly, and the walls were a good three feet above their heads. Grace stopped and waited for the others to come up next to her. Easing onto her haunches to give her back a rest, she felt the fronts of her legs sink into the compressed muck beneath the water. Her face felt heavy. When she touched her cheek, her finger skated through sweat.

She felt it in her legs long before she heard it – a low, throbbing vibration that traveled through the ground. 'They're coming,' she said quietly. 'Get down.'

The jeep seemed to thunder by above on their left, shooting grit from the road onto their backs, whipping the tall grass above them into a chaotic dance. And then the silence wrapped itself around them again.

Eventually, as soon as her heart slowed down, Grace started inching forward again, the other two following soundlessly in her grassy wake. The ditch became shallow again as they crawled up a slight incline until Grace's head topped the rise and she could see what lay ahead. She ducked down almost immediately and scrambled backward until she was with the other two.

She spoke downward, letting the ditch absorb her voice. Annie and Sharon had to tip their heads close to hear what she said. 'Another roadblock. More soldiers.'

Sharon whispered, 'Can we get past?'

'Too far away. Can't tell.' Suddenly, Grace realized that she could see Sharon's profile. Her eyes lifted and she saw the rim of a huge, rising moon topping the forest. A full, bright moon. 'It's getting lighter. It's time to get away from the road. We're too exposed here.'

All three of them raised their heads high enough to look over the edge of the ditch. There was a cornfield directly across from them, and beyond that, set far back from the road, the outline of a silo, its metal hood glinting in the moonlight.

And then suddenly there was a flicker of light up the road, less than twenty yards away. A suspended face appeared to be floating in the distance, and then a second one, moving close to the first. They heard the distinctive click of a lighter closing, then saw only two sparks of red in the darkness as the men drew on freshly lit cigarettes.

The three women slid silently down into the ditch to lie in the water again. Male voices, surprisingly clear, rode the thick, still air to where they lay.

'I don't like this. We should just clear the hell out.'

'Won't do much good if someone got in.'

'Christ, if somebody had gotten in, we would have found them by now. That car was outside the perimeter. It could have been there for a week, for all we know.'

'There was luggage inside. Nobody leaves luggage for a week.'

'So the car broke down, and whoever it was got a lift, and we sure as hell better be gone by the time they come back for it, or we're fucked anyhow.'

'At least the farm's done.'

There was a soft grunt of acknowledgment, and it frightened Grace that the sound carried so well. Then the soldiers' footsteps faded gradually as the men walked on the stony shoulder away from the women and toward the roadblock.

A minute passed, then another. There was the sound of gears grinding far up the road, and the labored growl of an engine, then nothing.

Grace closed her eyes. It was a little better than she'd thought. Yes, the soldiers had found the Range Rover, but they weren't sure they had company yet.

And the farm was 'done,' whatever that meant. Probably that they'd just finished searching it.

By the time the three women felt secure enough to creep back up the rise and peek over it, the moon was halfway over the tallest of the forest's giants, and a diffuse white light was rolling back the night. The corn across the road was full-grown, nearly ten feet tall, thick and dark and welcoming. *That way,* Grace thought.

A quick glance confirmed that the blinking yellow lights of the roadblock were still in place. The lights stuttered periodically as the shadows of men passed in front of them.

Grace's eyes shifted downward to where the white line of moonlight sliced the ditch in half. If they were going to cross this road, they had to do it fast, before the moon rose any farther.

They crossed the road on their stomachs, just beneath the rise so they wouldn't be visible from the roadblock, then rose to their hands and knees and scrambled deep into the cornfield. A few more rows in, and it was thick enough to block the moonlight, tall enough to allow them to stand in perfect concealment. The women stopped crawling and rose to their feet.

Homo erectus, Sharon thought as they started walking in a cultivation furrow. She pulled the soft fragrance of living, growing corn deep into her lungs and longed for the first bite of the season's sweet corn exploding sugary juice into her mouth.

Another week, she thought, *maybe two. If we live that long.*

The field angled to the right, leading them farther into the land, closer to the silo, and then suddenly only a single row separated them from a closely clipped lawn.

The farmhouse was a large, two-story cube sheltered by motionless umbrellas of old elms. The shadowy shapes of hollyhocks towered around the small back porch, leaning against it, making their own miniature forest. The three women stood at the edge of the cornfield, listening, watching.

The house looked solid in its darkness, as if there were no windows or doors, as if whatever lived inside could not bear the radiance of light of any kind.

Sharon caught a quick breath, suddenly understanding why she always left a lamp on all night long, in spite of burned-out lightbulbs and the battered bodies of moths that she had to sweep from the end table on summer mornings. It was for moments like this, for people like her who stood paralyzed in the night, affected beyond reason by the unshakable certainty that dark was evil and light was good.

This is a bad place.

13

By nine p.m., the lights were blazing in Halloran's office, the rich aromas of the chicken-fried steak Cheryl had brought over from the diner were already a fading memory, and wisps of Bonar's thinning hair were sticking out at all angles from his head. He slammed the phone down on the credenza and ran his hands through his hair again, making a bad situation worse. 'I swear to God, the collective IQ of all gas-station attendants drops about a hundred points on the weekend.'

'Nobody saw our cake lady?' Halloran asked from his desk. He had the phone cradled on his shoulder, and his pen was busy on the state map that was spread out on his desk.

Bonar exhaled noisily. 'Who the heck knows? Stopping at any one of those northern back-road gas stations is like jumping into a black hole. Hell, she could have stopped at every one of them, stripped naked, and danced around the pumps, and those bozos wouldn't remember.'

Halloran switched the phone to his other shoulder and rubbed his neck. They'd both been working the phones for more than two hours, trying to track the missing cake lady in the northern counties between here and the wedding in Beaver Lake, and throwing out a more casual net for Grace MacBride's car in the counties along the major routes from Minnesota to Green Bay. Halloran figured his ear would fall off soon. 'They'd remember Gretchen. That woman blocks out the sun.'

'One would think.'

'You sure you got all the stations? There's got to be a lot of them between here and there.'

'Forty-two, to be precise, and we pinned down the attendants that were on this morning for every one of them, which was no mean feat, I might add. Tracked down half of them at some bar or other in the middle of their second or third or tenth Saturday-night beer, almost too stupid to live. One kid asked if I was going to arrest him, and when I reminded him I was on the phone, calling from fifty miles away, he asked me if I wanted him to wait until I got there. You know, I don't get it. We have a drink or two on occasion, and I do believe we get more brilliant with every swallow.'

Halloran managed a smile. 'I agree absolutely. So maybe Gretchen didn't stop for gas at all.'

'No chance. Ernie said she left with under a quarter tank, and that old guzzler she drives gets about five miles a gallon max. You on hold?'

'For most of my life.'

Bonar grinned and stood up, arching his back to work the kinks out. 'So true, but who are you waiting on this time?'

'Ed Pitala.'

'Over in Missaqua?'

'Yeah, I've been trying to reach him for the past two hours. His dispatch is having some trouble patching me through.'

Bonar snorted. 'Good luck. Missaqua's serious toolies country. They've probably still got phones with cranks up there.'

'I know. Bothers me a little, though, not being able to reach Ed. He's old school, never out of touch for long, and this isn't like him.'

'I can't imagine Gretchen taking that route to Beaver Lake anyhow. The roads curlicue all over the place. Adds about thirty miles.'

'I'm just trying to cover all the bases. Maybe she cut across Missaqua County to stop at a friend's or something.'

'You are a good and thorough officer of the law. So isn't the lovely blooming Dorothy still working night dispatch there? She'll put the word out on Gretchen with or without Ed's say-so.'

'Well, that's the thing. She said she would normally, but not tonight. Got real tight-lipped when I asked why, and I got the feeling she was running pretty close to the edge, for some reason.'

Bonar stretched out his legs and scowled down at the scuffed toes of his duty boots. The northern counties were pretty relaxed about some of the rules, and if one Sheriff called in a missing person, they all usually hopped on board without looking at the clock or jumping through chain-of-command hoops. 'Maybe Ed dressed her down again for stepping on his star. That woman gives more orders in that department than he does.'

'Maybe.'

'How about all the counties Sharon might have come through? You get the word out there?'

Halloran nodded. This was a different set of counties, south of the ones Gretchen would have passed through. He'd called Sheriff Bull Rupert three counties over first, who'd laughed about him looking for women who were only a few hours late, and asked if he wanted him to stake out garage sales, which really set Halloran's teeth on edge. From then on, he'd asked everyone to pass on a callback to a Deputy Mueller he needed to reach fast, and under those circumstances, every Sheriff between Green Bay and the Minnesota border was happy to put Grace MacBride's Range Rover on the watch-and-stop list. 'No problem with those . . .'

Suddenly he ducked his mouth down to the phone again. 'Yeah, Dorothy, I'm still on, you got him? Uh . . . sure, that's fine.' He hung up the phone and shrugged. 'Ed's calling me back on his cell.'

Bonar's brows shot up. 'Ed Pitala's calling you on his own nickel?'

'It is a wonder.'

'More like a miracle. Bound to be a short conversation then. Be right back.' Bonar hitched up his pants and headed for the restroom.

He scared himself to death when he looked in the mirror, and spent over a minute wetting down his hair and combing it smooth. He still had high hopes of getting over to Marjorie's before she finally gave up on him and went to bed alone.

By the time he sauntered back into Halloran's office, Mike was sitting very still at his desk, his hands flattened on the open map, staring at the opposite wall.

'Man, I wish you wouldn't do that. I hate when you sleep with your eyes open.'

Halloran's eyes shifted to his. 'I talked to Ed.'

There was nothing ominous about the words, but the way Halloran said it made the hairs on the back of Bonar's neck stand up. 'And?'

'And he said he'd called on his cell because the FBI is crawling all over them up there, and they put the lid on radio transmissions. He was real nervous telling me that much, even on his own phone.'

Bonar took a breath that strained the buttons on his brown shirt, then walked over to the desk and pulled up a chair. 'The FBI's just popping up all over the place today, isn't it?' he said quietly. 'So what are they doing up in Missaqua County?'

Halloran shook his head. 'Ed didn't know for sure, but they called all his patrols in. Not that they have that many on the road up there – you got a thousand square miles with about that many people – but they still called them in. There's one deputy on his way home; other than that, there's not one cruiser on the road in the whole damn county, and Ed's having a real hissy fit.'

Bonar was tensing up. 'They can't do that. Can't strip a whole damn county of police protection just because they feel like it.'

'Apparently, they can, under certain circumstances. Ed tracked down the Attorney General at his lake cabin and got the word.'

'What circumstances?'

'That's the kicker. They don't have to tell during an active operation, and that's apparently what's going on. They didn't want some cruiser on patrol stumbling into the middle of it while it was ongoing, blowing the lid off.'

Bonar looked positively vapid for a minute – a very rare expression for that broad, wise face. 'That doesn't make any sense. An operation that covers the whole damn county?'

'That's exactly what I said. Ed figures they've got somebody on the roads they don't want to spook.'

Bonar leaned back in the chair and pulled a roll of breath mints out of his breast pocket.

Halloran arched a brow and glanced at his watch. 'Your optimism is amazing.'

Bonar popped a mint. 'I figure if we find Gretchen and Sharon's crew in the next five minutes, I'll still make it over to Marjorie's before she gets the night cream on.'

Halloran's cell rang from its holster, and with only a handful of likely callers, he felt a brief, foolish surge of the kind of optimism that Bonar lived with all the time. And then he heard the voice on the other end.

'Simons? What the hell are you doing calling in on my cell? What's wrong with the radio?' There was a short pause while Halloran listened. 'Hang on a second while I find the speaker on this thing. I want Bonar to hear this.'

'You've got a speaker on your cell?'

'That's what they said. It's a new one, haven't figured it all out yet . . . There it is.' He pushed a button and Simons's voice filled the room. It sounded a little like a chipmunk on speed.

'. . . guys crawling all over, so I don't . . .'

'You're on speaker, Simons. Start over.'

Bonar leaned closer to the desk and heard Simons take a deep breath.

'Okay. This is the deal. I was off Twenty-three, running patrol south past the lime quarry, saw the crime-scene tape broken and what looked like lights through the trees, decided I'd drive in there and kick some kids' asses and haul 'em in for underage, and then I get down to the quarry and all of a sudden there's about a dozen suits around the car with their weapons out, screaming at me, and those big lights on stands set up all over the damn place, and a bunch of other people in white coveralls crawling over our scene like a bunch of friggin' ants . . .'

'Hold it,' Halloran interrupted. 'Are you talking FBI?'

'They told me to get out, Mike. Just like that. Get

out of my own damn crime scene on my own goddamned patrol in my own goddamned county, and when I went for the radio to call in, this asshole gorilla reached right inside my unit and took the mike out of my hand, said if I put it out over the radio that they were there, I'd spend the rest of my life looking out the wrong side of a concertina fence. Shit.' He paused and took another breath, this one shaky. 'I reached for the cell phone then, and next thing I knew I was looking into the muzzles of about half a dozen nines pointed right at my head . . .'

Bonar's eyes opened wider than Halloran would have thought possible.

'. . . and all I could think of was to tell the big muckety-muck that I'd already called the stop in to you directly, and if I didn't check back within the next minute like I was supposed to, they'd have twenty patrol cars out here, and how the fuck would they like that?'

Bonar grinned. 'You lied to the FBI?'

'I did.'

'Simons, you are my hero.'

'Yeah, well, I don't feel like no hero right about now. I feel like a man who ought to go home and change his shorts . . . Oh, Christ on a crutch. Here comes the big A now. You're gonna have to talk to him, Mike.'

There was a spurt of static as Simons's cell changed hands, and then Halloran heard a deep male voice that he didn't recognize.

'Sheriff Michael Halloran? This is Special Agent in Charge Mark Wellspring. I want you to listen carefully.'

Halloran bristled instantly, straightened at his desk, and squared his shoulders as if he were facing the man head-on. 'No.' They could hear a sharp intake of breath through the speaker. 'First, I want an okay from my deputy that he's checked your credentials, and then I want to run them, and if they check out, then maybe I'll listen to what you have to say. Until that happens, you're just a bunch of thugs trampling my crime scene and drawing down on my officer, and that's exactly what I'll be putting out on the radio when I bring every other patrol I've got on the road down on you.'

He and Bonar stared at each other during the long silence that followed, then they heard Simons's voice again.

'Sheriff Halloran? This is Deputy Simons, sir.'

Halloran raised his brows at the 'sir.' Simons wasn't big on titles or proper forms of address – no one in the department was, really – and in that moment, Halloran understood the extent of his fear and felt sorry for the man. Like a lot of men of small stature, Simons did a lot of strutting, but right now he sounded like he'd dropped about six inches, and when you were only five-six to start with, that was a blow.

'Didn't have a chance to tell you, but I checked the creds first thing, Sheriff, and as far as I could tell, they're legit. And I took a careful look at the warrant. It's Federal, Judge Peakons out of Milwaukee, got the right seal and everything, and the number's in the computer.'

'Okay, Simons. Good work. Put him back on.'

'Satisfied, Sheriff Halloran?'

'Enough to listen to what you have to say, Agent Wellspring, and then we'll run our own check from here.'

'As you should. Firstly, this is no longer your crime scene. It is ours, and we are fully authorized and prepared to protect it by any means necessary. Are we absolutely clear on that?'

He wouldn't say another word until Halloran finally grumbled, 'We are.'

'Good. Secondly, this is a national security operation, our very presence here is closely guarded . . .'

'Not very.' Bonar couldn't help himself.

Agent Wellspring cleared his throat but held his temper. 'Your man may have gotten in, Sheriff – that was our mistake – but I hope you notice that he hasn't gotten out yet.'

Halloran was turning bright red, and Bonar's forehead was so furrowed you could have planted corn in it.

'As I was saying, our presence here is guarded, and that's the way it will remain until our operation is concluded, at which time we will share with you any pertinent information gleaned from the crime scene, according to law. Until then, your transmissions are being monitored, and mister, your whole department is under a microscope. Are you hearing me?'

Halloran took a breath so he wouldn't explode. 'Loud and clear, Agent. I want my man back here in fifty-seven minutes. That's how long it will take him, if he leaves in the next sixty seconds.'

'Then you'd better hope he doesn't hit a deer on the way back. We're disabling his radio and confiscating his cellular phone.'

There was a sharp click of disconnection, and then silence.

'Jesus, Mike,' Bonar finally murmured. 'I'm starting to feel like we're standing in the path of an avalanche here.'

14

Gino was riding shotgun in the posh cockpit of the Monkeewrench RV while Harley maneuvered the massive rig over a dark, twisting Wisconsin country road that wasn't much wider than his driveway. They'd turned north off the freeway a half hour ago, but it hadn't taken that long for the absolute darkness of the empty countryside to swallow them. There were no signs of civilization, no happy green road signs that told them they'd ever see civilization again, and Gino was starting to feel anxious. 'How much further to the gas station?'

Harley reached over to press a display button on the GPS console. 'Five-point-six miles, give or take thirty feet.'

Gino relaxed a little and leaned back in the plush leather captain's chair, tweaking the lumbar support, just because he could. 'Good. This is starting to get a little too Lewis-and-Clark for me.'

Harley nodded, his face glowing in primary colors from the dashboard lights. 'I can't figure out what the hell they were doing on this road. This thing heads due north all the way to Canada. They should have headed east on Twenty-nine.'

Gino rummaged for the map Roadrunner had

printed out after he'd traced Sharon's credit card to Badger State Feed and Fuel, and examined the network of red and blue lines. 'Yep, you're right. They should have stayed on Twenty-nine, but let me tell you from experience that there is no way of predicting what females will do once they're in a car. If there's an Amish sweatshop or a house made of beer bottle caps within a thousand miles, they're drawn to it like moths to a flame.'

'Those three aren't exactly the tourist-trap types.'

'They're women, aren't they? Hell, Angela's loaded with common sense, but the last time we took a road trip together, she made me drive sixty miles out of the way to see Bob's Kettle Moraine Grotto.'

Harley gave him a blank look, and Gino just shrugged. 'No clue. Still can't figure it out.'

Magozzi, who'd spent most of the trip in the office with Roadrunner, walked up from the back and knelt down on the console between Harley and Gino. 'The clerk who works the day shift at the gas station is on his way over there now to talk to us. He says he remembers them.'

'Let's hope like hell they asked him for directions, otherwise we're driving blind,' Harley grumbled. 'There's gotta be at least fifty weird little shortcuts from here to Green Bay they could have taken.'

'That's what Roadrunner's working on now,' Magozzi said. 'As soon as he started using probability equations, I checked out.'

Up ahead, the ugly glow of fluorescent lights

seeped into the night and Badger State Feed and Fuel came into view. Harley eased the rig into an ample fueling area obviously built to accommodate semis, tractors, and sundry other heavy equipment, and before he'd even lowered the stairs, a wiry, sun-cured old man wearing a trucker cap that advertised Purina Feed ambled over, giving the RV a reticent once-over while he waited for the occupants to disembark.

Magozzi, Gino, Harley, and Roadrunner all clambered down, a motley group if there ever was one, but if the old man noticed, he didn't let on.

'Dutch McElroy,' he said, offering his hand to each of them as they came off the bottom step, as if they were visiting dignitaries.

'We really appreciate you coming back here to talk to us tonight,' Magozzi said.

'No problem. Gives an old man something to do on a Saturday night.' He eyed the RV again. 'That's a beaut you got there. Need to top off your tanks?'

Harley shrugged. 'Sure, why not?'

Dutch winked at him and unhooked the fuel hose. 'Thought so. Rig like this sucks down the juice faster than an Irishman on Saint Paddy's.'

Magozzi took a closer look at Dutch's bulbous red nose and decided he was speaking from experience.

'So, you boys are after some women who were in here today?'

'Yes, sir,' Magozzi said. 'Three women in a Range Rover. On the phone, you said you remembered them.'

'Not likely to forget. I may be old, but I ain't dead yet, and when three lookers like that come into a little backwoods place like this, you stand up and take notice, if you know what I mean.'

Magozzi decided to take the last comment at face value so he didn't have to hit a geriatric. 'Did you talk to them?'

'Talked to one of them – a big gal, real pretty, real friendly. She came in for a pit stop, bought some water and a few lottery tickets, and we got to chit-chatting about weather and such.'

'Did she happen to mention where they were going or what they were doing?'

Dutch shrugged. 'Not right off, but she was wearing some kind of dress that looked like a wildcat had got to it – I figured it for a costume, so curiosity got the best of me and I asked where they were heading. When she told me Green Bay, that gave me pause. This place ain't exactly on the way to Green Bay, and I told her so, offered her a map. She didn't take it, though.' He sounded disappointed.

'Why didn't she take it?'

'Said they weren't lost. Said one of her lady friends was from around here and knew where she was going.'

'She didn't mention why they were on this particular road when they were supposed to be going to Green Bay?' Gino asked.

'Nope. I wondered, sure, but I'm not the nosy type.'

At that point, Magozzi knew they'd hit a wall. Honest, salt-of-the-earth folks might make polite conversation by asking where you're headed, but they wouldn't push it further than that unless you offered.

'So these women,' Dutch said. 'Are they dangerous?'

You don't know the half of it, buddy, Magozzi thought, but he just shook his head. 'No, but they are missing.'

'Sorry to hear that. Wish I could be of more help.' He finished fueling the RV and replaced the nozzle while Harley peeled off some twenties to pay him.

'One more thing,' Magozzi said. 'Did you notice which direction they went when they left?'

'Sure did. They pulled out and kept heading north. Now, if they had a local with them, she'd probably know that there are only a couple good ways to cross back over east and head to Green Bay, so I'd take a look at those. Come on into the station, I'll show you on a map.'

The four men followed Dutch into the station and waited patiently while he took a new map from a cardboard stand on the counter and spread it open. 'These used to be free for paying customers, but now we have to charge for them. This one's on me, though. Doesn't make sense, does it? Back in the old days, gas was cheap and you got real service – we'd pump your gas, wash your windshield, check your tires . . . plus you got a free map. Now gas is through the roof, nobody does squat for you except take your money at the register, and they charge you for maps on top of it all.'

As Dutch painstakingly highlighted roads with a felt-tipped marker, Magozzi's cell rang. When he answered, he heard the distinctive, prehistoric sound of coins being plunked into a pay phone, then the background noise of clinking glasses, multiple conversations, and country-western music. 'It's Halloran. Are you still at Harley Davidson's place?'

'Actually, we're all at a gas station in some place called Medford now. Me, Gino, Harley, and Roadrunner.'

'Medford, Wisconsin? What the hell are you doing there?'

Magozzi colored a little, still half feeling that he'd jumped the gun a bit, hoping that's what he'd done. Grace wasn't in trouble, absolutely couldn't be in trouble, and even if she was, she didn't need him or anyone else on some imaginary white horse tearing across the country looking for them. Grace took care of herself. Always had, always would. 'Making an ass out of myself, most likely,' is what he told Halloran.

'Women-hunting?'

'Yep. Roadrunner traced Sharon's credit card here. Last transaction.'

'Medford? That's totally out of the way . . . shit. This is getting weirder and weirder.'

'Where the hell are you, anyway? Sounds like a bar.'

'That's exactly where I am. I've got FBI ears all over the place here. Can you call me back? I've only got two quarters left.' He read off a number.

'No problem,' Magozzi said, then waved the others back to the RV.

The minute Magozzi mentioned FBI, Harley went into black-op mode and insisted that they call Halloran back on the sat phone. 'It's fully encrypted and trace-proof.'

'The FBI's monitoring Halloran, not us.'

'You can never be too sure with those sneaky sons of bitches. Besides, Roadrunner can patch the sat phone through the audio so we can all hear him loud and clear. It'll be like he's in the room with us.'

They all moved into the RV's back office while Roadrunner took his place at his computer station to set up the call. As his fingers flew over the keys, Magozzi tried not to look at the gnarled joints and crooked fingers of his hands.

Suddenly, Halloran's voice filled the room like surround sound in a theater. 'You there, Magozzi?'

'We're all here.'

'Uh . . . this is making me a little nervous. I'm getting this weird delay on the line . . .'

'We're calling you via satellite. No chance this phone is covered, so don't worry.'

'Jesus. Cops get satellites in that big city of yours?'

'No, we're in the Monkeewrench RV. This thing has more electronics than the Kennedy Space Center.'

'I'll be damned. And I was excited because I just figured out my cell phone had a speaker on it today. Probably just as well you've got an alternative. That cell of yours isn't going to be much good if you go any further north.'

'That's what Roadrunner told us,' Magozzi said.

'Okay,' Halloran continued. 'Here's the long and short of it. This morning, we pulled three bodies out of a local swimming hole, no IDs. Our ME said it was automatic rifle fire. So we run the prints and nothing comes back. Next thing we know, the FBI snatches our sinkers right out of the state lab, and they won't tell us beans.'

Magozzi's brows shot up. 'They took your bodies?'

'Right off the damn slab, according to the ME down there.'

Harley folded his beefy arms across his chest. 'This is getting interesting.'

'That's just the start of it,' Halloran said. 'A couple hours after that, the cake lady comes up missing.'

'What's a cake lady?'

'Gretchen Vanderwhite, sixties, bakes wedding cakes. She was delivering one over to Beaver Lake in Missaqua County this morning, never made it there.'

Magozzi grunted. 'You got the dogs out?'

Halloran took a noisy breath that came through the speakers like a hurricane. 'This is where it really starts to get weird. Apparently, the FBI pulled every one of Missaqua's patrols in from the road a couple hours ago, won't even let a uniform out on the street.'

Gino actually stood up. 'What the hell? They can't do that. That isn't even legal, is it?'

'We're getting the word that it is, but that's not the end of it. I just got a call from one of my men who found a couple dozen Feds crawling over our crime scene at the swimming hole. They kicked us out, made some pretty nasty threats, and now they're monitoring our radios and God knows what else. Christ. If they nail this phone call to me, I'm toast.'

'Rest easy, friend,' Harley said. 'Can't be done; we got you covered.'

'I sure as hell hope so. Anyway, now you tell me Sharon and the others were in Medford, and that far north, anything that heads to Green Bay runs smack-dab through Missaqua County.'

Roadrunner had been typing busily while he listened. He had a map of Wisconsin on one side of the big monitor with certain areas highlighted. In another open screen were endless lines of text that Magozzi couldn't begin to understand. 'So this whole thing started when you ran the prints on those three bodies, right?' he piped up.

Halloran waited a beat. 'Right. That's when the FBI moved in and took them.'

'Did you scan those prints into a computer file?'

'Sure did.'

'Can you send them to me? I might be able to access some other databases for you.'

'Son, nothing would make me happier. How about that facial-recognition software? Can you run that from your rig?'

'Sure,' Harley said, 'but how far are we from you?'

'About two hours,' Halloran said.

'So we'd have to work off a fax, which is less than ideal. And that program is damn slow. Let's try the prints first.'

Gino was pacing, scrubbing at his brush cut. 'Can we get back to the ladies here for a second while I get this straight in my head? We've got Grace, Annie, and Sharon off the radar, and you've got a missing cake lady, and if they aren't all in Missaqua County, they sure as hell could have been headed that way?'

'Right.'

'And the cheerless horde of Huns just shut down that whole damn county.'

'Right again.'

Gino stopped pacing and looked at Magozzi. 'We gotta go there.'

15

Grace, Annie, and Sharon were crouched in the deep shadows beneath some kind of weeping bushes that crowded against the back wall of the farmhouse. The quick run from the protection of the cornfield had left them all breathless.

There was a towering light pole close to the driveway, the kind that illuminates barnyards all across the Midwest, but thankfully, it was dark. Fortunate, and yet strange, Sharon thought. Normally those things were set to come on automatically at nightfall, or even during storms if the clouds were thick enough to block the sun. Burned out? It didn't seem likely in a place this well-kept.

Someone shut it off.

The three women hadn't spoken aloud in a long time, but through gestures, they had all agreed to bypass the house and head for the weathered barn that loomed across the drive, so enormous that it ate up a huge chunk of the sky.

Annie was hoping for sanctuary. Her heels were already blistered from the ill-fitting purple high-tops, and her muscles were screaming from tension and all the unaccustomed exertion. All she wanted was a few blessed minutes to stay in one place and let her heart slow down, and the barn seemed like a logical place to fulfill that fantasy. Even if the soldiers did come back, it would take a hundred of them to search every nook and cranny in a building that big.

Sharon was hoping for some kind of drivable vehicle behind the giant tractor doors, since there hadn't been a single one in town. Every old barn she'd ever been in contained a vehicle of some sort, from old hot rods buried under decades of hay dust to pristine classics preserved under heavy tarps. This was no bachelor pad; this was a family farm, and if there was one thing farms had in abundance, it was vehicles. Normally they were scattered all over the yard, tucked in long grass behind buildings, sheltered under an open shed, and certainly lining the drive. But there wasn't one of any kind in sight here, and that, almost more than anything else, seemed so dreadfully wrong. Surely the people who lived here couldn't have driven away in every single car they owned.

Grace was staring intently at the barn. Too big, she thought. The damn thing had to be at least eighty feet long, and that was too long to be out in the open. But if the inside was safe, they could travel through the barn to the back and, she hoped, a way out of this godforsaken town. She took a breath, glanced at the others, then moved.

They all darted from shadow to shadow across the moon-washed yard to the barn, and although the actual distance they covered was less than fifty yards, they were all breathing hard by the time they pressed against the cool blocks of the building's foundation. Hollyhocks grew here, too, leaning against the side of the massive structure as if the weight of their flowers was too much for the thick stems to bear.

Sharon's nostrils flared at the sharp, musky fragrance of the plants, and she remembered the hollyhocks that had grown on the side of her mother's potting shed.

'Oh, shit,' Annie whispered from right behind her.

'What?'

'Shit. Literally.' She grimaced and scraped the bottom of her shoe through the grass.

Sharon started to shake her head, then stopped the motion abruptly. She straightened against the side of the barn, lifting her head on her neck, then looked all around without saying anything.

'Did you hear something?' Grace asked.

Sharon jerked her head to look at her. 'Nothing. I don't hear anything. That's the problem.' She was preoccupied, eyes still busy. 'Look at this place. Fenced paddock, those big hay bales stacked in front of the barn, feed sacks on that trailer over there, and now manure.'

Annie snorted softly. 'It's a farm, honey. What did you expect?'

'Animals. Where are all the animals?'

Grace felt a prickle at the back of her neck.

The three of them were perfectly silent for a long time, each one straining to hear the slightest sound. 'Maybe they're in the barn,' Annie whispered.

With her blue eyes narrowed and focused, Grace started to creep along the edge of the barn toward a door. It was man-sized, cut into one of those big, rolling tractor doors hanging from a metal track. She pressed her ear flat against the wood, listening, then eased back and reached for the rusty latch. The door opened smoothly, without a sound, and the unfamiliar rotting smell of cow manure filled her nostrils. She stood in the doorway for a moment, listening to her heart pound in her ears, then stepped inside.

There was a huge overhead loft filled to the rafters with sweet, green alfalfa hay. To the right, there were open pens and box stalls filled with straw that looked freshly laid. To the left, a concrete walkway bordered with gutters and lined with metal stanchions led to a closed door at the far end of the barn.

But there were no animals. Not one. Even the dozens of mud nests clinging to the rafters overhead were empty. Not a single sleepy swallow peeped at the intrusion.

Sharon looked left down the aisle lined with stanchions. Sloppy, wet piles of manure deteriorated into brown dots, heading for the door at the far end of the barn, a bovine dotted line. 'That's where the cows are. There's probably a huge pasture behind the barn.'

'Maybe we can get out that way,' Annie whispered. 'Through the fields with the cows.'

The cold glow of moonlight made white vertical

stripes out of the cracks in the siding as they walked tentatively past the medieval-looking stanchions. The door at the end was a double-Dutch affair, each half latched with a simple hook and eye. As Annie and Sharon crowded in on either side of her, Grace popped the top one and pushed the door open.

The women stared out at a large, empty paddock with a sturdy three-rail fence. The dirt was ice-rink smooth and totally barren. 'Shit. No cows,' Annie whispered.

'No shit, either.' Sharon's eyes coursed over the strangely pristine surface.

Grace was leaning over the bottom half of the door, squinting into the distance. Moonlight laced the top rail of the fence at the far end, except for a broad gap of darkness directly across from them. 'It looks like there's an open gate down there. Probably pasture beyond that. Are you ready?'

Annie looked to the left and right of the paddock, at the grass on either side of the rectangle of smooth dirt. Tall, but not tall enough to hide a man standing upright, or even hunched over. 'Looks okay.'

But Sharon felt her stomach caving in as she stared out at nothing, her expression bleak. This was wrong. Just like the lack of a yard light and the absence of vehicles. No way cows didn't leave hoofprints.

Grace glanced at her, then touched her arm. Sharon blinked, then her head jerked once in a reluctant nod.

Grace unlatched the bottom half of the door and

pushed it open, and they all stepped down nearly a foot onto soil so hard-packed it felt like cement. 'What's that?' she whispered.

Sharon followed her gaze to the far end of the paddock. Something big. And . . . green? She squinted at the shape hulking in the opening in the paddock fence, trying to bring it into focus. 'Tractor. One of the big ones. A John Deere.'

Annie frowned, took a few tentative steps forward, then stretched her head forward on her neck like a turtle. The huge shape was just beyond the back fence line, cold light glinting off dirty green metal. She took another step forward, then another.

Mother may I? Mother may I take two giant steps? They'd always played 'Mother May I?' on the playground at recess – how old had she been then? Eight? Nine? – and no one would ever let roly-poly Annie take a giant step, because nobody wanted the fat girl on their side, as if fat were a disease you could catch by standing too close. Well, she could take goddamned giant steps now, she thought, stretching her right leg out in a long stride, grunting softly when her foot sank promptly in soil so soft, it seemed to suck at her shoe. She made a tiny cry, pinwheeling her arms to keep her balance as she brought her left foot forward. It sank, too, down over the laces of the purple high-tops, past her ankle, halfway up her calf, and then suddenly she was flat on her face with her arms stretched, her nose and mouth jammed into dirt that tasted of manure, her chest aching from the impact.

She raised her head, sputtering, spitting, furious with herself at the momentary loss of grace that made her trip over dirt. She tried to bring a knee under her, it sank, and she almost panicked. The stuff was like quicksand. Oh, Lord, maybe it was like one of those sinkholes that kept sucking up houses in Florida, and maybe that's what happened to the cows, and maybe that's what was going to happen to her.

She floundered halfheartedly, afraid to move, afraid not to, tugging at the foot that had somehow gotten jammed into the hole it had made. When she tried to brace herself, her arms sank to her elbows, but by then Grace and Sharon were on either side, grabbing her upper arms, pulling her back up onto her haunches.

'Damnit,' she panted, brushing the dirt from her chest and arms.

Grace was looking down to where her own feet had sunk into the earth. 'What *is* this?'

'They must have just plowed it up.'

Annie was using her hand like a trowel to move the dirt away from her trapped foot.

Grace looked out at the undisturbed surface beyond them, so smooth it looked as if it had been ironed. She started to say that it didn't look plowed, but then Annie made a funny sound and she looked down. 'What?'

Annie was just sitting there in the dirt, staring straight ahead. Grace followed her gaze but saw nothing. '*What,* Annie?'

Still, she didn't say anything. It didn't look like she was even breathing.

Grace fell to her knees and peered into Annie's face, her whisper tense. 'What *is* it?'

Annie's eyes shifted a fraction to look at Grace, then dropped to look at what her hand had grabbed instead of soft, mucky earth. She felt a little pop inside her head, as if something tiny and fragile had just been disconnected.

Her fingers were wrapped around a smooth, plump human forearm, half buried in the dirt. It was a strange, grayish color, and tiny grains of soil were caught in the downy hairs along its length.

Annie knew those barely audible, high-pitched sounds were coming from her throat, and then as Grace and Sharon bent to examine what she'd seen, she heard other sounds join in with the ones she was making. They were all tiny sounds, as if she were standing on the shore, listening to someone drowning far, far out in the ocean.

Sharon pressed the fingers of both hands so hard over her mouth that the skin around them seemed to glow white.

Grace was staring down at the arm, not blinking, not moving, the only one of the three not making a sound. Very, very slowly, she lifted her eyes and gazed down the full length of the paddock, and it seemed to go on forever.

The sounds coming from Annie's throat began to form the words of a frantic chant: 'I have to go,

I have to go, I have to go . . .' And suddenly she was scrambling in the loose soil like a panicked crab, the purple high-tops digging long, shallow trenches as she struggled. 'Come on, come on.' Her voice came out tiny and staccato, like a little girl screaming in a whisper as she shot to her feet and began to stumble-run headlong down the center of the paddock.

Behind her, Grace and Sharon saw her feet unearth another tubular shape of grayish, ghostly white, but this one was broad and muscular and sprinkled with dark, coarse hair, and it wasn't the mate to the first, it didn't belong, it wasn't a matched set. God, how many? *They're here. They're all here. Welcome to Four Corners.*

They both cried out at the same time to stop Annie, but Annie couldn't hear them anymore.

Dirt sprayed from the holes that her tennis shoes punched in the ground, like tiny volcanic eruptions marking her passage. Sometimes she could take as many as three strides without falling, then suddenly she would sink almost to the knee in an air pocket, her foot sliding against spongy lumps that shouldn't have been there. She tripped again and again, caught herself with her hands, touched things she wouldn't look at, and pushed herself up to plunge forward again. Finally, near the end of the paddock, she fell hard. She felt the searing pain of lungs emptied of air and simply lay there with her right cheek pressed to the dirt, trying to gasp.

If I move my arms and legs, I can make an angel in the dirt. It would have a head, a long skirt, wings, and very big boobs. That's why you never make angels in the snow on your stomach, because then they would show body parts that angels aren't supposed to have.

Then she heard Grace and Sharon floundering toward her from the back. She heard the tiny gasps and cries that meant they'd seen something, felt something, stepped on something . . .

She lifted her head and gazed at the great concave blade that faced her from just a few feet away. Clods of earth stuck to its shadowy surface, and behind and above that, the cab of the enormous tractor gleamed in the moonlight.

Sharon and Grace collapsed to their knees on either side of her until she sat up and looked at them both.

Her lungs tugged at the sodden air while she wiped her face with the heel of her hand, leaving a ragged white streak in the grime. 'They buried them with that,' she said, pointing at the tractor that seemed to crouch like some great beast waiting to spring on unsuspecting prey.

Grace was sucking in deep breaths. She felt strangely light, like a helium-filled balloon in the slippery grasp of a child's hand. She looked over her shoulder at the pockmarks behind them and shuddered at the tactile memory of softness that wasn't soil.

Annie was sitting there, staring back in the direction of the barn, at the holes and furrows that opened up into the land of the dead. Her eyes drifted a yard to the right, where the last ghostly shape lay exposed. She felt empty now, numb, staring at a little jeans-clad leg, trying to make her mind connect it to a body she knew had to be a child. Very close to it, a long, silky, brown-and-black ear lay on top of a soil clod like a disconnected thing she couldn't make sense of.

After what might have been a few seconds or ten or twenty, she took a deep breath and moved on her hands and knees. Two paces. Two little, soft, round knee holes in the dirt, and she was there. She sat back on her heels and looked down, and with a trembling hand, she reached out like a child trying to make herself touch a snake for the first time. *It's not slimy, it's dry, really,* and the moment her fingertips brushed against the little leg, she started to cry.

In all the years she had known her, Grace had never seen Annie cry, and this, more than anything that had happened this day, scared her to death.

The leg was cold. *This was a person,* Annie kept telling herself. *This was a person. This isn't a horror movie, and this isn't a monster or a ghost, just the empty body of the little person it used to be. And it isn't scary at all. It's just very, very sad.*

Sharon was kneeling right next to her, hands away from her mouth and covering her eyes now. *See no evil, see no evil; hail Mary, full of grace, the Lord is with thee, blessed art thou among women . . . Where are you, Mary?*

Where were you when all these people died? Did you watch from some heavenly perch with your plump little hands folded in front of your flowing blue gown, and did that Mona Lisa smile falter just a little when they shoveled dirt on top of the bodies, and how about when my own mother stuck a gun in her mouth? WHERE WERE YOU THEN?

She was vaguely aware of Grace murmuring to Annie in the background, a whispery, soothing drone of comfort that rang horribly false, seemed almost as evil as what had happened here. *Quiet, Annie, hush. It's going to be all right* . . . and that was such a dreadful lie. She took her hands away from her eyes and gazed dully past the corner of the barn toward the farmhouse, couldn't see very well anymore because her vision was blurred. When she blinked, water fell from her eyes onto the front of her little filthy FBI suit, and now it looked like one of the farmhouse windows was winking at her. She blinked again, her head tipped curiously. The window winked again, and then the window next to it winked, flashing a circle of light like the pupil of a large eye reflecting the sun.

Suddenly, her fuzzy thoughts sharpened and splintered away from one another. She jerked her eyes left, looked past the corner of the barn down the long drive, and breathed, 'Oh my God.'

Grace and Annie grunted when Sharon crashed into them, her hands clutching and pulling, her feet digging trenches into the soil around them. 'Quick, quick,' she hissed frantically. 'Headlights, cars coming down the driveway, hurry, hurry . . .'

. . . and then they were all scrambling in the loose soil, hitting the solid ground outside the paddock fence and into the tall grass on the other side.

Sharon was flying, number-one hunchback in a party of three, racing away from the barn and the paddock, past the dirty, green tractor at the end, over the lip of a hill, and onto a downward slope. She could hear Grace and Annie close behind her, their breath like thunder. Ahead of them, the moonlit tops of tall grass marched down a hill to mingle at the bottom with the oblong heads of cattails.

'Down!' someone hissed, just as headlights pierced the gloom above their heads like fingers of light jabbing into the dark sky. They all crashed to their bellies in the grass, facing the crest of the shallow hill, their nostrils flaring at the ripe smell of a midwestern lake in midsummer.

The still night air carried the sound of jeep doors creaking open up near the barn, then slamming shut.

'Jesus Christ,' a man said aloud after a moment, his voice even closer than the sound of the jeep's doors. 'Look at this shit. Looks like someone tried to dig them all up.'

The women flattened themselves even farther into the long grass, pressing their faces close to the fragrant earth beneath.

'Get on the radio,' the voice said to someone else. 'Get the Colonel out here, fast.'

With her left cheek smashed into the bent stalks of grass, Grace stared at Sharon and Annie on her right, staring back at her. *They'll come now. They'll all come.*

Her arms were stretched out in front of her, her left hand cradling the right. She continued to stare into Sharon's eyes as her right thumb moved up the Sig's grip to the safety and flicked it off.

16

Within ten minutes of the harried radio call announcing the mess in the paddock, the disturbed mass grave was striped with the yellow beams of headlights. Half a dozen jeeps nosed up to the paddock's fence, engines murmuring as their drivers stared solemnly at the things their headlights illuminated in the disturbed soil.

Like hunting dogs coursing for a scent, a dozen men spread out over the farmyard and surrounding land. They used flashlights indiscriminately, and the small noises of their movements carried clearly in the still night air.

From just inside the paddock fence, Colonel Hemmer glanced up at the five-man squad approaching the fence, ammo pouches and canteens clattering softly against their pistol belts. He squinted against the glare of the headlights, his grizzled face reflecting an unearthly glow beneath the black shadow of his field cap. 'Anything, soldier?'

'No, sir. Nothing in the house or barn.'

'What about the loft?'

'The loft, sir? The loft is empty.'

'That loft is full of hay. You ever play in a barn loft when you were a kid?'

'Uh . . . yes, sir.'

'Get your men up there. Check it again. Move every bale.'

Hemmer looked back at where Acker was sweeping the ground with the beam of a flashlight. Parts of the paddock were still smooth, the punched holes of running feet dark and jarring on the surface, like black blemishes on an otherwise flawless face. In a few places, there were compacted depressions where someone had fallen, surrounded by the gouges and scattered soil of panic. In each of those places, something better left buried protruded from the dirt, as if the residents of Four Corners had been trying to dig themselves out.

'No doubt someone was here, sir,' Acker said soberly.

The Colonel's eyes narrowed. *Jesus Christ. Goddamn women, stupid enough to leave their silly purses behind and right out in the open, walking all over this goddamned stupid town as if they owned the place . . .*

'Looks like they ran down to the end near the tractor, sir, but they could have come back this way. The dirt's a hell of a mess, makes them hard to track.'

And if they weren't running scared before, they sure as hell were now. Hemmer's mouth moved in disgust as he watched Acker's light arc across the paddock. 'How long could these tracks have been here?' he asked.

'The men have been making rounds since we found the Rover, but the last time would have been before moonrise. We weren't showing light then We could have missed it.'

The Colonel's jaw tightened. That meant this could have happened more than an hour ago. Goddamned women. Where the hell were they? *Where the hell were they?*

'Sir?'

He started, then blinked rapidly. Had he said that out loud? Suddenly, he was aware of the still-idling jeeps, the drivers with nothing to do but look at the horror in their headlights. 'Get those men out in the field with the others, Acker.'

'Yes, sir.'

Acker hustled away while Hemmer strode back down the length of the paddock toward the tractor. Pausing next to the hulking machine, he laid a hand on the cold ridge of a tire tread and closed his eyes for a moment, waiting for revelation. The tractor knew where the women went; the tractor saw them. But the goddamned fucking tractor wasn't talking.

He sucked air in through his teeth and moved to the edge of the slope. The flashlight picked up the parallel tracks of flattened grass off to the right, where the ill-fated truck had been rolled into the lake. Directly in front of him, the grass was smashed and slick in places where the cows had gone over. *They'll pop up to the surface soon,* he thought.

His eyes lifted and traveled around the uneven circle of the moonlit lake, saw several dots of light bobbing around the circumference as the men continued to search.

Three years, he thought. *Three years of meticulous planning, training, preparation, all at risk now because some stupid woman's car had broken down.* 'For want of a nail,' he murmured under his breath.

'Sir?'

Hemmer's heart leaped at the sound of Acker's voice at his left shoulder. *Jesus.* The kid had crept back up on him like a shadow. He was losing it – that second sight that saved you in the field. If this had been the Gulf, he would have been dead by now.

He pretended to be deep in thought, staring out into the black distance while his heart slowed down. After a moment, he started down the slope, Acker right at his heels. He stopped when his boots sank into the soft mud next to the shoreline and scoured the ground with the beam of his flashlight.

Pointless, he thought, looking up again. Between the cattle and men who had tried to manage that rolling stampede into the lake, the ground was ravaged.

The cattails towered over him here. He glared at them, wishing he had a machete to slice them down to size. 'Place is a goddamned jungle,' he muttered.

'Yes, sir,' Acker said, startling him again.

He snapped the light on Acker's face, making him squint. He kept it there for a moment, watched his baby face twitching in discomfort. When he spoke again, his voice was disturbingly quiet. 'We should have found them by now.'

Acker tipped his head, trying to avoid the light. 'They can't get out, sir. And we've got their purses and their cells, so they can't call out, even if they could get a signal. I'm sure we'll find them soon.'

'Are you?'

'Yes, sir, of course, sir.'

'Then you're a fool.' The Colonel scowled and looked away, clenching his jaw so hard his teeth hurt. *Take it easy,* he commanded himself. *Losing your temper is the first sign of losing control. Relax. Take a deep breath. Take command of yourself first, then your men.* 'We must find them,' he said evenly. 'They've seen too much.'

'Yes, sir.'

The Colonel turned to regard Acker's soft features, the sometimes startling innocence of his young face. 'These women are not the enemy. Not any more than those people in the paddock up there were the enemy. Just unfortunate souls who happened to be in the wrong place at the wrong time.' He paused, met Acker's eyes. 'They were all dead by the time we got here. There was absolutely nothing we could do. But this will be very different. Intentional. Could you do it, Acker? If you were the one who found them, could you shoot innocent women to save the mission?'

Acker was facing the Colonel, his back to the lake. 'Of course, sir,' he replied instantly, offended that the Colonel had to ask.

Directly behind him, less than ten feet into the forest of cattails and down near the surface of the stagnant water, a pair of terrified blue eyes stared up through the stalks.

Grace was kneeling in the sucking mud that anchored the roots of the cattails, her gaze riveted on the shadowy figures straight ahead. Their bodies were dissected crazily by the thick stalks that she peered through, as if they weren't real men at all – just scattered pieces of men whose conversation was as surreal as their visages.

Don't move. Don't breathe. Don't make a sound, because there's a very young man out there who's ready, willing, and able to shoot you dead. And this is what happens when you let little boys play with G.I. Joe dolls.

Only her head protruded from the stinking water; that, and her right hand. It was pressed next to her ear, gripping the Sig. The barrel was tangled in her hair, pointed skyward, still dry.

Directly next to Grace, Sharon couldn't feel her feet anymore, couldn't feel the cold muck seeping through her shoes and clothes, pasting them to her body like glue. Terror had numbed her senses long ago, focused the sum of her awareness on the simple life-and-death struggle to remain perfectly still.

It was pleasantly dark in this black nest of rigid stalks, and if it was dark, no one could see her, and she would be safe. Whatever evil was out there wouldn't be able to find her if she stayed perfectly still. She kept staring straight ahead, pretending she didn't see or hear or exist . . .

'... *Come on, honey, you have to come out. Come to Daddy. It's all right, I'm here. Daddy's right here ...*' *But Daddy was out* there, *where everything bad lived. Nothing bad was in here. Just her mother's faint scent lingering, silky dresses brushing the top of her head, her mother's shoes upside down on the metal rack, waiting patiently for her mother's feet. The dresses didn't know; the shoes didn't know; the hats and boxes, the terry robe on the hook – none of these things knew what had happened out there. In this tiny fragrant closet, her mother still lived, and Sharon wanted to stay here forever ...*

Next to Sharon, Annie's mouth was open an inch above the water, an orifice only slightly larger than her eyes. She could feel the blurred racing of her panicked heart, beating so fast it was a buzz in her chest, and she wondered absently if it would hurt to get shot.

The cow was still behind her, braced against her, its bloating, rigid body stuck in the mud of the shallows. She'd bumped into it, nearly fallen on it when they'd first slid into the concealment of the cattails together, but she hadn't screamed. She was very proud of that. She'd bumped right into this terrible, disgusting, dead *thing* and she hadn't screamed.

Her eyes were bright with tension, her face stiff with fear as she watched and listened to the two men. All the muscles in her body seemed locked into immobility. *That's why the deer freeze in the headlights. You always wondered why they didn't leap out of harm's way, off the side of the road, into the safety of the woods, and this is it. This is the reason. The survival instinct breaks down when danger gets too close. You can act only up to a point, and then you can't act at all.*

She concentrated, sent the paralysis draining down her body into the water and out through the soles of her shoes, and then, at last, she was free to blink.

Colonel Hemmer's smile was faint, barely there. Acker was a good soldier. All of his men were good soldiers. His smile faded. If they were all such goddamned good soldiers, how the hell had these women gotten this far? He clasped his hands behind his back and began to pace back and forth along a ten-foot stretch of shoreline, his combat boots slurping in the mud. 'Any chance they could have slipped away from here, across the lake, for instance?'

'Absolutely not, sir. The cordon around the lake has been tight. We treated it as a funnel point.'

Hemmer had known the answer before he'd asked the question, and the question hadn't really been necessary anyway. He knew the women were here. He could feel them the way you feel a cold starting deep in your throat. Soft, silly women who could never understand the concept of dying for your country or killing for it, so short-sighted that the term 'acceptable losses' would horrify them. These were the kind of people who had let the world become such a dangerous place. 'At ten hundred hours, those two trucks will blow, a thousand people will die, and the world will start changing. Unless those women get away.'

'That will not happen, sir.'

Colonel Hemmer stopped pacing and looked up at the silhouettes on top of the slope. A dozen soldiers stared down at him. Christ. They looked like goddamned Indians lining the canyon wall in an old Western, watching with that endless, alien patience, waiting for the proper moment to charge down. 'What is it, soldier?'

'They're gone, Colonel,' a man called down. 'We've searched the buildings, every inch of the farm, and around the lake. Shall we start the search pattern again, sir?'

'No.' The Colonel flashed blue eyes up the slope. 'Trying to track them in the dark is pointless. But they're still here, and we goddamned better keep them here. I want every man back out on the perimeter. Every. Single. Man. And we'll stay on that perimeter until dawn, and then we'll move in fast and start to tighten the circle.'

The soldiers on the slope saluted as a unit, then turned and double-timed away.

Acker waited until he could no longer hear their footsteps, then spoke hesitantly. 'You don't think it's risky, sir? Keeping this town closed off until dawn?'

Hemmer turned slowly to face him, and spoke with amazing control. 'Yes, Acker, I think it's risky. But riskier still to leave holes in the perimeter while our men fumble around in the dark, trying to find them. If they get out, others will come, and once they see this place, they'll figure it out in a hurry. They'd have a nationwide alert out on the other two trucks in a matter of hours. We'd lose them before they blow. We'd lose the gas. We'd lose the element of surprise. *We'd lose the war, Acker.*'

Acker closed his eyes and lowered his head in embarrassment. 'Yes, sir. Sorry to question you, sir.'

The apology made the Colonel feel magnanimous, almost paternal. 'It's all right, Acker. None of us expected this kind of duty. We're all on the edge here.'

'And what about the hourly patrols, sir?' Acker put in timidly.

'Cancel the patrols. All of them. Let the women have the whole goddamned town if they want it. For a few more hours, anyway.'

17

Deputy Douglas Lee arched his spine away from the seat, grimacing at a sharp twinge in his lower back. And it was no wonder, he thought. He'd pulled the empty northern sector for his patrol tonight, and taking a leak was about the only reason you ever had to get out from behind the wheel on this run.

He'd written up only two tickets in eight hours – one for a burned-out taillight on a '56 pickup, and another for a rusted-out Grand Prix pushing forty in Gill Lake's twenty-mile-per-hour zone. Lord, no wonder Wisconsin cops had a reputation for nuisance tickets. Unless you were highway patrol on the interstate, there wasn't a whole hell of a lot else to do. Thank God.

He eased back when he felt the lap belt press against his stomach. Never used to do that, he thought, patting the belly that had been rising like a loaf of Paula's bread ever since he married her last year. He was going to have to start the nightly sit-ups again, get himself back in some kind of shape before he had to endure the humiliation of moving up to a larger uniform size.

He yawned and rubbed at the black stubble sprouting from his chin, wondering what Paula had waiting for their late supper tonight. Who knew that a Phi Beta Kappa with about a million med schools vying for her favor would turn into a gourmet chef? For that matter, who would expect that a drop-dead looker with that kind of future would choose to put everything on hold while she took a year or two to be the stay-at-home wife of some bumpkin cop with a size-forty-eight shirt and a size-six hat? Lee figured he was about the luckiest man in the world, and then some.

He slowed the cruiser at the intersection of Double-P, then, at the last minute, decided to turn south. He automatically looked up and down the black crossroads, even though traffic on this stretch was as scarce as hen's teeth. It weaved in and out of the edge of the state forest, and basically, you could go nowhere in either direction. With only four cars per shift and hundreds of miles of roads to cover, trouble-free roads like this one rarely saw a patrol. But a trouble-free road was exactly what Lee was looking for tonight. Officially off duty for the last seven minutes, the last thing he wanted was to come across anything that would interrupt a straight run home.

Twenty miles to Paula's arms, he thought, smiling. He had to concentrate to keep his foot light on the accelerator and his eyes busy on the far edge of the headlight beams. The deer were everywhere this far north, and they thought they owned the roads.

Too bad he hadn't spotted the Range Rover. It

hadn't been an official call, really – just nosy Dorothy at dispatch, eavesdropping earlier this evening on the highway patrol frequency, passing along some poor bastard's worry about a car full of rich women – surely rich, because the Rover was out of Minneapolis, pretty new and pretty pricey. Lee liked stopping Minnesotans, with their tough cars and city attitudes. He might be a county deputy living in the sticks, but he had the ticket book and the authority, and in a way he knew wasn't healthy, that made him feel better about himself.

He eased up on the accelerator and frowned. Yellow lights were flashing through the trees up ahead on the left, and there was no reason in the world for them to be there.

His headlights caught the black cross on a yellow intersection sign, and his frown deepened as he drew close enough to see the barrier blocking the narrow strip of asphalt on his left.

It was rare enough to see highway-maintenance crews up in this neck of the woods – the most wear these roads ever got came from deer crossing from one side to the other – but to see a road closed overnight was damn near unbelievable, especially a narrow little country road like the one that passed through Four Corners. Hell, he could probably repave the full length of it in a single day all by himself – with a teaspoon and a tar bucket.

He slowed to a crawl as he neared the intersection and squinted out his window, puzzled. There should have been some kind of a detour sign on the highway, and the boys at County Highway knew that. He shook his head and clucked his tongue, then cranked the wheel left. The headlights glared on the barrier's reflective paint and nearly blinded him as he braked a few feet back from the blinking yellow lights.

He shoved the gearshift into park and let the car idle while he tried to squint past the light. No highway equipment that he could see, no signs explaining the barrier. And now that he thought about it, it wasn't one of those fence-like barriers the county always used; it was just painted sawhorses stretched across the road, battery-operated lights jury-rigged to the tops, and no room on either side for local traffic.

He sagged back in the seat to puzzle it out, wrists draped over the top of the steering wheel. Finally, he reached for the clipboard to make a note to call Dorothy when he got home and ask if she knew what the hell was going on . . .

'Sir?'

'*Jee-zuz!*' Lee gasped, dropping the clipboard and spinning his head toward his open window. His heart rate doubled within the space of a second. A man was standing there, right next to the car, and Lee hadn't heard so much as the scuff of a boot on asphalt.

'Sorry, sir. Didn't mean to startle you. Deputy . . . ?'

'Lee, goddamnit! And where the hell did you come from?' he bellowed furiously. Damn. He hadn't been surprised like this since his older brother had popped out of his black closet and scared the shit out of him when he was eleven.

'Glad you're here, Deputy Lee. We were beginning to wonder if anyone was ever going to respond to our call . . .'

'What call? What the hell are you talking about? I didn't get any call.' Then Lee colored a little, remembering that he'd been in one of the county's infamous dead zones since he'd left Gill Lake, twisting around the roads that dipped through the northern hills that played havoc with straight radio transmissions. 'Shit,' he muttered, then squinted up at the man's face, trying to make out his features in the reflected glow of the dashboard lights. He'd already seen the camouflage fatigues, the familiar shape of a field cap . . . *Jesus Christ. Was that an M16? What the hell?*

'I don't understand, sir. Your dispatch didn't send you?'

Lee moved his hand to unsnap his seat belt slowly. 'Dispatch didn't send me anywhere. I'm off duty, on my way home, just stopped to see what the roadblock was for. Now what the hell is going on here, and who the hell are you?'

The man's brow furrowed. 'I don't understand. We called the highway patrol some time ago . . .'

'Sheriff's Office and the patrol don't always automatically share calls up here. Besides, I've been off the air for the past half hour.'

'Well, that explains it, I guess.' The man nodded.

'But I'm still glad you're here. We're on a blackout weekend maneuver up here . . .'

'Who's "we"?'

'National Guard, sir.'

Deputy Lee took a breath and relaxed a little.

'And about forty minutes ago, a dark blue Dodge Ram blasted through our roadblock doing about eighty, and when one of our men fired a warning shot, the passenger fired back. Shotgun, we think.'

Lee closed his eyes and shook his head. Some out-of-season deer-shiner with too many beers in his belly and too many shells in the chamber taking on the U.S. National Guard. 'You get a plate?'

'No, sir. He was moving too fast, and to tell you the truth, he had us pretty shook up. We have to assume he was shooting live ammo.'

Lee eyed the man's weapon. 'Shotgun or no, I'll bet he wasn't as armed as you are.'

The man looked down at his rifle with a rueful shake of his head. 'Blank cartridges, sir. They don't issue live ammo for weekend maneuvers.'

Lee released a sigh of relief. 'I suppose not.'

'But he went straight out of here and down that way.' He pointed south, the direction Lee had been headed anyway. 'The Colonel would sure like to see a man who shoots at U.S. troops in custody.'

Lee grabbed his clipboard, unsnapped his holster as he did whenever he left the car, and opened the door with a jerk, oddly pleased when the young soldier had to scramble back out of the way. He took another step back when Lee climbed out and stood upright, facing him. Six-foot-four and built like a linebacker, he towered over most men, this one included. He rested his hand on the grip of his nine, just for effect, and kept it there.

'Uh . . . aren't you going to go after him, sir?'

'In a minute. You know how it is. Seems I'm back on the clock, and I'm going to need a little information before I call this in. You saw the truck?'

'I did.'

'Good. In the meantime, call whoever's in charge of this little show – Colonel, you said?'

'That's affirmative.'

'Well, call him on up here so I can get some kind of confirmation.'

The soldier stared at him for a moment. He was young, Lee noticed, and he looked scared to death. Probably some accountant from Wausau who never in a million years had actually expected to get shot at. 'We appreciate that, sir.'

Lee turned his back and reached through the open window of the car to turn off the ignition. When he tipped his head inside the car, he swore he could smell the stick of peppermint gum in the glove box and the oil on the muzzle of the shotgun on the rack above the cage. He heard the irregular breathing of the young soldier behind him . . .

Just as his fingers brushed the key, he saw . . . something. A reflection in the closed passenger window, moving too slowly, too purposefully, and suddenly he remembered things that had seemed silly at the time. Academy runs, slinking through the darkened training house where cardboard gunmen popped out of every doorway or dropped from the ceiling and your heart beat so hard that your chest wall ached for days afterward . . .

His head and his hand remembered those days like they were five minutes ago, which surprised him a little. He spun sideways, flinging his back against the door frame just as the report of the M16 exploded in his ears. His nine-millimeter was in his hand long before his brain would have thought to initiate the gesture, and then he had a split-second image of the young soldier standing there with the muzzle of the rifle leveled at Lee's head, and then there was another gunshot, so close on the heels of the first that they blurred together.

For a moment that seemed to stretch into eternity, Deputy Lee and the young soldier stared at each other in disbelief. Then Lee gaped down in horror as the soldier sank slowly to the pavement, a black-red circle spreading on his chest. The M16 clattered uselessly to the asphalt.

'Jesus,' Lee muttered stupidly, unable to tear his eyes away. 'Jesus.' The muzzle of his nine dropped toward the ground.

'Becker!'

The hiss came from the trees on the left side of the road, and as instinctively as Lee had spun and drawn his weapon and fired his first shot into the young soldier's chest, he sprinted around to the other side of the car. A bullet kicked up stones from the road just behind him, then another zinged by his left ear with a whining whistle. He ducked down next to the car and reached for the door handle as a volley of shots hit the pavement just behind him. Lee didn't believe for one minute that they were blanks.

He dashed down the berm into the forest, blood streaming from where the young soldier's first shot had grazed the side of his head.

18

Bonar walked into the Hunter's Inn, spied Halloran hunched over in a back booth, and made a beeline for him. He slid into the cracked vinyl seat with a heavy sigh. He looked every minute of the long day they'd put in so far. 'Okay. I sent the prints for our bodies off to that Roadrunner character and moved all the stuff you wanted into my ride, but why you want to drive all over the north woods in a 'sixty-nine Camaro is beyond me.'

Halloran tapped the eraser of a stubby pencil on the map he'd been studying. 'We're going to meet up with Magozzi and the rest of them at Hamilton, right?'

'Right. I figured we'd pop down to the state highway and make some good time, but you know darn well the Camaro's Smokey bait. They wouldn't stop us in the county SUV. If we kept the lights going, we'd have clear sailing.'

Halloran leaned back and rubbed at his eyes. 'We've got about a half an hour on Magozzi's crew. Thought we'd take the northern route.'

Bonar worked his thick eyebrows halfway up his forehead. 'Through Missaqua County?'

'Might as well take a look-see on our way. If the

Feds are hot enough to pull Ed Pitala's patrols off the road, I'm guessing they'll have some blocks set up to stop any other cops that might wander in. Civilian traffic is another thing. No way they can stop that. And a 'sixty-nine Camaro's about as civilian as you can get.'

Bonar puffed his cheeks in a miserable exhale and signaled to Joe over at the bar. 'If we get stopped at the Missaqua border by a few hundred gentlemen in really nice suits, I think the uniforms might give us away anyhow. Unless, of course, you're planning on just mowing them down with the shotgun and riot gun you had me stash in the backseat.'

Halloran slurped a sip of the best coffee in Kingsford County. 'After the way they've jerked us around today, I'm beginning to think that might be a pleasant way to spend a Saturday night.'

Bonar rolled troubled eyes up to the stuffed jackalope mounted to the wall over the booth and grimaced. 'Man, what're we doing here? You know I hate this place.'

'Best food around, and you wanted to eat before we took off. The diner's closed, and there's nothing on the road where we're headed. Cheeseburger rare, heavy on the onions, and every side old Joe's got back there on the grill.'

Bonar smiled a little. 'You got me onions when we're riding together?'

'I figured you'd be real polite and hold your breath the whole way.'

‘At least you didn’t pick the booth with the stuffed cat.’

‘Even I can’t stand that one. Used to pat that cat every time I came in here.’

Bonar took a quick look around the dark interior, then wrinkled his nose and pretended he hadn’t seen a thing. The place was made from hand-hewn pine logs pulled down by Joe’s grandfather a hundred years ago, and every few feet, the glass eyes of some dead animal or other stared down at you. It gave Bonar the creeps.

There was the two-headed calf one of Barkley Widen’s prize Guernseys had dropped back in the ’70s, a loose-lipped moose with a giant, moldy rack, and every other woodland animal you could think of, including a family of chipmunks fastened to a wall plaque with fake moss falling off. To the best of Bonar’s knowledge, Joe hadn’t killed a single one. The man couldn’t bear the thought of taking the life of any creature, but the animals had been hanging since his grandfather’s day and, as he put it, taking them down would be a pure waste of good taxidermy.

And then there was the cat – the one and only dead thing Joe himself had contributed to the grisly décor. Lord, how he had loved that cat, every one of the twenty-three years the tabby stray had prowled around the bar, taking the occasional swipe at a paying customer with his long, untrimmed claws, relenting only when he licked enough suds from where the beer tap dripped to put him to sleep.

Seemed a strange way to honor the memory of a companion, Bonar thought – stuffing it and having it mounted on a wall.

'I don't think I can eat here,' he said unhappily.

Halloran gave him a tired grin. 'You'll eat in your coffin.'

'This is like eating in someone else's coffin.'

His discomfort slowed him down, and it took him a full ten minutes to put away the cheeseburger, and another five to polish off the french fries, onion rings, and coleslaw.

Halloran watched him eat, sipping a fresh cup of coffee to keep him awake on the road. When Bonar pushed his plate away, he threw down a handful of bills and slid out of the booth. 'We need to go.'

Bonar nodded, reluctant to move. 'Man, I'm tired. You want to check with Green Bay again before we take off?'

'Called them before you got here. Sharon and the others still haven't shown up. The detective I talked to earlier went home an hour ago, but the patrols up there are running a watch-and-stop on the Rover.'

Bonar held his gun tightly in the holster as he got up. 'Not so long ago, I was thinking we were like a couple of old ladies, worrying about a woman who won't even give you the time of day just because she's a few hours late. But I started counting those hours while I was loading the car, and there's just too many of them.'

Halloran gave him a steady look and nodded.

'Damn, Mike, this is scaring me to death.'

The good thing about Bonar's Camaro – aside from the 427 big-block Chevy – was that he'd put in one of the county's new radio units just last year.

There was the usual weekend chatter coming out of Kingsford County – a couple of drunk-and-disorderlies, a bar fight with minor injuries, and poor old Ron Rohner, who saw aliens landing in his back forty almost every Saturday night – but when Bonar switched over to Missaqua's frequency, there was nothing but dead air.

'Ah,' Bonar sighed. 'The soothing sounds of the FBI.'

'Why don't you put out a prank radio call to that jackass Wellspring up at the lime quarry? They'll never catch us in this car.'

'Not with you driving.'

'I'm not even going forty-five, which is just about impossible in this thing.'

'Seems like you're going faster.'

Halloran reined back the Camaro's 450 horses even further as they hit the Missaqua County line, which was a cruel irony, since this was the one place in the state they knew for sure didn't have a single patrol on the road. They both kept a close watch for Gretchen Vanderwhite's car, Grace's Range Rover, and anything else out of sorts, but the roads across the county were as quiet as the radio.

Exactly two minutes on the other side of Missaqua County and still twenty miles from Hamilton, Bonar fell sound asleep, and judging by the depth and volume of his snoring, he would probably stay that way for a while. He didn't even stir when Halloran pulled into the gas station where they were meeting Magozzi, got out and slammed the door. By the time Halloran finished his calls in the station and came back out, there was a shiny silver thing big enough to be its own tourist attraction pulled up in the truck lot. Bonar was walking around it with his hands in his pockets, his head tipped back and his mouth open. Harley Davidson, bearded, tattooed, and leathered, looking like a biker version of the gigantic Paul Bunyan statue in Bemidji, walked next to him. Magozzi and his partner, Gino, were stretching their legs in the lot, heads close together as they talked, and Roadrunner was bent in half under one of the big station lights, a collection of sticks hanging on to his ankles for some reason Halloran didn't even want to think about.

They gathered in a circle in the far corner of the lot. Greetings and quick handshakes were exchanged before Halloran got into it. 'We've got a new wrinkle. I just talked to Ed Pitala – the Sheriff over in Missaqua County that the FBI shut down – and sometime in the last ninety minutes, one of his deputies went missing. Guy was off shift on his way home in his patrol and just disappeared.'

Bonar's face tightened. 'Which one?'

'Doug Lee. Know him?'

'Hell, yes, I know him. That guy drank me under the table with the most god-awful sloe gin you ever tasted at the association dinner last year. What the hell was he doing on the road, anyway? I thought the Feds pulled all the patrols.'

Halloran scuffed at a stray stone on the asphalt. 'He was already on his way home and in one of the radio dead zones when the order came down. As far as Ed knows, Lee never even heard about it. Thirty minutes ago, Lee's wife called in a panic and the agent that set up shop in Ed's office tried to keep him from sending out his officers to look, so Ed slammed the guy against the wall and gave him a black eye.'

Bonar grinned happily. 'Good old Ed. Pushing sixty-five, and he's slamming Feds against the jail-house wall and looking at twenty years. They just don't make them like that anymore.'

'Amen,' Magozzi added.

'So the agent finally agreed to let him put all his people on the road, as long as they used their personal cars,' Halloran continued. 'No patrols. No radios. They're all checking in on landlines, and they all have the descriptions of the Rover and the cake lady's car, too, but you know they're looking hardest for their own man.'

Gino threw up his hands. 'Jesus Christ, they've got four women and now a cop gone missing in that cluster fuck they've got going on over there, and they won't tell us what the *fuck* is going on?'

Halloran started to shake his head, then stopped abruptly. 'That agent who took over our scene at the lime quarry said it was a national security operation. I didn't put a whole lot of stock in that, because that's what they told me five years ago when they were trying to bust some morons who were running a multistate dog-fighting ring out of Wisconsin. Back in those days, the Feds hollered national security whenever they wanted the local law to butt out. Thinking anything they ever said was a load of crap was a way of life. Hell, maybe this time they really meant it. Maybe something bigger than missing people is going on here, and we're about to storm right into the middle of it.' He looked around at each of them. 'Anybody here have a problem with that?'

'Hell, no.' Harley spoke for them all. 'As far as I'm concerned, Grace, Annie, and Sharon missing is about as big as it gets. I don't give a shit what kind of operation the Feds are running, national security or not. But if those women are somewhere in the middle of that operation, and figuring out what the hell is going on will help us find them, then I say let's just get down to it.'

Magozzi said, 'Any way you and Roadrunner can tap into the landlines coming out of the Missaqua County Sheriff's Office?'

Roadrunner bobbed his head enthusiastically. 'No problem.'

'I want to catch every report from the officers Ed has out on the road when they call in.'

‘We’ll trap all the calls, in or out.’

Harley spoke up, looking at Halloran. ‘And the Feds are crawling all over that county, right?’

‘So Ed says.’

‘Well, they’ve gotta be talking to each other somehow, operation that big. We need to figure out what kind of a network or frequency they’re using, tie in, and find out what the hell is going on and where.’

‘You can do that from this rig?’

‘You bet we can.’

‘Let’s move, then,’ Magozzi said. ‘We’ll head for the middle of Missaqua County, park this thing in a wayside somewhere, and be ready to move in any direction the information points us.’

‘We’ll follow in our car,’ Halloran said. ‘In case we have to head out somewhere fast.’

Harley smiled at him and jerked a thumb toward the rig. ‘She may look like an elephant, but she runs like a cheetah. You aren’t going to need your car.’

Bonar gave a short nod and started to walk away. ‘I’ll grab our stuff and load up.’

Harley trailed along to help while the others climbed into the RV. ‘We’ve got about everything you need in there already.’

Bonar kept walking. ‘I got a riot gun, a shotgun, goodies like that.’

‘Cool. Where’s your car?’

Bonar pointed. ‘That one. Couldn’t take the county vehicle through Missaqua.’

Harley's mouth hung open. 'Jesus Christ. That's your ride?'

'That's it. The old clunker.'

Harley laid reverent hands on the Chevy while Bonar leaned into the backseat. 'Old clunker my ass, I'm touching the Hope Diamond here. The Holy Grail. Hose me down and hang me out to dry, this is a Yenko Camaro.'

Bonar passed Harley the shotgun and reached in deeper for the riot gun. 'I don't know what Yenko is, but this is Charlie Metzger's old car. No real beauty, but it runs nice. Here, take this.'

Harley grabbed the riot gun without looking at it. He was still staring at the car. '427-cid L72 engine, front disc brakes, ducted hood, heavy-duty radiator, special suspension, and a 4.10:1 rear axle. Quarter mile in the high elevens. I'll give you a hundred right now.'

'In your dreams.' Bonar chuckled and slammed the door hard.

Harley winced. 'One twenty-five.'

'You're a penurious son of a bitch, aren't you?'

Harley tightened his mouth and stomped after Bonar toward the rig. 'All right, all right, you hard-ass, a hundred and fifty.'

'Give me a break, Harley. I paid three thousand for this car and you want to give me a hundred and fifty dollars for it?'

Harley stopped and looked at the man. 'A hundred and fifty *thousand*, you moron.'

19

The dead, empty weight of perfect silence lay over the little lake behind the barn. Beyond the broad clumps of cattails, the water's black surface reflected the full moon's stark light like a bottomless mirror. No water bug skated on its surface; no frog sang from its shore; no cricket scraped the hairy bow of one leg across the other. There was no night music.

For several moments after they heard the last jeeps pull away Grace, Annie, and Sharon remained perfectly still, kneeling in the water like three soggy penitents.

Annie's nose itched. Were they really gone? If she lifted her hand to scratch her nose, if a drop of water plunked back to the surface, would a dozen men leap from hiding and start shooting?

Slowly, carefully, she lifted her left hand from the water and raised it to her nose. It was covered with thick clots of swampy mud. She scratched her nose and no one shot her. 'Can we get out yet?' Her whisper was barely a breath.

Grace's shoulders lifted under the surface, and the water around them rippled. 'Carefully,' she whispered back.

Annie rose from her knees, wobbling, water

sheeting from her tattered dress, her eyes almost screwed shut when the body of the cow behind her shifted. 'There's a cow in here.' She moved aside to show them.

'Good Lord,' Sharon whispered, staring at the thing. It looked peaceful lying there, only a portion of the belly rising above the water's surface like a hairy black-and-white rock. 'That's where all the animals went. They pushed them into the lake.'

The three of them waded hurriedly out from among the cattails onto the mud-flattened grass of the shore, water running from their clothes to puddle at their feet. Sharon and Annie both sagged to the ground like dazed, broken-stemmed flowers pummeled by a heavy rain. Grace stayed upright a moment longer, standing straight and tall and still, a motionless vessel for her busy eyes. Finally, she took a deep breath, and Annie knew it was safe. 'That's what happened here,' she said. 'They were moving some kind of gas in trucks, something went wrong, and they killed a whole town.'

'Oh, shit.' It was the first time Grace had ever heard genuine panic in Annie's voice. 'So we've been sitting in a lake filled with animals that died from poison gas?'

Grace sat down next to her, lifted a soggy piece of silk away from her neck, and laid it back on her shoulder where it belonged. 'It's been hours. Those soldiers weren't worried, so we shouldn't be. Whatever it was isn't here anymore.'

'So I don't have to strip down and look for lesions?'

Grace shook her head. 'There wouldn't be lesions, anyway. It wasn't a chemical agent. It was nerve gas.'

Sharon looked at her. 'How do you know that?'

'Chemical agents are all corrosive. From what I saw of that cow, it was clean, and there wasn't a mark on that dog back in the house, either.'

Annie thought about that for a second, then breathed out and nodded, completely satisfied, and Sharon wondered how the hell she learned to do that. She shivered, hugging her knees, feeling the very careful world she'd created for herself crumbling around her. Suddenly, what she had chosen to do with her life, profiling one killer at a time, maybe saving a life or two along the way, seemed terribly insignificant. While she was so busy – and Grace and Annie, too, for that matter – tracking single serial killers all over the country, mass murder was happening right in her own backyard. 'Christ, I don't believe this. Nerve gas? This is Wisconsin, for God's sake, not the Middle East. Where the hell did they get nerve gas?'

Annie patted her on the knee. 'Actually, Wisconsin's a pretty good place to get the stuff. It's pretty much pesticides on steroids. You've got the main ingredient on every farm in the Midwest, and instructions on how to make it all over the Internet.'

Sharon closed her eyes. 'It just can't be that easy, or every nutcake on the planet would be using it. We're not talking about fertilizer bombs here.'

'It isn't that easy,' Grace said quietly. 'But it isn't impossible, either. Remember the sarin release in the Tokyo subway? They didn't buy that stuff from an arms dealer. They made it themselves.'

Sharon rubbed at her eyes and took a couple of deep breaths, thinking that this was what had killed all the people and animals here. Just breathing. 'They've got two more trucks filled with the stuff out there somewhere.' Her voice was trembling now, and her hand shook as she fumbled with the button to light up her watch face. 'And in about nine hours, they're going to gas a thousand people if we don't do something. We have to *hurry*.'

Grace's voice was maddeningly calm. 'We need someplace to hurry to first.'

'Out of here! We have to get out and let someone know what's going on!'

Annie grabbed Sharon's hand and shook it with a little scold. 'You have to calm down. Just think for a minute . . .'

'We don't have a minute!' Sharon hissed. 'This isn't just about us anymore. What are we supposed to do? Sit around here, thinking, while a lot of other people die?'

Grace blew out a sigh, reminding herself that this wasn't just a panicked woman talking – the cop in Sharon had just taken over, and as far as cops were concerned, immediate action was the answer to everything. 'Fine,' she said quietly. 'Just what would you like us to do?'

'Head for the roadblock, take out the men guarding it, steal one of the jeeps.'

'You and me with our nines against who knows how many men with M16s?'

Sharon didn't want to hear about problems, just solutions. She spoke quickly, fueled by the desire to make things happen. 'So first we try to pick them off from some kind of cover, even if we don't get all of them, we'll at least improve the odds, then we rush the jeep while we're still firing . . .'

'Honey, that's just plain suicide.'

Sharon glared at Annie. 'There's too much at stake here not to try it.'

'There's too much at stake *to* try it,' Grace corrected her, speaking very slowly, very clearly. 'Because if we die trying, a thousand other people die with us.' She let that sink in for a minute. 'We have to think of another way.'

'Goddamnit, there *is* no other way. We've been trying to get out of here since we got in and couldn't do it, and it's even worse now. Now they're all out there in a big circle, just waiting for us.'

'Then we have to break the circle.'

Annie nodded. 'What we need is a diversion.'

Grace eyed her. 'You've been watching old war movies again.'

'Lots of movies. And that's what you do. You get all the enemy in one place, then you slip out in the other direction.'

Sharon snorted. 'Great idea. How do you propose we do that?'

'Hell, I don't know. How do cops do it? If you're in the field, on the job, and surrounded, what do you do?'

'The one thing we can't do. You call for backup.'

Grace spun her head to look at her, went very still for a moment, and then a rare smile spread slowly over her face. 'Maybe we can do both.' She took a breath, looked up the slope toward the paddock, then back down at Annie and Sharon. 'What if we set the whole goddamned town on fire?'

Deputy Douglas Lee was in the one and only place he considered safe at the moment – twenty feet up in the knobby clutches of an old box elder tree.

He'd always hated the messy box elders and the massing, flying beetles they hosted. Damn things took root anywhere – in the sand or the clay, in the sun or the shade, in the middle of a cornfield or a crack in the sidewalk if you didn't keep after them. Even in the middle of a first-growth pine forest, thank God. One day a spindly sapling, the next day a monster like the one he sat in.

The lowest branches of the white pines had been too high for him to reach, and too well spaced for easy climbing. The box elder had been a godsend with its fat, sharply angled limbs and broad, cupped crotches. If he managed to live through this, he had the box elder to thank, and by God, he'd never uproot another seedling from his yard.

He didn't know how long he'd been in the tree – near half an hour, he figured. Long enough to doze off and jerk awake to a terrifying volley of gunfire that turned out to be only in his brain. The wound on the side of his head had run like a faucet while he was tearing like hell through the woods, and for long minutes after, he'd settled in the tree to listen to his heart thunder in his chest. He reached up and touched the side of his head with one of the few clean spots remaining on his bloody hankerchief. Hardly bleeding at all now. Maybe it wasn't too deep, just a bleeder like all head wounds.

He moved his head to peer down at the ground, then jerked back against the trunk when the ground moved.

Shit, Lee. You're a little woozy. Must have lost a little more blood than you thought.

Twisting his arm until the filtered moonlight hit his wrist, he peered down at the face of his watch, careful to move only his eyes and not his head. He blinked hard in disbelief, then raised his wrist closer to his face.

Jesus. Two o'clock in the morning. He'd been in this goddamned tree for *hours*, not minutes. He closed his eyes and thought it through. Maybe he hadn't been dozing. Maybe he'd blacked out. Maybe the head wound was a hell of a lot worse than he imagined.

His heart stuttered in his chest and his breath started to come faster. *Easy, Lee. You're okay. You've come this far, so don't panic now.*

He forced slow, deep breaths, and when he was calm again, he opened his eyes and looked around. If he moved his head very slowly, very deliberately, he found he could keep a measure of equilibrium.

Even with the dense canopy of branches blocking the moon, enough light filtered down to make spotty shadows on the ground below. None of them moved. There was no sound . . .

Son of a bitch. He remembered now. Earlier, he'd fluttered into wakefulness long enough to hear a disturbance in the forest beneath him. The sounds had been different than the frantic, whispered shouting of the men who had shot at him on the road. This time, the noises had been slow, more orderly. Soft murmurs, twigs snapping regularly under carelessly placed boots, underbrush swishing with the passage of a body. They'd come right under the tree, some of them, all dressed in camo like that bastard at the roadblock, all toting M16s and heading in the same general outward direction.

The direction you don't want to go, he told himself, and that was the first time he realized he planned to leave the safety of his perch.

Jesus. What the hell was going on here? No way they were National Guard on maneuvers. No way they were U.S. military of any kind, or by God he was moving to China. But there were a lot of them; they were organized; they were well armed. Christ, it was *somebody's* army.

He pressed his hand against his forehead and tried to rub some sense through his skin. *Think, Lee. You're in some deep shit here. If they wanted you dead back there at the roadblock, they want you dead even more now. Dear God. You killed one of them.*

The memory stunned him for a moment, left his eyes open and staring until he caught hold of his thoughts and made himself blink.

Never mind that. Don't think about that now. His right hand fumbled at his side until his fingers closed around his holster, and he sighed with relief. Thank God. Delirious or not, at least he'd had the sense to hang on to his weapon.

Suddenly, his mind went blank. Now what? What the hell was he supposed to do now?

Get out of here, of course. Get away from these bozos and call it in. Oh, Lord, wouldn't Dorothy just pitch a fit. Hey Dot, I've got an army out here by Four Corners trying to blow my brains out with automatic rifles. Send backup, will you?

He started to chuckle, then closed his throat, horrified by the sound. He'd sounded crazy.

Get a grip, Lee. Cheryl's waiting.

The thought of his wife paralyzed him for a moment. Ah, Jesus, poor Cheryl. Two o'clock already. She must be half mad with worry, bugging the hell out of dispatch . . . oh, hey. Lee, you stupid jerk, of course. Cheryl would have called in hours ago. They must have the whole force cruising by now . . . shit. He had to get out, get to a highway, get visible . . . But first, he had to get past the bad guys, and the problem with that was he didn't know where the hell they were.

Fifteen minutes gone, Grace thought when they finally started to move up from the lake toward the paddock. It took fifteen whole minutes to work it out and find the holes and agree on the timing, and if the damn thing worked and they were fifteen minutes too late for a thousand people, how the hell were they going to live with that?

After the illusion of shelter between the lake and the side of the hill that led up to the paddock, she felt dangerously exposed standing on top of the slope. They all did. They moved quickly to crouch in the tall grass next to the tractor and froze there, breathing through their mouths, straining to hear the slightest sound, to see the merest hint of movement in the lifeless landscape. Heat seemed trapped in the muggy air around them, as if a great, stifling lid had been clamped down on the world.

It's all right, Annie kept telling herself. He said the town was ours for the night, and he didn't know we were listening, so why would he lie? It wasn't a trick, it wasn't a trick, the soldiers really are waiting for dawn somewhere out there on the perimeter. It's safe to move. We have to move. We have things to do and places to go, and never put off until tomorrow what you can do today, and he who hesitates is lost

. . . Inane axioms crowded her thoughts in a traffic jam of words.

Finally Grace eased away from the tractor and moved quickly down the right side of the paddock fence toward the barn, with Annie and Sharon trailing her silently. They all kept their eyes averted from the ghastly things rising like a crop of horrors from the paddock's soil.

Annie glanced toward the open barn door once, caught a glimpse of moonlight laying a dirty glow on the oblong steel collars of the stanchions inside.

Horrible things, she thought, imagining what it would be like to be a cow and hear that brace snap closed around your neck for the first time, to try to back up and find to your amazement that what you'd put your head into, you couldn't pull your head out of. Probably not a whole lot different than what we're feeling right now, she decided.

They stopped at the corner of the barn. The setting moon washed the farmyard in a sickly crust of light that seemed bright after the shadowy recesses by the lake.

A few stones in the driveway reflected a dull gleam. Beyond that, the black windows of the house seemed to stare like the hollow sockets of a dead man's eyes. Shade trees stood in the yard like weary black sentinels, their leaves drooping and motionless in the still air. There was nothing to see, nothing to hear, as if someone had pushed the pause button on the world.

And apparently, they had pushed the pause button on Grace as well. She'd stopped moving in mid-stride, scaring Annie to death.

Suddenly Grace turned toward her, her face clouded with an emotion that was impossible to read. She was frantically digging into her jeans pocket, pulling out her tiny cell phone, flipping it open. Annie's mouth dropped open when she saw the screen, miraculously aglow, the phone shaking a little as it vibrated in Grace's hand.

20

When Bonar followed Harley up the steps into the RV, a big, wirehaired Slinky was creeping up the aisle on his belly. It took Bonar a second to realize it was a dog, and then he was all over him. He hadn't had a relationship with a canine since his boyhood dog had tangled with the wrong end of a badger, but it only took sixty seconds for Charlie to remind him what he'd been missing all these years.

'I get the copilot's seat; I get the dog.' It was Gino's voice, right behind him.

Bonar kept his arm around Charlie's neck and grinned as the big, wet tongue scraped at the blond stubble on his cheek. 'You can have the copilot's seat. I'll fight you for the dog. Where'd everybody go?'

'Halloran went in the back with Magozzi and Roadrunner. You ought to take a look. They got an office back there right out of a James Bond movie.'

Bonar found a seat on an upholstered silk sofa right behind Harley in the driver's seat. 'I'm good here. Besides, this is my neck of the woods. I'll be the navigator.'

Gino slid into the shotgun recliner and buckled

up. 'Hell, we don't need no stinkin' navigator. We got a GPS that'll knock your socks off.'

Harley gave him a look. 'You sure you got a handle on that thing?'

'Damn right. I spent the last two hours learning how, and I've got it down. You want to get out of the parking lot?' He pushed some buttons and peered at a screen. 'Straight ahead sixteen-point-three-seven feet, turn right, bearing north-northeast oh-point-one-one-eight-four . . . Jesus Christ, where'd you get this thing?'

'Took it off a nuclear sub,' Harley grunted.

'Seriously?'

'For Chrissake, Rolseth, of course not. They don't have anything this good. Now pull up Missaqua County and point me toward the center.'

'Hold on a minute.' Magozzi came striding up from the back with Halloran and Roadrunner. He looked paler than he had under the mercury lights in the lot, and his voice sounded like someone had wound it too tight. 'Roadrunner just ID'd your three sinkers from those prints you sent.'

Bonar, Harley, and Gino all turned to look at him.

'They didn't pop up on any of the databases because the Feds made sure they wouldn't. Those bodies were their boys – so far undercover they didn't even have names, just numbers.'

Bonar had the kind of sigh that could make a grown man ache just listening to it. 'Undercover agents. Damn me. It's the one thing that makes a little sense – why they snatched the bodies so fast, took over our crime scene, and shut us out – and it never once occurred to me.'

'Or me,' Halloran said.

Magozzi was standing rock-still, all his body parts quiet except for his brain. 'You said it looked like an execution, right?'

Halloran nodded grimly. 'Looked like they were lined up in a row, nearly stitched in half. Doc Hanson was thinking an M16.'

Magozzi tried to pace but couldn't find enough room with five big men cluttering up the place. 'So they were undercover and into something big – something worth killing three Feds over – and got caught.' He was thinking out loud now. 'Probably just dumped in Kingsford County, a good distance away from where they were operating, since all the Feds want there is the crime scene at the quarry. Missaqua has to be the source.'

'Which is where we were headed for anyway,' Gino complained. 'We may have another piece of the puzzle, but it doesn't tell us a thing about where to start looking. Doesn't do us a damn bit of good at all.'

Magozzi almost smiled. 'It might. It might make all the difference. Roadrunner?'

'Right here.'

'I need an off-the-books FBI number. Far as I know, it isn't listed anywhere. Think you can manage that?'

Roadrunner's grin was his answer.

Gino was on his feet in a second, brows cocked at Magozzi. 'You old dog. Don't tell me. You're going to call Plastic Paul.'

'That I am.'

'Who's Plastic Paul?' Bonar asked.

Gino was already following Roadrunner and Magozzi toward the back. 'That would be Special Agent in Charge Paul Shafer, back in Minneapolis. He and Magozzi have a special relationship.'

Halloran stumbled behind them, frowning. 'That guy we met when we were in Minneapolis on the Monkeewrench thing? I thought you hated him.'

'That's the special nature of the relationship.' Gino smiled as the four of them clustered around a communications console. 'Come on, Leo, have a heart, you gotta put this on speaker.'

It took Roadrunner thirty seconds to find the number. A sleep-thickened voice came through the speaker before the first ring was completed. It was the kind of phone the owner answered instantly, twenty-four-seven. 'Shafer here.'

'Paul, it's Leo Magozzi, MPD.'

There was silence for a moment. 'How the hell did you get this number?'

'Information.'

'Bullshit. This is a closed Federal line, Magozzi, and you just bought yourself a world of hurt. I'm hanging up now.'

'Good idea. After you hang up, you can write your

letter of resignation, or shoot yourself in the head. Your choice.'

Silence again. And then, 'You have thirty seconds.'

Magozzi took a quick breath. 'One of your agents is missing in an area where three other agents were found murdered.'

There was a lot of noise coming through the speaker then – covers being thrown aside, feet hitting the floor, a little static. 'Okay, you got my attention, Magozzi, but if this is bullshit, I will personally see to it that you get your first glimpse of sky in about forty years.'

Gino watched Magozzi's face redden and his chest swell, and wondered if he'd just blow up. You could almost smell the testosterone shooting right up to the satellite. 'Bullfight.' He nudged Harley.

But Magozzi's voice was deceptively calm when he spoke. 'Sharon Mueller's missing.'

'Oh, for Christ's sake, Magozzi, she's not missing. Is that what this is about? She went to Green Bay with those Monkeewrench women to do some profiling on her own time.'

'She never got that far.' Magozzi let that register, then went on to tell him about all the missing people, the dead undercover agents, the FBI taking over Missaqua County. 'We think Sharon and the others are somewhere in the middle of whatever the hell is going on, but it's a huge search area. We're on-site, or close to it, but we need your people to narrow it down so we know where to start looking, and they aren't telling law enforcement over here shit. She's your agent, Paul, not theirs. You have enough pull in that organization to get something done that might save her life? Because that might very well be what's at stake here.'

Shafer answered quickly. 'You have a secure line wherever you are?'

'We're on it.'

'Then give me the number and fifteen minutes.'

They'd only gone ten miles toward the Missaqua County line when Shafer called back. 'Do you know where Beldon is?' he asked without preamble.

Halloran nodded at Magozzi.

'Yes.'

'Missaqua County Sheriff's Office is there. They're setting up a command post. Talk to Agent Knudsen. He'll share what he can with law enforcement. Who do you have with you?'

'Rolseth and I are here, Sheriff Halloran, and Deputy Carlson' – he hesitated for only a second – 'and a couple others out of Kingsford County.'

'I'll give them the heads-up, then. Call from there if he gives you any trouble.'

Magozzi released a breath. 'What's going on over here, Paul?'

'I don't know yet, but I sure as hell am going to find out. And I want to hear from you people. You're riding on my rep now, and I want to know every step you take before you take it, understood?'

'You got it.'

Gino went back up to the copilot's seat and brought Harley and Bonar up-to-date on the word from Shafer. Harley was doing hands-on, eyes-on driving along a tar road that looked about six feet too narrow to accommodate the RV's width. 'So punch Beldon in on the GPS and take us there,' he told Gino. 'Shit. Saturday night with the FBI. I haven't had this much fun since I got mugged and Tasered during Carnival in Rio a few years back.'

Gino took a quick sideways glance at the size of the man behind the wheel, and marveled that a Taser would actually bring him down. 'One of these days, I'd like to hear the rest of that.'

Harley shrugged. 'It's an okay story. Nothing epic. Hey, Bonar, grab me a carton of OJ out of the fridge, would you?'

Bonar was still planted on the sofa; Charlie happily sprawled all over him. He turned his head to browse a kitchen area that was bigger than Margie's. It was all wood – teak, if he wasn't mistaken – and not a hint of enamel anywhere. 'You don't have a refrigerator in here.'

'Third drawer to the right of the sink,' Gino said without looking away from the GPS readout. 'We've got another two-point-seven miles on this one, Harley, then right on some road – County pee-pee is what it says, but that's gotta be wrong.'

Bonar eased Charlie off his lap and went to find drawer number three. 'That's County Double-P. All the county roads in the state used to be letters. Great idea back in the 1800s. Sort of went to pot when they built too many and ran out of alphabet, so they just started doubling up.'

Gino shook his head. 'I am a stranger in a strange land.'

Bonar was in deep reverence once he found the refrigerator drawers, completely concealed behind the polished teak fronts. A whole slew of them. One for liquids, one for produce, one for meat, and a big one that held more wine bottles than the cast-iron display rack down at the Municipal Off-Sale. 'Amazing,' he murmured, snooping without shame, finally grabbing an OJ for Harley. 'You mind if I grab a cherry soda for myself?'

'Anything you want, buddy,' Harley said, downshifting for a mean curve. 'You like the kitchen?'

'Are you kidding? Haven't seen anything this beautiful outside the pages of *Bon Appétit*.'

Gino rolled his eyes. 'Ah, Jesus, next thing you know, you two guys'll be trading recipes and watching *Oprah* together.'

Harley glowered at him. 'I love *Oprah*.'

In the back office, Roadrunner was running multiple programs full-blast, digging as deep as he ever had into closed Federal sites, looking for the tiniest piece of data on whatever operation the dead undercover agents had been running. So far he hadn't found a scrap, which was extraordinary.

Halloran and Magozzi were planted at a small booth next to the windows, alternating between looking over at Roadrunner when he cursed at the keyboard and looking out at what Halloran saw as a quiet country night, and what Magozzi saw as a black landscape of nothingness. 'Christ, somebody turned the lights out in the whole state.'

Halloran smiled a little. 'It's pretty empty up this way. The Silver Dome should be coming up soon, though.'

'What's the Silver Dome?'

'Supper club. Dining, dancing, tablecloths and everything.'

Another half mile around a long curve, and Magozzi saw what looked like a dollhouse-sized Vegas in the middle of a black hole. Christmas twinkle lights were strung all over a dirt parking lot jammed with pickups, and a pink-and-green sign with neon letters as tall as he was blinked on and off, announcing, 'Fine Dining, Dancing, Entertainment.' The sign was attached to a Quonset hut.

'What's the entertainment?'

'Bowling.' Halloran kept his eyes on Magozzi, who didn't even crack a smile. He liked him for that. He looked back out the window and sighed. There was nothing left to see for miles after the Silver Dome, just trees that blocked the moon and an occasional piece of empty land that didn't. 'I don't mind telling you, this is one of the few times on the job I've been seriously scared.'

And that, bizarrely, was when Magozzi smiled. 'Who are you kidding, Halloran? We're not on the job. What we really are is a couple of frantic guys chasing a couple of skirts. Saving our women. Caveman stuff.'

Halloran put his big hands on the table and sighed again. 'You, maybe.'

Magozzi raised a brow.

'Sharon isn't coming back.'

'To you, or Kingsford County?'

'Neither.'

'Well, Jesus, Halloran, she took a bullet in the neck. And like it or not, you and the job are all wrapped up in that. That kind of thing shuts you down for a while, makes you afraid to get back out there.'

Halloran was quiet for a long time, and then he said, 'I should give it some more time.'

'Damn straight. You know what, Halloran? Come to think of it, the last time we were together, we were busting into a gunfight, chasing after the same two women.'

Halloran blinked. 'My God. You're right.'

'Maybe we should get together a couple of times between catastrophes, break the monotony.'

Suddenly the shriek of an alarm blasted through the back of the rig and Roadrunner exploded out of his chair and stabbed a button on the console. 'GRACE!?'

Magozzi was halfway out of his seat, frozen, afraid to move, afraid to breathe. And then he heard the sound of a dial tone buzzing through the big speakers. 'What just happened?' he asked, his voice shaking.

'GODDAMNIT!' Roadrunner stabbed another button, and the sound of numbers dialing filled the rig. 'We had a sat line rigged on auto-dial to rotate every five minutes on all three of the women's cells. Someone just answered Grace's cell, and then I lost the signal . . . CHRIST, THERE IT IS AGAIN!'

The speakers hissed with white noise, then an ear-splitting shrill tone, and then, by God, Grace's voice, garbled and fuzzy and broken, coming through the speakers: '. . . need help . . . four . . . people dead . . . Roadrunner . . . ?'

And then, abruptly, nothing. The speakers went silent.

21

Twenty minutes after hearing Grace's disconnected message, the atmosphere inside the Monkeewrench RV was supercharged, almost electric.

Even working together with all the legal and illegal computer resources they could muster, Roadrunner and Harley hadn't been able to reconnect with Grace or pinpoint the tower that had picked up the call from her cell. Not one of the cell-provider sites they'd hacked into had registered any activity from Grace's cell in the past hour. After fifteen frustrating minutes on the side of the road, Harley was back behind the wheel, driving toward Beldon at an alarming clip on the dark, twisting road, praying that this trip to hook up with the Feds wasn't taking them in the wrong direction.

Bonar was riding shotgun, holding Charlie in his lap with one hand, manipulating an outside spot with the other, supposedly lighting the road beyond the headlights to spot deer. A useless venture at this speed, he thought – they'd never be able to stop in time – but it never occurred to Bonar to suggest that Harley slow down. The call from Grace had been chilling.

Gino was in the back office, poring over a map of

Wisconsin cell-phone towers that Roadrunner had printed out. As far as he could tell, there wasn't a single one anywhere near Missaqua County. After ten minutes of working the map and abusing his haircut, he was absolutely convinced that they were way off track, and almost afraid to say it aloud. Roadrunner already looked insane, attacking the computers, spewing profanity like a Marine, and Magozzi and Halloran both seemed so brittle that it was a miracle they hadn't snapped into pieces. Gino went back to the map, looking at the sites marked for upcoming cell-tower construction, wondering how current the map was.

Halloran was monopolizing one sat phone line, trying to find the tower that had picked up Grace's call the old-fashioned way, by calling all the cellular providers in the state, pushing his badge on sleepy flunkies on weekend duty, trying to get some help from part-time workers with an average IQ in the single digits who thought they could coast through the late shift. He'd finally connected with someone who seemed to know what he was talking about, who proceeded to tell Halloran how it was possible that no one had a record of a call that had obviously gone through. The explanation gave Halloran a headache. He hung up and tried to rub the lines out of his forehead.

'Did you get anything?' Gino asked him.

'Yeah, I found out why there's no record of the call. The guy who runs the whole network for

Wisconsin Cellular just told me it was black magic. How's that make you feel? The people who run the system can't even explain why it works the way it does. Christ. He said if the conditions were perfect, there's a solar storm or sunspots or maybe goddamned Jupiter aligns with goddamned Mars, then sometimes a phone can snatch a tower's signal way beyond the normal range. And if the connection is short enough or distorted enough, it might not register in their software at all.'

'I tried to tell you that,' Roadrunner called from across the room.

'Yeah, well, this guy said it in English.'

They all looked up when Magozzi started to raise his voice. He'd finally gotten through to Minneapolis SAC Paul Shafer, and now he was snapping out an exact quote of Grace's call. He'd memorized every word. He stood up and yelled down the aisle toward the front of the rig, asking how far they were from Beldon, totally forgetting they had an intercom, then he went back to the phone, listened for a second, then exploded: 'Jesus Christ, Shafer, were you listening? She said *dead people,* at least four of them, and they're right in the middle of it . . . Fuck tracing the call; we already tried that, and if these guys can't do it, your guys sure as hell aren't going to be able to manage it . . .' And then he shut up and just listened for a long time before replacing the receiver and looking helplessly at Gino. 'You aren't going to fucking believe this.'

Everybody in the office stopped what they were doing.

'Shafer's been rolling some people out of bed, pretty much laying his career on the line, calling in favors, and when that didn't work, making some threats. He says the Wisconsin Feds moved their undercover guys in when a few of the people they were watching made some unusual purchases. They think they might be making nerve gas.'

Halloran's pencil froze on a pageful of scribbles. Roadrunner sat perfectly still, staring at lines of data scrolling by on the monitor, seeing nothing.

'How sure are they?' Gino asked, his voice tense, his words clipped.

'Shafer didn't know, but he called the agent in Beldon, gave him some background, told him about the call from Grace.' He took a breath, upset by the mere mention of her name. 'He'll fill us in on what they know when we get there.'

Up front in the cab, Harley listened to the exchange on the intercom and pushed the accelerator to the floor.

Ten minutes later they drove into Beldon, flying past a speed-limit sign so fast that Bonar couldn't read it. The streets were dark and quiet, but the parking lot of the Missaqua County Sheriff's Office was lit up like one of those casinos in the middle of the prairie, crowded with dark, nondescript sedans. Magozzi suspected the inside of the cinder-block building was equally crowded with dark, nondescript suits. Harley rocked to a stop and within seconds, all of them exploded from the RV's front door like fizz from a punctured pop can.

Sheriff Ed Pitala was waiting for them outside the front entrance, a cigarette smoldering at the corner of his mouth. He looked lean and mean and nowhere near his sixty-plus years, and it wasn't a stretch to imagine him slamming a Federal agent up against a wall. But he was all smiles when he saw Halloran and Bonar.

'Mike Halloran, it's been too damn long. You missed the Association golf tournament . . . Jesus, Mike. You look like roadkill that isn't quite dead yet. What the hell is going on?'

Halloran grabbed his hand and kept shaking it the whole time he was talking, as if he'd forgotten to let go. 'The women we're looking for are in big trouble, Ed, and we've got no time at all. Anything we should know before we go in there?'

Ed crushed his cigarette out in a flowerpot of dirt that was sprouting Marlboro filters. 'Just a bunch of spooks running around chewing up my place and bossing me around for no reason they'll tell me. That phone call from your friend in Minneapolis shook 'em up some. It was chilly in there to begin with, but now I'm skating on a real thin patch of ice. But I'm still the head rooster. I got my people out looking for Doug Lee, and that's all I care about.'

'Have you heard anything from the road?' Bonar asked.

'A couple deputies have called in. Nothing yet.'

Agent Knudsen intercepted them in the lobby, and, given the circumstances, he was surprisingly cordial. Magozzi figured him for one of the public relations front guys that the FBI used to smooth ruffled feathers while they ran interference. His expression remained neutral until Magozzi introduced Harley and Roadrunner.

'And this is Officer Davidson and Officer . . . Road.'

Harley tried his hardest to look legit, but Roadrunner didn't even bother – it was hopeless for him.

'Undercover,' Magozzi added quickly.

Knudsen still looked skeptical.

'Computer crimes,' Harley said, and Knudsen nodded as if that explained everything.

Knudsen glanced at the sat phone clutched in Roadrunner's hand. 'Did you have any luck reconnecting with your women?'

Magozzi shook his head. 'No luck reconnecting, no luck tracing. You've got to give us something, Agent Knudsen. They're in the middle of this somehow, and we need every scrap of information you've got so we know where to start looking.'

'That's already been negotiated. I'll give you what I can, although I don't think it will help. But you gentlemen need to understand something up front: This is our show. Paul Shafer and the Minneapolis Field Office have no jurisdiction, and we call the shots. Letting you in so you can find your missing agent is a personal favor, but if you interfere in any way with our operation, we'll pull you off the road, is that clear?'

Everyone nodded.

'As you already know, we've lost three agents, and we certainly don't want to see the Bureau lose another one, but we're talking about many more lives at stake here, and that *will* take priority.'

And that was the sentence that brought it all home. Everyone was momentarily shocked into silence. Magozzi was thinking that just a few hours ago, he'd been pelting softballs at a circular target, trying to send Gino into a dunk tank, rubbing a stomach abused by more deep-fried food than he normally ate in a year. A few hours. Apparently, that was all it took for the world to tilt on its axis and send everything that made sense sliding off.

'Well, Christ, man, then give us something we can use.'

Knudsen's eyes went over his head. 'Sheriff Pitala? May we use your office?'

'Why the hell not? You'd use it anyway. But gee, thanks for asking.'

Sheriff Ed Pitala was in his office even when he wasn't. The place was cluttered with dozens of family photos, most of them featuring big, dead fish on stringers.

Agent Knudsen helped himself to the desk and chair while the others stood. Harley and Roadrunner hung back by the door, Halloran and Bonar kept a respectful distance, but Magozzi and particularly Gino were in-your-face close to the desk.

'As of this moment, you're an official part of an FBI operation, and you will remain in Missaqua County after this wraps up for debriefing.' Knudsen looked at each of them. 'All of you. Understood?'

'Understood,' Magozzi said, and everyone nodded.

'All right. We've had a watch on a cell up here for over two years.'

Halloran, who had some familiarity with Wisconsin's penchant for creating and attracting fringe groups, frowned. 'What kind of a cell? White supremacists? Militia?'

Knudsen made a face. 'That's the problem. They don't fit the standard profiles. They're farmers, business owners, working-class men, some of them decorated veterans, and no history on any of the men that attaches them to groups like that. No suspicious activity of any kind, except what attracted our attention in the first place.'

'You found out they were making fucking nerve gas.'

Knudsen's eyes twitched at Gino's interruption and his language. He found a photo of an obscenely whiskered fish on the wall and just stared at it. 'We do not have any confirmation on that, and I will not discuss the details of our investigation. All you need to know is that something they did rang a lot of bells in Washington recently, and we immediately sent in three men to try to infiltrate the group. Three days ago, those men called in their first success and gave us two things: next Friday's date and the letter E.'

'What's the E mean?' Magozzi asked.

'Event.' He paused a moment, let that sink in, then gave Sheriff Halloran a nod. 'The next thing we knew, you had our agents on slabs down in Wausau.'

Magozzi watched the man take a breath. It was the first visible break in his demeanor, and he wondered if Knudsen had known the murdered agents personally, if maybe they'd been friends.

'So,' Knudsen continued, 'we moved in fast, really fast. Within four hours, we had every agent we could get on the ground here. We had a few names of people our agents thought were key. We just finished executing warrants on the homes and businesses of all of them. If there was anything there in the first place, it's not there now. Neither are the men. We've got the county locked down tight, and we're watching every vehicle in and out.'

'Oh, yeah?' Harley challenged him. 'Well, we just drove in here in a rig big enough to carry a hundred if we packed them in, and we didn't have any trouble.'

Knudsen gave him a nasty smile. 'You've had two cars on you since you crossed the line.'

Gino's brows went up to impressed height, a place they'd never been when the FBI was involved.

Magozzi said, 'So something's going down, and you've got until Friday to stop it.'

'It might be worse than that. We suspect the call from our agents was intercepted – that's what got them killed – so they could have dismantled the entire operation and moved it somewhere else . . . or, worst-case scenario, maybe they moved up the schedule and we don't have until Friday anymore.'

Magozzi felt his stomach drop. 'You have a target?'

'No.'

Gino was dumbfounded. 'Jesus Christ, these people are going to hit something and you don't even know what?'

'Correct.'

Magozzi felt like he was swimming through Jell-O. 'We need the names of the men you identified and the sites you raided.'

Knudsen shrugged. 'You can get them from the man out at the front desk, but if you ask me, it's a waste of time. Agents are still crawling all over every site, and for miles in every direction, and we haven't turned up anything. Listen. We appreciate your concern over your missing people, and we're impressed with what you've put together so far. So impressed, in fact, that we're going to have a long talk with you all later about how you managed to do that. But we can't see any kind of a possible connection between your missing people and our operation. Just a freak coincidence.'

'The coincidence is the connection,' Magozzi said.

'Whatever. At any rate, we're willing to give you the run of the roads in the county, as long as you keep watch for a few things we're looking for and report back immediately if you see them.'

'So what are we looking for?'

'Milk trucks.'

Knudsen stayed in Sheriff Pitala's office to make some calls while the others went out to the lobby. Harley strutted up to the suit at the front desk to collect the names and raid sites that Knudsen had promised.

Halloran signaled Sheriff Pitala with a jerk of his head, and the rest of them went outside.

Halloran was face-to-face with Sheriff Pitala, but both men had their hands in their pockets and were looking down at the ground.

'That little twerp in there ask you to do anything for him?' Pitala asked.

'Yep.'

'He told you to look for something, right?'

'Right.'

Pitala nodded, looking off into the night. 'Yeah, well, he told us to look for something, too. That was the only way he'd let my people out on the road to find Doug Lee. Wonder if it was the same thing.'

'Milk trucks,' Magozzi said, and Sheriff Pitala smiled and pulled out a Marlboro.

'Thank God. Didn't know how long I'd be able to keep that one under my hat.'

Harley burst out the door and thrust a sheet of paper at Magozzi.

Magozzi glanced at the sheet, then passed the paper to Roadrunner. 'Three names, three places of business, three houses. Maybe you can do some computer magic with these the Feds can't, but to tell you the truth, I think it's pretty much a dead end.'

'No shit,' Gino said. 'The Feds are all over those sites already. No reason for us to travel down that road. So once again, we get a piece of the puzzle, and we aren't any farther ahead. We still don't have a clue where to start looking.'

Magozzi turned to Sheriff Pitala. 'You have your people covering the whole county, looking for Deputy Lee?'

'I've got thirty-five people out there, including a couple of secretaries.' He raised his eyes to Magozzi. 'It's a small department. That's damn near my whole roster. Most of them are concentrated in Doug's patrol area – that was the northern sector tonight. Five hundred square miles.'

'Jesus,' Gino murmured. 'You could have a thousand men out there who'd still miss him if he was standing behind a tree.'

'Yep.'

Halloran was looking out at the cars in the lot, rubbing the underside of his lip the way he always did when he was thinking hard. 'On the phone, you said you tried to radio Lee when the Feds first pulled your patrols.'

Sheriff Pitala nodded. 'Tried to. Couldn't reach him, but didn't worry about it. Figured he was on his way home anyhow.'

'But you said you thought he was probably in a dead radio zone, that's why you couldn't reach him.'

'That's right. We've got a few of those in the hollows where we don't have enough repeaters around, and some more near the high tension lines . . . oh, shit. Goddamnit. God*damn*it.'

'It might not mean anything.'

'Maybe not, but it's a connection I should have made. Stay put. I'll be right back.'

Gino nudged Bonar with an elbow. 'That was a nice call your boss made.'

Bonar beamed like a proud parent. 'That boy shines under pressure. Always did.'

Inside of a minute, Sheriff Pitala was back with a copy of a county map with all the dead zones marked; another two minutes, and he was inside, sharing the information with Knudsen, begging to contact the few people he had on the road who had radios in their personal cars. Knudsen wouldn't let him.

Pitala went over to a side desk and sat by the phone to wait for check-in calls on the landline, his head in his hands. By the time the first call came in, the RV was long gone.

22

Grace, Sharon, and Annie had been stunned into immobility by the startling cell-phone call. They'd heard a fragment of a single shouted word that Grace and Annie had been absolutely certain was Roadrunner calling Grace's name, and then nothing but static. Grace had talked into the phone anyway, words tumbling over one another, and then the cell had abruptly gone dark.

They tried everything they could think of to get the phone to work again, to recapture that fragile connection, not knowing if anything that Grace had said went through.

'It's not the signal,' Grace finally said. 'The phone's dead. It's a miracle it ever connected after being in the water that long.'

Annie was glaring at the useless phone in frustration. 'I didn't even know you had that thing with you.'

'I always have it with me.'

Sharon sagged against the corner of the barn, devastated to have been so close to salvation, only to have it snatched away. 'Stupid. *Stupid,*' she hissed bitterly. 'We finally find a place high enough and open enough to catch a signal, and we don't have a goddamned phone because we were so stupid that we left them where those guys could find them.'

Grace took Sharon's arm and shook it a little. 'We don't have one second to think of things like that. We've wasted too much time already. We have to hurry.'

They backtracked the same way they had come: into the cornfield at the side of the farmhouse, between the rows, green leaves rustling at their hurried passage, down onto their hands and knees when they broke out of the corn into the tall grass of the field that abutted the road.

This used to be fun, Annie thought as she crept ahead on all fours. When you're a child, dropping to your hands and knees and scrabbling through the grass was something you did for the sheer joy of it. But once you reached a certain age, the posture implied degradation, submission – 'he was brought to his knees,' 'she came crawling back on her hands and knees' – even the language recognized that somewhere between age five and ten, crawling ceased to be fun and became humiliating.

Grace paused at the edge of the field while the others came alongside. They all dropped to their stomachs and peered through the last fringe of tall grass before the land sloped gently down into the ditch, then up onto the road.

To their left, the asphalt climbed the small rise that kept them out of sight of the roadblock; to their right, it rolled gently down into the deeper blackness of Four Corners.

Grace held her breath, listening, watching, caution pressing on her back and tapping her on the shoulder. Crossing the road was the only time they would be totally exposed. She clenched her jaw and concentrated on the evidence of all her senses.

Nothing. No sound, no lights, no sign of life.

She nudged the other two, then held up a forefinger. One at a time. They'd cross one at a time, just in case all the soldiers hadn't gone to the perimeter, just in case they'd left an odd one here and there to keep watch, just in case anything.

Annie and Sharon nodded understanding, then watched with wide eyes as Grace slipped down into the ditch, up the other side, hesitated, then darted across the road and disappeared into the ditch on the other side.

Sharon caught a deep breath, then followed; Annie went a few seconds later.

On their bellies once more, single file, they wriggled like the disconnected segments of a crippled worm back toward the deserted town.

The ditch seemed like an old friend now, its banks rising as if to shelter them from the road. Annie made a face as they slipped into the rank water puddling around slimy grass stems, and it occurred to her that she had to go to the bathroom. Bad. It seemed preposterous. You shouldn't have to go to the bathroom when you're busy running for your life and the lives of a thousand other people.

Certainly Superman never had this problem.

Gradually, the ground beneath them began to rise again, and they were on dry grass. A few more yards, and the old lilac hedge bordering the café and house behind it popped into view on the left.

Grace scrambled around into the deep shadows between the café and the hedge, the other two close behind. For a moment, they all huddled close to the lilacs, blunt-nosed twigs poking their backs. The wall of the café blocked their view of the town, and the only thing they could hear was the sound of their own labored breathing. Eventually, even that quieted and the world was perfectly still.

The peculiar silence of this place had become normal, almost restful. Grace was kneeling comfortably, hands on her thighs, eyelids at a heavy half-mast as she rested her body and mind. In a minute, they'd head back toward the basement to gather what they needed. In just a minute . . .

'I have to go to the bathroom,' Annie whispered. 'Right this second.'

Sharon rolled her head to look at her, amazed to feel a smile come from somewhere. It didn't make it to her mouth, but it was there, on the inside. A stupid smile, really, and all because there was something strangely comforting about Annie having to go to the bathroom. It was so wonderfully ordinary, so damn *normal*.

Without thinking about it, she reached out and

touched Annie on the arm, one of those priestly gestures that seem to convey some kind of a blessing: *Go to the bathroom in peace, my child.*

Annie pressed back into the embrace of the lilacs' greenery while Grace and Sharon crawled a few feet away, more to get out of the splash zone than to give her privacy. They hunkered down close to the hedge, facing each other like two Aborigine elders in the bush. They grinned like guilty, eavesdropping children when the silence was broken by the unmistakable sound of a stream of liquid hitting dirt.

Annie's black lace underwear was puddled around her ankles, her eyes closed in almost euphoric relief, her bare backside jammed against the impenetrable tangle of the lilac hedge's thick, horny trunks. After the first few seconds, the muscles in her legs started to quiver with the strain, and she thought she'd finally found something else that a penis might be good for.

She wiggled her butt in a vain attempt to shake herself dry, then, discouraged, started plucking glossy leaves from the tangle of branches. It was more noise than she'd made crawling all the way from the farmyard, but for the first time, she was beginning to believe they really did have the town all to themselves. She could make a little noise gathering makeshift toilet paper, she decided, and no one would shoot her.

She had almost enough when a huge, calloused hand shot around from behind her and clamped down hard over her mouth, jerking her backward.

23

Grace and Sharon were crouched by the side of the lilac hedge, waiting for Annie to finish. It seemed to be taking her forever.

Sharon shifted her shoulders anxiously. The skin on the back of her neck seemed to be moving. She shuddered and pulled the sides of her mouth down. Lord. So that's what it felt like when something really made your skin crawl. It was this blasted, deadly-silent town. The slightest noise sounded malevolent, like Annie jerking leaves off the branches to use as toilet paper. And just when you got used to the noise, it stopped, and that seemed more malevolent still.

'Annie?' Grace leaned forward on her knees, peering back along the hedge at the spot where Annie was still hidden in greenery.

Silence.

Sharon frowned and moved a little closer to Grace. If she'd been an animal, her ears would have been pricked forward. 'Annie?' she echoed Grace's whisper.

More silence.

Grace hadn't moved; she was barely breathing, her eyes fixed on the wall of leaves where Annie had been just a moment ago – where Annie absolutely, positively still was, still had to be . . . 'Annie!'

'Be quiet.'

Sharon shrank back and her mouth dropped open. The voice had sounded like God – big and booming, even in a whisper, coming from a bush, no less. *God isn't really a bush, Sharon, honey. That's just how he talked to Moses.*

She could feel Grace's arm pressed tightly against hers. They trembled in unison, shudders passing from one body to the next, because somebody else was in there with Annie.

Sharon slammed her mouth closed, trapping a scream that belonged to a woman, not a cop. Out of the corner of her eye, she saw Grace fall to her belly, elbows braced on the ground, the big Sig pointed at the bushes before Sharon's gun had even cleared the holster. Grace's expression was tight and hard, and her eyes were so big that they looked like they were eating her face.

The big whisper, definitely male, sounded again. 'Who are you?'

Sharon swallowed. It was one of them. God in heaven, one of the soldiers had Annie.

Grace moved her hands slightly, drawing a bead on the sound of the voice, but she kept her eyes forward, her gaze laying right on the barrel of the Sig.

There was a little squeaking Annie-noise from deep inside the hedge, and Grace nearly fainted with relief. Annie was in there, she was alive, but then there were muffled grunts and sounds of a struggle and oh, God, he was hurting her. 'Let her go!' Grace's voice was the one that boomed now.

'Quiet! I have a gun to your friend's head. How many of you are there, and what are you doing here?'

There was a sudden commotion in the bushes – a loud cracking of branches, a gut-deep grunt, then a high, whistling sound as branches burst open and Annie came tearing out on her hands and knees like an enormous motorized toddler, her underwear tangled around her ankles, her face horribly contorted. She plowed into Grace and nearly knocked her backward. 'That goddamned son of a bitch grabbed me while I was *going to the bathroom,* for Christ's sake. What kind of a person does that? Shoot the bastard.' She tugged furiously at her panties, struggling to pull them up while she was still kneeling. 'I got him a good one with my elbow, but he's still wiggling. Go on. Shoot him!'

'Don't shoot,' the man's voice said weakly. 'Don't . . . please . . . Jesus . . . I'm already shot . . .'

Grace's eyes narrowed. He was lying. He wasn't shot. She hadn't pulled the trigger yet.

'. . . your friends . . . already shot me . . .'

Grace frowned. *Their* friends? Not his? Was he telling the truth? Or was it a trick? Was he sitting in there perfectly all right, pretending to be shot so she'd creep over and peekaboo in and then he'd yell, 'Surprise!' and blow her off?

'Who are you?' she demanded.

'. . . deputy . . . deputy . . .' the voice faded.

The three women exchanged glances, then jumped when something small and metal sailed out of the bushes and landed in front of them. Moonlight glittered on it, outlining it on the dark grass blanket. It looked like a perfectly shaped star had fallen from the sky.

'Oh, God,' Sharon murmured, leaning forward to pick up the Missaqua County badge. 'Who are you? Who's the Sheriff of Missaqua County?'

No answer.

'Hey, you. Throw out your gun.'

Silence.

Grace glanced at Annie. 'Did you see him? Is he one of them?'

Still outraged, Annie shrugged. 'He grabbed me from behind.'

Sharon was already moving cautiously up to the hedge, creeping forward to where Annie's exit had left the greenery in disorder. She stopped just shy of the spot, then led the way in with her 9mm. It was a thoughtless act, automatic. She'd done it a million times before. Sure, she'd been stuck behind a desk for the past several months, hiding from the memory of what it felt like to have a bullet plow through your neck, losing her edge and dulling her senses, but she was back in full cop mode now.

She saw him behind the tangle of thick branches at the roots, slumped into it, his arms snaked around from behind as if he were hugging the hedge. His shirtsleeves were light tan, not camouflage. His gun had fallen from his hand and lay in the dirt in front of the bush, beyond his reach.

Sharon released a soft breath, looked at his head, and saw blood. His eyelids fluttered and he groaned.

It took them ten minutes they didn't have to get him down into the basement.

A miracle, Grace thought, grunting as they negotiated the last step down. He had his right arm over her shoulder, his left over Sharon's, and Grace wasn't sure he'd been entirely conscious during the halting trip from the lilacs. Her back ached from the weight of his arm. He was a big man.

'Maybe if I could just sit for a minute,' his voice strained.

Annie closed the doors behind them while they eased him down to the dirt floor. He leaned back against a wooden support beam and closed his eyes.

He was Deputy Douglas Lee, according to the County Sheriff ID card in his wallet. They'd gone through it hurriedly while he was blacked out under the hedge. Grace thought they must have looked like criminals, peering at their booty in the moonlight.

She looked him up and down while his eyes were still closed, thinking that unless the local Sheriff's Department was involved in this whole thing, he probably wasn't one of the psycho warriors. Then again, identification could always be faked, and the uniform could just be part of an elaborate disguise.

She closed her eyes and pinched the bridge of her

nose hard. Nothing was what it seemed anymore. What looked like pretty Wisconsin countryside was really a bloody battlefield; men who looked like U.S. soldiers were really stone-cold killers who shot women in print dresses and wanted to shoot them, too.

Suddenly, the man's chin sagged to his chest and his eyelids went still.

Annie peered down at him. 'Is he dead?'

'He's not dead,' Grace said, watching his chest rise and fall. 'He just blacked out again.'

'You think he's really a deputy?'

Sharon shrugged. 'The badge looks legit. Which doesn't mean anything.'

No, Grace was thinking. We can't trust anyone except ourselves. 'I don't know,' she said aloud, looking at the wound on his head. One side of his face was streaked with dried blood – a lot of it – and fresh, shiny seepage trickled over it. *See that? That's real. And even a crazy man wouldn't shoot himself in the head as part of a disguise, right? So he is a deputy. One more for our side. The odds are improving. We're now up to four against . . . how many?*

'Lord God,' Annie murmured, staring at the wound. 'Who would have thought I could do that much damage with one little ol' elbow.'

Sharon had already wet a rag at the sink and was bending from the waist to dab ineffectually at his wound. 'Your elbow didn't do this. Might have made it worse, but he really was shot. See the graze right here?' When she pressed a little harder, he groaned awake and leaned forward, grabbing his head in both hands. 'Ah, shit, that hurts.'

Sharon jerked back involuntarily, holding the rag out at arm's length. He reached for it with a shaky hand and pressed it against his head.

'Who shot you?' Grace said.

'You tell me.'

There wasn't much moonlight filtering through the high, narrow windows, but there was enough to show the steadiness in Grace's hand as she raised the Sig and let him see it. 'You first.'

His eyes widened a little at the gun. 'Christ, who are you people? Your goddamned soldiers at the roadblock shot me. I thought they were Guard. Are they?'

Sharon dropped to a crouch and looked right at him. 'Who's the Sheriff of Missaqua County?'

'Ed Pitala.'

'Tell me something about him a stranger wouldn't know.'

The man looked at her hard. 'Sixties, hard as nails, two tours in 'Nam, wife Pat, who's about four times tougher and ten times smarter than he is. Loves his wife, his kids, and Jim Beam, in that order. Smokes Marlboros. And he's stone deaf in his right ear.'

Sharon raised a brow. Anybody could know most of what he said, except for the deafness. That was under wraps, information for good friends like Halloran, and maybe this man, because if the county commissioners ever found out, old Ed would be out of a job. She held out her hand. 'Deputy Sharon Mueller, Kingsford County.'

It took a second for Deputy Lee to absorb the information. 'Mike Halloran's woman?'

Sharon reddened. 'One of his deputies.' She looked up at Grace. 'He's okay.'

'You sure?'

'As sure as I can be.'

Grace still didn't trust him. 'How'd you get here?'

Surprisingly, Lee felt a nudge of angry indignation. He'd never been on the wrong end of an interrogation before, and he didn't like it. But there was an undercurrent of fear in the woman's voice, and that tempered his response.

'I told you all that . . . didn't I?' He frowned hard, squinting at the dim outline of his legs sprawled before him on the dirt floor, trying to remember.

'You started to, then you passed out.'

Lee sighed and squinted as his pupils tried to find enough light. He could almost see her now – see them. Three woman-shadows in this strange, shadowy place. A basement, he decided. Of course. They'd told him they were taking him to the basement, or had that been a dream? 'Is there water?'

One of the shadows moved, and he heard water running into something metal. A moment later, a tin cup of some sort was pressed into his hand. He drank, tasted soap, then suddenly remembered grabbing the woman in the hedge. She'd gone immediately rigid – he remembered what that had felt like, like when you pick up a wounded bird and it freezes in your palm, terrified – but then later, she'd started to flail, and . . . had he hit his head on something? He had a vague tactile memory of sticky warmth coursing down his cheek, then nothing.

'Tell us!' the interrogator woman hissed. 'How did you get here?'

Still scared, he thought. And scared people were dangerous people. He felt for his gun, panicked when he found his holster empty. 'I was at the end of my shift, heading home, stopped at a roadblock that shouldn't have been there. The soldier guarding it shot me as soon as I turned my back.'

'How'd you get away?'

His head turned toward a new voice. 'I killed him,' he said, and although his tone was flat, there was a tremor beneath it.

It made Grace feel better. It made her believe he really had killed one of the soldiers, and that killing wasn't something he was used to.

She felt her way to the sink, filled a hand with water and drank, then crouched next to him and met his eyes in the near dark. She could see only the whites. 'We don't know who we can trust.'

He almost smiled. 'Join the club. Are you supposed to be a Kingsford Deputy, too?'

'Sharon's the deputy. Annie and I are from Minneapolis.'

Something clicked in Deputy Lee's head, and he

struggled to focus on it. 'Shit,' he muttered, almost to himself. 'Three women in a Rover.'

Grace caught her breath. 'How do you know that?'

'Highway Patrol had a watch-and-stop on three women in a Minnesota Rover. Figured it was some rich housewives got lost on the way home from antiquing or something.' His eyes moved down to Grace's weapon. 'But I don't expect all Minnesota housewives carry guns like that.'

'Sure they do,' Grace told him, because he deserved that after the assumptions he'd made. She hesitated for a moment, then thought, What the hell. If they told him everything and he turned out to be one of the bad guys, they'd just shoot him again. So she let him hear all of it: the car breakdown, the deserted town, the murder of the young couple in front of the café, but when she got to the mass grave in the paddock and the things they overheard at the lake, Lee interrupted.

'Wait a minute, just wait a minute.' He was pressing his hands to the sides of his forehead, trying to take it all in. 'You're trying to tell me this group of whackos accidentally killed the whole damn town with some kind of gas, and now they're killing more people just to keep it quiet? Do you realize how crazy that sounds?'

Grace lost her patience instantly. 'You stupid man. One of them shot you in the head. Did you think that was an accident?'

He was glaring at her for calling him stupid, but

her gun was still right out there, so he kept his voice soft and even. 'No, I do not think it was an accident, ma'am. Right-wing crazies, militia types – Lord knows we have enough of them in this state – but nerve gas? Mass murder? I'm having a little trouble getting my head around that.'

'Well, you'd better hurry up,' Grace snapped. 'Because at ten o'clock, two more of those trucks are going to blow somewhere.'

Lee's mind stumbled through all the information she'd fired at him, his thoughts rattling around in his brain like bumper cars at the county fair. His head was killing him. He wasn't a hundred percent sure he could trust his own judgment at the moment, but one thought kept rising to the top like oil on water, and that's the one he focused on. 'We've got to get out of here. Tell someone what's going on.'

Annie elbowed Sharon. 'Gee, why didn't we think of that?'

Lee recognized the voice of the big one he'd caught in the bushes – the wild one. Who the hell was she? And who the hell was the one with the gun and the attitude, and what were they doing with a Kingsford deputy? Do they have husbands, kids? Hell, he didn't even know their names. Someday, when he got them all out of this, they'd all go out for beers and he'd ask them those things and a million others, but not now.

'I told you, we already tried to get out of here,' Grace said rapid-fire, angry and impatient because the fool didn't listen. 'Twice. There are too many of them, and right now they're all out there on the perimeter, just waiting for us to try again.'

Lee gritted his teeth against the pain in his head, against the nausea that rose like a black bubble when he pushed himself away from the post and sat erect. He didn't pass out, though. *Good. Step one, get it together, Lee,* he told himself. *It all depends on you.*

'The road that runs through Four Corners is almost a mile long. It's too big an area for any kind of effective perimeter. They'd have to have a thousand men to keep it tight.'

Annie snorted. 'Do the math, honey. Line-of-sight average, oblong, not a circle, they could do it with less than a hundred.'

Lee blinked in the general direction of the voice. The wild one again. Christ, what was she, a math teacher? 'I was raised in these woods, ma'am. Unless there's enough of them to hold hands, there's a hole in their line somewhere. I'll find it.'

Annie just closed her eyes in sad resignation. You couldn't talk to a man when he was thinking like a man. He wanted there to be a hole in the perimeter, therefore there was a hole in the perimeter. Penis is genius.

Lee was trying to stand now, fingers hooked around the post to pull himself up. There was an instant of dizziness, then Sharon was next to him, supporting his elbow. 'We already decided that was too dangerous. We have another plan.'

Lee shook his head with a smile but immediately regretted the motion. He breathed deeply, waiting for the nausea to subside. 'I'm sure you do, ladies, but I'd feel a whole lot better if you just sat tight and waited for me to come back with help.'

'Oh, for Christ's sake,' Grace said, totally disgusted and then infuriated when Lee started to talk again with one of those condescending tones a lot of men still used on women.

'Listen,' he said gently. 'I know you think trying to walk out of here is hopeless, or you would have done it yourselves. Hell, there's a bunch of boys out there with automatics; that's enough to intimidate anyone. I understand that. But you have to know they're not supermen. There has to be a way past them; you just haven't found it yet. I need to go look. It's my job.'

Sharon took a step away from him and tried to keep her voice from shaking. 'What do you think you're dealing with here? A bunch of simpering women in long dresses waving white hankies, waiting to be rescued? I had the same training you did; I'm a deputy sheriff and an FBI agent to boot, and as far as the other two go, they're just plain scary. I get the serve-and-protect impulse. I know what you think you have to do and why you think you have to do it. But we did not veto trying to walk out of here because we're intimidated. We vetoed it because it's suicide.'

Lee waited a moment before he spoke, responding

to that singular male sense that instinctively retreats from the murky, unspoken undercurrents that sometimes pass between women when they've decided that men are idiots. Once they got to this point, trying to talk some sense into them was like beating yourself over the head with a hammer. It was better to just slip away and do what needed to be done, and let them see the right of it later.

'I'm going to need my gun,' he said quietly.

Grace took a step closer so he could see her eyes. 'That's too bad, because we could use another weapon after they kill you.'

Lee actually smiled, although no one could see it very well. 'Tough lady,' he said, then held out his right hand. 'Deputy Douglas Lee, Missaqua County Sheriff's Department. I didn't catch your name.'

The hand hung there alone for a moment while Grace tried to process the gesture. Tough, maybe. Rude, never. She shifted the Sig to her left hand and gave him the other one. 'Grace MacBride.'

'Pleased to meet you, Ms MacBride.' His face searched the darkness in the basement. 'And the woman I met in the bushes?'

A drawl answered him. 'Annie Belinsky. The woman you *attacked* in the bushes.'

Lee dropped his eyes. 'I do need to apologize for that. Never once in my life did I think I would lay violent hands on a lady.'

Grace handed him his gun, butt-first, and he slid it into his holster in a smooth, powerful movement.

Then he moved toward the door, his gait growing more steady with every stride.

He's huge, Grace thought as his shadowed form passed her. And he seems stronger now, almost whole. Rationally, she knew that just because they were bigger and stronger didn't automatically make men more competent, more capable of accomplishing what a smaller person could not – but sometimes it was a comfort to wish it were that way. It was part of the male mystique so deeply ingrained in women that you grew up wanting to believe it, even though it didn't make any sense at all. Or maybe there was a God and miracles and truth in biology, and Deputy Lee would find a way out and come back and save them all. Wouldn't that be lovely. Grace closed her eyes. *You think of Magozzi that way, too. Even you, with all you've seen and all you know, still want desperately to believe the lie of fairy tales.*

Deputy Lee opened the wooden door that led to the concrete stairs, then turned and looked at them, standing there in a pathetic little semicircle, watching him leave. It occurred to him then that he hadn't really seen their faces, not clearly; that he wouldn't recognize one of them on the street; that if he didn't make it back in time and, God forbid, they disappeared forever in this town, he wouldn't even be able to give a description. At least he'd gotten their names.

He gave them a bleak smile. 'Well, I guess I'll see you later.'

The three women watched in desolate silence as he crept up the steps and slowly raised the slanted storm door on the outside. A slice of fading moonlight came down the stairs and lay a lighter stripe on the black dirt floor in front of their feet. They all stared down at it, listening to the storm door's soft thump as it was closed.

Lee straightened, releasing a long exhale, then looked around carefully. Shadows. Nothing but black, silent shadows everywhere. He had his 9mm back in his hand, safety off, and he could smell the sweat of his own fear. Still, it felt better out here than it had in the clammy basement – better to be moving, to be taking action, than to be hiding and waiting for the bogeyman to come.

And it felt better to be alone again. There was a small twinge of guilt as he realized how glad he was to be away from the women.

He was a short distance into the trees when a small yellow fireburst bloomed in the woods directly ahead. His brain never had time to process the sound or the image that his senses recorded, or even the great pressure of the projectiles that drilled into his body.

For an instant that imitated life, he remained erect, then he toppled backward slowly, his body rigid, like a giant redwood severed from its trunk, reluctantly yielding to gravity.

Back in the basement, all three women closed their

eyes at the same time. 'M16, triple burst,' Sharon murmured. 'No nine millimeter. He didn't have a chance to shoot back.'

24

Grace, Annie, and Sharon stood immobile in the dark basement for a full minute after they heard the triple burst from the M16.

Grace's eyes were fixed on some distant point in the blackness as she remembered how ready she'd been to kill Deputy Lee when he'd been holding Annie in the lilac hedge. Not a quiver of guilt, not a single thought of hesitation, finger tight against the trigger. And then she remembered the big man stretching out his hand to her less than an hour later, and the way that hand had felt in hers. '*Pleased to meet you, Ms MacBride.*' She gave herself that full minute to think of these things. It was all she had to give.

Sharon was scowling at the floor, damning her mother, her upbringing, the religion that had pounded the mantra into her head day after day, year after year, because for the second time this terrible day she was hearing it pop to life inside her brain and she didn't know how to make it stop. *Holy Mary, Mother of God, pray for us sinners now and at the hour of our death. Amen.* And once again, holy Mary was just sitting up there, watching the innocent and maybe the foolishly brave get killed, and it was such a lie. It was such a goddamned fucking lie, and oh, Lord, she'd never said that word before, never even let it form fully in her thoughts, because that was a sin, and there was no confession for little Sharon Mueller, not now or ever again, and they were innocent, and now they were about to do something foolishly brave, and did that mean they would die, too, with the sin for thinking the f-word so fresh and unforgiven?

Annie was just plain furious, because that was the one emotion she really had a handle on. They told him flat out that he was going to die if he went out there, and the stubborn fool went on ahead and got himself killed anyhow. Sure, she'd been thinking about killing him herself in the lilac hedge, and she'd thought about it again when he'd fluffed out his strutting ruff like some randy grouse hell-bent on beating the shit out of some other randy grouse, but then the bastard had shown his true colors as a good and decent man and apologized. It was a purely mean thing to do. Annie didn't know what to do with sadness.

Grace was the one to break the silence. 'We're down to six hours and ten minutes. We've got to hurry.'

The three of them felt their way to a workbench on the stairway wall. Grace and Sharon stooped to pull out the filthy wooden crate under the bench they'd seen earlier, the first time they'd been in this basement. While they were dragging the thing out into the open, Annie found treasure on top of the workbench and flicked the switch. The old flashlight shot a beam across the floor and startled them all.

'Good find, Annie,' Grace said. 'You have any pockets in that dress?'

Annie shone her light down on the eight-thousand-dollar ruin and sighed. 'I have a bra.'

'Same thing. Tuck a couple of these in.' She handed her two of the old Coke bottles, and Annie struggled to find a place for them.

'Could probably sell these things for some serious money on eBay.'

'The bottles or the boobs?' Sharon asked, and the second the words were out of her mouth, she snapped it shut in horror. Oh, God. Had she really said that? A thousand people were going to die, poor Deputy Lee was already dead, and a minute later, she was making jokes? What kind of a person was she?

Annie had slapped a hand to her mouth to cover the laugh, but it kept squirting through her fingers in little breathy snorts. Not funny, not funny, none of this is funny, she kept telling herself, but once she'd started to laugh, she couldn't seem to stop. It didn't help that Grace was laughing, too. Grace hardly ever laughed. It was scary. 'Omigod,' Annie gasped. 'We're hysterical.'

And that made Sharon start laughing, too, because she'd seen hysterical, and this wasn't it. Hysterical was when your mother raced stark-naked through the house, wailing at the top of her lungs, wringing her hands, settling briefly in this chair and that, until finally the chair she chose was the one behind the desk with the big, ugly gun in the center drawer. *That* was hysterical. And then there was the ten-year-old daughter crouched on the floor, legs scrambling as she tried to push herself into the wall she was leaning against, her mouth open in a silent scream, her eyes fixed on her mother's blood and brains sliding down the plate-glass window behind the desk. *That* was hysterical, too. But not this.

She took a deep breath that erased everything. Displacement behavior, she remembered, was the body's defense against stress. People laugh at funerals. Cats stop fighting and spontaneously groom themselves. Cats licked, people laughed.

Annie and Grace were letting out the last long, shaky exhales, letting it all go, and then Grace was passing out bottles again, and it was as if the laughter had never happened.

They started upstairs to leave the house by the front door – not out through the basement and into the backyard. The perimeter was out there, in the woods but closer than they'd thought. Deputy Lee had proven that. There was less chance that they would be seen with the protection of the buildings between them and the trees.

Grace was in the lead, shining the flashlight down on the risers, making the climb easier.

It's the flashlight, Sharon thought as she followed. Whoever has the flashlight is automatically the leader, as if light was some kind of royal scepter, even more powerful than a gun. Maybe in the Bible, she thought wryly.

In the feverish religion that her mother had practiced, plowshares were mightier than swords, and things like light and goodness and mercy always won out over the lesser weapons, like atomic bombs. *God's sword will not be beaten, Sharon. Man's weapons are puny in the face of the Word of God . . .* But in the end, her mother hadn't stuck a Bible in her mouth and blown her brains out, now had she?

'Wait a minute,' she whispered, thinking of something as Grace prepared to open the door at the top. 'We don't have a lighter, or matches.'

'There are matches in the glass display case at the gas station,' Grace said.

Christ, Sharon thought. She sees everything. The tiniest detail. And never forgets it. Like a really excellent cop. She saw all the things that you should have seen, drew all the conclusions that you should have drawn, and that's how she knew that this town was wrong before we ever walked into it. You're not just a good cop scared off the street by a bullet in the neck – you were never that good to begin with. And Grace isn't the leader because she's carrying the flashlight – she's the leader because she just is. Something big and dark seemed to open a little in Sharon's head, and her next breath felt like the first one she had taken in a very long time. It almost made her smile.

Grace opened the door to the upstairs and turned

off the flashlight, and they were all lost in a black void. They felt their way to the front door and slipped outside. The moon was below the tree line now, and the darkness seemed to have texture, it was so impenetrable. Grace could barely identify shapes more than ten feet distant. This must be what it's like to be blind and deaf, she thought – no sound, no light, no motion, not even a breath of air stirring in the hot, still night.

The hulking outlines of the café and gas station were barely visible, but the outside air had that sweet, wet, predawn smell that seems to gather in the last hours before sunrise on a hot summer night. We have to hurry, Grace thought.

They carefully crept across the broken asphalt between the house and the gas station – this was the one place they would be fully exposed to any line of sight from the woods. Once inside the gas station, Grace felt around the display case until she found the matches, tucked them into her jeans pocket, and they all moved into the adjacent garage bay. There were no windows in here; even the narrow back door was solid, and it was safe for Grace to turn on the flashlight.

Ten minutes gone, six hours left.

Grace found a red gas can with a gooseneck nozzle next to the hydraulic lift, checked it and found it nearly full, then swept the walls with the beam of light. 'Can't see it.'

'Give me the light,' Sharon said. 'They're usually

somewhere near the counter.' She found the master switches that turned the pumps on and off under a shelf near the register that held about a decade's worth of dusty Veterans Day poppies. She pushed the two levers to the off position and hoped they worked.

When she came back to the garage bay, she shined the light on Annie and Grace, who were filling the Coke bottles with gas by touch. The smell was cloying in the closed space. Grace looked up at her. 'Pumps off?'

'Yes.'

'There's a box of disposable rags on the bench behind you. I couldn't find them in the dark.'

'Got 'em,' Sharon said after a few seconds with the light.

Annie gave up crouching after a few minutes and sat down on the filthy garage floor, fat legs crossed, expertly twisting and stuffing rags into the bottles. 'Haven't done this since I tried to blow up Cameron DuPuy's BMW convertible sophomore year in Atlanta. Remember, Grace?'

'No. I had nothing to do with it. I wasn't there.'

Annie chuckled softly and kept stuffing, and Sharon wished for a moment that she had been there, committing a felony with these two women. Maybe life would have been different then.

When the bottles were ready, they moved out to the pumps. Sharon removed the nozzles and locked them open, watched the trickle of gasoline that remained in the hoses seep out onto the concrete, then stop. The shut-off switches had worked.

Annie started laying a trail of rags from where the nozzles lay on the concrete back to the big garage bay door. Grace followed, soaking the rags with gas from the can. Back inside, they cracked the big garage door, then Grace continued the flammable trail, sloshing gas over cases of motor oil and cans of solvent stored inside the garage. She felt the cold, slimy wetness on her hands as she continued the trail out the back door, through the junked cars behind the station. They piled more rags there, and then all three of them stood, looking down at the pathetic pile of dirty, pale blue.

'No way we are ever going to hit that little bitty pile,' Annie said worriedly, glancing over her shoulder at the woods behind them.

'Softball,' Sharon murmured. 'All-state pitcher, three years in a row.'

'Honey.' Annie gave her a soft punch in the shoulder. 'Way to go.'

It was too dark to see her face – they didn't dare use the flashlight out here – but Sharon thought she might have been smiling.

While Grace soaked the pile of rags with gasoline, hoping it wouldn't evaporate too fast, Annie and Sharon collected the Coke-bottle Molotov cocktails from the gas station and carried them back to the edge of the woods. The reek of gasoline was in their mouths, their noses, bathing their sinus cavities, and by the time they were finished, it seemed that there was no fresh air left in the world. But they were ready.

Carefully, carefully, but hurrying now, graceless and more daring in their haste, they skittered back to the house, in the front door, and on to the kitchen.

They clustered around the big, old four-burner gas stove, the fumes from the pilot lights mingling with the gasoline stench in their nostrils. Sharon thought it was probably a miracle the three of them didn't just burst into flames.

Grace lifted two heavy skillets off hooks behind the stove and placed them on the burners. 'Cast-iron,' she murmured. 'Makes the best hash browns in the world.'

Sharon pulled her one and only spare clip out of her blazer pocket, fingers tight around it, reluctant to let go. God, what were they doing? What if they needed these to save their lives? 'Are you sure this is going to work?'

Annie felt for the clip, tugged it away from Sharon, then expertly started ejecting bullets into the two skillets. They made tiny, clinking sounds. 'Don't ask me, darlin'. I haven't cooked bullets in years.'

Sharon half believed her.

'Lord, we must look like the three witches in *Macbeth*.' Annie turned on the burners, and there was a soft *poof* as blue flames sprang to life beneath the skillets, warming all the little bullets inside. 'Bubble, bubble, toil and trouble.'

'Let's get the hell out of here,' Grace said, glancing at her watch.

Five and a half hours left.

25

Grace and Annie waited at the open door of the gas station while Sharon went in with the flashlight to turn the pumps back on. Before she came outside, the sound of liquid hitting concrete broke the silence of the night, and the smell of gas polluted the sweet air.

'Lord, that sounds like it's coming out fast,' Annie whispered.

'It's a lot of gas,' Grace said. 'It's going to hit the woods.'

Great, Annie thought. Even if we do manage to get out of here, they'll slap us in Federal prison for setting a forest fire. Unless, of course, we burn to a crisp first.

Grace was squinting into the dark, trying to pick out the rag trail that led from the pumps to the garage bay. How long for a fire to follow that trail? Two seconds? Two minutes? Would it take too long, or move too fast?

By the time they all had crept back to the edge of the woods where they'd stashed the Molotov cocktails, Annie was beginning to understand the truth of the old saw about it being darkest before the dawn. As a rule, she was seldom up this late, and never up this early unless she was in Vegas, and they didn't have any windows there anyway, but this was ridiculous. She was staring right down at her feet and couldn't even see the white trim on the purple high-tops. Not that the trim was all that white anymore. Not after crawling through that ditch and crouching in that filthy lake with that positively disgusting dead cow . . . the memory made her shudder, but it also took her back to the paddock where the real heart of this godforsaken town lay buried under four inches of manure, and that was good. It was a reminder of why she was huddled in the dark woods like a barbarian, next to a row of IIDs, as Sharon called them back in the garage.

'*What the hell is an IID?*'

'*Improvised Incendiary Device.*'

'*Don't talk in initials. You sound like a man. Drives me crazy the way they make up acronyms for everything. It's exclusionary, that's what it is, little boys talking in code. For heaven's sake, it's just a gas-filled Coke bottle with a rag stuck in the top, and they've got to put initials on it so it sounds like some technological marvel. Damn, now look what you've done. You got me all riled up. Let's just get out there and KSA.*'

Grace was staring into the darkness, eyes wide open in a futile search for light. She couldn't see the rag pile. It was too dark, and the pile was too small and too far away. Sharon's collegiate softball career seemed like a very fragile thing to carry the entire weight of what they intended to do, but there weren't a lot of choices.

They'd decided to risk the flashlight once, just to spot the pile and give Sharon something to aim at. When the time was right, Grace would hit the rags with the light, Annie would strike a match to one of the bottle wicks, then Sharon would hit the gas-soaked pile on the first throw and they'd all live happily ever after. *Yeah, right.*

But first the bullets had to work.

It was a simple plan, really. Primitive. First, the diversion. Bullets exploding in the house, soldiers running in from the perimeter to see what was going on, getting distracted by the fire in the garage before they realized it was following a trail that would make it a hell of a lot bigger, giving the women enough time to run out the way the men had run in.

Simple. *If* the bullets went off. *If* the men ran in. *If* Sharon could hit that pile with one of the bottles. Grace closed her eyes. For a woman who left nothing to chance, this was agony. Too many ifs, and this time, there were no contingency plans.

The three of them waited there in the dark, breathing through their mouths, hoping for noise and hearing nothing but silence. It was taking too long. Grace felt a trickle of sweat roll from her hairline down her cheek as she revisited the argument Annie had made at the lake, back when they were putting all this together.

'*Why mess with the bullets at all? Why not just open the pumps right away, let the gasoline fill the whole damn town, and then light it up?*'

'Would you run into a burning town? If the fire starts too big, they'll just sit out there on the perimeter and wait for us.'

Sharon and Annie were both on the edge of panic. Sharon was holding out a bottle toward Grace in question. Grace shook her head strongly. No. The bullets had to go off first. They had to.

Back in the kitchen of the dark house, there was no noise save for the soft, breathy sound of flame. They'd turned the burner under one skillet higher than the other, hoping to prolong the noise, and ever since that moment, the immutable laws of physics had been at work, transferring heat from flame to skillet to bullets. When the proper temperature had been reached, the primer and powder so tidily contained within each bright, brassy casing ignited and then exploded.

Popcorn! Annie thought instantly, jumping at the sharp crack that split the silence. The second crack seemed louder than the first, but it didn't really sound like the shots Annie fired off at the range – more like the explosion of a small firecracker, which was just fine with her. The louder the better. Another one went off, then a short, chattering salvo, like stuttering, and then nothing.

One skillet down.

Annie opened the matchbook and peeled off the tiny cardboard strip with the sulfur tip. Her hands were shaking.

Sharon crab-walked a few steps out of the sumac

thicket that sheltered them and held a bottle at arm's length, back toward Annie. Grace pointed the flashlight like a gun, her thumb on the switch.

The seconds ticked by as their ears hummed in the silence. Then the first bullet in the second skillet did what it was supposed to do, and Annie struck the match and leaned forward to touch it to the cloth wick. It exploded into flames instantly, with a foul stench and an accompanying puff of oily smoke. Grace turned on the flashlight and trained it on the rags as Sharon jumped to her feet and flung the bottle toward the gas station in a panic. It hit the dirt, bounced, then rolled, but it didn't shatter and it didn't explode. Gasoline spilled out through the cloth into a puddle of fire that made a soft whooshing sound, a good ten feet from the pile of rags. It burned merrily on the ground, harmlessly contained by the bare dirt around it. 'Shit,' Sharon hissed, grabbing another bottle.

Annie was scrambling with a second match, trying once, twice, then ripping off a new one, goddamned cheap gas-station matches, and then there was another soft explosion from the house, the third match blossomed, and almost immediately a man's voice from the woods behind them, shouting, and it sounded so close, so damn close . . .

Sharon let the second bottle fly toward the rags, arcing it upward, a flaming arrow soaring through the air, then coming down. It hit the ground with enough impact to shatter, and the explosion of fire seared the back bumper of an old junked Buick, but it didn't spread to the trail of gas leading into the station.

Her eyes were watering from the smoke and the terror because there were more voices now, closer still. They'd be here in a minute, and then they'd see the bottle flying, they'd see *them,* and Grace and Annie would die because the all-star pitcher of the women's Badger softball team choked the one time in her life that it really mattered.

She held out the third bottle for the kiss of flame, tears running from her eyes, then took a breath and turned her back on the woods and gave the bastards a better target. *Concentrate, Sharon. Focus. Men can always do that better than women, so narrow that brain bridge, be a man. Y chromosome, come to Mama. You're Robert Redford in* The Natural. *You're Kevin Costner in* For Love of the Game, *and there is nothing else in the world except this single pitch. Bases loaded, two outs, full count, bottom of the ninth, but don't think of any of that. Just think of the ball and the strike zone, and black out everything else . . .*

The flaming bottle wobbled through the air, end over end, whishing like a huge pendulum, writing with a jagged contrail of black smoke. It shattered on impact within inches of the rags, and instantaneously, the pile exploded in a pillar of fire, sucking oxygen out of the air with the throat-deep woof of the world's biggest Great Dane.

In that first second of combustion, Sharon imagined that she could actually feel the change in air pressure, feel herself being sucked toward the column of black smoke and fire.

Strike three.

Shouts. Lots of them. Much closer now.

'Hurry!' Grace hissed from behind her.

But Sharon hadn't moved. She was standing perfectly still, a paralyzed lawn-ornament woman, grinning fiercely, her gaze fixed hypnotically on the circle of fire.

'Sharon!'

The rags were burning furiously, noisily, but there was no fiery snake rushing toward the station, no fire at all along the trail of gasoline they'd poured from the rags to the inside of the garage, and *how many soldiers does it take to put out a burning rag pile? Fifty? A hundred? I don't think so.*

There would be no trail of fire to the garage. Goddamnit, too much of the gas had soaked into the dirt or evaporated or God knew what, but now there would be no explosions as cans of flammable liquid blew up, no danger at all of a raging conflagration spreading to the pumps and the gas pouring out of the hoses. There was just a little circle of flames now, burning in the dirt – a little girl's campfire, that's all it was. *Bring hot dogs.*

Grace and Annie were hissing-whispering-squealing at her, panic fragmenting their words into unintelligibility, and now Grace was starting to scramble away from the trees on her hands and knees to come and get her . . .

Sharon spun and dipped and grabbed another bottle and shoved it at Annie. 'Light the goddamned thing and get out of here!'

Annie lit the rag wick and smiled at her, looking genuinely wicked in the reflected flames. 'KSA, honey.'

Okay, Sharon, here you go, Kicking Some Ass. So throw long – very, very long, all the way to that back door, because if God is great, God is good, then there would still be gasoline on the concrete floor.

She hurled the bottle, and as she dove back into the shelter of the trees, the interior of the garage flashed with a great *whoosh,* a sudden and early sunrise in Four Corners.

Instantly, the shouts in the woods behind them multiplied and increased in volume. The women crowded together, peering out through the spaces between the sumac, their hearts hammering.

Within seconds, a line of men pounded down the cartway less than twenty feet away through the trees. Just as the first of these darted out onto the broken asphalt of the cul-de-sac, dozens of others seemed to materialize magically from every direction, popping from the forest, appearing around buildings, all converging on the fiery furnace still contained within Dale's garage. They seemed to pour into the once-quiet clearing of Four Corners, as if someone were spilling bottomless bottles of men into the town.

Grace stared without blinking at the cartway, waiting for it to clear. Breathing fast, her hand clenched around the Sig, every muscle in her body tensed and ready to run. *Hurry up, hurry up,* she screamed at the men in her mind. By the time it seemed safe to slip out the back and into the emptying woods, the heat from the fire was rolling over them in palpable waves.

Doubled over their bent knees, their faces running with sweat, the women clambered from their hiding place, dodged from tree to tree until they were on the other side of the cartway, then plunged into the deepest part of the forest.

Colonel Hemmer and Private Acker were at the back of an old hay field five miles from Four Corners. An overgrown, two-track field road led deep into the property, where a large metal machine shed stood crumbling into its own rust. Meryll Christian had stored some of his farm equipment there, back when the old bachelor had still been alive and farming, but with no heirs to claim the property, the State took possession. Hemmer had picked it up for back taxes five years ago, thinking he'd reseed that field one day, never dreaming of the grand purpose it would eventually serve.

Acker and Hemmer were in a jeep in the middle of a cluster of other vehicles parked in the long grass. Acker had the field radio mike off and held it to his chest, waiting for Colonel Hemmer to speak. He'd been silent for almost thirty seconds – Acker timed such things on his watch – and he'd served the man long enough to dread the silences that almost always meant that the Colonel was quietly seething, mentally busting some heads.

In this case, the heads Hemmer was wishing he could bust belonged to women he'd never met. Jesus. They'd set the goddamn gas station on fire. 'Is it contained?' he asked suddenly, making Acker jump.

'Sounds like it's just in the garage bay at this point, but there are a lot of flammables in there, and the pumps out front were running full blast. The men shut them off, but there's a lot of gasoline everywhere.'

Hemmer puzzled over that for a second, then shook his head in disdain. 'They were trying to set the whole town on fire.'

'Looks that way. They had some half-assed trail running from the garage to the pumps, but the men took care of that. They're using some on-site hoses to keep the fire down in the back so it doesn't hit those dry pines, but as soon as daylight comes, you're going to be able to see the smoke from the garage for miles if they can't get it under control.'

Hemmer's pale eyes rolled skyward. It wasn't exactly light yet, just showing a little indigo in the black, but even that was too close for comfort. They had maybe an hour tops. 'They're certain the gunfire came from the house?'

'Yes, sir.'

'And no one got out?'

'No, sir. They were in sight of the house within seconds, and we've still got men around it.'

Hemmer nodded, pleased and a little troubled, all at the same time. 'So the women are still in there.'

'They have to be. We've got them, sir.'

'Possibly.'

'Sir?'

Hemmer rolled his head toward him. 'Doesn't it bother you at all, Acker, that they would set the gas station on fire and then try to hide in the house next door?'

Acker's shrug was hapless. 'They're women, sir.'

Hemmer had a deep scar on the left side of his mouth that pulled it down a little when he tried to smile, which he didn't do often. Very few people realized that the resulting grimace when he heard something that pleased him was a sign of approval. Acker was one of them.

'You want to send some men into the house, sir?'

'No. Everybody on the fire. You and I will take care of the women.'

This time Acker smiled back at him.

26

Every single man in the Monkeewrench RV was running on adrenaline, and not much else. They'd covered only two of the seven dead zones in Deputy Lee's patrol sector in the past hour, no joy in either, and the next one was a good twenty miles away. They'd run through four pots of coffee and all the high-energy snack food left in the bus from the last trip, but it wasn't doing Harley much good. He'd been night-driving since Minneapolis, and his eyes were starting to look like two pinwheels spinning in opposite directions. Bonar, who'd been riding shotgun with Charlie in his lap since Gino went in the back with Magozzi, Halloran, and Roadrunner, feared that the shoulder harness was the one and only thing holding the tattooed giant upright.

Back in the office, Roadrunner looked up from his computer station for the first time in an hour. Up until now, he'd been in some strange cybertrance, punctuated by occasional violent outbursts of furious typing. He was running multisite cross-checks on the suspect men and sites on the FBI raid list, hoping to find things the Feds had missed, printing them out, then feeding the papers to Magozzi, Gino, and

Halloran. 'Goddamnit, this is going nowhere!' His voice was a frustrated whine. 'I didn't get a single red flag on any of those men, and unless you can find something I didn't, they're just as clean as Agent Knudsen said they were. Just ordinary people.'

Magozzi tapped one of the papers he was speed-reading. 'If the Feds are looking for milk trucks, this Franklin Hemmer has to be the primary target.'

Gino fanned through the sheaf of papers he was holding. 'Which one's Hemmer?'

'The guy who owns the dairy.'

'Oh, yeah. Christ, what kind of a sick fuck would fill up milk trucks with nerve gas? I'm never going to be able to eat cereal again.'

Roadrunner punched the print key, and more papers started spewing out. 'This is kind of interesting. I just pulled the county tax rolls on Hemmer, and it seems he has about a thousand acres scattered all over the place.'

Halloran held up his own stack of papers. 'His tax returns list him as businessman and farmer, which explains the thousand acres.'

Magozzi grunted. 'The only thing I see on the raid list is Hemmer's house and the dairy. How come none of that acreage was searched?'

'The FBI must have done drive-bys. It's probably all just cropland, and there's no way he's cooking nerve gas in the middle of a hayfield.' Halloran sighed, setting the papers aside for a minute. Roadrunner was right. This wasn't going anywhere, and it wasn't getting them any closer to finding the women.

He looked out the back window to rest his eyes. The sky had been gradually lightening for the past half hour, as if someone had spilled a big bottle of bleach on it.

He glanced over at Magozzi and wondered if he looked that bad. The skin across Magozzi's face was taut, as if he were about to jump out of it, he had a black five o'clock shadow twelve hours gone, and it was getting hard to tell where the beard ended and the black circles under his eyes began.

They'd talked the case inside and out nonstop since they left Beldon, like tired dogs chasing their tails, never getting anywhere. Every scrap of information they had blew into a brick wall, and the frustration was building to that dangerous point where you start thinking that there just isn't a goddamned thing you can do. If they didn't find Sharon, Grace, and Annie standing in the middle of the road in one of the dead zones, they'd be right back where they started with no clue where to look next, getting eaten alive by the thought that the women were out there somewhere in a bad place.

He turned back toward the window and looked out at the kind of wild country he'd loved all his life, and thought he'd gladly blow up every square inch of it if that would put them one step closer to the missing women. He wondered how old you had to get before you stopped making mistakes. He shouldn't have let Sharon go into the Monkeewrench warehouse last fall. He shouldn't have stopped trying to call her, just because she never answered. And he sure as hell shouldn't have sent that goddamned form letter that said she was going to be fired. Christ. Hurt feelings could mess up a man's head beyond recognition. And pride. *Pride goeth before the fall, Mikey.* It was another one of those blasted Bible quotes that his mother and Father Newberry had been so fond of spouting when he'd been a kid, and it had taken him twenty years to hear the truth in it, because he surely was taking a tumble now.

He wasn't all that sure he could stand it if he lost another deputy.

No, goddamnit, that wasn't right. He wasn't sure if he could stand it if he lost *Sharon.*

The admission, even to himself, was almost his undoing. He rubbed at his eyes because they were tired and starting to water, blurring the colors that were beginning to show up outside the window.

'Dead zone coming up,' Harley's voice boomed through the RV intercom. 'And this is a big one. We've got about five square miles to cover. Eyes front.'

They all got up instantly and started to head for the front of the bus and the big windows. By the time they got there, Bonar and Harley were looking at a smear of smoke on the horizon.

'I wonder what's burning,' Harley was saying.

Bonar shrugged. 'Could be anything. Folks still burn garbage up this way, and every now and then, one of those hundred-year-old barns with hundred-year-old hay in it goes up. And it's been real dry. Could be a grass fire. Long way away, though.'

Magozzi was half listening to their conversation, but most of his attention was focused on the road ahead and the passing countryside. It was a lot lighter now, and the sky was taking on that early-morning frosted-blue color that promises heat to come. He could see patches of woods, fallow fields, and not a single sign of human life anywhere. It seemed that you could call a place like this a dead zone for a lot of reasons.

His eyes kept going back to that smudge of gray on the horizon. For no good reason he could think of, the smoke bothered him.

By the time Hemmer and Acker got into Four Corners, the town wasn't quiet anymore. Dozens of shouting men had converged with shovels and hoses on the fire that had once been Dale's garage bay. There were still occasional minor explosions as something inside reached ignition point, but they were beating it.

Jesus, there was a lot of gasoline. An unbelievable amount of gasoline around the pumps and all over the road, but other men were shoveling dirt on it as fast as they could. To a civilian, it would have looked like mass confusion, but Hemmer recognized it for what it was – ordered chaos. Yes, it was loud, but there was no one for miles around to hear the noise, so that didn't bother Colonel Hemmer. The smoke cloud did.

The damn thing was huge; acrid, black smoke billowing into an enormous, oily, reeking mass spreading over the town like a visible, airborne cancer. It boiled into a huge cauliflower shape directly over the station while its edges sank toward the ground, a dark and deadly blanket settling onto a fiery bed. Soon enough, someone would see it and raise an alarm, if they hadn't already. But he didn't need a lot of time. The women in the house were the last loose end, and with the deputy dead, the last witnesses. Even if outsiders did come in, it was going to take them far too long to find out what had happened here. He glanced at his watch. The two trucks they had left on the road were already nearing their destinations. Innocent, lumbering things that looked like they belonged where they were going, and there they would sit, benign, unmanned, unnoticed – until ten hundred hours, when they would automatically send out a wake-up call that the whole world would hear.

Gagging against the smoke and the odious stench of burning rubber, Acker and Hemmer crept up to the house and slipped inside, their minds and bodies in full fighting mode. Well, not fighting exactly; this time, it would really be murder, but it was necessary. Christ. Goddamned women. Setting a gas station on fire as if it were a fucking flare and now they were cowering in a dark hole somewhere inside this house while his men were risking their lives trying to undo what *those stupid bitches had done* . . .

Don't do that. Rage is a distraction. It slows reaction time and dulls the senses. Let it go.

Colonel Hemmer fought for control, but he kept a small bit of the rage going, too, so what he had to do would be easier. He wasn't a killer, not by nature, and he found no pleasure in it. But he had never shirked in his duty. Not once.

With the door closed behind them, the house was almost blessedly quiet after the din outside. He and Acker moved silently, carefully, like the soldiers they were, from room to room.

Hemmer shivered a little beneath his sweat-soaked shirt, disturbed beyond all reason that the house was so still, so oddly pristine, while all hell was breaking loose just outside. His thoughts galloped down that never-forgotten path of memory where he was lost in the blowing sand, separated from his unit until a smiling American soldier came out of nowhere to lead him to safety. Only it hadn't been a fellow soldier, and although the soldier looked and talked and dressed the part, he hadn't even been an American, not in the way it mattered. One goddamned turncoat in the entire U.S. Army, and he had managed to find Hemmer and lead him right to a cage in the middle of the desert, where things happened that he'd never told a living soul. He'd seen and felt the horrors of extremism in that cage, but that wasn't what had opened his eyes. It was the American who'd led him there.

Hemmer shuddered as that particular memory surfaced, sensing on some primal level that at this moment, the house he was standing in and that smiling American face, they were the same. Good and right on the outside, quivering with evil just beneath.

Something was wrong here, and for the first time in a long time, he was afraid.

He pushed that fear back, reminding himself that a lot of people would think what he was doing was evil. But they hadn't learned the lesson yet: that sometimes pure evil hides beneath apparent goodness, and sometimes it was the other way around. His own government hadn't learned that lesson yet. So dogmatic in their adherence to human rights that the founding fathers had mandated hundreds of years ago that they were afraid to take the single, pathetically simple action that would end the threat instantly. When people were trying to get into your country to destroy it, you *closed the goddamned door*. It was so easy, and yet unbelievably, they wouldn't do it. So good Americans – faithful, loyal, patriotic Americans like Hemmer and all his men – had to do it themselves, because the government had also forgotten another thing that the founding fathers had said about power reverting to the people when their government failed to provide protection: '. . . *it is their right, it is their duty . . . to provide new Guards for their future security.'*

Hemmer and Acker found a few things that were glaringly out of order in the otherwise tidy kitchen. Acker's flashlight beam picked up brassy bits of shrapnel glinting from odd points all around the room – punched into the plaster and scattered across the counters and floor like tiny, sharp sequins flung at random, and the room was filled with mingled, rank smells. Empty metal skillets left on open flames, old fat smoking and vile, and something else elusive yet oddly familiar. Only the skillets weren't entirely empty. There were a few bits of brass in them as well.

'Oh, shit.' Hemmer closed his eyes the moment he finally identified the strange, underlying odor as the gas that escaped from his grandmother's stove when the pilot light went out. But the pilot lights weren't out on this stove, because the burners were still producing flame.

It came together in a hurry. The women were not in this house – they'd left long ago. And the bullets that went off in here hadn't come from any gun. They'd been fired from two goddamned stupid skillets, and at least one of them had pierced a gas line.

He could almost imagine narrow streams of invisible vapor shooting from tiny cuts in the line, gathering in a dense mass in the confined area of the stove, sinking inexorably toward the burners.

And then, very suddenly, he didn't have to imagine anymore.

The soldiers fighting the fire in the garage bay had been feeling pretty good about themselves. By the time the Colonel was finished in the house, he would be very pleased to find the fire almost totally under control. And sure, the sky was lightening by the minute, but the coming dawn had brought a breeze with it, and already the huge cloud of black smoke was beginning to dissipate. By full sunrise, it would look like the remnants of a smoky garbage fire.

And then something inside the house had exploded, and the back half of the building seemed to suck in a huge breath and swallow itself. That was the funny part – that the damn thing had seemed to explode inward. And the Colonel and Acker were still in there.

A few of the stunned soldiers called out and made hesitant moves toward the house, but others had their eyes lifted skyward, watching in horror as minor debris from the roof – pieces of flaming shingles, mostly – initially flew away from the blast, over their heads, and into the forest. More ominous yet were the ones floating down toward the lake of gas that had collected on the other side of the pumps and spread onto the road. They'd shoveled dirt between the garage bay and the pumps, soaking up what they thought was the immediate danger, but they hadn't worried about the gas out by the road. Hadn't they been silly.

27

The sound of the explosion stopped the women in their halting run through the still-dark woods. They were all breathing hard from both panic and exertion, and sweat soaked their clothes and streamed down their faces the instant they stopped moving.

They turned and looked back toward the town, eyes lifting to see the tower of fire they had hoped for. 'Damn,' Grace said softly. *Something* had exploded, but it hadn't been all that loud, and she could barely see the new fire through the trees. Even the oily cloud from the initial fire was beginning to dissipate. There wasn't a chance in hell that someone miles away would think it was worth traveling to.

'Was that the pumps?' Annie asked, and Grace shook her head.

'The pumps won't blow. Too many safeguards. Something in the garage, maybe. It's probably not going to bring in help, but our chances of getting out are a whole hell of a lot better. Keep your eyes open, though, just in case they left some soldiers out here somewhere.' She turned and started running through the forest again.

So help was not on the way – no fire trucks, no police cars, no gawkers, bless them all, coming to see the show, because the plan hadn't worked. The goddamned fire hadn't been big enough.

It was a bitter pill for Annie. As independent and self-reliant as she was, this was one time when even she wished the cavalry would come riding over the hill – preferably with a martini.

She kept trying to swallow, but she didn't have enough saliva left to soothe the soreness in her throat. They should have stopped for a drink. Yes, indeedy, that's what they should have done. Stopped somewhere between cooking bullets and committing arson to have a glass of iced tea or something.

She wondered how far they had come and, at the angle they'd traveled, how much farther before they'd hit the highway that they'd been on when the car had broken down. My God. She'd almost forgotten the car breaking down. Was that only yesterday?

Dodgeball, Grace thought, twisting and weaving through the spindly trunks of second- and third-generation pines packed closely together, starving for light beneath the canopy of their giant parents. A great many of them were already long dead, canted and leaning against their siblings, propped up in a sorry parody of life simply because there wasn't room to fall down. Kindling waiting for flame.

She misstepped only once and stumbled, but Annie's voice was quick behind her.

'Careful, careful!'

Grace almost smiled at that, even though she

kept right on running. Annie was protecting her again. (You've got to eat more. You're not sleeping enough. You didn't wear a hat? What is this? You think pneumonia is a joke?) She hadn't seen that side of Annie since this whole nightmare had started. It was almost as if Four Corners had sucked away part of her identity, and it was only now, as they were finally leaving that place behind, that the old Annie was coming back.

After five minutes of running, even Grace, who was in amazing physical condition, felt a searing pain in her side, and every breath she drew seemed to contain less and less oxygen. They hadn't covered very much ground – the woods had been damn near impassable at first – but she felt like they'd been running for hours.

'Stop . . .' She heard Annie panting breathlessly from a few yards behind her. 'I've . . . got . . . to . . . stop . . . for just a minute.'

They all stumbled to a halt and just stood there with their heads bowed, chests heaving, breath rasping through dry throats. Finally, they turned and looked back the way they had come. They listened for the sound of crazed men crashing through the woods in hot pursuit, but all they could hear was a faint crackling sound far behind them, and the answering wheeze of their own ragged exhalations.

They stumbled on, running as long as they could, finally slowing to a gasping dog-trot, then to a walk through trees that were starting to thin. The only noises they heard now were the ones they made with their feet and breath.

Around them, the forest floor had begun to open again, the canopy of old pines so thick overhead that there wasn't enough light to support undergrowth and they were able to walk abreast.

'We must be close to the highway now,' Grace said. 'But we'll have to stay out of sight of the road. Some of them might drive out this way, and they still want us dead. More than ever. We're the only ones who know what really happened back there.'

Annie made a disgusted noise with her lips. 'Terrific. So what are we going to do? Hike all the way to the next town through the woods? Do you remember how far that was?'

'We need to check out anyone who comes along before they see us.'

Damnit, damnit, not fair, Annie thought, watching the filthy toes of the purple high-tops as they popped into view in front of her. *Left, right, left, right, onward Christian soldiers, marching, still marching, goddamnit, off to war.*

'Hold it.' Grace stopped, her eyes fixed straight ahead. 'There it is.' She pointed through a curtain of trunks to a ribbon of asphalt less than a hundred feet away, riding high on the top of the berm, separated from the woods by a ditch full of wild grass.

Less than five minutes after they'd started walking parallel to the highway, just inside the cover of trees, all three women heard the car. A big car, not a jeep,

Grace thought, roaring up the other side of the hill they were walking toward.

Sharon was through the trees and into the ditch in an instant, peeking through the dewy grass to catch first sight of the car as it topped the rise. And when it did, she jumped to her feet and walked smack-dab into the middle of the road and started waving like crazy.

She turned toward the woods with a fierce grin and looked straight at where Grace and Annie were standing. 'It's a goddamned fucking police car!' she yelled happily, and turned to face the oncoming car as it slowed, still smiling so hard that her cheeks hurt.

Grace looked at her watch.

Five hours until Armageddon.

28

Grace and Annie watched from the trees as Sharon stood patiently in the middle of the road, her gun holstered, her badge held high. She didn't move when the patrol car stopped ten feet from her and idled there for a moment while the man inside checked her out.

Damnit, she should have left her gun with Annie. She was trying to stop a cop car with her holster clearly visible by holding up an FBI badge that probably looked like a Cracker Jack prize at this distance. 'Sharon Mueller, FBI!' she hollered.

Another moment, and the driver's door opened and a man slid out to crouch behind it. She could see his eyes over the window frame and not much more. Good cop, she thought. Careful cop.

'Both hands over your head, ma'am!' he shouted. 'Higher!'

Sharon complied, holding rock-still as he rose slowly and moved toward her. His weapon was drawn and in both hands, pointed straight at her.

'Now step forward, put your weapon on the hood, please, then step well back.'

Sharon did exactly as she was asked, careful to point the gun away from the man.

Back in the trees, Grace had a bead on the man's forehead, hoping like hell this was a seasoned, steady cop who was just taking precautions and not the kind who got nervous, got twitchy, and sometimes made tragic mistakes, like shooting a fellow officer who'd been running for her life all night from other men with guns.

He took a look at Sharon's 9mm, then tucked it into his belt. 'Thank you, ma'am. You can put your hands down now.'

Grace saw Sharon frown for a moment, then lower the hand that held her badge very, very slowly to hook it back on her jacket pocket. Both the cop and Sharon moved around to the driver's side of the car and had a rapid conversation that Grace couldn't quite make out.

Sharon darted around to the side of the car that faced the woods and shouted down, 'Come on, hurry!'

Grace looked at her. She looked a lot different than she had a few minutes ago. Still filthy, still exhausted, still like a woman who'd been through hell, but . . . happy. For Sharon Mueller, a cop car *was* the cavalry. One of her own had come to take her home.

Grace stood up slowly, and when the man walked around the front of the car and approached her, she automatically raised the Sig. Sharon scowled down at her. 'Damnit, Grace, put that down. He's one of us.'

No, he's one of you. Not me, not Annie, not us.

'He's a cop, Grace, just like me. Missaqua County Deputy.'

Grace never took her eyes off the man. He'd spotted her almost the second she'd stood up, and stopped dead when he'd seen her weapon, his hands up, palms out. But he was wearing jeans and a T-shirt, and cowboy boots that looked like they'd seen a lot of wear. He looked like anybody. Put him in a patrol car, instant cop; put him in camouflage, instant soldier. 'Where's his uniform?'

Sharon actually rolled her eyes. 'He was off duty, at home, when a call came through on the fire.'

Grace kept the gun steady, her lips folded inward.

'Come on, Grace, give me some credit. I asked him all the right questions; he had all the right answers.'

So why is your heart beating so fast, Grace? What are you afraid of? Well, that's pretty simple: Everything. Everyone. Just like always.

Annie remained hunkered down in the bushes, looking up at Grace's face, waiting. She didn't have Grace's instincts about certain people and situations, and she knew it. If Grace was nervous, there was probably a damn good reason.

'Uh, ma'am?' the man called to Sharon. 'Your friend there seems a little nervous. We've got a lot of units on the way. You all want to just sit tight here 'til you're feeling better about things, that's just fine, but I've got to get to the staging area and report for duty.' He took a couple hesitant steps backward, hands still up, harmless, which finally eased Grace's mind a little – that he was willing to drive away without them.

Sharon raised an impatient brow. 'We started a goddamned forest fire, Grace. Get out here and take a look. And for God's sake, holster your weapon. Cops don't like civilians pointing guns at them.'

Grace thought about it. He had his gun holstered, and even if he went for Sharon's, an easier draw from the belt, she could still put him down.

She slipped the Sig back in the holster but didn't fasten the snap, released a long breath, and started forward. Annie rose out of the bushes to follow her, a fat, wild-looking woman in a tattered dress, and the man's eyes widened to see a third.

'Jesus,' he breathed in an aside to Sharon as he watched Grace and Annie approach. 'Your partner looks pretty wired. This must be some case you're working.'

Grace stopped two feet away, enough room to get at her weapon, close enough to use her hands if she had to. 'You don't look like a cop.'

That irritated him. 'Deputy David Diebel. Missaqua County Sheriff's Department. And as far as that goes, you don't look much like arsonists, either. But if you really did start this thing, you've got a lot of explaining to do.'

Grace and Annie looked back toward Four Corners and saw what Sharon already had. Black billows of smoke stained the morning sky, and tongues of orange flame rose above the trees and pixellated into sparks that swirled in a vortex overhead. And now they heard it, faintly – a low, distant roaring sound, like an enormous animal just coming awake.

'Oh, dear Lord,' Annie murmured, thinking that Smokey the Bear was going to be really pissed. She stepped out of one of the high-tops and felt the burn when the air hit her heel. The blistering had bled a little into the shoe. Sharon was going to be pissed, too.

'Listen, ladies, we're in a bad spot here, and I need to get moving. You can call whoever you need to from the staging area, and while you're there, you can explain your involvement in this fire to Sheriff Pitala.'

'Sheriff Pitala?'

'My boss . . .'

Grace glanced quickly at Sharon, who gave her an almost imperceptible nod.

'. . . and my guess is, he'll be mighty interested in whatever you have to say. We've got a town right in the middle of that fire, and you better pray to God that everybody who lives there got out.'

His voice was a little shaky now, with understandable rage, Grace thought. This is his county, and those were his people in Four Corners, and he thought they set the fire that might have killed some of them. Something inside her that had been tight since the car broke down finally loosened. Let it go, she told herself. He's a cop. For God's sake, he's a cop. It's over. You're safe. You're all safe now.

The sound of an explosion made the deputy look

up in alarm. 'Shit, the big pines are going. That thing is moving fast. Get in the back, now.'

'I need my weapon, Deputy,' Sharon said.

'Later,' he said, running to the car and opening the back door.

Sharon stopped at the open car door. 'I'm a Federal officer, Deputy. Cops don't take guns from cops.'

He hesitated for an instant, then pulled her 9mm out of his belt and handed it over, grip first. 'Sorry. Holster that. We're going to be moving, and the roads are rough.'

Sharon crawled all the way across the backseat, moving the deputy's hat up to the back window ledge so they didn't smash it. Halloran would climb all over me for blocking the window, she thought in a sudden pang of nostalgia. Actually, Halloran would have given Deputy Diebel an even more serious dressing down for storing his hat in the backseat in the first place. Things must be a lot more relaxed in Missaqua County.

Annie clambered in next to her, feet splayed on either side of the hump, one of them bare. 'Shit, my shoe . . .' But by that time, Grace was already slamming the door, the deputy was behind the wheel, stomping on the accelerator, and the rear tires were squealing.

It was a frantic sound, a sound of panicked haste, and Grace felt her stomach knot as she stared straight ahead at the cage between the front seat and back, then at the doors without handles. Being locked in your own tiny, safe place was one thing; being locked in someone else's was altogether different.

She leaned forward, closer to the cage. 'We need to get patched through to a landline as fast as you can.'

'We're in a dead zone,' he snapped back. 'Radios and cells don't work. But the staging area's less than five miles from here, and like I said, there's landlines there. You better buckle up. Another mile or so and we have to take a farm road. It's straight washboard.'

Grace sat back and buckled the lap belt, and felt the wind from the deputy's open window buffeting against her face, lifting her hair away from her ears. Relax, she told herself. There's not a single thing you can do for five more minutes anyway. She glanced at her watch. Dear God. Only four hours and forty-five minutes left. Was that enough time to find two particular trucks out of the millions across the country? And even if they found them, was it enough time to disarm them?

Suddenly, the weight of a thousand lives came down on her, and five short mintues seemed like a lifetime. She tried to look forward to the end of it, when they'd get to the staging area and a phone . . . Her thoughts stuttered to a halt. Who were they going to call? Who did you call to report something like this? She went through all the possibilities, starting with Magozzi, the one and only cop she really trusted, and she smiled when she ended up at the only real choice they had. She'd run from the FBI for ten years, maligning them every chance she got, hating them almost constantly for what a few bad agents had done to her once, and now she was sitting next to one of them, planning to call the rest in for help.

And the wheel goes round and round, she thought, rolling her head to look at Annie. The woman was going to kill herself the minute she got a look in a mirror. She didn't do disheveled. But Grace envied Annie's ability to disconnect instantly, to throw back her head and close her eyes and go from total terror to total relaxation in the space of a few minutes.

Sharon was a different story. She was buckled in but sitting straight up, her back nowhere near the seat, and that surprised Grace. Of all of them, she should have been the most relaxed in a police car with a fellow officer. Then again, maybe she was never caged in the backseat before, or maybe she was as screwed up after getting shot last fall as Grace was after Atlanta. Maybe the two of them were more alike than Grace knew.

The deputy braked suddenly and cranked the wheel to the right.

Annie's eyes flew open as she felt herself thrown forward, and her heart pounded. *God, take it easy, fat woman, you're going to have a heart attack. He just made a turn, that's all.*

'It's going to get bumpy now, ladies,' Deputy

Diebel called over his shoulder as he turned sharply off the highway and onto a dirt road carved into the forest. 'Hang on.'

The car's axles tap-danced over the washboard surface, jostling the women against one another in the back. Annie had her arms folded under her breasts to support them. Stupid things were about to pop out of their sockets, or whatever the hell held them in there, and they *hurt.*

The car jittered over another series of bone-jarring washboards and something hard and narrow stowed under the front seat poked at Sharon's toes. She moved her foot and looked down as her eyebrows crept toward one another.

There was a ghastly scraping sound as the car suddenly bottomed out on a hard ridge of dirt, and the deputy's hat bounced off the ledge and slid down between Annie and Sharon. Sharon grabbed it automatically and set it in her lap, but her eyes were on the fields and woods and great clouds of dust flashing by the window.

Another minute, and they turned off the dirt road onto a highway. 'Another mile, ladies, and we're there.'

Annie patted Sharon's knee. 'Relax, honey, it's almost over.'

Sharon nodded slowly, turning the deputy's hat over and over on her lap, fingering the familiar rigid brim, finding an odd sort of comfort in this small piece of a uniform just like the one she used to wear.

It looked just like the one sitting on her hall closet shelf, waiting for the day she might return to her job in Kingsford County, except for the size, of course, and the name on the inside label. She took a very deep breath and let it out slowly. Her hands were shaking.

'These are the last bumps now,' the deputy said as he turned onto another farm road. 'We set up in a machine shed at the back of this field. Only place close enough to the fire with a phone line.'

The machine shed was corrugated steel, large enough to house a lot of farm equipment, and it looked old and faded and uncared for. Cars were jammed in the long grass off to the side, but there were no people in sight.

Grace was leaning forward against her seat belt. 'Where is everybody?'

Deputy Diebel actually gave her a smile over his shoulder. He was where he wanted to be now, and considerably more relaxed. 'A few of them are inside running communications, but most everybody is out fighting the fire. We drop our personal vehicles here, load up in an emergency unit, and take off.'

He pulled to a stop next to the other cars, turned off the ignition, unfastened his shoulder harness, and reached down to unsnap his holster. It was an absolutely normal thing for him to do. You make enough road stops when you ride solo, unsnapping your holster before you got out of the car to confront God knows what becomes a habit.

Grace glanced over just as Sharon was raising her 9mm to the back of Deputy Diebel's head.

And then she pulled the trigger.

29

Sheriff Ed Pitala had forcibly pulled Dorothy away from the dispatch desk and sent her home at two a.m., a full three hours after her shift had ended. Trying to pry her loose any earlier had met with about as much success as trying to get her to retire for the past ten years.

Dorothy had a face like a topographical map of the Rockies, a body like Aunt Bea, and a voice like a blowtorch. Her pictures hung on the wall with three previous sheriffs, all of whom she'd outlasted and outlived. Sheriff Pitala figured that if she ever up and died, he'd just slap a 'closed' sign in the window and nail the door shut, because this place sure as hell couldn't run without her.

She was back by 5:30 a.m., shoving a plate of ham, eggs, and biscuits under his nose. 'Get away from my desk.'

'Lord almighty, Dot, now I know how all my predecessors died. You scared them to death.'

'You were sleeping on the job.'

'Dozing. It's been quiet since you left, except for the boys checking in by phone. And before you ask, there's no sign of Doug yet, or those women the Minneapolis cops are looking for. And what the hell are you doing here? I just sent you home.'

'Hmph. Three hours ago. I walked home, took all the snooze I needed in the recliner, then showered and made you breakfast. Eat it, you skinny old man, before it gets cold or you keel over. Don't know which is likely to happen first, the way you look.'

She rolled him, chair and all, over to the other desk and grabbed the card-table chair she'd been sitting in for more than forty years. Not a single light was lit on the patrol board. It had been that way since the FBI pulled the cars off the road, and Dorothy thought looking at that black board was like looking at the end of the world.

'Don't know how you can sit in that damn thing,' the Sheriff said around a mouthful. 'There isn't a lick of padding left in that seat, if there ever was any to start with.'

'If you carried a little more padding in that skinny butt of yours, it wouldn't be a problem.'

Ed smiled, lips sealed shut with the honey she'd put on the biscuits. When he pulled them open again, he said, 'Swear to God, Dorothy, if Pat ever kicks me out, I'm going to run right to your house and marry you.'

Dorothy snorted. 'I'm twelve years older than you. It wouldn't work out. You're too immature.'

'You gotta get with the times. People do that stuff all the time now. We could be like Cher and whatever-his-name-is, or that Dimmy woman and her young fella.'

'Dim-*eee*. How often do I have to tell you that?'

He didn't answer her, and when she glanced over to look at him, he was holding a bite of food in his mouth, not chewing, just looking at her with his eyes half screwed shut.

Dorothy cocked her head at him. 'What? Don't tell me there was a bone in that ham, because it was a boneless ham. Born and died in a can, as far as I know.'

It took a slurp of cold coffee for him to get the bite down his gullet. 'Funny thing. I thought I heard you say you were twelve years older than me.'

'So?'

'So that makes you seventy-seven years old, Dorothy, and as I recollect, the birth date on your records puts you at sixty-nine. If the county commissioners ever found out how old you really are, they'd make you retire.'

'Who's going to tell them?'

'Not me.'

'Allrighty, then. You quit jawing now, because I've got an honest-to-God light coming up on the 911 board, and I'm so excited I can barely stand it.' She adjusted her headset and punched her buttons at the same time that the phone on the desk started ringing.

The phones kept ringing off the hook for the next half hour and Dorothy's 911 board was so lit up, even she was starting to get a little frazzled. By the time Ed Pitala had finished his fifteenth call, his face was red and his eyes were hard, and he was ready to start making some calls of his own. He stood up quickly and said, 'Dorothy, you've got to cover the board and the phones for a minute. I've got to talk to Knudsen. You think you can manage?'

'Probably not. I'm seventy-seven years old.'

'You don't look a day over sixty-nine.'

She shooed him away with her fingers, and he crossed the outer office to the door that had his name on it. He rapped hard and stormed in before he got an answer. Agent Knudsen was talking on that peculiar thing he'd brought with him that looked something like a phone and a lot like something else. It didn't plug into any wall or phone jack, and as far as Ed knew, the thing probably ran on a can of baked beans. He raised his eyes and held up a finger, which the Sheriff thought was pretty laughable. Fingers never stopped anyone unless they were on a trigger.

'You can put that damn thing down or not, I don't care, because I've got a whole goddamned forest on fire, and I'm about to send out every goddamned truck in the county whether you like it or not.'

Knudsen just stared at him with his mouth open for a second, and it was the first time Ed noticed that he was little more than a kid. It made him nervous to think of kids in positions of responsibility with law enforcement, but not as nervous as the other expression Knudsen was hiding behind the one that just looked surprised. This boy was scared.

'Stay put. I'll get back,' Knudsen said into the

phone, then gave Ed his attention. 'I know all about the fire, Sheriff. It's under control.'

'The hell it is. The last call I got was from one of my deputies who damn near drove into the thing, and it is nowhere near under control. That fire's crowning, and it's going through thirty-foot dry pines like they were matchsticks, and I did not walk into my own office to ask for your permission, I am just telling you that I am calling in every one of my people and getting them out there in patrol cars, because we are going to need every emergency vehicle we've got . . .'

'Understood, Sheriff.'

That stopped Ed's rant cold. Damn. He hated working his hackles into a bristle and then getting them hosed down like that. 'What happened to all that crap about our patrols scaring off whoever you were trying to find?'

'We are not here to impede public safety; we're here to protect it.'

Ed narrowed his eyes. 'You already found what you were looking for, didn't you?'

'No, we did not.'

'Any chance whatever it is has anything to do with this fire?'

'Anything's possible, but we don't think so. Your fire started small. We had smoke sightings a while ago that didn't raise any major alarms. The real fire started a bit later, with a few small explosions. Could have been propane tanks, something in the gas station . . .'

Ed caught his breath. 'What gas station?'

Knudsen frowned. 'I don't know. Is there more than one in Four Corners?'

'Four Corners?' he repeated stupidly, and Knudsen looked at him sideways.

'You didn't know the fire was in the town?'

Ed shook his head. 'My people weren't close enough yet. I knew the general area, that's all.'

'Oh. Sorry. We did a fly-over a few minutes ago, that's who I was talking to. All he could make out was that the center of it looked like it might have been a gas station, and it spread out from there. I'm afraid there isn't much left of Four Corners.'

Ed blanched and felt his knees start to give way. He grabbed the nearest chair and nearly fell into it.

'Hazel?' The whisper came from the doorway. Dorothy was standing there with her eyes and open mouth making three circles in a face that didn't look sixty-nine anymore, or even seventy-seven – it looked a whole lot older.

Knudsen's face went still. 'You knew someone in that town?'

'My sister,' Ed said. 'Well, half-sister. She owns the café next to the gas station.'

The agent caught his breath and took a minute, then spoke very quietly. 'Remember, Sheriff, it started small. She would have had time to get out. Everyone would have.'

Ed looked like he was shrinking in that chair, as if the fire were right there, sucking all the moisture out of him. 'You think so? We got over fifty calls on that fire in the past half hour, and not one of them came from Four Corners or anyone who lived there. If they had all that time, why didn't one of them pick up a phone?'

Halloran and Roadrunner were in the back of the RV – Roadrunner back at the computers, Halloran on the satellite phone, trying to get through to Sheriff Pitala about the fire. Everyone else was in the front, looking out the big windows at the smoke cloud that had gotten more and more ominous the closer they got. The damn thing was huge now, right in the middle of the next dead zone, and they were still at least five miles away. The center of it was black and nasty and halfway up the sky; the sides were gray, expanding outward by the minute.

'That's no grass fire,' Bonar said. 'Something dirty's at the center of it, and that means man-made. Buildings of some kind, for sure.'

Gino grunted from the sofa behind the driver's seat. Charlie sat next to him, looking out the window. 'We had a big swamp fire north of the Cities a few years ago. Never could figure that one out. I mean, there's about fifty acres of waterlogged frog city burning like it was dry kindling. Anyway, the smoke was black like that.'

Bonar said, 'Peat.'

'Who's Pete?'

'Very funny. There's a high peat content in

swamps, rotting vegetation and all that. Oil in the making. Burns like a son of a gun forever once it gets a good start. Smells bad, too.'

Gino sighed. 'I'm on a road trip with Mr Britannica.'

Halloran came up from the back and looked out at the smoke. 'I finally got through to Sheriff Pitala's office. His phones have been jammed with calls on the fire. That FBI agent who gave us the raid sites said they've got a lot of their people heading our way, fire trucks from all over the county, plus Pitala put the patrols back on the road, so we might be running into some serious traffic when we get close. There's a little town dead center in that fire. Sounds like it's gone.'

Magozzi had been standing behind Harley, watching him punch commands into the GPS. He looked over his shoulder at Halloran. 'What about the residents?'

Halloran shrugged. 'He said it started small. They're assuming everyone had a chance to get out.'

'They're not sure?'

'No. Ed's on the way for a closer look. His sister lives in there.'

'Oh, Lord,' Bonar murmured.

Gino stroked Charlie's back absently. 'How shook up was the Fed you talked to?'

'Pretty much. But there's a lot going on up there with the phones ringing off the hook and people yelling in the background. Why?'

'Nothing. You just gotta wonder if whatever the Feebs are up to has anything to do with a fire that suddenly pops up out of nowhere.'

'It's fire season, Gino.'

'Yeah, well, nothing's ever that simple.'

Harley had his face close to the windshield now. 'Jesus. I think I just saw some flames shooting up in the middle of that cloud.'

'Could be,' Bonar said. 'When those pines are dry enough and hot enough, they literally explode, and the flames can shoot straight up like bottle rockets.'

'Shit. I gotta pull over. We are not driving into that thing unless I know we can get the hell out fast if we need to, and this damn GPS map is telling me there's only one turn off this road for the next ten miles, and that's the turn that leads right into Four Corners.'

'Four Corners?' Magozzi asked.

'That's the name of the town in the middle of all this,' Halloran said.

'We could turn around,' Bonar offered.

'In this rig? On this peanut road? Are you kidding?' Harley pulled the RV to one side of the road and stopped.

Bonar was actually wringing his hands. 'There's probably lots of little dirt roads cutting off this one that won't show up on that map. The county's checkered with them.'

'"Probably" doesn't cut it for me. What if we get in there and the fire jumps the road behind us?'

'We'll all cook in here like pork roasts.'

'You got that right. And can anybody tell me why we're planning to drive straight into hell anyhow? We're looking for our ladies, and I can guarantee that the one place they're *not* is in the middle of that shit up there.'

'Like Gino said, it's just one more coincidence in a long string of them,' Magozzi said behind him. 'We know for sure at least one of our missing people disappeared in a dead zone, and now there's a big fire smack in the middle of one. If we're going with coincidence and a possible connection to the Feds' operation, we've got to take it all the way. We've got no place else to go. And my gut tells me those women are somewhere near that fire, either running from it, trapped by it, or –' He stopped dead, but nobody seemed to notice.

Harley grunted derisively. 'No way they're trapped in there. They're just too goddamned smart.'

Magozzi looked at him. 'Smart enough to send up a flare? What if Grace wasn't saying four people were dead. What if she was trying to say "Four Corners"?'

Harley stomped on the accelerator.

30

Barely a moment had passed since Sharon Mueller had raised her gun and blown away Deputy Diebel's head.

Annie couldn't hear anything over the ringing in her ears, and she couldn't see very well, either, because she hadn't blinked in a long time.

Blink. You have to blink, or your eyeballs will dry up and fall out, and then you'll be blind – blind and deaf, and your last memory of sound will be the thunderous roar of a gun, and your last memory of sight will be this shocking thing that Sharon just did. Don't look.

She was actually staring at Sharon's face – the side of her face, actually – sort of three quarters, sort of profile, and she didn't recognize her at all. She blinked at last, but that didn't help. She moved her jaw, trying to clear her ears, and then someone turned down the ringing sound. It was still there, but it was softer, hiding way behind the eardrum, muffled like a jangling phone under a pillow. Another noise began to tiptoe in. Sharon, she realized, making the oddest little sound, like she was screaming as loud as she could with her mouth closed, screaming through her nose.

Oh, dear. Poor Sharon. She was staring at

something awful in the front of the car, on the other side of the cage, and Annie knew what she was looking at. She'd had just a glimpse, just the tiniest flash on the back of her retina before she'd shifted her gaze to Sharon's face and refused to look forward again, just like when you went to a horror movie. You didn't keep looking at the screen when something gross happened. You just shifted your eyes a little to one side, not so far that anyone would notice, just far enough, and then later, when people asked how you could watch that stuff, you just shrugged and said it wasn't so bad, really. It was a trick, a secret trick. She should have told Sharon about it, because Sharon was still staring at all the blood and little pieces of matter sliding down the windshield.

'Sharon.' Grace reached across Annie to touch Sharon's left hand, which had fallen into her lap like a dead thing. It was ice-cold. Her right hand still held the 9mm, still pointed at the place where Deputy Diebel's head had been before his body slumped to the right, over the console. 'Sharon.'

Annie watched Sharon's eyes move just a little, hardly far enough to notice – maybe she did know the trick. Hello, Sharon. Anybody in there?

The noises stopped, and Sharon's throat moved. Her mouth opened and a whistle came out, then a whisper: 'Sorry about the noise.' And then her right hand started to shake, hard, and she lowered it slowly to lie in her lap with the left one. She felt Annie and

Grace looking at her, and she turned her head to meet their eyes.

'I'm sorry,' she said, her tone calm, perfectly controlled, pretending to be normal but sounding hideously abnormal coming from her face. It was a ghastly gray color, and all the skin looked loose.

Grace didn't know what to say to that. Sharon had just killed the man who was driving them to safety, a deputy just like her, and now she was apologizing as if she'd burped at the dinner table.

'I have to do it again,' Sharon said suddenly, lifting the gun so fast that Grace couldn't believe it, firing two quick shots and blowing out her side window.

Annie slammed her hands over her ears, but it was too late. Instant deafness. She couldn't hear the safety glass falling to the ground as Sharon pounded at it with the butt of her gun, desperate to reach for the outside door handle, to crawl through the window opening itself if she had to, anything to get out of the car.

In the end, she couldn't manage it. Not just yet. She was simply too tired. Funny how pulling a little trigger could wear you out. But that wasn't really true, either. On the range, she could get a hundred shots off without feeling the strain in her finger or the muscles in her forearm quiver. Killing an actual person was surprisingly exhausting. Sharon had never done it before, had never dreamed she would ever have to do it, in spite of all the training and preparation. She sat there on the edge of the seat, ready to do something she couldn't quite remember, her thoughts tripping away to touch on things, losing focus almost immediately. The psychology major inside her head put a finger to her mouth and nodded sagely. Oh, yes. She was going to need therapy.

'Sharon?' Grace's voice, tentative, filled with tension.

'Right here.'

'Look at me.'

Sharon turned and gave Grace her eyes, and then Annie. Why were they looking at her so oddly? Why did they still look afraid? She'd taken care of everything, hadn't she?

'Why?' Grace said.

Oh, that. She felt a bad, naughty smile trying to form . . . *Don't do that, don't smile, can't excuse smiling after you killed a person, not even with displacement behavior or any of that gobbledygook . . . oh, shit. I forgot to tell them why.*

A wave of clarity rolled over her mind, washing away all the silly, disgusting, normal human reactions to trauma you were allowed to have when you were just a person and not a cop. She took a deep breath and came back to the here and now.

'He didn't check my badge,' she said simply, because that was when it had started. That had been the first thing to bother her. 'He should have looked that thing up and down and sideways, made sure I was FBI, but he didn't. All he cared about was getting my gun.'

Grace and Annie were still staring at her, saying nothing. It wasn't enough.

'He had another gun under the front seat. A long one. Part of it's probably in plain view in the front, and I was too goddamned stupid to check out the car before we got in. Too goddamned relieved to see a cop to even think about checking the car. My fault.'

'Cops all carry shotguns,' Annie said carefully, and Sharon nodded impatiently.

'In the trunk. Always. Unless it's racked. Besides, the barrel was all wrong.' She pulled an untidy memory from her brain, and her voice got hard. 'I know guns. My father was a collector. Don't know where he got half of them; now they'd be illegal as hell. But one of them was an M16. Just like the one under the seat. Our Deputy Diebel was one of *them*.'

Grace was very quiet, her gaze turned inward, trying to decide if Sharon had jumped too fast and way too far, or if all her vigilance had failed her once again.

'And there's this.' Sharon lifted the hat from where it still sat on her lap, undisturbed by shooting and window-breaking and madness. She flipped it over and showed Annie and Grace the inside.

Annie looked down at it stupidly. 'It's a hat.'

'Look at the name tag.'

Grace grabbed the hat and squinted down at the small, faded printing that read 'Douglas Lee.' 'Oh my God.'

'What?' Annie snatched the hat and held it close to her face. 'Oh, Lord. This is *his* car, isn't it? This was Deputy Lee's car . . .' Her eyes jerked to the front seat, then quickly darted away. 'Jesus God in heaven. We went right with him. We just hopped in the car and let him drive away with us.'

Sharon's neck was starting to hurt from looking to the right for so long, but she couldn't look anywhere else, she just had to keep looking at Grace and Annie because her thoughts were slipping again, like marbles on ice. 'I killed him,' she said matter-of-factly. 'Just like he was going to kill us. They killed Deputy Lee and took his car and his hat, and that bastard up there is probably carrying Deputy Lee's gun, so I killed him right in Deputy Lee's own car.' She leaned forward and hissed toward the bloody ruin that had been the man's head. 'How's that for poetic justice, Deputy Fucking Diebel?' And then she scrambled right out the open window and tumbled to the ground and started to suck in huge breaths.

It was the first time Sharon had really scared Grace, even more than when she'd fired the gun in the first place. *She's losing it. She's forgetting everything. Damnit, she didn't even look before she went out there.*

Annie had her arm out the window, reaching for the outside door handle, but Grace was looking everywhere frantically, around every car, the sides of the building, through the tall grass, and into the trees beyond.

She was positive of only one thing – if this was where that imposter in the front seat wanted to take them, she didn't want to be here.

31

Except for Roadrunner, who was still back in the office, all of the men were in the front of the RV, looking worriedly at the towers of flame in the woods on their right, moving steadily toward the road.

Less than a mile from the Four Corners turnoff, Harley eased the rig to a stop at a makeshift roadblock that some firefighters had set up. There were two fire trucks ahead of them, pulled as close to the nonexistent shoulder as they could get, and it still left only about an inch of clearance for the RV to get by. One of the engines looked like it should have been pulled by horses.

Two men in heavy yellow firefighting gear were gesturing wildly for Harley to back up the rig, which was just plain ridiculous. Magozzi and Halloran went outside with their badges and guns and attitudes, and it still took another minute before they could talk the firefighters into letting them pass through. Charlie slipped out the open door before anyone noticed.

'Your dog's loose.' Halloran pointed on the way back to the RV, and Magozzi saw Charlie rooting around in the ditch, running back to the woods toward the fire – stupid dog – then back up to the road again to plunge his nose into a piece of debris he'd found.

'Charlie, come!' Magozzi slapped his thigh.

Charlie looked up, then back down at whatever treasure he'd been examining, then snatched it up in his jaws and raced toward Magozzi and dropped it at his feet.

Magozzi picked up a battered, filthy, purple high-top tennis shoe and held it with two fingers. Christ. All hell was breaking loose, and the dog wanted to play fetch with a piece of someone's discarded trash. He heard Halloran whisper, 'Oh, shit,' and turned to look at him. The man was staring at the shoe, looking like he was about to double over.

'That's Sharon's.'

Magozzi looked at what he was holding. 'It's a shoe. It could belong to anyone. It could have been here for months.'

Halloran was shaking his head back and forth. 'It's a Converse. Lavender high-top. They stopped making them years ago. Sharon loved those stupid, ugly shoes. It was one of the first things she asked me to bring from her place when she was in the hospital in Minneapolis.'

Magozzi looked into the shoe and felt his stomach turn. There was blood in there. 'Shit,' he murmured, glancing up as Charlie raced away. He called after him, but the dog ignored him and just pressed his nose down hard on the tar and started trotting, the dog who was afraid of anything and everything, who hid between Grace's legs when toddlers on tricycles approached, and there he was, weaving past fire engines and stepping over hoses, dodging scary, shouting men in big yellow coats, oblivious to everything except the twin streams of air and scent going in and out of his nostrils.

'Goddamnit!' Harley shouted from inside the rig, banging his hand on the wheel. 'Roadrunner! Get your ass up here and get that dog!'

Roadrunner came racing up from the back, clutching a forgotten piece of paper in his hand, and jumped clear of the narrow steps instead of trying to negotiate them in his size-twelves. Gino was right behind him, both of them hurrying to catch up to Magozzi and Halloran, four grown men chasing a mangy mongrel down a road while the world was burning.

Harley and Bonar were in the RV, staring at the spectacle in disbelief.

'What the hell?' Bonar said.

'It's Grace's dog,' Harley explained. 'Anything happens to that dog, she'll kill us all.' He moved the rig forward slowly, easing past the two fire trucks while Bonar held his breath, waiting for the sound of metal screeching against metal. A hundred yards farther, and Harley stopped to pick up the men. It had taken the dog less than a minute to leave them far behind.

'What the hell got into him?' Bonar asked when the others were back inside, panting and sweating.

Magozzi nodded at where Halloran was clutching a filthy shoe against his chest. 'Charlie found that. Halloran says it belongs to Sharon.'

Bonar looked at it more closely, and his face fell. 'Oh my God.'

Gino was banging on the back of the driver's seat. 'Goddamn, that dog is a friggin' genius. I swear to God he's tracking, and there's only one thing in the world that dog would be interested in finding, and that's Grace MacBride.'

Roadrunner was staring out the big front window as Harley eased the RV forward to keep pace with the dog. Charlie was moving at a dead run, covering ground at an astounding pace for a dog who sat upright in chairs and took his meals at the table like any other fat, slow human being.

Gino was bent over, still breathing hard, waiting for the heart attack. 'That dog nearly killed me. How far has he gone?'

'Over a mile – maybe two.'

'Jesus, he's fast.'

Roadrunner caught his breath when Charlie made an abrupt right onto a narrow dirt road.

'Harley,' he whispered. 'I know where he's going. And you gotta catch him. He's got another three miles to go, and he'll be dead by then.'

'Three miles to where?'

'I just pulled up an old deed on one of those pieces of property Hemmer owns. It has a building on it, and it's less than five miles from Four Corners.'

32

It didn't take long for Grace to decide that this overgrown field was deserted, and that all the cars parked in the high grass were empty. There were two doors accessing the corrugated steel building – a large, rolling one for heavy farm equipment, and a smaller, man-sized door next to it. Both were chained and padlocked from the outside.

'Stay on her; stay down!' she'd commanded Annie when her friend had tumbled out of the car onto the ground next to Sharon, and Annie had done what Annie always did best . . . wrapped her arms around Sharon and held her still, kept her safe, just as she had held Grace on a few occasions, back in the days when she was the strong one.

While Annie and Sharon lay there next to what had once been Deputy Douglas Lee's patrol car, Grace did what had to be done. She crawled out the back door, around to the front, and pulled the man who had called himself Deputy David Diebel off the console so she could get to the radio and computer. The computer didn't work, and no one answered her desperate radio calls.

'He was telling the truth about the dead zones,' Sharon finally called up from where she lay in the comfort of Annie's arms. Except for the few times that Halloran had touched her, each erotic memory seared in her mind, she hadn't felt genuine caring from another human being in years. Annie had been holding her close – probably to keep her still and silent – but the effect was identical to when her mother had held her as a child, chasing away the demons of the night. Mute tears leaked out of her brown eyes and onto Annie's plump forearm.

While Sharon was sitting up, wiping the embarrassing tears from her cheeks, Grace was wiping blood from her fingers. The radio had been covered with it. She looked up toward the building and wondered if Diebel had been telling the truth about the landline inside. 'I'm going to try shooting off one of those padlocks.'

'There should be bolt cutters in the trunk of the patrol.'

Grace looked at Sharon, a little surprised by the strength she heard in her voice. 'You okay?'

Sharon was already on her feet, collecting her weapon from where it had fallen in the grass beside her. 'Better than that. I'm pissed.' She extended a hand to Annie to help her up, then went to the car, reached into the front seat, and popped the trunk without glancing at the body a few inches from her arm, without even letting her brain acknowledge that it was there. She wiped her hand on her slacks when she was finished, but she never looked at what she was wiping off. Grace and Annie found the bolt cutters in the trunk, then the three of them moved toward the steel building together.

The inside was pitch-black and dead silent, except for a low, distant hum that they couldn't identify. Grace wished for the flashlight, wondered where she had dropped it. She found a bank of electrical switches on the wall and started flipping them up. The annoying buzz of a hundred fluorescents flickering to life overhead, lighting the enormous space, ended the silence.

The women just stood and stared.

Seven enormous tanker trucks were neatly parked in a row facing the big rolling door. 'Good Health Dairies' was emblazoned in bright blue across their silvery skin.

'Funny place to keep milk trucks,' Sharon murmured.

Annie was frowning. 'I thought milk trucks were those cute little white vans with the cute little bottles jangling inside.'

'These are the bulk carriers. They travel from farm to farm to pick up raw milk and transport it to the dairy . . . oh, shit. Do you think these are the trucks?'

Grace looked at the lumbering, innocent-looking things with their happy blue lettering, thinking what better way to transport something lethal without detection? She pushed the thought to the back of her mind and turned away.

An elaborate computer setup on a desk against the far wall explained the humming sound. She couldn't see the phone but guessed it had to be there. By the time Annie and Sharon joined her, she had tracked the single phone line to the back of the computer and nowhere else.

'No phone set,' she told them. 'The only hookup runs through the modem.'

Annie shrugged. 'Good enough. We'll just sign on and text message Roadrunner, who is probably out of his mind by now.' She jiggled the mouse impatiently and waited for the screen to wake up.

'Don't you need a password or something?' Sharon asked, and Annie chuckled.

'Oh, child, we have so much to teach you.' She sat down in the cracked vinyl chair, frowned at the nonsense appearing on the monitor, then lifted her hands to the keyboard.

'*ANNIE, STOP!*' Grace shouted suddenly.

Annie jerked her hands up and back and froze. Sharon's eyes were wide, following Grace's terrified gaze around the side of the monitor to a rectangular box of the same color. Only it wasn't exactly a box, just a whitish brick of something that looked like modeling clay, with wires that led to the back of the computer.

'Oh, shit,' Sharon whispered.

Annie was still frozen in position with her hands up by her shoulders. 'Can I move?'

Grace's voice was shaking. 'Just don't touch the keyboard or click the mouse.'

Annie pushed well away from the desk and rolled

the chair to the side to see what Grace and Sharon were looking at. She didn't trust her legs yet. 'Oh, Lord in heaven, that's not Play-Doh, is it?'

Grace actually thought about it, but it didn't make sense. Why would anybody set up a dummy explosive and conceal it?

Sharon was coursing through her memories of the bomb squad demonstrating plastic explosives in her Academy class. 'It looks like the real thing.'

Annie laid a hand over her heart, as if to hold it in.

'Did you see this clock?' Sharon asked.

'What clock?' Grace moved to get a better look at the monitor. Red numbers were blinking at the top of the screen, counting down. Three hours, thirty-seven minutes, forty-two seconds, forty-one seconds . . .

'This thing is counting down the time until ten, when the other two trucks are supposed to blow.'

Grace was staring at the monitor, speed-reading through the lines of text, taking quick, shallow breaths. 'Look at those names halfway down the screen.'

Annie and Sharon scrolled down with their eyes and saw the words that had caught Grace's attention.

Schrader – off-line
Ambros – target acquired
Ritter – target acquired

Grace hugged her stomach and whispered, 'Oh, Christ, not that,' then broke down and ran toward the trucks. She jumped up on a running board, peeked in the window, then ran to the next truck to do the same thing, then disappeared around the other side.

Annie and Sharon found her on the far side of the trucks, staring at the three empty spaces right next to the big rolling door. She was still clutching her stomach, but now she was rocking back and forth. 'Every one of these trucks has a small computer unit on the dash. The ones in here are turned off, but there are three trucks missing. See the tread marks? Three sets, going right out the door. Back at the lake, that soldier said the Four Corners thing was an accident – truck number one. But he was waiting for two others to get where they were supposed to be, and according to that computer, they're on target. That computer is the control. It sends the signal for the other trucks to blow, and unless we find somebody who can disable that bomb, we can't get into it to stop them.'

In the next second, they were all running back toward the little door, out onto the grass, and toward the cars.

'If we can't find any keys, a couple of those look old enough to hot-wire,' Sharon panted.

'We don't have time.' Grace veered back toward the patrol car. 'There are already keys in this one.'

Sharon closed her eyes.

33

Harley had the RV pushed up to forty on a road that any sane man wouldn't have tried to negotiate on foot. Where it wasn't washboard, the dips in the hardpan were so deep that a few times, the rear wheels almost left the ground. An enormous rooster tail of dust followed them.

Everyone was holding their jaws open to keep their teeth from clattering together, hands grasping whatever was nailed down. Bonar had Charlie next to him on the sofa, one beefy arm wrapped around the dog's wriggling body to keep him from flying into space. No one told Harley to slow down. They had tied the thinnest of threads together in an impossible tapestry of hope, every one of them willing to believe at that moment that every *Lassie* episode they had ever seen was real, and that Charlie was even more amazing than Lassie had ever been, because without believing that, they had no hope at all, and no idea where to go.

Roadrunner was clutching the back of the driver's seat, angled like a Tinkertoy man to peer out through the windshield, breathing lime over Harley's shoulder. 'Okay! You're almost there! Slow down, then take a right,' he shouted over the noise of the big rig.

The washboard jittered his voice, making him sound like Porky Pig.

Harley slowed long enough at the intersection of dirt and tar to make sure there were no fire trucks coming, then slammed the accelerator to the floor when rubber hit asphalt and found some traction.

'Two miles, maybe less,' Roadrunner said, as Halloran, Magozzi, and Bonar all stood, jamming into the space closest to the door, every heart beating fast and hard.

Charlie was weaving between their legs, whining, tap-dancing, tongue dripping doggy sweat. He gave one short howl, which frightened Magozzi. Once you started to believe in any kind of dog magic, you had to consider it all, like those stories about dogs howling when their masters had died, long before anyone else knew it.

'There it is! See it? See it?!' Roadrunner shouted. 'That dirt track into the field! Slow down! Slow down!'

Harley slammed on the brakes and cranked the wheel hard to the right, fishtailing the fifty-foot rig as if it were one of his Porsches. It wasn't really a road, just two tracks through the grass of an overgrown field, and this time he had to slow down.

They all saw it at the same time. Some kind of big building at the back of the field with a bunch of cars parked around it. One of them was a patrol car with the driver's door open. Three filthy, haggard people were tugging a bloody body out of the front seat.

One of them straightened and turned to look in their direction, and Magozzi felt a vise tighten around his heart. He moved his lips, but no sound came out: *Thank you.*

'Lord Almighty, I don't believe it,' Annie murmured as she watched the RV lumbering toward them.

'What is it?' Sharon asked, gaping at what surely had to be a mirage, or else a Rolling Stones tour bus. *Special engagement, one night only, right here in this Missaqua County farm field . . .*

'The Monkeewrench coach,' Grace said, bloody hands hanging at her sides, refusing to believe what she was looking at until the rig stopped and Charlie shot out like a soaring, hairy meteor to race toward her, smiling like he always did. She wiped her hands on her jeans and caught Charlie, all eighty pounds of him, in midair. During the few seconds that she permitted this disgraceful display, she saw the men clambering out of the rig.

Her breath caught when she saw Magozzi, and then, oh my God, Gino, Halloran, and even Bonar, right there with Harley and Roadrunner. She glanced over at Sharon and saw her lips quivering and her eyes threatening to fill, staring at Halloran like he was the only thing in the world to see, and she had to look away fast.

Goddamnit. This was totally bizarre, just like all those stupid fairy tales when the men come riding in to save the women in the nick of time and the women cry and throw their arms around them.

Too bad they didn't have time for any of that.

The women sprinted toward the bus, and the men stopped as a unit, startled. Grace didn't look in any faces – she wouldn't have been able to stand that – as she raced past them up into the rig, and down the long aisle to the office. Apparently Sharon and Annie hadn't stopped, either, because they were right beside her when she grabbed the headset for the sat phone and punched frantically at the buttons.

Magozzi and Halloran were standing outside, staring at the empty air where the women they'd come to save had just raced by them as if they weren't there. It wasn't quite the reunion either man had pictured. Harley, Roadrunner, Bonar, and Gino were already following the women into the RV while the two big, tough guys trailed behind, just a little off-balance. They could hear Grace yelling the second they came through the door.

'What's the matter with this goddamned thing! It won't connect!' She was pounding one hand on the console, banging numbers uselessly with the other. No one in that room had ever seen Grace that out of control. It was Roadrunner who gently took her blood-smeared hands in his and said quietly, 'Let me do it, Grace. Who do you want to call?'

'The FBI, Roadrunner,' Annie said quietly. 'We need them right now.'

Roadrunner had Agent Knudsen on the line within ten seconds, and then all the men listened as

Grace began to talk very fast. Before she finished, a hundred emotions had crossed every face in the room. Harley grabbed three bottles of water from the office fridge and handed them to women who had been through more than he could imagine – more than he'd certainly heard, because Grace was condensing everything. He came to Annie last.

She stood there in her tattered, manure-covered dress with her chaotic hair and filthy face and said, 'What took you so long?' She took the opened bottle, drank from it, then reached out and patted his cheek. Harley had to look down at the floor, because that was the nicest thing she'd ever done to him.

He saw her feet – one bare, the other in a purple high-top. 'Jesus, Annie. You look like friggin' Cinderella.'

Agent Knudsen had been in his car when Grace had called, only a few miles from the fire that had troubled him ever since he got the first call in Sheriff Pitala's office. Maybe Magozzi had been right: coincidence *was* the connection.

Knudsen made a dozen calls in the ten minutes it took to get to the machine shed. By the time he arrived, an astounding-looking collection of people were running from a big RV toward the shed, led by three women who looked as though they'd been to hell and back, and a dog that looked like he'd gone with them.

Knudsen joined them at the door. There was no time for introductions, but a tall, black-haired woman nodded to him brusquely, as if she fully expected he would know who she was. The woman on the phone, he decided.

'Don't touch one thing in there,' she commanded them all, then opened the door and led them all to a computer against the far wall. 'Just read.'

The men crowded in a circle around the screen as she started to explain what was on the monitor. Every face looked ashen and ghastly under the fluorescent lights – Knudsen's most of all, and, surprisingly, Bonar's.

Agent Knudsen bolted from the building without explanation. The rest of them continued to stare at the screen, at the ominous row of trucks, at the block of plastique sitting placidly next to the computer.

An irritated Gino shoved his hands in his pockets, trying to make sense of what he'd just read on the monitor. 'I don't get all the numbers. Or the stupid names. "Schrader – off-line, Ambros – target acquired." What the hell does that mean? I don't get any of it.'

'Schrader, Ambros, Ritter,' Bonar recited in a flat voice. 'They're missing one – Linde – but that doesn't count for much. Germans. Those were the men who discovered sarin in the thirties. They named the trucks after them.'

Every face turned toward him.

'Sarin?' Magozzi whispered.

Bonar pushed his lips out and nodded. 'One of the first-generation nerve gases.'

'Jesus Christ, the Feebs got it right,' Gino said, looking over at the trucks, then back at the blinking numbers on the monitor: 03:14:17 . . . 16 . . . 15 . . .

34

They found Agent Knudsen pacing a furrow in the long grass near his car, phone clutched in one white-knuckled hand that swung back and forth as he walked. Sharon hung back a little – the agent's car was a little too close to Doug Lee's patrol – and Halloran stayed with her.

'We've got to get rid of that bomb so we can get into the computer,' Grace was telling Knudsen. 'Those trucks in there all have remote computer units. The one inside that building is the host, and obviously it already sent out the detonation command. There's got to be an abort in there somewhere.'

Knudsen gestured with his phone. 'Nearest bomb squad is in Green Bay. We'll get them on a chopper, along with some computer experts.'

'How long?' Magozzi asked.

'Two hours. At least.'

Grace checked her watch and moved her head impatiently. 'Not fast enough. There's less than three hours until those trucks blow.'

Knudsen shot her a furious look, as if she were the enemy. Why the hell was the woman wearing riding boots? Damn things had to be hotter than hell. And that big ugly mutt glued to her leg looked like he wanted to rip his throat out. 'You think I don't know that? I'm waiting for a callback from Bill Turner. He's the best bomb man in the country, but he's in D.C. and we're having trouble locating him. It's Sunday morning. He's probably in some goddamned church somewhere.'

Magozzi looked at the agent who looked both twenty years younger and a thousand years older than he had ten minutes ago, a little surprised by his choice of adjectives. He was starting to sound more like a person and less like FBI, and that was not necessarily a good sign. 'Even if you find this guy in the next few seconds, what's he going to be able to do from D.C.?'

'He can walk me through deactivation.'

'You've done this before?'

Knudsen narrowed his eyes at Grace. She sounded like an interrogator. 'No. But we've run out of options. We don't even know where the targets are, those two trucks are already on-site . . .'

'And filled with sarin,' Bonar said matter-of-factly, and Knudsen jerked his head to glare at him.

'You want to tell me how you know which nerve gas it is?'

Bonar opened his hands. 'The names they gave the trucks, of course.'

Knudsen closed his eyes. Too many people knew too many things these days. The information age was killing them.

'What about all the other information on the

screen in there?' Gino asked. 'A bunch of those numbers keep changing. Maybe that's latitude or some of that shit that tells where the trucks are.'

Knudsen shook his head. 'The trucks aren't moving anymore, according to that computer. Besides, I know what those tables are. I've seen them before. They estimate initial dispersal distances based on a lot of factors, like wind speed, direction, humidity . . .'

'Hey.' Roadrunner turned to Harley. 'We could plug those numbers into that stat program and link up with the National Weather Service. What are the chances that any two locations in this country are having exactly the same fluctuations in weather conditions at exactly the same time?'

'Sounds good, but it'll take a while.'

Knudsen was frowning at the two of them, then his face cleared. 'Oh, yeah. I almost forgot. Kingsford County undercover computer crimes, right?'

Grace and Annie looked sideways at their partners.

'Right,' Harley said.

'It was a good thought, but even if we found those trucks in the next ten minutes, chances are they're in an urban area and we won't be able to get them to a safe disarmament location in time.'

'So we're right back where we started,' Grace said. 'We have to get into that computer and find the abort.'

'Looks that way . . .' Knudsen's phone rang, and he jammed it up to his ear so hard that Gino thought it was a miracle it didn't go all the way through his head.

'Knudsen!' he shouted, listened for ten seconds, then threw the phone down on the ground. 'Apparently, Bill Turner took a goddamned fucking Sunday drive in the country with his family.'

Suddenly, Grace jerked her head to look at something, then took off at a run. She stopped at Doug Lee's patrol car and nearly ripped the passenger door off the hinges when she opened it to dig inside. A second later, she was running toward them, carrying a dripping black case. She wiped it on the grass and set it in front of Roadrunner.

'Whose laptop?'

'The guy in the car. He was one of them, but he wasn't wearing fatigues like the others. His job was something else, maybe that setup in the building, since this was where he brought us – someplace he was familiar with, someplace he knew was empty so he could kill us without any interference . . .'

Roadrunner smiled faintly and popped open the case. 'So he was the geek.'

Annie and Harley had already crowded close to see the screen. 'And geeks always have backups,' Annie said.

The monitor came to life and proved them right.

By that time, everyone else was kneeling or crouching around them, all watching the little laptop screen like wide-eyed kids examining an exotic bug. Sharon was behind Annie, her hand on her shoulder, for balance of many kinds.

Magozzi recognized the first image as a duplicate

of what had been on the computer inside the building. 'So it's a sort of a mirror image?'

'It had better be.'

Roadrunner punched a few keys, accessed the programming code, and scrolled down at warp speed.

'What are you looking for, precisely?' Knudsen asked from the back of the group. He was on his knees, getting grass stains on his nicely pressed pants.

Harley answered without looking around. 'All this stuff scrolling by? This is the brain that runs the whole shebang, and somewhere in here, there are command lines that control whether or not that bomb goes off.'

Bonar was staring, shaking his head. 'It all looks the same.'

Gino nodded. 'Alphabet soup with numbers in it. My kid eats that stuff. How the hell do you tell when you find the right line? There must be a million of them in there.'

Roadrunner stopped the scroll and pointed. 'Here.'

Harley looked, then nodded. 'One of those two, anyway. Funny that this guy would be that sloppy on the bomb command lines, when the rest of it looks so tight.'

'They didn't expect Four Corners,' Grace reminded him. 'This was a last-minute setup when they thought they might be discovered.'

'Man, I don't know.' Harley was shaking his big head. 'Could be either one of those two command lines, and fifty percent are some pretty bad odds when you're talking plastique. Let's get this thing in the rig and online and see if it's a talker. If it is, we can work on it on the road while we get the hell away from that building.'

The only bad part of that good idea was that it didn't work. After thirty minutes in the RV trying to connect the laptop to the computer in the building, Roadrunner disconnected the thing from his software analysis unit in the bus and headed for the door, laptop tucked under his arm. 'If there ever was a communications program in here, it's been wiped. No way we can talk to the trucks through this thing, no way we can get into the main computer to stop the clock.'

Magozzi was hurrying after him. 'I thought it was a mirror image.'

'Yeah.' Harley stomped behind. 'But somebody broke a piece off, and that was the piece we needed. Roadrunner, where the hell are you going?'

'To shut off the bomb.'

'Roadrunner.' Grace's voice stopped him when no one else's might have. He turned back and looked down the aisle at her, and then he smiled, which seemed an odd thing to do under the circumstances.

'What is it, Grace?'

'We've got two possible command-line sequences hooked up to that plastique. We don't know which one it is.'

'I'll figure it out. Be right back.'

Knudsen was just outside the RV, talking into his

sat phone; Halloran was a respectful distance away, smoking. Knudsen was flapping his hand in front of his face as if all the outside air in the world weren't enough to save him from the ill effects of second-hand smoke. Halloran thought that was pretty funny, since they might be standing a few yards from a building that was full of nerve gas.

Suddenly, Roadrunner jumped the steps out of the RV, with Harley, Magozzi, and the women right behind him.

'You'll figure it out?!' Harley was bellowing. 'You've got a fifty percent chance that you're going to blow yourself to the moon, you goddamn stupid Lycra stick!'

Roadrunner stopped right in front of Knudsen, who put down the phone and said, 'Bomb squad, one hour out.'

Roadrunner shrugged as if it was meaningless information. 'You're some kind of a bomb expert, right? That's how you recognized those weather stats on the screen.'

Knudsen didn't answer.

'So if that building over there blew, how far away do you have to be to be safe?'

'If all those trucks are full of sarin, it could be as far as seven miles . . .' He stammered to a halt, understanding exactly what Roadrunner was going to do and what he was asking. 'If you know a way to disarm that plastique, tell me what to do and I'll go in there.'

Roadrunner smiled like a boy. 'No offense, Agent, but that would take way too long.'

Knudsen just looked at him for a second. 'Five, ten minutes on these roads.'

Roadrunner looked around worriedly. 'Do a lot of people live around here?'

'Four Corners was about it. This is mostly state forest.'

Roadrunner nodded, still troubled but resigned. It was the best he could hope for. 'You've got to make everyone else leave. I'll wait ten minutes from right now,' was the last thing he said before he turned around and walked toward the building.

They stood there with stricken expressions, watching Roadrunner walk away. Magozzi turned to Grace and Annie and Harley a second too late. They were already gone, following quietly in Roadrunner's wake without saying a thing. Charlie was right by Grace's side.

Roadrunner turned on them when he heard Harley's leathers swishing against the grass. 'Get the hell out of here, Harley. Take Annie and Grace and get the hell out of here.'

'Fuck you, you fucking fuck.' Harley stomped past him, seething. 'What if you hit the first line and it calls up a chain? That screen shows thirty lines at a time, and you're going to need more eyes to find the right one before it shuts you down.'

Roadrunner had to trot to pass him. 'That's bullshit, Harley. I'm better than any of you, and you know it.'

'The hell you are. You've only got a fourth of a brain, you dumbshit. The other three fourths are right behind you. Keep walking. We're running out of time.'

Sharon had automatically started to follow Annie and Grace. Part of it was some twisted sense of duty, part of it was guilt, and part of it was just knee-jerk. The three women had been following one another for what seemed like forever. Separating now didn't seem possible. She'd gone two paces before Halloran grabbed her by the upper arm and turned her to face him. 'Not. This. Time. You get that, Sharon?' His words blew across her face. 'This time, I'm not letting you go.'

Sharon felt something ripping inside, pulling her in two different directions, felt Halloran's fingers tight against her arm, and figured she'd have to shoot him to get him to let her go. She decided not to.

Magozzi, Gino, and Agent Knudsen stared after the Monkeewrench people, thinking things that none of them would ever say out loud. Finally, Knudsen spoke.

'Between the three of us, we could probably take down all of them and drag them back to the RV. Except maybe the big guy.'

Magozzi smiled a little, watching Grace. Funny. It should have looked like she was getting smaller, walking away like that, but instead she seemed to look bigger. 'Don't follow me, Gino.'

Gino didn't look at him. 'You go, I go.'

'Don't be an ass. Everything I've got is walking into that building right now. Everything you've got is back in Minneapolis.'

Gino watched him walking away. *Not everything, buddy.*

35

Magozzi walked across what seemed like an endless expanse of concrete floor toward the desk, the computer, the bomb, and the entire Monkeewrench crew. All he saw was Grace – and Charlie, of course. Goddamnit, she was going to get the dog killed, too.

She felt him coming. 'Get out of here, Magozzi,' she said without looking at him when he moved up beside her. 'Go with the others. You've only got eight minutes left to get out of range before Roadrunner starts hitting those keys.'

It was the first thing she'd said to him directly, and for reasons that defied logic, they made him ridiculously happy. He waited until she got tired of his infuriating disobedience and turned on him, glowering. Then, the second he had her eyes, he smiled and said, 'Hello, Grace.'

She jerked her head back toward the computer screen almost immediately, but the corner of her mouth twitched just a little. 'Seven minutes.'

'Okay. You want to make out?'

Outside, Gino, Bonar, Halloran, and Sharon had piled into Knudsen's bare-bones sedan. Knudsen hadn't started the car yet. Dying in the line of duty was one thing. You accepted that the minute you put on any kind of badge. Dying senselessly was another thing. No agency pretended there was glory in pointless self-sacrifice, not even the FBI. And this would be pointless. Living to fight another day was the ticket, and this was his case. Getting blown up and gassed right at the beginning wasn't going to do anybody any good, which was why he was driving out of here. So if the unthinkable happened, he'd be around to sort through the aftermath, find the bad guys, if there were any left, and uncover the things they'd know to look for the next time, so it never happened again.

Except he wasn't driving out of here. He was just sitting like a slug behind the wheel while the seconds ticked away, thinking of the civilians and the cop inside that building who happened to think that this particular self-sacrifice wasn't that pointless after all. He waited for one of the other four people in the car to start banging on the seats and screaming for him to get the hell out of there, but none of them said a thing.

'How much longer?' Annie asked.

Harley looked at his watch. 'Five more minutes.'

The waiting was killing Magozzi. Grace hadn't exactly jumped on the making-out idea, and the others were preoccupied with the programming language on the laptop screen, which left him with nothing to do but stand there and contemplate his own death. He could have been working on what he would do with the rest of his life if Roadrunner picked the right command line instead of the wrong one, but it seemed safer to go with the worst-case scenario. Grace had taught him that.

Suddenly Roadrunner slapped his forehead, said 'Duh', of all things, then moved the mouse and clicked.

Magozzi sucked in a breath and watched numbers flying by on the screen, waiting to blow up and die and see the light at the end of the tunnel or whatever else was supposed to happen.

After a few seconds, the monitor blinked black, then a new screen came up. The rest of them released a collective exhale that sounded like the wind. Magozzi looked down at his body. He wasn't dead, and he hadn't blown up. Not even a little.

'What just happened?' His voice sounded squeaky, and his face colored.

'Harley said the guy was sloppy on this. I just didn't read far enough, the command sequence was so long.' Roadrunner pulled the screen back up and pointed. 'It's right at the end; see those four letters? B-O-O-M at the end of this sequence' – he paged down a little – 'and M-O-O-B, that's boom backwards, at the end of this one. Christ. That's absolutely puerile.'

Harley looked a little tense. 'So which one did you punch in?'

'Moob, of course. Boom sets the bomb, boom backwards unsets it. I mean, how obvious can you get?'

Harley smacked him across the back of the head. 'You dumbshit. What if the guy had set it the other way around so it wouldn't be obvious?'

Roadrunner rubbed his head. 'Shit. I never thought of that.'

Harley smacked him again, lightly. 'That's the trouble with you linear thinkers. You have no imagination, no understanding of human psychology, and psychology rules the world, man. Magozzi, you want to get out there and call the others – tell 'em it's safe to come back?'

Magozzi looked down at his shoes. Sure, he could do that. Just as soon as he could get one of his legs to move. 'So the bomb's disabled?'

Annie gave him one of her slow, signature smiles. 'Of course it's disabled, sugar. That's why it says "Bomb Disabled" on that screen.'

Agent Knudsen's car was still outside when Magozzi walked out of the shed. Knudsen was standing next to it with his phone pressed to his head; everybody else was inside the sedan.

Magozzi was furious. He stormed up to the passenger side and jerked open the door where Gino sat. 'What the hell are you still doing here?'

Gino glanced at his watch. 'We've still got three, four minutes.'

'The hell you do. And what the *fuck* is he doing on the phone?'

'Calling off all the people coming in, keeping them away from this place.'

'He couldn't do that when the goddamned car was moving?' Magozzi was nearly spitting.

'Well, it's a bumpy road. Makes it hard to dial.'

'God*damn*it, Gino . . .'

'Take it easy, buddy. You're going to stroke out. Glad you changed your mind about leaving, though. Hang on. I'll move over and make room.'

'I didn't change my mind about leaving, goddamnit, I came out to call you and tell you it was safe to come back!'

'No fooling?' Bonar said from the backseat. 'They deactivated the bomb?'

'Yeah.'

Halloran and Sharon both closed their eyes at the same time. They looked like a couple of Kewpie dolls going to sleep.

Gino looked down at his knees for a minute and just breathed. When he looked up again, he was grinning. 'Knudsen's going to be pissed. Now he'll have to call back all those people he just told to stay away and tell them to come back, and I wouldn't blame one of them for not believing him. What about the trucks in there? Any chance they'll blow when the two on the road go?'

Magozzi dropped to a crouch in the grass by the car, arms across his thighs. 'Grace says no. There are only the two trucks online. The computers in the trucks in there aren't even linked up, which probably explains why they aren't on the road with the others.'

'So we don't have to worry about dying in the next couple hours.'

'No. Just about a lot of other people out there somewhere dying. Roadrunner thinks there has to be a fail-safe in the program – some kind of an abort command. They're trying to find it now.'

Gino stared out the windshield and shook his head. 'Godspeed.'

They waited outside as the minutes ticked by. Their guns, badges, and law-enforcement expertise – even the hotline to D.C. – were utterly useless. Everything depended on one skinny guy inside that machine shed finding one single circuit in a dizzying maze of computer language.

Halloran, Sharon, Magozzi, and Gino paced in mindless patterns close to the shed door while Halloran smoked one cigarette after another. Knudsen continued to walk his own private circles around his car, phone pressed to his ear, putting on the miles.

'You sure they don't want us in there?' Sharon asked Magozzi for the tenth time.

'They were pretty specific about *not* wanting us in there. This is their thing. There's no way we could help them. We'd just get in the way.'

'This is driving me crazy, not doing something. Anything.'

Magozzi saw the hollows under her haunted eyes

and thought it was all getting lost. Everything the women had been through in the last eighteen hours – things the rest of them would never be able to imagine, no matter how many times they heard the story – was getting lost in what was happening right now, and what was going to happen if they couldn't find a way to stop it. And yet there were Grace and Annie in that building, right in the thick of it, and here was Sharon, pacing around like a caged animal because she wasn't in there with them. She reminded Magozzi of a combat vet who signed up for another tour through hell because he couldn't stand the thought of his comrades fighting without him.

'You did good, Sharon Mueller,' he told her on her next pass.

She stopped where she stood and looked at him, and what he saw in her face almost made him wish she hadn't. 'Thank you, Magozzi,' she said, and then started to pace again.

Knudsen finally signed off the phone and walked over to where Halloran was sitting. He scowled down at the burning cigarette, and Halloran glared back at him. 'What?' Halloran growled. He was spoiling for a fight, any kind of a fight. They all were.

'You got another one of those?' Knudsen pointed to the cigarette.

Halloran handed him the pack. 'Never in a million years would I have pegged you for a smoker.'

Knudsen lit up, took a drag, and coughed for a long time. 'There are no nonsmokers in this business.

Just people trying to quit, and people who haven't started yet. They've got the fire under control. My people are starting to move into what's left of Four Corners. The bomb squad and the computer expert should be here in thirty minutes.' He took another drag and looked back toward the RV. 'Monkeewrench,' he recited the name painted on the side. 'Those are the people traveling all over the place, donating their programs to law enforcement, right?'

'That's right.'

'Huh. And you've got two of them on your force.'

Halloran looked him straight in the eye. 'They're kind of subcontract.'

Knudsen almost smiled. 'How good are they?'

'From what I hear, the best in the world.'

'They'd better be. We're running out of time.'

Within a few minutes, the field started to fill up with the people Knudsen had called in: a couple of HAZMAT vans, sedans with more suits, and an ominous-looking black helicopter that had emptied out some ominous-looking men in black suits in the last five minutes. That contingent was standing in a tight, motionless group near the building. As far as Magozzi knew, they'd said a few words to Knudsen and hadn't talked to anyone since.

'Those guys give me the creeps,' Gino said. 'They all look like the bad guy in *Matrix*. Who are they, Knudsen?'

'Friends.'

'Gee, could you be a little more specific?'

'No.'

In the next minute, the sky filled with noise and a big, dirt-brown sky pig came in fast, beating all the grass in the far corner of the field down into a crop circle. It had barely touched down before men started tumbling out, then lumbering toward them. They were already in full gear – bulky, padded suits, sealed helmets, ninety pounds of protection weighing down each man.

'Don't they know the bomb's been deactivated?' Magozzi asked.

'They know,' Knudsen said. 'But there's still a brick of plastique in there. They'd come in like that if it were floating in the middle of a swimming pool. As far as they're concerned, no bomb is deactivated until they say it is.'

'Goddamnit, that plastique is not going to blow, whether they believe it or not. You cannot let them go in there and start messing around while the Monkeewrench people are trying to . . .'

'For God's sake, Magozzi, I'm not a complete idiot,' Knudsen interrupted, then trotted over to meet the bomb squad and the other men who had disembarked.

Magozzi sighed and looked at the trio from Kingsford County. Halloran and Bonar were standing close on either side of Sharon, who looked wired enough to start snapping apart. Magozzi figured they all looked a little bit like that.

There was a flurry of activity and voices for a

few minutes while Knudsen made the rounds of the arrivals, barking out instructions like a drill sergeant. By the time he was finished, the field was remarkably silent. Magozzi looked around and felt the hairs on the back of his neck stand up. There had to be at least fifty people standing in a ragged semicircle around a building that looked as benign and harmless as a thousand other old farm buildings dotting the midwestern countryside. Nobody was doing anything; nobody was saying anything. They were all just staring at the door, waiting for it to open.

Inside the machine shed, Grace, Annie, and Harley hunched around Roadrunner at the computer, every unblinking eye fixed on the screen as pages of command codes scrolled by. A sheen of sweat washed Roadrunner's face as his twisted fingers talked to the keys, and then suddenly, his fingers froze and the scrolling stopped.

'*What?*' Harley demanded. 'Did you find it? Is that the abort?'

Roadrunner closed his eyes for a moment, then swiveled his chair to face them all. 'There is no abort,' he said quietly.

Outside the machine shed, the semicircle of silently waiting people let out a collective gasp as Harley came barreling out the door. He was moving at a perfectly amazing speed for a man that size, a blur of beard and tattoos and black leather as he raced past all of them into the RV. He came out five seconds later waving a disk and hollering, 'There's no abort – we've gotta try something else!'

He was back in the building so fast that it was hard to believe he'd ever been out. Everyone was standing up, hearts pounding, legs ready to run somewhere if they only had a little direction.

'What do you suppose was on that disk?' Knudsen asked.

'God knows,' Gino said.

'I'm going back in there,' Magozzi said abruptly, heading for the door. He had license, he reasoned. He'd been in there before when things were really tense and hadn't messed anything up. Besides, this was driving him crazy. He had to know what was going on. He had to feel like he was part of it. He'd be very quiet. They'd never know he was there.

Sharon stared after him for a moment, muttered, 'Well this is just bullshit,' and followed him.

It was as if she had taken a cork out of a bottle. One by one, everyone in the field started to move toward the building and slip silently through the door.

36

Roadrunner's lycra suit was soaked with sweat, and his leg jiggled furiously under the desk while he pushed the disk Harley had retrieved from the RV into the computer drive.

Grace eyed him worriedly. 'Anything you want to run by us before you try this thing, Roadrunner?'

He shook his head hard and fast, keeping his fingers over the keyboard and his eyes fixed on the screen. 'No time.'

'Is this what you wouldn't let me get a look at in the office yesterday?'

'Yeah. It's just something Harley and I have been working on.'

Annie forced herself to take a breath and blew the exhale up toward her bangs. 'Are you saying you don't even know if it *works*?'

'Are you kidding me?' Harley rumbled. 'Of course it's going to work.' He clapped Roadrunner on the back. 'Go for it, my little chickadee.'

Roadrunner pushed a few keys and started the disk loading, but Grace's eyes were on Harley. His voice had sounded strong and full of confidence, but there were bloodless white lines tracing around his moustache and down into his beard, and his eyes looked sad, almost hopeless.

'How much time does it take to load?' she asked quietly when Roadrunner had finished typing.

He punched a single key and brought up a time bar that started filling with blue color, millimeter by millimeter. 'Five minutes, maybe. I don't know. We only did one test run.'

'And then how long to execute?'

'I don't know.' Roadrunner pulled his hands away from the keyboard and stared at the time bar. Everyone else was staring at the red countdown clock in the upper-right-hand corner of the screen.

37:22:19 . . . 18 . . . 17 . . .

Jesus, Magozzi thought, moving a little closer to Grace, sensing her rather than seeing her because his eyes were fixed at the damn clock as it ticked down. *It had to be wrong. It was going too damn fast.*

'Well, what the hell is this thing?' Annie demanded harshly, but her hands were on Roadrunner's shoulders, kneading through bunched muscles that felt like tangled tree roots.

'Uh . . . sort of a virus . . .'

'*What?* You wrote a *virus*? You went to the dark side?'

'No, no, no, it's not like that.' Roadrunner's mangled fingers were twisting together. 'It's not really a virus. Well, it is, but it's not a bad virus. It's a good virus.'

Annie dropped her hands from his shoulders.

'There are no good viruses. That's why we call them viruses, for God's sake.'

'It's not contagious,' Harley broke in. 'We only direct it to specific sites, and it can't go any farther. All it does is just eat away the guts of the computer we send it to, while the computer doesn't know it's getting eaten. It doesn't replicate, the recipient computer can't send it to anyone else – it's perfect.'

'But it destroys computers.'

'Boy, does it ever.'

Magozzi's eyebrows shot up. Behind him, in the back of the vast room, a lot of other eyebrows were doing the same thing.

'Oh, for God's sake, you guys,' Annie chastised them. 'Who were you sending this to?'

Roadrunner muttered something unintelligible down at his lap.

'What?'

Harley was staring at the countdown clock, and then at the time bar, shifting back and forth on his worn-down boots. 'Oh, for Chrissake, it's no big deal. We send it to the kiddie-porn sites. Shut down a big one last night.'

Annie thought about it for a minute, and then said, 'Oh. Cool.'

Grace was looking down at the floor, saving up a smile for later. When she looked up again, the time bar was almost entirely filled with blue, and the countdown clock was at twenty-nine minutes.

*

In a suburb of Detroit, Michigan, a Good Health Dairies truck sat outside the entrance of a vast, sprawling building. Hundreds of people were skirting the truck as they went inside, eyeing it curiously, irritated by the group of playful neighborhood children who were gathered around the truck. They were climbing the running boards, pressing their noses against the window glass, chattering, and squealing in a most inappropriate manner.

The oldest of these children, a boy closing in on eleven years, fixed his gaze inside the truck cab and gestured to a friend. 'There's a computer in there,' he whispered, tapping his finger against the glass, pointing to the glowing screen that was flashing numbers in bright blue pixels. 'That's gotta be worth a bundle.'

His friend shaded his eyes and peered inside. 'What do you suppose those numbers mean?'

'Hell, I don't know. You want to bust the window and do a grab-and-run?'

His friend looked around at all the people streaming past and the cars still pulling into the lot. 'Too many people around. Wait 'til they all get inside.'

They both climbed down and sat on the running board to wait, guarding their treasure.

Magozzi was frantic, watching that goddamned clock count down second by second. Finally, the last slice of blue ticked into the time bar, filling it completely, and he couldn't stand it any longer. He broke the promise he had made to himself to stay silent and out of the way. 'Is that it? Is it finished? Is it over?'

Harley glanced quickly in his direction and registered a little surprise to see him there. The computer screen had been his total focus for so long that he hadn't noticed anything going on around him. None of them had. 'It's loaded.'

Roadrunner's fingers suddenly started flying over the keys. Grace and Annie were leaning over his shoulders, watching the text appear on the screen as Roadrunner typed.

Magozzi nodded rapidly. 'Great. That's great. It's loaded. Now you execute, right?' He jumped when Grace reached back and touched his hand.

'Not yet, Magozzi. If we execute now, we destroy this computer, and this computer is the only way we have to talk to the trucks.'

Magozzi tried to make sense of it, his mouth open like a fish, gasping for air. 'I don't get it, goddamnit, I don't get it.'

Harley took pity on him. 'We're just piggybacking the virus through this computer to the trucks, Magozzi. Get it? Those truck computers are already set up to accept data from the host computer and no place else. We're just sending them a package from Mama. So we download the program here without executing, have this computer send it on to the trucks, then send the execution command.'

'And what the *fuck* does that do?' Magozzi demanded, and Harley actually smiled at him.

'It destroys the truck computers, and that, my friend, destroys the detonate command.'

Magozzi finally took a breath. 'Okay, okay. I get it. So how long does it take?'

'Roadrunner just finished sending the virus program to the trucks. Another five minutes at least to execute, maybe a little longer.'

Magozzi's eyes were glued to the computer screen, watching the countdown clock. 'Christ, man, we've only got twelve minutes left.'

'Yeah, I know. It's going to be tight . . . oh, Jesus.' Harley was gaping at the screen.

Magozzi had to force himself to look. The monitor had gone black, and big, red letters were flashing in the center:

DETONATION SEQUENCE INITIATED
DETONATION SEQUENCE INITIATED

No one around the computer station moved. They just stared at the monitor, hanging on the meaning of red letters in the black box. Magozzi wanted to ask something stupid, like, What the hell does that mean? but he knew damn well what it meant, and he couldn't move his mouth, anyway. What really scared him was when Roadrunner's hands started shaking visibly.

'*Fuck a duck!*' Harley shouted, bulldozing closer to Roadrunner, shoving his face at the screen.

The people gathered in the back of the room – Knudsen, the suits, the HAZMAT squads – all moved en masse to get closer, then froze when they were within sight of the screen.

'What's that mean?' Knudsen breathed, his face a deathly white.

Roadrunner didn't even look to see who had asked the question. 'They must have rigged the detonation sequence to upload at a specific time in the count-down. It initiated when we were still executing the virus, and because the truck computers can't upload more than one program at a time, they kicked one off.'

'Which one?' Gino whispered.

'Hard to say. Normally, they'd take them in order, which means they'd keep executing the virus and kick the detonation command, but if that were happening, that message shouldn't be there.'

Grace closed her eyes. 'The detonation sequence was a priority. If I'd set this up, I would have put an automatic override on it, so it kicked everything else off.'

'Yeah. Me, too.' Roadrunner's voice was shaking almost uncontrollably.

At that moment, Magozzi felt something let go in his head, then his neck, his shoulders, all the way down to his gut. A strange sense of serenity followed. He thought it was probably a lot like what terminal patients felt when they acknowledged their impending death, relaxed their resistance, and let it walk in. A thousand people somewhere had less than five minutes to live, and there wasn't a goddamned thing they could do about it. So you just shut down, let it go. Roadrunner was still talking, but Magozzi caught only the last part.

'... so the only hope we've got is that part of the virus got through, and that it will corrupt the computer enough to keep the detonation sequence from finishing ...'

Suddenly, 'DETONATION SEQUENCE INITIATED' disappeared from the screen, and a new message took its place: 'DOWNLOAD COMPLETE.'

'Which download?!' Magozzi shouted. 'The virus or the detonation code?'

Roadrunner's lips were sealed against a held breath. He raised a shaky, deformed finger toward the countdown clock in the upper-right-hand corner of the screen. The numbers had frozen at just under two minutes.

Magozzi had no clue what that meant. Neither did anyone else in the room. They were all leaning forward, like people bucking a strong wind, eyes wild and unblinking. Had the detonation code gone through? Was the clock wrong? Were a thousand people dead? Magozzi looked frantically from Grace to Annie to Harley, who all looked perilously close to meltdown, and figured it couldn't mean anything good. He almost turned away when Roadrunner started swiveling his chair, afraid to see the look in his face, but he made himself stand there. It was the least he could do.

And then Roadrunner finished his turn, and the eyes he met first just happened to be Magozzi's. 'We did it,' he said. And then he smiled. 'We shut it down.'

Suddenly, a tremendous noise shattered the silence. Roadrunner looked up with a baffled expression at the dozens of people he hadn't even realized were there. Harley, Annie, and Grace turned around in amazement. The place was filled with people. All of them were cheering, banging one another on the back, and moving together toward the Monkeewrench crew like out-of-control groupies at a rock concert.

Harley, Annie, Grace, and Roadrunner watched as the crowd surged toward them.

The cheering went on for a long time.

37

It was a blindingly sunny morning in the field outside the building that had housed death and hate and destruction. Magozzi drew in a deep breath that smelled of smoke from the Four Corners fire, but even that smelled good.

His hand was glued to Grace's arm as surely as Charlie was glued to her leg, and he felt pretty good about that. He had hands and the dog didn't. Advantage Magozzi. He squinted in the sunlight and looked around at the mess of cars and trucks and choppers and people, and thought what a goddamned beautiful place the world was.

He looked at Grace's face, trying to read her expression, and realized what a fool's errand that was. He looked at Roadrunner's face instead, which always gave away emotions for free. But even that reliable countenance was impossible to read. He looked like somebody had pulled the plug on his head and there was absolutely nothing left inside.

Harley was frowning at all the confusion around him, looking like a man who had just woken up naked in a crowded room. Then he shrugged and walked over to Knudsen and handed him a piece of paper. 'Here are the coordinates for the two trucks.

I don't know where the hell they are; it's just a bunch of numbers to me.'

Knudsen accepted the paper without taking his eyes off Harley's. He looked like he was about to burst into tears, but then suddenly, he smiled.

He had an astounding number of teeth, Harley thought. He looked a little like a mule getting ready to bray.

The field got even busier after that. A few more choppers came in, and a lot of cars and vans. A large team of what might have been men or women dressed in bulky white self-containment suits finally got permission to swarm all over the building, and disappeared back inside to take a look at the plastique and the trucks. Another HAZMAT team swarmed with equal purpose over everyone who had been in the building, sweeping them with wands from a dozen different instruments, then taking them into the back of the van for other tests.

Halloran and Magozzi watched helplessly as Sharon, Grace, and Annie got the once-over about a hundred times.

'It's just a precaution,' Knudsen tried to reassure them. 'Knee-jerk. They're at the highest risk. Not only were they in that building with the trucks, they were in Four Corners where the first one crashed; they've got to be cleared.'

'We don't even know if there's anything in those other trucks,' Magozzi complained.

'The team inside is checking on that. Until we get

confirmation from them that there's no danger, we act as if there is.'

'Well, that's just plain dumb,' Halloran grumbled. 'We were all in that building.'

'Yeah, I know. We'll be next.'

Gino made a face. 'Shit. Are there needles involved?'

Knudsen just smiled at him.

When Gino and Magozzi were finally released from the testing van, Gino rolled down both sleeves and stomped away in search of his manhood. 'Well, that was about the most humiliating experience of my life, and that includes the time when my pants split in the middle of the medal ceremony for the Monkeewrench murders. I feel like aliens just harvested my eggs or something.'

Magozzi smiled, but Knudsen looked almost as distressed as Gino. His face fell when he saw a Missaqua County cruiser coming up the farm road. 'That's Sheriff Pitala,' he said miserably. 'His sister ran the café in Four Corners.'

'Did she get out?'

'Who knows? We're pulling a lot of bodies out of that place. No females yet, as far as they can tell.'

Magozzi nodded. 'So there's some hope.'

'I don't know. We need to talk to the women. They're the only ones who were in there.'

'So what the hell did you do with them?' Gino demanded. 'I haven't seen them since you dragged me into that mobile test tube and slammed the door.'

Knudsen looked a little nonplussed. 'Actually, they're in your RV. The big one with the bedroom eyes?'

Magozzi smiled in spite of himself. Every single man in the world reacted the same way the first time they saw Annie. And every time after that, in fact. 'Annie Belinsky.'

'Yeah, her. She said she'd whip the next man that tried to talk to her before she had a shower, and I swear to God she could do it. Especially with that big undercover tattooed guy from Kingsford County backing her up. Are those two married or something?'

'Not even close.'

'Whatever. Anyway, when they're finished in there, we're going to have to start debriefing. At this point, they know more than any of us. We've got three live ones in lockup we caught running from the fire in Four Corners. Camo, M16s, just like that woman said on the phone . . .'

Magozzi stiffened a little. 'The woman's name is Grace MacBride, Agent Knudsen.'

Knudsen looked at him for a second, recording the connection, finding his boundaries. 'Sorry, Detective. Anyhow, we need to hear what all the women have to say before we start interrogation.' He turned his head when a cruiser pulled up close beside them and Sheriff Pitala climbed out.

The man's uniform was covered with soot, his

face was drawn, and he walked with a stoop that Magozzi hadn't noticed before, as if a grief he wasn't sure he should be carrying was weighing him down. He nodded to the group, then turned to Knudsen. 'I can't find anybody that can tell me about Hazel,' he said. 'I thought maybe you could help me out with that.'

'Who's Hazel?'

The voice came from the steps of the RV. Everyone turned and saw Grace MacBride, black hair dripping on her shoulders, Charlie pressed against her side, smiling inappropriately. Stupid dog had no clue what was going on here, Magozzi thought; and then he realized that he felt almost the same way. As long as Grace was in it, the world was just as it should be.

Sheriff Pitala looked up at her and swept his hat from his head in manners so ingrained they transcended everything else. 'Sheriff Ed Pitala. Pleased to meet you, ma'am, and Hazel's my sister. Ran the café in Four Corners.'

Grace looked at him for a moment, then nodded ever so slightly. 'Why don't you come on in for a minute, Sheriff.'

Halloran and Bonar were wandering through the jumble of cars closest to the building, the ones that had already been there when they'd arrived. It was a motley collection of old and new, cars and trucks and vans.

'Who do you suppose these belong to?' Bonar asked.

'Sharon figured they were the cars in Four Corners when whatever went down went down. There wasn't a single drivable vehicle in the town by the time she and Grace and Annie got there.'

Bonar shuddered. 'You know, it's the little details that really get to you. Like walking into a town with no people, no cars, no sounds. That had to be weird.'

Halloran barely heard him. He was staring at a big faded blue sedan parked almost out of sight behind a pickup truck peppered with holes. He and Bonar walked over and looked at the side. There was a hand-painted logo on the driver's door, letters just slightly off, white paint bleeding into the faded blue.

'The Cake Lady,' Bonar read it aloud like a sigh, and they were both silent for a time.

'Probably stopped at the café for a bite on her way to the wedding,' Halloran said. 'That Gretchen, she loved her donuts.'

Bonar was looking across the field at nothing in particular. 'Ernie's going to take this hard.'

'Yes, he is.'

'So what kind of a world are we living in, Mike, where people put nerve gas in milk trucks and set out to kill a lot of other people they never even met?'

Halloran thought about that for a minute. 'Same old world, Bonar. Same old hate. Different weapons.'

38

It took a full seven hours for Agent Knudsen and the ominous black-suited men that came from the ominous black helicopter to debrief Grace, Sharon, and Annie. The *Matrix* look-alikes were well-mannered, soft-spoken, and absolutely unused to interviewing anyone with a mangy mutt at her side. Not one of them thought to ask the dog to leave. There wasn't a precedent for such a thing.

'You want to debrief them, fine,' Magozzi had said. 'But it'll be right here in this field, this RV, or that building. We go from here to home, and that's the only choice you have.'

One fool had tried to exert a little nonexistent authority, citing all sorts of statutes and policies that mandated an FBI debriefing at an FBI office with all the prerequisite equipment and witnesses. Agent Knudsen had silenced him with a single gesture. The kid, Halloran thought, had a lot more influence than any of them had realized.

When it was all over, Agent Knudsen personally escorted the three women back to the RV. By that time, the sun was setting on the chaotic day, and most of the choppers and vehicles had already left. Magozzi met them at the door. He was wearing a dishtowel apron and a stern expression that didn't go with it. He looked at Knudsen, then at Grace. 'Do we feed him or eat him?'

Charlie had made some decisions about Agent Knudsen in the past few hours. He walked over to the agent, sat down next to his leg, and lifted his head to be patted. Knudsen hated dogs. Always had, always would. Except for this one. He laid a hand on Charlie's head, and Charlie's stump of a tail wiggled.

'Feed him,' Grace said.

They should have fed him sooner, Magozzi thought a few hours later, because all the fat and carbs and protein that Harley and Bonar had managed to whip up in a cooking frenzy had done little to mitigate the three glasses of Bordeaux Agent Knudsen had slammed before the meal, and they sure as hell weren't affecting the glass he was drinking now.

Grace, Sharon, and Annie had all been frighteningly quiet during the meal, and everyone else had been quiet, too, mentally tiptoeing around them as if they were recently returned combat vets, which, in a way, they were. The women were pressed close together on one side of the table, the men crowded on the other. Magozzi felt a chasm running right down the middle, and wondered how hard it was going to be to cross it. The only thing that gave him hope was when the women excused themselves and went to the back of the RV to crash on the hidden beds that pulled down from the office walls. Grace hadn't actually smiled at him, but she'd trailed her fingers lightly across his hand as she passed.

Just before Annie disappeared down the broad aisle, she paused at the doorway with a pink flounce of the chiffon-and-marabou dressing gown she'd donned after her shower. It showed a lot of cleavage and a lot of plump, delicious leg when she moved, and Gino had been wondering ever since he dropped his jaw at the first sight of it how the hell the FBI had managed to debrief a woman who looked like that.

'Not so long ago,' she said, 'this body was neck-deep in a scummy lake, butting up against a dead cow.'

Every man in the front of the RV smiled at her. Of the three women, Annie was truly the ultimate survivor, the only one who could live through hell, then immediately let it go. Magozzi wondered what it was in her past that made her able to do that – besides knifing a man to death when she was seventeen, of course.

Agent Knudsen, who was already four or five sheets to the wind, brandished an off-center smile. He held up his glass to her. 'Not so long ago, dear lady, you were neck-deep in a scummy lake next to a truck filled with nerve gas.' His glass wobbled, and a dribble of wine fell to the table.

Annie gave him a quick curtsy and disappeared down the aisle.

'What truck? What lake? What the fuck are you

people talking about?' Gino demanded. He looked a little blurry-eyed and aggressive.

'Have you called Angela?' Magozzi asked him.

'About twenty thousand times.' He rolled his eyes toward Harley. 'I sure as hell hope you get free minutes on your sat phone.' He moved his head back toward Knudsen. 'So what's all this lake shit?'

Knudsen was making the mistake a lot of non-drinkers make when they have a little too much. He was gesturing with his glass, and Roadrunner was frantically blotting up spills as they happened. 'There were three trucks originally – three targets. The first one had some kind of accident and crashed in Four Corners. They shoved it into the lake the women ended up hiding in. It's a really long story.'

Harley was immediately alarmed. 'Are you shitting me? They were really exposed to that gas?'

Knudsen stuck his lips out. 'No worries. You would not believe how fast sarin hydrolyzes, and there probably wasn't a whole lot left in the truck anyway.' He dropped his chin and raised his eyebrows almost up to his hairline. 'Now, if it had been VX, that would have been a whole different story. Big trouble. Big problem.' He grinned foolishly, inappropriately, a lot like Charlie.

Up to this point, Roadrunner had been pretty quiet for a man who had literally saved the day. 'What were the targets?' he asked Knudsen. His voice was polite, almost deferential. He was asking about the people he'd saved.

The question sobered everyone. Even Knudsen put down his glass, and his gaze seemed to sharpen. 'I really can't tell you that.'

Gino bristled a little. 'You can't tell the man who saved your ass? Who has a better right to know?'

Knudsen fiddled with the stem of his glass for a minute, then laid his gaze on Roadrunner, right where it belonged. 'One of the trucks was parked at a mosque outside Detroit – one of the biggest in the country, by the way. The other was at an Immigration Services field office in a Chicago suburb.'

No one said a word.

Magozzi looked down at his hands on the table, thinking how accomplished they were in some things, how versatile, and ultimately, how helpless. 'They were sending a message.'

Knudsen nodded. He looked one hundred percent sober. 'That's what it looks like. They were very careful with the target sites. The mosque and the immigration office were both quite isolated, which makes the targets pretty specific.' He dug in his pocket, pulled out a wrinkled business card, and smoothed it flat on the table. 'We found about a thousand of these in Hemmer's desk at the dairy.'

All the men leaned over to read it. There was no name on it, no address, no logo of any sort – just a simple quote:

> '*. . . it is their right, it is their duty . . . to provide new Guards for their future security.*'

'Sounds familiar,' Halloran murmured.

'It should,' Bonar replied. 'It's from the Declaration of Independence. What the forefathers said you had to do when the government wasn't doing enough to protect you.'

Knudsen nodded sadly.

And this, Magozzi thought, was the dreaded black place. The desperate place where people always went when anger and fear couldn't find any other answer, the place that obliterated logic and compassion and reason and all the other higher functions of the human mind that civilization had fostered.

No one wanted to talk after that. They found their rest in leather recliners, or doubled up on the sofa beds. Roadrunner was mothering again, covering everyone with blankets before he stretched out in the middle of the aisle and immediately fell asleep.

To his everlasting shame, Harley woke up in the middle of the night on one of the sofa beds, with both arms wrapped tightly around a happily sleeping Agent Knudsen.

39

Sharon Mueller was up at dawn, shrouded in a big terry robe from the RV's closet, standing near Deputy Douglas Lee's bloodied patrol car.

It was quiet in the field. Dew sparkled on the seeded heads of tall grass, and a hawk flew overhead, screeching occasionally for its mate.

She heard the RV door close softly in the distance, then felt Halloran approaching. She didn't have to look to know it was him. She would never have to look to know he was there.

He moved up beside her, hands shoved in his pockets, light eyes fixed on the car. 'Who killed the man who was pretending to be Deputy Lee?'

'I did.'

It was amazing how easily it slipped out – no guilt clouding the issue, no lingering questions, none of the doubts that used to fill her mind whenever she held a gun so similar to the one that had ended her mother's life, hesitant – always hesitant – to pull the trigger and end someone else's. It was part of the reason she'd been shot in the Monkeewrench garage all those months ago. She hadn't been too slow to get at her gun and pull the trigger to keep a killer from shooting her. She'd just been paralyzed by the past, and that had made her a bad cop. But that was over. She could go back to Kingsford County now if she wanted. She could go back on the street. Maybe she could even go back to Halloran.

Halloran didn't even bat an eye. He just nodded. 'It was a righteous shooting.'

'I shot him in the back,' Sharon said.

'Even so.'

'I know. I'm okay with it.'

Halloran swallowed hard and wondered how people did this. *You did it when you were a kid,* he told himself. *You did it every time you stepped to the edge of that cliff at the lime quarry, swung the rope out over the water, and hoped you didn't shatter yourself on the sharp-edged rocks that were waiting below, always waiting.*

'I was thinking maybe we should get married. Have kids. Do the whole thing.'

Sharon bent in half almost immediately, laughing out loud, and Halloran thought either he'd just proposed to an absolutely insane woman or he'd screwed this up just like he'd screwed up everything else in his life.

'Oh, God, I'm sorry, Mike,' Sharon finally gasped, straightening, at least making an attempt at a sober face befitting the occasion. 'But we haven't even had a real date yet.'

'Okay. We could do that first if you want.'

She turned toward him then and grabbed his whiskered face in both hands and pulled it down to hers. Then he felt the woman beneath the thick terry robe and saw in his mind's eye the woman in the red dress, high heels, and lips like colored water, who had laid her hand on his heart in the Kingsford County Sheriff's Office way back last October, and refused to let go.

Five hours later, Gino and Magozzi were leaning against the side of the RV, staring across an empty tar road, across a field at a huge barn. Grace's Range Rover was parked right behind them. The road was so narrow that both vehicles blocked it, but from what they'd seen in the past hour, chances were slim that another vehicle would ever come along. Northern Wisconsin was the end of the world, according to Gino. They could hear a single blackbird calling from a cornfield next to the barn, and not much else.

'So that's what started all this,' Magozzi said, tipping his head to get a different angle on the barn.

Grace walked up from the Range Rover and leaned between them. 'That's it.'

Gino shook his head in disbelief. 'Sharon took you fifty miles out of your way to see this?'

'That's right.'

Gino pushed away from the sun-heated metal skin of the RV. 'Well, it's about the dumbest thing I ever saw in my life,' he said, heading back inside for a little liquid refreshment and some more of that gooey chocolate crap with the unpronounceable name that Harley had made last night. He hadn't wanted to make this side trip. He'd been anxious to get home to Angela.

'I think it's pretty amazing,' Magozzi said after Gino had left.

The whole side of the barn was painted in a huge, amazingly accurate replication of Leonardo's *Mona Lisa*, wearing a T-shirt with 'On Wisconsin' emblazoned across the front.

Grace smiled at him like the Mona Lisa on the barn. 'The thing is,' she said, 'if we hadn't gone out of our way to see this barn that Gino thinks is about the dumbest thing he ever saw in his life, we never would have gotten lost. We never would have ended up in Four Corners, and a thousand more people would have died.'

They both stared at the barn for a while longer, Grace thinking of things that had happened and things that might have been, Magozzi thinking of things that were to come.

'You want to make out now?' he asked.

Grace looked down at the ground and smiled, thinking that you never knew how short your time was. But sometimes, if you were really lucky, you got the faintest glimpse of how you should spend it.

Acknowledgments

Long, long ago, back when P.J.'s body parts were all still relatively close to their original locations, we sent an unfinished manuscript over the transom. The agent who read it saw through the problems to the possibilities, and championed the story and the author in spite of the book's flaws. We spent the next ten years promising ourselves that one day we would send our thanks in the form of a book that the poor woman could sell. That book was *Want to Play?*. We were not sure what a 'good' agent was, so we settled for an amazing one. Ellen Geiger of Curtis Brown Ltd., this one's for you, babe.

Amazing people apparently gather in packs, because Ellen Geiger led us straight to Christine Pepe, executive editor, vice president, and all-around wonder woman at G. P. Putnam's Sons. We know what you're thinking – that every author says really nice things about his or her editor in these acknowledgment pages – but you have to understand that this woman has already earned any accolade you can think of. She is a truly gifted editor with laser-sight judgment who makes everything we write better. We respect her professionalism, we admire her intelligence and talent, and, most of all, we value her friendship.

We began the Monkeewrench series with these two women and their colleagues in their respective firms. At Curtis Brown, a very special thank you to David Barbor, who tolerates our nonsense with inimitable grace; to Ed Wintle, who parries our nonsense with surprising skill; and of course, to Anna Abreu, who can brighten the darkest day with the sound of her voice. You people are the best.

At Putnam, we are indebted to Carole Baron, president, a consummate professional and truly a class act; to dedicated, delightful Marilyn Ducksworth, who won us over in about two seconds; to the patient and talented Kara Welsh and the New American Library family; to Dr Michael Barson, who babies us on tour, and his staff, Megan Millenky and Lisa Moraleda. And a thousand thanks to tireless, sweet, unflappable Lily Chin, assistant to Christine Pepe.

We are deeply grateful to Penguin UK for giving our books a wonderful home across the water, and to all their talented people who created such a brilliant presentation for our debut and continue to wow us. A special thank you to our truly amazing editor, Rowland White, for being one of our first champions overseas, and for shepherding us along the way with such grace and good humor.

And most importantly, thanks to all of our readers

far and wide – we never dreamed our work would be so well-received outside the U.S. and we are grateful to each and every one of you for letting us share our stories.

An exclusive extract from

Snow Blind

The new thriller by

P. J. Tracy

Published by Michael Joseph May 2006

Prologue

They had to sit for a time after dragging the body so far in this heat – two young women in sleeveless summer dresses, hugging their knees on the hillside while the hot wind danced in their hair and crept up their skirts and a dead man lay behind them. They both looked straight ahead across the rolling fields of prairie grass, and nowhere else.

'We should have tied him to a board or something,' Ruth said after a few minutes, 'so he wouldn't get tangled up in the grass like he did.'

Laura opened her mouth, then closed it abruptly. She'd almost said they'd know better next time. She closed her eyes and saw big, raw hands dragging through the grass, fingers curled, almost as if he'd been trying to hang on. It was high summer and the grass was long, whipping in the wind and wrapping around the rough fabric of his sleeves.

'Shall we start?'

Laura felt her heart skip a beat. 'In a minute.'

But it was impossible to keep Ruth still for very long. She was like one of those little birds whose wings beat so fast you couldn't see them, darting here and there like they were always on the edge of panic. She was trying to be still to please Laura, but her hands were busy, almost frantic, shredding one piece of grass and then another. 'I have a headache.'

'It's those combs. They always give you a headache.'

Ruth took the combs from her hair and shook it free, lovely blonde curls falling down her back like liquid sunshine. Silly Ruth, as old-fashioned in appearance as the name she'd been saddled with; hair too long, skirts too short, and maybe that was what had brought this whole thing to a head. She managed to sit for almost a full minute, and then the fidgeting started again.

'Stop fussing, Ruth.'

'Don't yell at me.'

Laura heard the hurt in her voice, and knew without looking that Ruth's lower lip was starting to tremble. Soon the eyes would spill over. She hadn't yelled, exactly, but perhaps her tone had been too sharp. That was wrong. Ruth had always been the fragile one, even before her belly had started to swell, and you had to be careful. 'I'm sorry if it sounded that way. Have you thought of a name for the baby?'

'Stop trying to distract me. We have to dig this hole.'

'I just want you to be still for a bit. Rest.'

'Rest?' Ruth looked at her as if she'd just uttered a profanity. 'But we have so much to do.'

'Just this one thing.'

And then Laura smiled and felt herself relax for

the first time in years. It was true. Kill a man, bury him – that was all that was on their list today.

After a few seconds Ruth said, 'Emily.'

'What?'

'Emily. I'm going to name her Emily.'

'What if it's a boy?'

Ruth smiled. 'It isn't.'

This was the story Emily was remembering on her last day, and it amazed her that she could remember it at all. She'd only heard it twice in her life – once from her Aunt Laura, who'd told her on the sly when Emily had turned thirteen, as if it were a strange and secret birthday present; and again from her mother on the day Emily had left the home farm to marry Edward and make her own life. Her mother had giggled during telling, which her aunt had never done, and that had frightened her a little. And then she told her to remember the tale, that it wasn't really so funny, in case a day should come when she would need it.

Today she needed it, Emily thought, wondering if she could finally do it, after all these years. And if she did, what would all those wasted years have been for?

It was the last day; the last day of secrets. She lay on her back in bed, right hand pressed against her flat stomach; pushing, pushing the pain back inside; holding the evil, growing mass that writhed inside with hungry tentacles reaching for open nerves. God, it hurt.

A perfect, thin line of light pushed up the black curtain on the horizon outside her bedroom window, and the quality of dark began to change inside the room. This room, where love and hell had happened, all in the same lifetime.

Emily's feet were on the floor before the first chirp of the earliest rising bird had sounded, and the rush of agonizing pain pushed her head to her knees. She squeezed her eyes tightly closed and saw rolling, sparking pinwheels of light.

Old, ravaged huddle; tiny woman; folded into a small package of gray hair and sharpened knees, alone in a chamber of agony where, inexplicably, birds welcomed the morning in gay, sporadic disharmony.

She did things that seemed odd, considering her chore list for the morning. Prepared and ate her oatmeal; drank her precious single cup of coffee; carefully washed the bowl and cup and saucer with their faded rose patterns, knowing those patterns had always been there, amazed at her years of indifference. Everything seemed sharper, clearer, as if she had seen the world for years through a lens just barely out of focus.

And then she walked to the old gun cabinet in the dining room.

The pistol lay in her right palm, and she folded arthritic fingers around it. It felt good. It felt right. She hadn't used it for years. Five? Six? Since she shot the squirrel the oil truck had left panting and mangled, eyes glazing in the driveway.

Emily was an excellent shot. Edward had seen to that, back when fox and bear still wandered freely in and out of the chicken coops and the isolated barnyards of rural Minnesota. 'You will learn to shoot, Emily, and you will shoot if you have to,' he had answered her shudder when he first lay the new pistol in her palm; and she had. How impossibly far from her mind then was the final use to which she would put this gun. How inconceivable it would have been. To kill, with careful thought and planning; with only cold, dismal dread, as for any other unpleasant task.

Appalling, evil woman, she thought as she stepped out onto the back porch. To feel no remorse; no guilt. How hideous. How deeply sinful.

The sun had not yet topped the cottonwoods when she walked out from the house toward the looming barn, and the path through the tall grass was still dim with early morning.

She saw in her mind an image of how she must have looked at that moment, and laughed aloud at the sight – a crazy old woman, hustling in a faded dress and orthopedic shoes, gun in hand, out to kill quickly, out to finish the job before it was too late.

She stopped when she rounded the turn at the bushy hydrangea, just as the enormous, ancient barn sprang into view, tractor door gaping like a bottomless black mouth.

Suddenly the pain in her belly moved. Now it

was a bright piercing in her head, and then, without warning, a deadness spread down her arms.

It didn't get the gun, she thought senselessly. It didn't get the gun. I can still feel it. It's heavy, hanging so heavy from my hand.

But the pistol was on the ground, winking sunlight off the long, polished barrel, mocking her as Emily fell beside it. Her lips wouldn't move, and the scream stayed inside her head.

No, God, please no. Not yet. I have to kill him first.

I

Minneapolis hadn't had much of a winter. Every promised storm had veered far to the south, dumping Minnesota's fair share of snow on states that neither wanted nor deserved it, like Iowa.

Meanwhile bitter Minnesotans watched their lawns green up in the occasional rain, and their snowmobiles gather dust in the garage. A few die-hard riders made the short trek to Iowa to try out new machines, but they never talked about it at the water cooler on Monday morning. It was simply too humiliating.

Today was going to change all that, and the whole state was giddy with anticipation.

The snow started at ten o'clock in the morning, falling with a gentle vengeance, as if to apologize for its late arrival. Within an hour there wasn't a blade of grass visible in the whole city; the surface streets were slick with new snow hiding the black ice beneath it, and the average freeway speed had dropped to seven miles per hour. Reporters' minicams picked up shots of lunchtime drivers behind the wheels of cars barely inching along in the kind of stop-and-go traffic that normally fosters road rage, but all the drivers were smiling.

In City Hall, Detectives Leo Magozzi and Gino Rolseth were totally oblivious to the little surprise nature was cooking up outside. They sat at their facing desks in the back corner, grinning at each other. It wasn't the kind of picture you saw often in Minneapolis Homicide, but this was a banner day.

Gino propped his feet on the desktop and laced his hands behind his head. 'We are never going to have another day this good. Not on the job, anyway.'

Magozzi pondered that. 'Maybe we should retire right now. Go out in a blaze of glory, get jobs as golf pros on some course in Hawaii.'

'Golf pros never get a high like this.'

'Probably not.'

'And neither one of us knows how to golf.'

'How hard can it be? You hit a little ball into a little hole. Pinball on grass, is what it is.'

Gino's grin widened. 'We are probably the only homicide detectives in history where the homicide victim lived.'

'Nah. Must have happened a hundred times before.'

Gino made a face. 'Yeah. I suppose. But not in this department. And she could just as well have died, if it weren't for the two greatest detectives on the planet.' He shook his head in happy disbelief. 'Man, this is almost better than sex.'

Magozzi thought that was a load of crap, but he was feeling too good to take issue with it.

They'd been called out on a probable homicide

four days ago. Bloody bedroom, drunken ex-husband with a history of abuse and assault, and a missing woman who'd had a restraining order against the dirtbag ever since the divorce. Magozzi and Gino had found her early this morning, locked in the trunk of a car in the long-term lot at the airport, barely breathing. The docs at Hennepin General said she was going to make it, and they'd been floating ever since.

Gino rolled his chair around to face the window, and his silly grin turned upside down. 'Oh crap. That stuff's still coming down.'

'Good. People hardly ever kill each other when it's snowing.'

'Oh yeah? Homicides were up six percent last quarter.'

'Because there was no snow. It'll get better now. Man, look at it come down.' Magozzi walked over to the window and looked down at the mess the storm was making of the street.

Gino joined him, shaking his head. 'Those homicide stats never made sense to me. Should be the other way around. Winter in this state is enough to make anyone homicidal. Boy, this better stop soon.'

Magozzi shoved his hands in his pockets and smiled. 'We're supposed to get at least a foot.'

'Aw, jeez, come on, don't tell me that.'

'Sorry, buddy. Looks like there's going to be a Winter Fest after all. Baby's got snow.'

*

By noon there were six inches on the ground, most of the city schools had started bussing the kids home, and people were cross-country skiing on side streets the plows hadn't hit yet.

Intrepid youngsters gifted with an unexpected snow day were trolling the residential neighborhoods, shovels in hand, picking up a little extra cash for a lot of hard labor. There were a lot fewer of these baby entrepreneurs these days; most kids were parked in front of the TV or a PlayStation, hands out for allowances earned by their mere existence. The few who worked the small, older houses on Ashland Avenue in St. Paul never bothered to knock on Grace MacBride's door.

She'd had high-tech heating grates built into her sidewalks and driveway before she bought the place six years earlier, and you could Rollerblade on those sidewalks in a blizzard. Not that Grace had minded physical labor, but she'd been hiding from a lot of people in those days, and there was no way she would expose herself long enough to shovel a path through a Minneapolis winter. Supposedly no one was trying to kill her anymore, but it was just plain silly to take chances.

Today, inside the snug little house she'd converted into a fortress, she was practicing the MacBride version of slovenliness.

No one ever saw Grace dressed like this, except Charlie, of course, and since human speech was the only trick the dog hadn't mastered yet, he wasn't talking. The flannel pajamas had been a gift from Roadrunner; soft and warm and, bless the stick man, black. Clearly a lot of thought had gone into the purchase, because the pants were wide enough to provide easy access to the derringer she kept strapped to her ankle when she was working at home. But the very softness of the lightweight flannel felt dangerous. Grace liked weighty fabrics between her and the rest of the world. Jeans, riding boots, her heavy duster, even her thick terry robe. If it had been anyone but Jackson, she wouldn't have opened the front door.

She didn't even have to look at the monitor linked to the front porch camera when she heard the heavy knocking. Charlie told her Jackson was here before the kid had made it halfway up the walk. The clever dog had very distinct signals that identified everyone. He announced Jackson with an immediate and shameful loss of dignity, reverting to rolling-on-the-floor puppyhood. Grace suspected the dog considered the child a litter mate.

But the kid was two hours early, irritating little monster.

'What are you doing here?' she demanded when she opened the door. 'Did you skip?' Grace needed a little work on her hostessing skills.

'Jeez, Grace,' Jackson muttered, smart enough to shake the snow off his silly pom-pom hat before he pushed past her, stepped inside and fell immediately to his knees on the mat, arms open. Charlie was all over him in an instant, tongue and nose and big wriggling body all at high speed. Charlie loved licking Jackson's face, hands, any exposed skin. Grace wondered if black skin tasted better than white. 'You gotta start watching some TV or listening to the radio. This storm's a honker. Schools let out right after lunch.'

Grace scowled out at the snow that had dared to fall when she wasn't looking, disrupting her routine. And then she remembered tomorrow's contest, how much Gino Rolseth hated winter, and caught the smile just in time.

A few hours later, Jackson sat at the kitchen table while Grace monitored the mysterious sauce she had simmering on the stove. 'Smells good. Did I mention I was starving?'

Grace said nothing.

'Did I mention that Charlie was starving?'

That got her attention. She turned with the spoon halfway to her mouth and looked at the silly dog sitting on the ladder-backed chair, an appetizing stream of drool hanging from his jaw, threatening the table. Damn dog still insisted on sitting in a chair at the table like a person, waiting with all the patience he could muster for the alpha female to serve. It wouldn't have been so bad if he'd been smaller, but there was a big Shepherd somewhere in Charlie's lineage, and at the table he was taller than most men. 'Give him a dog biscuit. This needs another ten minutes.'

'How about me?'

'You can have a dog biscuit, too.' Grace turned back to the stove. She was making capon au bourbon tonight. Just because Jackson was a streetwise foster kid didn't mean he couldn't develop a familiarity with and appreciation for dishes a bit more exotic than Hamburger Helper. Suddenly she stopped stirring the sauce and reconsidered that thought. What the hell was she thinking? Jackson was not her kid, luckily for him, because Grace didn't have a maternal bone in her body. His education in any area, culinary or otherwise, was not her responsibility. Damn kid.

Grace wasn't quite sure why she'd let him into her life. One day there had been no Jackson in her world; the next he had pushed himself in, all because she'd made the stupid mistake of intervening when his foster brothers were beating the crap out of him.

Grace didn't like kids. Didn't want to like anyone, really. She looked at Jackson, sitting at the table next to Charlie as if he had every right to be there, and tried to resent him for that. She glanced at the clock, thought that his foster mother was probably home from work now, and that she should just shoo him out.

'I think Charlie's a genius, trapped in a dog's body, what do you think?' he asked suddenly, and Grace felt a little something inside give way again. Dammit.

'I think you're nuts. He's just a dog.'

Jackson's face was so deeply brown that when he

grinned, his ten-year-old teeth made a white sunrise. The two front ones were big; the rest were in transition. He hadn't done much smiling when Grace first met him. Neither had she, for that matter. But now they shared one occasionally – a guilty secret between them both.

'Bad juju, this snow.'

Grace sighed and started spooning wild rice onto plates. 'You're a kid. You're supposed to love snow.'

'Not tonight. I got a feeling.'

Grace set a plate in front of Charlie, and then Jackson. Priorities were priorities. 'So now what? You're a ten-year-old psychic?'

Jackson's brown eyes got bigger as he looked down at his dinner, but he didn't touch his fork, and wouldn't, until Grace sat down and lifted hers. His mother had died a few months before Grace met him, but the woman's good-manners stamp was all over the kid. 'Something bad coming down with this snow.'

Gee, Grace hated it when he said things like that.

Toby Myerson kept drifting in and out of a delicious sleep, and each time his eyes fluttered open, the landscape had changed, as if someone had pushed fast-forward on a movie.

Earlier, the big sledding hill across the field had been a rush-hour kiddie freeway, jumbled with the primary colors of a hundred miniature snowsuits, and the air had been sweet with the delighted squeals of children. Happy music that warmed him from the inside out.

Toby loved watching the little bodies sailing down the snowy hill, tumbling off saucers and sleds and the occasional toboggan at the bottom. They rolled like balls and then skittered up the slope like colorful insects; so animated and tireless, so very alive. Occasionally he would focus on one child who seemed a little taller and more coordinated than the others, and he would wish with all his heart that the child would cross the stretch of open parkland and walk up to greet him. He was feeling a bit strange at that point, and worried that he might seem intimidating. Youngsters frightened so easily, and if they were frightened, they would run from him, and Toby thought he would just die if that happened, because he had to tell someone about . . . something . . . something bad. He just couldn't remember what it was.

Things seemed darker when he opened his eyes again. At first he thought the park lights had been turned off, but that couldn't be it, because when he moved his eyes up to look at them he could still see pinpoints of brightness, as if none of the light could get out of the bulbs. Odd.

Only a few shadowy stragglers remained on the sledding hill now, and the only sounds he heard were the shouts of the last parents calling their kids up the hill, home to bed, because the park was closing.

Don't go. Please don't go.

And then Toby realized he was very, very cold. He'd been still for so long, watching the children. Probably hours. My God, what had he been thinking? He had to move, get the blood flowing, get home and warm.

Funny how the scenery remained exactly the same, no matter how far he went. And the really funny part was that his mind recorded every movement of his legs and arms, and yet he couldn't feel the snow sliding beneath his feet or the good stretch of his triceps.

That's because you're not moving, Toby.

Oh my God.

There was a brief flutter of heat as his body tried to find some adrenaline to send to his heart, and he concentrated on not blinking, on screaming as loud as he could to the last kid climbing up the hill. Omigod, he was almost to the top, screaming, screaming, splitting the silence with terror and outrage because now he knew he was dying and he couldn't move and WHY DIDN'T THE KID TURN AROUND?

At the top of the hill, the last child grinned up at his father, and the two of them turned to look out over the empty, absolutely silent park.

2

Traffic on Theodore Wirth Parkway was an unmitigated disaster – the twelve inches of yesterday's fresh snow had been churned into treacherous slop before the overworked battalion of snowplows had been able to catch up, and when the temperature had plummeted overnight, the slop froze into icy furrows. Instant bobsled track. Magozzi had stopped counting fender-benders long ago.

Still two blocks from the park's main entrance, he'd been sitting in his car at a dead standstill for almost five minutes, watching enviously as throngs of pedestrians waddled cheerfully and unimpeded past the gridlock in their warmest winter garb, heading for the Winter Fest Snowman Sculpting Competition. There were too many to count, all of them braving the wind and cold and traffic just so they could watch people play in the snow, and, amazingly, they all looked happy about it.

This town was absolutely nuts for winter. Or maybe they were just nuts; Magozzi hadn't decided. Once there was enough snow on the ground, streets were always blocked off for one thing or another – sled dog races, cross-country ski marathons, hockey demonstrations, or bikini-clad residents making a big fuss over the idiocy of diving into a frozen lake or river. Every winter sport the world had ever thought of had a home base here, and when they ran out of sports, they took art outside.

Give a Minnesotan a block of ice and they'll harvest 20,000 more from whatever lake is handy, and build a palace. Give them a little snow and you're likely to find a scale replica of Mount Rushmore or the White House on someone's front yard. But ice and snow sculpture had been elevated to artistry here, and competitors came from all over the world to participate in any number of winter festivals. Who would have thought that a snowman contest the department sponsored just for kids would attract this much attention?

He moved another half-block by inches, past a wooded section of the park, and got his first glimpse of the open field that fronted the boulevard. Like all the drivers before him, he slammed on his brakes and stared out his window in amazement.

The park opened up here onto a good thirty acres of empty, rolling land that looked a lot like a golf course in summer. Today it looked like a blindingly white battlefield for an invading army of snowmen. Magozzi gaped at what looked like hundreds of them sprouting up every few yards, up and down the hills, staring out at the boulevard with their black, lifeless eyes and silly carrot noses.

When he finally got into the park, he pulled into the first illegal spot he could find, between a Channel

Ten satellite van and a NO PARKING AT ANY TIME sign. He grabbed his gloves and a thermos from the passenger seat, and stepped out in time to catch a frigid gust of wind square in the face.

Hundreds of spectators were milling around the park, watching piles of snow take shape under frozen hands, and Magozzi wondered how he was ever going to find his partner in such a vast sea of anonymous bipeds swaddled head-to-toe in fur and down and Thinsulate.

Gino Rolseth was the very reluctant fall guy for every charity gig the MPD sponsored, thanks to some anonymous donor that kept doubling the proceeds, as long as Gino participated. Even the computer wizards at Monkeewrench hadn't been able to trace the culprit – or maybe they had, and realized Gino would kill the guy if he ever found him.

He finally spotted Gino on the far side of the field, his modest five-foot-nine-inch frame cutting a towering figure amidst all the crazed, screaming little munchkins who swirled around him in a rainbow of brightly colored coats, scarves, and hats.

Gino, on the other hand, was dressed all in black, as if in mourning, bundled up in a huge down parka so puffy he could barely bend his arms. He had some kind of animal on his head, and his hands were encased in leather snowmobile mittens that were big enough to be pizza paddles. It was obvious that his mood was even blacker than his outerwear, because he was planting nasty kicks to the base of his nascent snowman.

'Nice parka, Gino. How many ducks died for that thing?'

'It's about time you showed up. And to answer your question, not enough. I can't feel my extremities. I think I have frostbite. And hypothermia. Goddammit, I hate winter, I hate snow, I hate cold. Remind me why I live here again?'

'Because you love mosquitoes?'

'Wrong answer.'

'Must be the change of seasons, then.'

'No, it's because every goddamned winter, the brain cells that know how miserable it is here freeze and die. It takes 'em all summer to grow back, and then it's winter again and the whole ugly process starts all over.'

'But you look great – most places you just can't get away with ear flaps anymore.'

Gino adjusted the black pelt on his head a little self-consciously. 'Laugh now, freeze your ass off later, Leo. The wind chill is about fifty degrees below zero, and dressed like that, you're going to be running for the car in five minutes. What, are you shopping with the Chief now? You look like a mobster.'

Magozzi smoothed the front of his new cashmere overcoat – a Christmas gift from Grace MacBride. 'I heard it was supposed to warm up. Look, the sun's coming out already.'

'When the sun comes out in Hawaii, it warms

up. When the sun comes out in Puerto Vallarta, it warms up. When the sun comes out in Minnesota in January, you just go snow-blind.'

'And therein lies the real truth as to why you live here.'

'So I can go snow-blind?'

'No, so you can complain about the weather.'

Gino mulled that over for a good, long time and finally nodded. 'That's actually a good point, Leo. The only thing worse than bad weather is boring weather.' He bent down and swept up a mitt full of dry, powdery snow. 'You want to tell me how the hell I'm supposed to build a snowman out of this?'

Magozzi gestured toward a group of kids who were working with spritzer bottles full of water. 'Watch and learn. You use the water like glue.'

'Okay, Michelangelo, go pull your gun on them and requisition a water bottle for the MPD.' He looked hopefully at the thermos Magozzi was carrying. 'Tell me you got Schnapps in that thing.'

'Hot chocolate. You're not supposed to drink in the cold. It dilates your blood vessels and you get hypothermia faster.'

'I already have hypothermia, so what's the difference?' Gino turned back to his misshapen, pathetic half-snowman that was shedding vast portions of its body with each gust of wind. 'Christ, look at this. This is the worst snowman in the whole contest.'

Magozzi took a few steps back and eyeballed it.

'Maybe there's a conceptual art category. You could enter it as Snowman with Psoriasis.'

'You're just full of wisecracks today, aren't you?'

'I'm trying to cheer you up. Aren't Angela and the kids coming?'

'Later, for the judging. And I want to at least get an honorable mention, so help me out here.'

'Okay, I'm ready. Where do we start?'

'I think we need a theme.'

Magozzi nodded. 'Good plan. Like what?'

'Hell, I don't know. Maybe we should do something cop-related since we're cops.'

'I'm with you. I think a cop snowman would be appropriate.'

'But nothing too flashy. See that one over by the woods?' Gino pointed to a nearby snowman that had cross-country skis sticking out of its base, ski poles propped against its torso, and a pair of Elvis-style reflective sunglasses perched atop a carrot nose. 'It's too skinny if you ask me, but nice execution overall. I'm thinking we could use it as a template.'

'Whatever you say. You're the visionary, I'm just the free labor. Tell me what to do.'

'Make me a head that won't fall apart.'

Gino and Magozzi started working fast, rolling and molding and shaping. The sun was on their side, because it was bright and high in the sky now, softening up the snow and making it easier to work with. A half-hour later, they had a respectable-looking, basic snowman.

'That's a damn fine start,' Gino said, stepping back to admire their handiwork. 'A few details, maybe a couple trimmings, and we'll have ourselves a contender, what do you think?'

'I think its butt looks fat.'

Gino rolled his eyes. 'Snowmen are supposed to have fat butts.'

'Maybe some arms would balance him out a little.'

'Great idea. Go get some twigs from those bushes over there.'

'It's illegal to pick foliage in parks.'

'I don't give a shit. I'm not signing off on this thing until it has some limbs. And don't make any smart-ass remarks about the Disability Act.'

Magozzi wandered over to the straggly thicket that bordered a margin of woods, stopping to look at the skiing snowman on the way. The sun was hitting it full on now, and its left side was starting to look glazed and a little mushy. With any luck, it would melt before judging and they'd have one less competitor.

'This yours?'

Magozzi looked down at a little red-haired kid who'd suddenly appeared at his side.

'No.'

The kid couldn't have been more than eight or nine, but he was circling the snowman with the critical eye of a seasoned judge. 'It's pretty good. Better than that one the fat guy's working on.' He pointed to Gino.

'That's my partner you're talking about.'

The kid looked up at him, nonplussed. 'You don't look gay.'

The ever-evolving English language, Magozzi thought. Seemed like every word had multiple meanings nowadays. Somebody was going to have to make up some new ones eventually. 'Not that kind of partner. We're cops.'

Now the kid was impressed. 'Did you ever shoot anybody?'

'No,' Magozzi lied.

'Oh.' Disappointed, the kid turned back to the skiing snowman, dismissing Magozzi as quickly as he'd engaged him. Clearly, inanimate objects were more interesting than cops who didn't shoot people.

Magozzi looked around to make sure Park Service wasn't hovering in the bushes, waiting to ambush him, then started harvesting illegal arms for their snowman.

A few seconds later the screaming started. Magozzi spun toward the source, his hand on his holster even before the pivot, and saw the red-haired kid standing in front of the skiing snowman, staring up at it with wide blue eyes and an impossibly wide mouth.

He was at the kid's side in seconds, looking at the carrot nose tilting downward in the melting face, the sunglasses sliding down the carrot, and the big, terrorized milky eyes the sunglasses had been hiding. The real nose behind the carrot was a waxy white, right off the color palette of the dead.

Oh. Shit.

The kid was still screaming. Magozzi put his hands on his shoulders and turned him gently away from the snowman that wasn't a snowman, toward the red-haired man and woman running frantically toward their terrified son.

ALSO AVAILABLE FROM P.J. TRACY

He just wanted a decent book to read …

Not too much to ask, is it? It was in 1935 when Allen Lane, Managing Director of Bodley Head Publishers, stood on a platform at Exeter railway station looking for something good to read on his journey back to London. His choice was limited to popular magazines and poor-quality paperbacks – the same choice faced every day by the vast majority of readers, few of whom could afford hardbacks. Lane's disappointment and subsequent anger at the range of books generally available led him to found a company – and change the world.

'We believed in the existence in this country of a vast reading public for intelligent books at a low price, and staked everything on it'
Sir Allen Lane, 1902–1970, founder of Penguin Books

The quality paperback had arrived – and not just in bookshops. Lane was adamant that his Penguins should appear in chain stores and tobacconists, and should cost no more than a packet of cigarettes.

Reading habits (and cigarette prices) have changed since 1935, but Penguin still believes in publishing the best books for everybody to enjoy. We still believe that good design costs no more than bad design, and we still believe that quality books published passionately and responsibly make the world a better place.

So wherever you see the little bird – whether it's on a piece of prize-winning literary fiction or a celebrity autobiography, political tour de force or historical masterpiece, a serial-killer thriller, reference book, world classic or a piece of pure escapism – you can bet that it represents the very best that the genre has to offer.

Whatever you like to read – trust Penguin.